A MOUNTAIN TOO STEEP

ROBIN PATCHEN

JDO PUBLISHING

For the people who saved my son's life: the drivers who stopped on that lonely road in Utah, the helicopter pilot and paramedics, and the doctors, nurses, and support staff at Primary Children's Hospital in Salt Lake City. Every single one of you played a part, and we are eternally grateful.

I never wanted to marry.
And then I did, because I loved him desperately.
I never wanted to be alone again.
And now I am, because he loved me more.

CHAPTER ONE

CAMILLA WRIGHT WAS ACQUAINTED with late-night phone calls. The first had ripped her world apart. The second might well destroy her.

That evening it happened, the house was quiet. Zoë was at work. Jeremy was in Utah at Marcy and Kevin's for spring break, hanging out with his cousin, giving Camilla the perfect opportunity to deal with his room.

It took her three evenings to get it clean. Her teenage son was a lot of things, but tidy wasn't one of them. Once she cleared out the trash—empty soda cans, bags of chips, and candy wrappers—she dealt with his clothes...hanging, folding, and tossing the outgrown items into a box.

When it was clean and organized, she hung the painting she'd been secretly working on for weeks. It showed nine-year-old Jeremy wearing Grandpa Roger's too-big fedora. Beside him, Daniel had crouched to his level and adjusted the hat so it angled to the side. He'd declared it perfect, and they'd looked at Camilla for confirmation.

She'd snapped the picture, catching father and son with wide, natural grins. It was Jeremy's favorite photograph.

Camilla had painted the image on a canvas, eliminating the chaotic background to focus on the faces.

She stepped back to admire it. The Jeremy who occupied this room had the same natural grin as her little boy. On the surface, he'd recovered from his father's murder. But deep in the shadows, where secrets and fears flourish, Jeremy was changed. The eyes that stared at her from the portrait, glowing with joy and confidence, now held wisdom gained through pain. And grief.

But her little Jeremy was still in there.

And the man she'd loved was never far from her heart.

She felt arms wrap around her from behind, Daniel's body warm against hers. She could almost feel his breath on her cheek. Almost hear his voice. *It's a masterpiece, but not as beautiful as you.*

Her phone rang, shattering the illusion.

She pulled it from her pocket, glancing at the screen unnecessarily. "Hey."

"How are you?" Paul's tone was kind and concerned, as always.

"Tired." She went to the kitchen, where she ladled leftover tomato-basil soup into a pan on the stove. "I was working on Jeremy's room."

He chuckled. "You're not happy unless you're redecorating something. You think he'll like it?"

"Once he gets over the fact that I was in there, definitely. Especially the painting."

They chatted until her soup was warm. "I'm sitting down to eat. We'll talk tomorrow?" A silly question, since he checked on her every evening. She didn't need him to take care of her, but it was nice to know somebody cared.

"How about dinner Wednesday?" he asked. "There's that new Italian place."

Paul had been Daniel's best friend back in St. Louis, before her life had fallen apart. He'd stayed by her side as the police had searched for Daniel's body, not that anybody ever believed they'd find it.

She and Paul had grown close, closer still when he'd followed her to Oklahoma City. But he wanted more than friendship now.

What did she want? She spun the wedding band on her left hand. She'd tried more than once to take it off, but though it was big enough, she couldn't get it to budge. "Meet you there at seven thirty?"

"I thought I'd swing by and pick you up."

Like a date. "That's okay. I've got some errands."

She could feel his frustration in the long pause that followed, but his tone was kind when he spoke. "That'll work. See you then."

She'd successfully kept it casual, again. And disappointed Paul, again. She tamped down the twinge of guilt. She cared for him, but she wasn't ready. She didn't know if she ever would be.

After dinner, Camilla settled on the couch in the living room and found the TV show she'd been binge-watching. When Daniel was alive, they would often linger at the dinner table for hours, talking about their days, their children, his cases, her charities. That last year, though, there'd been few intimate conversations. Rather than enjoy each other's company, they'd argued. A lot. She'd often wondered if they'd ever get past their disagreements.

Their stupid, petty disagreements.

When she started to feel sleepy, she reclined on the couch to drowse until Zoë got home.

The ringing of the phone woke her.

She sat up and glanced at the wall clock. Eleven? Where was Zoë?

Camilla swallowed a surge of panic. She'd left her phone on the kitchen counter. She snatched it and looked at the screen.

Marcy.

Terror swelled as she connected the call. "Is everything—?"

"Camilla, the boys have been in a terrible accident. They're being life-flighted to Salt Lake City. They're both alive. That's all I know."

The words, delivered as if her sister had rehearsed them, hardly penetrated before Camilla found herself on her knees. She hadn't fallen. She'd just...gone down. As if her body knew she wouldn't be able to shoulder the load. She couldn't fight the invisible pressure that pushed until she lay facedown, phone pressed to her ear.

Jesus. Please... "What happened?"

"We don't know exactly. The car flipped." Marcy's voice shook. "I got a call from someone who stopped to help. He said Evan was talking. I don't know about Jeremy. They wouldn't tell me much. We're on our way now. I'll call you when I know more."

An accident. Life-flighted. Serious.

She couldn't do this again.

Please, please...

"Camilla?" Marcy said.

"I don't know what to do." Her voice was high and squeaky.

"Get a flight. As soon as you can. I'll be in touch." Marcy ended the call.

Camilla didn't move while her mind flicked through image after image. Daniel's blood everywhere—on the steering wheel, the windshield, the console. The memorial. The photograph. No casket. No body.

"Mom?"

She opened her eyes to her daughter's black shoes, her

denim-clad legs. Zoë crouched beside her, terror evident in her expression.

Camilla sat up, wiping moisture from her cheeks.

Zoë's long brown hair was pulled back in its typical ponytail, the checkered button-down she wore for work wrinkled after a long day. Though she couldn't have known what happened, tears streamed from her daughter's eyes. "What is it?"

Camilla would do anything to protect Zoë from this. She'd been through enough. She'd carried enough burden on her narrow frame to last a lifetime.

"Sit down, sweetie." Camilla didn't have the strength to stand yet, so she tugged Zoë down on the tile across from her and took her hands. "Jeremy and Evan have been in an accident." Her voice shook. She needed to hold herself together for her daughter's sake. "It sounds serious. They're being taken to the hospital."

Zoë's lower lip trembled. "Are they going to be okay?"

"I don't know." Camilla pulled her daughter into a hug. She wanted to lie, to promise Zoë they wouldn't have to go through this again. She wanted the world to be different than it was, to be kind and gentle, not harsh and painful.

Zoë pulled back. "We have to go."

Those words had Camilla pushing to her feet. "*I* have to go. You have school and work."

"Mom, I need to be there." Even though she was twenty-one, every once in a while, Zoë's demanding teenage voice surfaced. Now, she stood and crossed her arms. "I'm going with you."

Camilla couldn't handle an argument right now. "Let me think, please. Let me just..." She opened her laptop on the kitchen island and navigated to a travel site, trying to figure out why she didn't want Zoë to go with her.

She loved Zoë and craved her presence. Zoë and Jeremy were close. No doubt he would want her there.

Zoë hovered at her side.

"Did you eat dinner?" Camilla asked. Zoë often didn't have time to eat during her shift. "You could warm up some soup."

"I can't eat right now, Mom. Be serious."

Camilla forgave her daughter's tone and studied the flights. There were too many to choose from. She couldn't think.

What she wanted was to get in the car and start moving, to get closer to her son now. But it was a nineteen-hour drive to Salt Lake. Surely flying would be the fastest way.

She didn't have the wherewithal to figure it out. She dialed the airline directly.

And was put on hold.

The music grated on her nerves. She needed to do something.

And then she knew exactly what. She opened a text to her best friend and typed.

Jeremy and his cousin were in a car accident.
It's serious. Please pray.

Her friend responded immediately.

Praying now. Keep me informed.

If she'd learned nothing else in the years since Daniel's murder, she'd learned the power of prayer.

She copied the message and sent it to everyone she knew would pray. Within seconds, her phone was dinging with responses. How many people stayed up later than she? How many had she awakened?

Praying. How can I help?

Oh, sweetie, I'm so sorry. Lifting the boys and you to the Lord.

I'll start a prayer chain at church.

She closed her eyes. *Thank you for my friends. Please spare my baby. Please...*

She was still on hold with the airline when her call-waiting beeped. Paul, of course. She rejected the call and texted that she couldn't talk.

"What are you doing?" Zoë asked.

"Asking for prayer."

Zoë's low *pff* told Camilla what she thought of that. After Daniel's death, Zoë had shrugged off her faith like an ill-fitting jacket. *Lord, use this to draw Zoë close.*

Please save the boys.

"I want to come," Zoë said.

Camilla closed her eyes to think, and then she realized why she didn't want Zoë to go with her. Because that would mean the accident was very serious. And she couldn't handle that right now. She needed life to go on—Zoë's life here. Jeremy's life...

She opened her eyes and took Zoë's hands. "Sweetie, you have that big project due at school, don't you? You can't just take off."

"That doesn't matter!" She yanked her hands away. "I need to be there. What if he dies?"

"Don't say that." Camilla's words were harsh. She swallowed the tone and started over. "He's going to be fine."

"What if he's not?"

"He will be." Zoë argued, but Camilla spoke over her. "If we find out there's a chance that... If I think you need to be there, I'll fly you out. Please trust me. Right now, I need to get there, and I need to know you'll be here, managing your life and this house."

Zoë opened her mouth to retort, but then her shoulders drooped. "You promise?"

"I promise."

"I'm going to warn my professors tomorrow and get that project done, just in case."

"Good idea."

On the phone, a man asked if he could help her, and Camilla explained the situation, cursing the tears in her voice.

The agent was kind and patient as he booked her the eight o'clock nonstop flight.

Until then, Camilla just had to survive.

CHAPTER TWO

AN HOUR LATER, Camilla called her sister back, unable to wait another moment. Marcy and her husband, Kevin, lived thirty minutes from Salt Lake, and the traffic would be light at this hour. They had to have reached the hospital.

Marcy answered. "I'm sorry I haven't called. Evan was examined and taken for a CT scan. He's awake and seems all right."

"And Jeremy?"

"I don't know." Marcy's voice pitched high. "They're still working on him. We only saw him for a second. He was struggling to breathe."

Camilla needed details. Any details. "Was he awake? Was he...?"

"I don't... Wait. The doctor's coming. I'll call you back." Marcy hung up.

Camilla stared at the phone, willing it to ring.

Her baby couldn't breathe.

Please, God. Please.

She didn't know what to ask for, But God knew what Jeremy needed.

Phone in hand, she went to her bedroom and tried to pack. Instead, she found herself wandering, empty-handed, from her closet to the suitcase, over and over. What did one pack for such an occasion? How long would she be gone? Where would she sleep?

Would she sleep?

What clothes would she want in the hospital?

What if she had to make arrangements to transport his body?

No. Please, God.

She tossed clothes in the suitcase. Jeans and sweaters, yoga pants and T-shirts.

Daniel's letters.

She grabbed the stack from her nightstand and put them in her carry-on. She needed Daniel with her. She couldn't do this alone.

Finally, Marcy called back. "The doctor says the boys are stable for now."

For now? What did that mean?

"They're moving them to ICU," Marcy added.

"What do they think?" Camilla asked. "I mean, are they going to be okay?"

"They don't know or they won't say." Marcy's voice hitched. "I think we'll know more when we get to ICU. I'll call you then."

Information dribbled in over the next few hours. The CT scans showed no spinal injuries, thank God. Evan was complaining of pain in his head and more in his abdomen.

Jeremy had a broken wrist and thumb, not to mention three broken ribs, but the biggest issue was the trauma to his lungs.

Serious trauma. Unable to breathe on his own. Intubated.

The words repeated in her head like a mantra from a horror film.

As Camilla was climbing into bed a few hours later, Zoë knocked on her door and stepped inside. She wore pajamas and carried her pillow with its bright purple pillowcase. "Can I sleep with you?"

Zoë had slept with Camilla for two years after Daniel's death. Many of those nights, Jeremy had slept on an air mattress on the floor in her room. They'd needed each other then. They needed each other now.

"Of course, baby." She patted the mattress beside her. "Climb in."

Zoë did, turning so her back was to her mom, and Camilla switched off the bedside lamp.

"Do you think you'll sleep?" Zoë asked.

"I'm going to try."

"How?"

Good question. She rolled over and stroked her daughter's long hair. "Do you mind if I pray?"

Zoë's head shook beneath Camilla's fingers.

"Father, we're scared. We don't know why this happened, but we trust You. You are good, and You are powerful, and You will accomplish Your will." *Please, God. Please. Have mercy.* She waited until the rush of emotion passed. "Lord, we need to rest. We entrust Jeremy and Evan to Your hands tonight. Hold them, protect them, heal them. Be with Marcy and Kevin and all the doctors and nurses caring for the boys. Give them wisdom and insight. Protect us here as we wait. Grow our faith, Lord. Draw us near."

At the sound of Zoë's sobs, Camilla pressed close and wrapped her arms around her daughter. "Comfort us tonight. Help us to trust You."

She finished the prayer and kissed her daughter's head. "I know you're not sure about God these days, but He's sure about you, and He loves you. Hang onto Him right now. He can get you through."

Zoë said nothing, and Camilla rolled back to her side of the bed. She had a lot of practice trying to sleep when worries and fears assailed her. Scriptures she'd memorized over the years came back to her. She recited them silently, hanging onto God's Word, the only solid thing in her life. One verse came to her, and she took it as a promise. She repeated it over and over and willed herself to believe.

I will contend with those who contend with you, and I will save your children.

CHAPTER THREE

CAMILLA SETTLED in her window seat. The couple of hours of sleep hadn't been enough, but there was no way she'd drift off now. She opened her bag and took out the first of the letters Daniel had left for her in his desk at the hospital before he was murdered.

Dear Camilla,

I hope you never need to read these. I hope, soon, we'll be back to normal or at least safe somewhere, together. But I've made my decision. I have to testify, and that might lead to... Well, if you're reading this, then you know exactly where it led. I hope you can forgive me.

They say your life flashes before your eyes when your death is imminent. Ever since I walked into that hospital room, the memories have been coming. Faster now as the end draws near.

I see Zoë, our darling firstborn, who was always studying the world around her as if there might be a test. Remember the pigtails? The purple sweatshirt? She wanted to wear that ratty thing every day, even after she grew so much we could barely peel it off her. At seventeen, it's clear she has the heart of a caretaker. Maybe she got that from me. Maybe I won't leave her with only the bad.

I see Jeremy with his winsome smile and contagious laughter. Our son was born to bring joy to the world. To me, it seemed like he went from crawling to running in seconds, though maybe I just wasn't around enough to notice the transition. Maybe that was my first mistake, thinking they'd always be there. Thinking there'd always be time to be a daddy. Believing the lie that my work was more important than my family.

Camilla, I am so sorry.

You were right about everything. I should tell you that. When we get through this, I will. But if we don't get through it, I hope these letters will suffice.

If this is the end for me, I want you to know your face, your beautiful, beloved face, will be the image I take into eternity with me.

And our memories.

Remember the first time we saw each other?

October, second year of college. The pre-med classes were getting harder, but I was smart. My scholarship covered my tuition, and my parents covered my books and living expenses, which left me with plenty of time to study—and party.

I did too little of the first, too much of the second. The night that changed my life started out like so many other Friday nights. My fraternity had thrown a bash. The air hung heavy with the scents of liquor and weed. I prided myself on my self-control and good choices back then. I wasn't doing shots, after all. I wasn't smoking or snorting or injecting anything. A couple of beers never hurt anyone. But when the beer flowed so easily from the keg, nobody was counting the ounces. I'd built up a decent tolerance, but I was still a skinny kid, not even twenty. That night, I was past the point of good decisions.

I don't remember how I met Lynne. I know we ended up on the back patio—which was no more than a bunch of uneven pavers shoved unceremoniously into soft Missouri soil. Somebody had lit a fire in the pit and after the heat of the party, it was a refreshing place to have a quiet conversation. Though Lynne and I didn't do much talking. She was tipsy and hot. I was drunk and, well, let's say eager. After what felt like an appropriate amount of time—I'd known Lynne about thirty minutes—I led her up to my bedroom but found my roommate and his girlfriend there.

Lynne took my hand and asked me to walk her home.

Sounds so innocent, doesn't it?

Her apartment wasn't far, one of the newer buildings just off campus. When we stepped inside, I froze.

No hand-me-down furniture like in most students' apartments, but well-made furnishings and high-end decor. Just inside the door, I took it in—the couch and love seat and upholstered ottoman that, with a fancy tray on top, served as a coffee table. Lamps placed just so on end tables were surrounded by decorations that added light and life. On the walls hung canvases, works of art in bright colors that drew me in. Though the room was dim, the space felt peaceful, surreal. After the frat party, I felt as if I'd stepped off campus into my parents' life of order and privilege and faith.

I know now that the room was your doing. Your fingerprints were all over that beautiful place.

I'd thought we were alone, but Lynne's quick, "Hey, Camilla," had my gaze scanning the space again.

There you were, in the corner by the window beneath a dim lamp. Paintbrush in hand, studying the canvas. You glanced our way, gaze skimming past your roommate to land on me. Your lips squished together, and you leaned back. I didn't know what the reaction meant at the time. After years together, I recognize disgust on your face.

I deserved that.

You returned your attention to your painting.

"Ignore her. Come on." Lynne tugged gently to lead me toward the hallway, but I didn't move. And I didn't take my eyes off you.

You wore a ratty St. Louis Rams T-shirt and sweatpants. Your hair was pulled up in a messy bun, and you had on no makeup. Compared with your painted and coiffed roommate, you seemed downright dowdy. Except there was something about you, as if I'd seen you before. As if you'd mattered to me once, and somehow I'd forgotten.

Okay, I was drunk. That last bit feels like a memory I made up to make myself feel better. Sounded good, though, right?

So maybe it wasn't you that had me pausing. Your apartment reminded me of my mother and all the times I'd seen her on a similar sofa surrounded by similar decor, head bowed in prayer. My conscience, which had lain dormant for months, decided at that moment to rear its prying little head.

And unexpected words filled my mind.

Are you really willing to forgo a lifelong dream for one hour of pleasure?

How would one night with Lynne ruin my chances of becoming a doctor?

Maybe she'd pass along some debilitating disease. Or maybe my promiscuity would become a pattern. Later, when I reflected, I realized it had already become a pattern. Still, how would that prevent me from attending medical school?

I'd forgotten my other dreams, Camilla, dreams beyond work. Dreams that included a wife and children and serving the God I'd once been so devoted to.

At that moment, I knew God was warning me, and I trusted Him. Nothing that happened in the bedroom down the hall would be worth the cost.

Lynne tugged on my hand, but I saw her differently. She was high, in no better shape to make good decisions than I was. I kissed her on the cheek, made a lame excuse about an early study session, and fled.

It was the first time the Lord intervened in my relationship with you, Cammie, but it wouldn't be the last.

Yours always,

Daniel

CHAPTER FOUR

THE SEATBELT SIGN DINGED. Camilla was almost there, only—she glanced at her watch—twelve hours after the call from her sister. The longest twelve hours of her life.

How was Jeremy now? Had anything happened while she'd been in the air? She'd kept her phone on, against the rules, but hadn't had service for most of the two-and-a-half-hour flight from Oklahoma City. She glanced at it now. As they descended into Salt Lake, her service connected and text messages flashed. Mostly friends checking in, reminding her of their prayers.

Nothing from Marcy or Kevin. Which meant that Jeremy was the same.

Not that they'd text if he'd gone downhill since she'd talked to them that morning. They'd wait until she arrived and tell her the bad news in person.

Stop it.

In the years since Daniel's murder, Camilla had been forced to learn to control her thoughts. If she hadn't, the fears and regrets would have driven her mad. She practiced those skills now, turning her worries into pleas and prayers. God had this. She would trust in Him.

Though Marcy and Kevin had offered to pick her up, she'd insisted they stay with the boys. She ordered an Uber, which took her to Primary Children's Hospital, where she dragged her suitcase inside the grand and spacious lobby.

Gazing around, she was trying to figure out where to go next when she saw Kevin stepping off the escalator.

She hurried forward and fell into his arms. He'd been her brother-in-law for over twenty years. Right now, his presence steadied her, comforted her.

He hugged her tightly, then pulled back. "They're both the same. Come on." He ushered her to the reception desk. "This is Jeremy Wright's mother," he told the woman.

She asked for ID, which Camilla produced, and then was handed a badge hanging from a lanyard. "You have to show that—"

"I'll tell her everything," Kevin said. "She needs to see her son now." Kevin took Camilla's suitcase. "Let's go."

Camilla and Kevin rode the escalator up one flight, and then she followed him along a maze of hallways. They took so many turns, she was sure she'd never remember the way. Outside double doors labeled *Pediatric ICU,* Kevin pressed a button. Over the intercom, a woman said, "Yes?"

"Kevin McMillan, Evan's dad."

The door opened automatically, and Kevin led the way. He paused at the desk inside the door, where a woman stood. "This is Jeremy Wright's mother."

The woman smiled at Camilla. "Glad you made it. Let me know if you need anything."

Camilla couldn't seem to form words. The woman accepted her quick nod.

Kevin led her around a corner, then another. They stepped into a bright, spacious area.

She'd barely taken the scene in when Marcy rushed to her, arms open.

Camilla pulled her older sister close and sobbed. "I can't believe this is happening."

"I know. I know." Marcy stepped back and took her hand. "Come on."

A huge nurses station sat in the middle of the area. Glass-fronted rooms lined both sides. Marcy passed one and stopped in front of the next. She squeezed Marcy's hand.

Camilla stepped through the open slider and approached cautiously.

Her son lay on a hospital bed beneath a dingy white blanket that covered him from the stomach down. A neck brace held his head unnaturally straight. Tubes poked from each nostril. A thicker one came from his mouth, fastened in place with tape that extended almost ear to ear. He wore no shirt, and little squares had been attached to his chest, wires coming from those.

His hair, usually perfectly styled, was pushed back, messy and dirty. His closed eyes were bruised. His left arm had a cast from his biceps to his fingertips. A bandage on his neck only partially covered a long gash. Not a cut, more like a serious scrape. From the seatbelt, she realized.

Above his head, a monitor displayed his heart rate, his blood pressure, and other things she didn't understand.

If Daniel were there, he'd know exactly what was going on. He'd hold her and tell her everything would be all right.

Camilla wanted to take Jeremy's hand, but the one not encased in plaster was attached to more tubes. She touched his shoulder and felt warm skin. "I'm here, baby." The words cracked, and she sniffed, pulling herself together. She had to be strong now. "I'm here. You're going to be okay."

Marcy stood at the foot of the bed, tears streaming down her face.

"Have you heard anything else from the doctors?"

On the far side of the room stood a man Camilla hadn't noticed before. He looked to be in his forties, had graying hair, cut short and receding, and a close-cropped beard. He wore royal-blue scrubs. "I'm Nathan, Jeremy's nurse. I'll let the doctor know you're here. She should be by shortly to give you an update." He grabbed a phone on the wall and stretched the cord as he stepped just outside the room.

Marcy said, "There's been no change."

"And Evan?"

"He has a terrible headache, and he's in a lot of pain"—she patted her lower abdomen—"where the seatbelt restrained him."

"Is he awake?"

"Off and on. He's on some pretty heavy painkillers."

Camilla looked back at Jeremy. She willed his eyes to open, then rethought that. He'd be miserable with that neck brace, a tube down his throat. It would be better if he slept.

Marcy's hand slid into hers. "I have to ask you something."

"Okay."

"They said they were going skiing."

She turned to Marcy. "Right. Jeremy was looking forward to it."

Marcy held her gaze. "The accident happened in the desert about forty miles south of our house."

What? That didn't make sense. Marcy and Kevin lived in Stansbury Park, a good half-hour drive west of Salt Lake. The mountains were to the east. Though Camilla had never been south of Stansbury, there was nothing but desert for miles, as far as she knew. "What were they doing out there?"

"I hoped you'd know."

Camilla turned back to Jeremy. "They lied to us?"

"Maybe they went skiing and then went to the desert."

"Why?"

Silence.

"Did you ask Evan?"

"He doesn't remember. The doctors say it's normal for him to have some memory loss."

It made sense that he wouldn't remember the accident and maybe a few minutes before it. But to not even remember why they'd been there? "Any idea where they might have been going?"

Marcy shook her head. "The accident investigator's going to come talk to us later."

Camilla focused on Jeremy again. What had the boys been up to?

A knock had her turning. A forty-something woman in green scrubs and a white jacket stepped in and extended her hand, which Camilla shook. "Dr. Henrietta Grayson. Just call me Hen." She was slender with curly brown hair that fell to her shoulders. "I'm the attending physician."

Hen was followed by a man—younger, dark-brown hair, also wearing green scrubs but no white jacket. He introduced himself. "Dr. Marcus Vincheti."

"Mark is a resident." Hen stepped to the opposite side of Jeremy's bed. "How's our patient?"

"He doesn't look good," Camilla said.

Hen smiled. "Not that this'll make you feel better, but he's looked worse."

The nurse—Nathan, she remembered—said, "His blood pressure's held steady."

"Good." Hen checked the tube coming from his mouth, then the ventilator. She studied the numbers and graphs before facing Camilla again. "Did they tell you his blood pressure dropped in the middle of the night?"

She glanced at Marcy, who said nothing.

"No."

"We pushed fluids and got it under control. It's risen now. If it starts to drop again, we'll have to wean him off the sedatives and wake him up. Sedatives lower blood pressure."

"Was it that serious?"

Hen tipped her head from side to side. "It can only go so low, and we were on the edge."

On the edge, as in... Jeremy had almost died? She didn't ask the question because she couldn't make her mouth form the words. And maybe she didn't want to know the answer.

"If we wake him, will he do what you tell him?" Hen asked. "Some patients will try to pull out the tube, which can cause serious damage. Will he listen to you and be calm and do what we say?"

Jeremy had a stubborn streak, but he trusted his mother. "He'll be fine."

"Good. We could always restrain him, but I hate to do that. He'll be distressed enough. Hopefully, we won't have to go that route."

"What's the prognosis?" Camilla asked. "What happened exactly?"

Hen rounded the bed to where Camilla stood. "Jeremy's chest was pummeled by the steering wheel. One of his lungs collapsed completely. The other didn't fare much better. We've inserted chest tubes on both sides." She lifted the blanket, and Camilla saw a tube extending from her son's side near the bottom of his ribcage to a clear plastic box hanging from the bed. The box had different sections. One was filled with blood. "We're draining fluid and air from the chest cavity. It's called a pneumothorax. Basically, air and fluid press on the lungs from outside and keep them from expanding, so we have to get that air and fluid out."

Camilla thought she understood. "So when you drain all

that stuff, he'll be fine, right? His lungs will heal, and he'll recover?"

Hen squeezed Camilla's upper arm. "That's the goal."

"But...?"

"No buts. But also no promises. Your son is young and strong." She took a breath. "Honestly, Ms. Wright—"

"Camilla."

"Camilla, Jeremy was in very bad shape when they brought him in. The fact that he's still here tells me he's a fighter."

There'd been a chance that...that he wouldn't still be there? It had been that close?

"Also, you might have noticed"—Hen patted Jeremy's arm—"we've got this huge cast on him. Ortho will be down to talk to you later today."

She tried to catch up with Hen's assessment. "Is the arm okay?"

"Nothing that can't be repaired." She joined Mark, who'd stood in the doorway silently. "If you have any questions, let Nathan know, and he'll get answers for you. Don't be shy. We want you to understand what's going on. Okay?"

"Thank you."

Hen nodded, and she and Mark walked out.

Marcy still stood in the corner of the room. "She's really good. Kevin says she's one of the best in the country."

Kevin wasn't a medical doctor but had a PhD in biochemistry. He understood this stuff more than Camilla or Marcy would.

Of all the things she needed to deal with, what came out of her mouth was, "It's weird she asked me to call her by her first name."

"They all do that," Marcy said. "I'm getting used to it."

Camilla focused on Jeremy. Until she'd walked in, it had all felt like a terrible nightmare. Now, at her son's side, seeing him attached to more machines than she had names for, it felt too real. It *was* too real. She'd hoped for a positive prognosis. She'd hoped for a promise. *He'll get better. It's just a matter of time.*

But that wasn't the sense she'd gotten from Hen, kind as the doctor had been. The sense she'd gotten was that Jeremy might be stable now, but there were no guarantees.

CHAPTER FIVE

AFTER MARCY WENT BACK to Evan's room, Camilla called Zoë to give her an update, then called Daniel's parents. Her parents already knew about the accident—Marcy was keeping them informed.

Though she couldn't see their faces, she heard the shock and horror in the voices of her in-laws. They'd never been the same after Daniel's death, and the prospect of their only grandson joining him... It was horrifying.

Please, God.

While Peggy tried to pull herself together, Roger promised to let the rest of Daniel's brothers know what was going on.

After that, Camilla stood at Jeremy's bedside and watched him sleep, begging God for his life.

She didn't know how much time had passed when Marcy poked her head in. "You all right?"

She forced her gaze away from her son. "Yeah. Can I see Evan? Where is he?"

"Right next door." Marcy held out her hand. "Come on."

Camilla glanced at the nurse, seated again on the far side of the room. "You'll stay with him?"

"Jeremy's my only patient. I'm not going anywhere."

His only patient? There was comfort in that, knowing the nurse would be solely focused on her son.

There was terror in that, too. Was Jeremy teetering so close to death that a nurse needed to stay with him constantly?

She didn't want to leave. But she needed to support Marcy the way Marcy had supported her. And she needed to see her nephew. "Thank you."

They walked to the next patient room, no more than ten feet away. If anything happened with Jeremy, would Camilla hear?

"Nathan knows where you are," Marcy said. "Everybody on this side of the floor knows what happened with the boys. Everybody knows they're cousins. They'll get you if they need you." She stepped into the room, which was identical to Jeremy's. A pretty blond nurse in blue scrubs was seated on one side of the room and focused on a computer screen.

Kevin was at his son's bedside. The head of Evan's bed was raised.

Camilla froze. The whites of her nephew's eyes weren't white but bright red. Bruises rounded them. He had a cut on his cheek. His lips were pinched in pain.

Over the shock of his appearance, Camilla crossed the room. "Evan, sweetheart. How are you feeling?"

"Is Jeremy okay?" His voice was weak and filled with dread.

"He's alive." Camilla took Evan's hand. "They're taking good care of him."

Evan turned away.

"How are you?" Camilla asked.

"I need to see him. I need to know..."

Camilla looked at Marcy, but her gaze was on her son.

"I'm so sorry this happened." Camilla brushed a lock of his dark brown hair off his brow.

He said nothing.

The room was silent and tense.

Evan pressed his hand against his abdomen, and the muscles in his cheeks ticked.

Camilla backed away as Kevin stood and said, "He's hurting. Is it time for those painkillers?"

The nurse glanced at the clock. "Not quite. I'll call the doctor and see what we can do."

The pain in her nephew's face caused Camilla's stomach to tense. Poor, sweet kid. She'd do anything to make this better for him. Right now, that meant leaving him alone.

"I'm going to sit with Jeremy." She kissed his forehead. "I love you."

He nodded but didn't seem able to speak.

Marcy followed her out.

Camilla peeked into Jeremy's room. The nurse was there. Jeremy was unconscious. She wiped the tears streaming from her eyes and turned to her sister.

"I'm so sorry."

Marcy was crying too. "This isn't your fault."

"Whatever happened, Jeremy was driving. Do you know anything—?"

"The investigator will be able to tell us more. I'm going back to sit with Evan now that you're here and can stay with Jeremy."

"Thank you." She pulled her sister into a hug. "Thank you for taking care of him."

Marcy nodded against her shoulder. "We didn't leave him alone all night. I stayed with him, and when medical issues came up, Kevin went in with Jeremy, and I sat with Evan."

The tears kept coming, but now they were tears of gratitude. She whispered a prayer of thanks for her sister and brother-in-law, for the hospital and nurses. *Please, please save our boys.*

"Excuse me, Mrs. Wright?"

She turned toward the voice. Jeremy's nurse was standing in the doorway to his room, the phone receiver in his hand. "Just Camilla."

He nodded. "There's a detective here to see you. Is it okay if they let him in?"

"Yes, please."

"I'll get my husband." Marcy hurried to Evan's room.

A moment later, an older, heavyset balding man rounded the corner and walked toward Camilla. He stuck out his hand. "Detective Hawkins."

"I'm Camilla Wright. My sister and brother-in-law will be here in a second."

"No rush." He looked to be in his midfifties and had a paunch that hung over his belt. His eyes were kind. He looked around, spotted a short, empty hallway that led to a corner beyond Jeremy's room. "I'll wait there. Come when you're ready."

She waited in Jeremy's room. Her son looked the same. The ventilator's soothing rhythm kept air in Jeremy's lungs. The numbers on the monitors... "His blood pressure's down."

Nathan glanced at the screen. "We're watching it closely."

She should let the nurses and doctors manage it. *Please, Lord...* How many times had she said that since she'd gotten the news? A hundred? A thousand? She felt like every exhale carried a prayer.

A few minutes later, Marcy stepped in. "They gave him something for the pain. He's asleep."

"Thank God."

They found Kevin with Detective Hawkins. After they'd all been introduced, the detective faced Camilla. "The boys were headed south away from the highway on a country road off

Route 36 about ten miles from Vernon. Jeremy was driving. Before I tell you anything else, I want you to know he was doing nothing wrong. According to the driver of the car behind them, he was going seventy in a sixty-five on a straight, dry, deserted road. No cop would have stopped him."

Marcy took Camilla's hand. "Just an accident."

The cop's lips pressed together. "Yes, well. About that." He pulled a little notebook from his pocket but didn't consult it. "There were reports of gunshots."

Marcy gasped. "Someone shot at them?"

"We don't know exactly what happened. The 911 caller said the shooter was still firing as he rode to the scene."

"Wait," Kevin said. "Still firing...at him? At the boys?"

"The caller didn't say, just that he was still firing."

"Did he see the guy?" Kevin asked.

"He didn't say, if he did. It seems the caller was more focused on the boys and getting them to safety."

"Who was he?" Kevin asked. "What was he doing out there?"

The detective shook his head. "The guy wouldn't identify himself, and when the helicopter arrived, he told the paramedics what he knew and then took off."

"How odd," Marcy said. "Why would he do that?"

"We're trying to locate him now," Detective Hawkins said. "The accident happened on a narrow road not a quarter mile from the main highway. Witnesses saw the accident from the highway and were there in minutes to help. A few of them told us about the man who was already at the scene. Together, they pulled Evan from the car and got him to safety, then lifted the car off Jeremy and—"

"*Off* Jeremy," Camilla said. "It was *on* him?"

"Sorry. Let me back up. It looks like a tire blew. The car

jerked to the right, and your son jerked it back to the left. He overcorrected and lost control. It's not that uncommon with teen drivers. The car spun, hit the lip on the far side of the road, and flipped." The investigator's gaze met all of theirs before he continued. "It flipped three times side-over-side, then shifted and flipped three more times end over end."

Marcy gasped.

Kevin pulled his wife close, but Marcy never let go of Camilla's hand.

Six times. They'd flipped six times.

Hawkins continued. "The car came to a stop about a hundred yards from the road. All the windows shattered, of course. Jeremy's arm flew out the window. The car landed on its side, pinning Jeremy's arm beneath it."

That explained the broken wrist and thumb. They were lucky his bones hadn't been crushed.

She thought of the cast. Maybe they had been. But the doctor said it was fixable.

The investigator consulted his notebook. "Other drivers who stopped to help told us the unknown man, presumably our 911 caller, knew exactly what to do. He was shouting orders, telling people how to care for Evan while he managed Jeremy. When someone challenged him, he told them he was a medic. Someone suggested he was an angel." One of the man's eyebrows quirked. "He's the one who insisted helicopters be sent. Good thing, too. The closest first responder was forty miles out. I was farther away than that when the call came in. That stranger saved their lives."

Thank You, God, for that man. Whoever he was.

"Nobody got a good look at him." The detective's lips pressed together for a moment, and he shook his head. "Fact is, he was no angel. I think he was the guy who fired the gun."

"Come again?" Kevin took a step back.

"Either that or he was associated with him. Maybe they were messing around. Maybe they were shooting at each other. What other reason not to identify himself? To take off? He must have been doing something wrong."

"Why report the gunshot if he was the one who'd done it?" Kevin asked.

"Maybe he was afraid someone else would report it and cast suspicion on him."

Kevin squinted. "It doesn't make sense."

"When I find the guy," the detective said, "I'll figure it out. I'm looking into the medic angle—how many medics could live out there? We've been canvassing the few homeowners in the area, trying to find him, but no luck so far."

"You think a bullet hit the tire?" Kevin shook his head. "Doesn't make sense. A tire is low to the ground. To fire that low—"

"We're just beginning our investigation," Hawkins said. "There's a ridge to the west of the accident site. To the east, where the car ended up, is flat. We're assuming the man was on that ridge, and we're assuming he wasn't trying to kill the boys, since he went out of his way to save their lives." His lips quirked in a smile. "Unless you think someone has it in for your kids."

He'd meant the words as a joke, but Camilla felt them deep in her gut.

Both Marcy and Kevin looked at her.

She shook her head, swallowed. "It can't be related."

The investigator narrowed his eyes. "Explain."

"Nothing. My husband..." Her voice cracked. Her hands trembled. She breathed through the rise of panic.

Detective Hawkins waited.

Marcy and Kevin said nothing, even though they knew everything. Almost everything.

"My husband witnessed a murder. He testified, and then he went missing. Technically, he's still missing, but it's been four years." The images came back. Blood on the steering wheel. Blood on the windshield. Blood pooled on the floorboards. "He was murdered."

The man stepped back. "Whoa. Okay. But... You don't think—?"

"I can't see why, now, they'd come after Jeremy. He was only thirteen at the time. He had nothing to do with anything. And the gang got its revenge on Daniel." She focused on her sister. "Why would a St. Louis gang come all the way to Utah to hurt him?" She shifted her gaze to Kevin, trying to sound confident and cursing the fear in her voice. "It doesn't make sense."

Marcy squeezed her hand.

Kevin said, "I'm sure this has nothing to do with that."

The investigator missed nothing. "You're probably right, but I'm glad you told me. We'll keep our eyes open for... What gang was it?"

"Sons of Vipers out of St. Louis. The murderer is Francis Campos. He's in prison, though he still has people on the outside. But it's probably not related." She looked at her sister, at Kevin, needing reassurance. "How could it be related?"

They looked as scared and confused as she felt.

"It's good to know." Hawkins handed her a business card, then gave one to Marcy and another to Kevin. "I'll need your contact information."

They recited their cell phone numbers, which the investigator wrote down. "How are the boys doing?"

Kevin gave him an update, and the man smiled. "When I got to the scene..." He shook his head, but his smile stayed in place. "Thank God they were wearing their seatbelts. Even so, it's a miracle they survived. I don't use the m-word very often, but it fits here. This is a story I'll be telling for a long time."

After he left, Marcy and Kevin returned to Evan's room, and Camilla returned to Jeremy's. She should feel better. Jeremy hadn't caused the accident. His injuries and Evan's weren't Jeremy's fault.

But she couldn't help the worry that crept into her heart. Were Francis Campos's people after them?

CHAPTER SIX

DEAR CAMILLA,

Maybe you don't want this walk down memory lane. I hope I haven't ruined things so thoroughly between us that you tear my letters up and toss them in the fire.

Just in case you don't read to the end—or I don't have time to finish—I need you to know the point. I need you to know the most important thing.

I love you.

That's never changed.

No matter what happens next, it never will.

I took you for granted. I assumed that you and the kids would always be there. That I could run off and do my thing and come home whenever it suited me, and you'd be there, happily waiting for me. It was wrong. *I* was wrong. I'm sorry.

I love you, and I want to fix it. All of it. Please?

Two days after I saw you for the first time, I found myself stepping into an older building on the edge of campus. I'd discovered the nondenominational church about two weeks into freshman year, back when I thought I could balance college life and faith. The experience Friday night had shown me that my so-called balance was anything but. I'd made time to go to class and study, to drink and meet girls—more than I could count, not that I wanted to. And I'd cut God out of my life. Not on purpose, of course. I still pretended my faith, but it wasn't real.

Most of that time, He was pretty quiet about the whole thing. But ever since His whispered words in your apartment, He'd been in my head.

Maybe Mom had stepped up her praying game. You know how she is. She probably asked Dad and her friends to join her. Though I didn't tell her how I'd been behaving, she has a sixth sense about these things. Like you do with Zoë and Jeremy. When it's you, I'm amazed and impressed.

When it's Mom, it's just creepy.

Saturday, the day after I saw you for the first time, between study sessions, a jog, and a late-afternoon workout in the campus gym, I wrestled with myself and my conscience. I didn't want to give up my lifestyle. Staying pure and sober were hard enough, but doing that while living in a frat house? Temptations surrounded me every day.

Okay, fine. I know what you're thinking. Yes, I was having fun. Anybody who tells you sin isn't fun is lying. It is. At least at first.

I was still in the fun part, and I didn't want to let it go.

Sunday morning, usually reserved for sleeping off headaches and exercising away the shame that lingered from Saturday's choices, I slipped into a seat near the back just as the worship team had the congregation stand. I read the words projected on the screen and sang along, feeling like the biggest hypocrite in the world. That feeling didn't fade as I listened to the sermon, wishing I'd stayed in bed.

I was ready to bolt from the auditorium the instant we were released, but then the older guy next to me introduced himself. Turned out he was a professor at the university, guessed I was a student, and invited me to a small group at his home. I was polite, of course, but there was no way this church thing was for me, not anymore. Not after the choices I'd made.

And yeah, I knew all the scriptures about grace and mercy and how Jesus paid the price. I'd decided to pretend none of that was true. Easier to wallow in sin than climb out.

The auditorium was nearly empty when I finally extricated myself from the conversation with the professor and turned toward the aisle to make my escape.

And there you were.

You'd shed the sloppy clothes and messy hair. You wore a pretty white blouse and slacks. Your dark-brown hair framed your ivory skin and set off the bluest eyes I'd ever seen.

You were on your way out, laughing at something the woman beside you had said, and I saw what I'd missed Friday night. You were gorgeous.

You still are, by the way. Sometimes, even now, when you smile at me, I'm blown away by your beauty. Your inside-and-out beauty.

When you saw me, your smile faded. I think you were trying to remember where you'd seen me before. Or maybe you knew exactly and were trying to figure out how I could stand in a church and not be struck by lightning.

I wanted to avert my gaze. Shame poured over me, hot and thick and sticky, and I was sure I'd never be able to get it all off.

"Everything okay, son?"

The professor settled his hand on my shoulder, and I focused on him, avoiding you, the one person who knew I didn't belong there.

You saw through my clean-cut facade to the ugly truth beneath.

"Come back next week," the professor said, "and maybe you'll get up the nerve to talk to her."

I didn't think I wanted to talk to you. But when he said that, I realized I did. I hurried to the lobby, but you were gone.

Thank God He didn't end the story there.

Yours always,

Daniel

CHAPTER SEVEN

CAMILLA HAD BARELY PROCESSED the conversation with the accident investigator when a man in green scrubs stepped into Jeremy's room. "Dr. Phillip Shreve. Phil."

She stood and shook his hand.

"I'm an orthopedic surgeon. They told you about Jeremy's injuries?"

"Wrist and thumb, right?"

"Yup. I don't want to wait too long to do the surgery. Probably tomorrow, assuming Hen agrees."

"Is it serious?"

"Not at all. The wrist is a clean break. The thumb's a little more complex, but I'll get it straightened right out." He lifted the blanket and tapped on the plaster cast. "We'll get him out of this. The last thing he'll need when he wakes up is to expend all his energy lifting that."

Seemed the least of their worries.

"Will it be dangerous to do surgery with all this"—she waved at the ventilator—"going on?"

"We can manage. The sooner we set those bones, the

better." He glanced at Nathan, the quiet presence on the far side of the room. "How's he doing?"

"Holding steady," the nurse said.

"Good, good." Phil regarded the screens before facing Camilla again. "Unless something changes, I'll see you tomorrow. Hang in there. We're taking good care of him."

The doctor left, and the nurse smiled at her. "He's good. All the doctors here are good."

"The nurses, too, I think."

Nathan dipped his head. "Did anyone show you where the food is?"

Food. She hadn't even thought about it, though at the mention, her stomach growled. She hadn't eaten since that bowl of soup the night before.

He must've heard the growl because his lips quirked up. "There's a Ronald McDonald room on this floor, which has some snacks and a microwave. The one upstairs is better stocked. Often, a group brings lunch or dinner, so you don't have to buy food. If they don't have anything, there's a cafeteria on the first floor, but most people walk across the skybridge to the building next door. They have a much better selection."

"I can't leave him."

"Eventually, you'll need to stretch your legs," Nathan said. "You're fortunate that you have other family here who can sit with Jeremy. There's a little snack room down the hall, just past Evan's room."

That Jeremy's nurse knew her nephew's name warmed her heart. He cared. All these people, though they didn't know Jeremy or Evan or any of them, cared about them.

Nathan continued. "The snacks are for patients' families, so help yourself. If you want to bring something to put in the fridge, just label it so nobody else eats it."

"Thank you." Gratitude for this man and all the people in this place overwhelmed her. They'd even provided food.

Camilla found the snack room and grabbed a yogurt, a granola bar, and a bottle of water and returned to the chair next to Jeremy's bed. "Is it okay if I eat in here?"

"Of course." Nathan inserted a tool into the tube going down Jeremy's throat and pulled it back out slowly. "It needs to be suctioned regularly."

There were so many moving parts in keeping Jeremy alive. If one of them broke down...

Stop it. Nathan and Hen and Phil—all the people caring for Jeremy knew what they were doing. Worrying wouldn't help anything. *Please, God, please heal him.*

The nurse sat again and typed on the keyboard sitting on the built-in desk.

Camilla's phone dinged. A text from Zoë.

How is he?

She stepped out of the room and dialed her daughter. "There's been no change. But we expect a full recovery." It didn't matter that the doctors hadn't said that, Camilla expected it. She would believe. And she needed her daughter to believe too.

When she hung up with Zoë, she texted her friends and updated them. She didn't tell anyone what they'd learned from the accident investigator except that the tire had blown out and Jeremy had lost control of the vehicle. They didn't need to know the rest. She didn't want to think about the rest.

She resumed her seat at Jeremy's bedside, trying to shake off the investigator's suspicion. It had been an accident, nothing more.

But in the quiet of her own mind, she couldn't make herself

believe it. Francis Campos was in prison, but the gang he'd operated was still going strong. At the time of Daniel's death, the FBI had estimated that the Sons of Vipers were responsible for more than a quarter of the drugs that came into St. Louis.

Daniel'd had more than enough contact with gang members as an ER doctor in the city. He'd always managed to steer clear of the drama they brought with them into the hospital. Daniel had tried to be a positive force in their lives, sharing his faith and kind words. Not that anybody'd responded, not that she knew of, anyway.

That day nearly five years earlier, he'd just been doing his job when he'd walked into one of the rooms and found Francis Campos standing over Daniel's patient, pressing a pillow against the man's face.

Daniel made himself a target when he reported the incident, even more of a target when he insisted on testifying. The whole family had relocated to a safe house until after the trial.

Daniel should have been safe. Would have been if not for Camilla.

Moisture swelled beneath her eyelids. She could never undo what she'd done that day. She would never forgive herself.

She snatched a tissue from a box on the adjustable table and dried her tears. She couldn't bring Daniel back, but she wouldn't let her fear or her negligence put her children in danger. Maybe the gunshots that resulted in the boys' accident had been random. Some irresponsible guy doing target practice too close to the road. Maybe it had nothing to do with Campos and drugs and murder. But she had to be sure.

Could she do it, though? Could she nudge back open the door she'd worked so hard to slam shut four years earlier?

She stood and watched Jeremy breathe. Details she'd missed the first time she'd looked at him became apparent to her now. Bruises around his eyes. A thin cut on one shoulder. There was dirt on his forehead and in his hair. More on his neck. She closed her eyes and allowed herself to imagine the accident. The car flipping on the hard desert floor, rocks and earth and debris flying everywhere, entering through those smashed windows. She tried to brush some of that dirt away with her tear-moistened tissue, but there was too much.

"Here."

Nathan was holding a folded disposable cloth toward her.

She took it. "I won't hurt him, will I?"

He glanced at the monitor. "If anything, your presence will comfort him."

She followed the man's gaze. "Is the blood pressure too low?"

"We're watching it."

She wanted to ask more questions. What blood pressure numbers would be too low? When should she start worrying?

As if that would help.

She wiped Jeremy's face and neck.

Behind all the tubes and bandages was her handsome, fun-loving son. She brushed a few hairs off his forehead and kissed it. *Please, Lord. Please heal him.*

Tears stinging again, she backed away. When Jeremy woke up, he'd want to know everything. He'd want evidence of what had happened.

She took her phone and snapped a photo. She knew him well enough to know he'd want to see it.

And she'd want to remember it later. When they were home, when Jeremy was healed, when they could look back on this as a time of restoration, of God's faithful hand, she would want to remember everything. When this was over, she'd be thankful for the photographs.

But if Campos was behind this, it wouldn't be over with Jeremy's healing.

Would it ever be?

She couldn't pretend. She couldn't just hope for the best. She wouldn't. The accident probably had nothing to do with the gang member currently serving a life sentence. But *probably* wasn't good enough.

She scrolled through her contacts until she found the name of the FBI agent who'd worked with them four years earlier. After a deep breath and a quick prayer, she dialed.

CHAPTER EIGHT

THE PHONE RANG TWICE before a man answered. "Special Agent Falk."

The sound of his deep, familiar voice stole Camilla's breath. She'd hoped never to talk to him again. Never to need him again.

"Mrs. Wright?"

She was surprised when he said her name, but perhaps her number was still in his phone as his had been in hers. She swallowed her fear and stepped into the hallway so Nathan wouldn't overhear. "You worked with us four years ago when my husband was—"

"I remember you." His voice shifted from businesslike to concerned. "I remember Daniel and his sacrifice. What's happened?"

He remembered? That made this much easier. "My son was in a car accident last night, and the local investigator believes someone was shooting at his car. Or maybe just shooting nearby. He thinks maybe a bullet hit the tire, but they haven't confirmed that yet. I'm probably just being paranoid, but what are the chances a stray bullet would accidentally hit the boys' car on a desert road? It seems slim. Anyway, you told me I should call you if I ever felt threatened. I mean, it's probably nothing but..." She was rambling. She forced herself to shut up and let him talk.

There was a long pause. She waited, knowing Lincoln Falk wasn't distracted or irritated. He was processing.

Finally, he said, "I'd say the chances are very slim that it was an accident. But slim chances happen every day. How's Jeremy?"

She stared through the glass at her son while she gave Agent Falk the short version of his and Evan's injuries. Try as she might, she couldn't keep the tears from her voice.

"Sounds serious," Falk said. "If somebody did it on purpose, he wasn't messing around."

"We're lucky they survived."

"This happened in Oklahoma?"

"Utah. He was visiting his cousin."

"Your sister still lives in Stansbury Park?"

"You have an impressive memory, Agent Falk." She'd liked that about him—his memory, his focus, his dedication. "The accident happened near Vernon on Route 36."

Another long pause, and then, "Looking at a map. That's on the outskirts of the middle of nowhere. What were they doing there?"

"We don't know. Jeremy's unconscious. My nephew doesn't remember. They were supposed to be skiing. If they went skiing and were on their way home, then they passed my sister's house to go into the desert. But maybe it was all a lie."

"As far as I can tell, there's nothing out there," Falk said. "Were they headed toward home or away?"

"I didn't think to ask that."

"No problem. I can't see anything interesting on that road in any direction."

Camilla waited. She could picture Agent Falk staring at a wall, a blank look on his face. But she knew that behind the goatee, behind the coffee-colored skin and black eyes, his mind was spinning, making connections, considering all he knew. She'd been impressed with him four years earlier when he'd worked on the anti-gang task force in St. Louis. When they'd been turned down for federal protection, he'd done everything in his power to keep them safe. Daniel's death hadn't been Falk's fault.

That had been all Camilla's doing.

In the silence, she stared through the glass at her son and prayed Falk would tell her it was very unlikely Campos's men were after them. She hoped he'd thank her for the information and tell her not to worry, that they were safe.

Through the phone, she heard tapping, a quiet, "huh," and more tapping. Then, "I'm not working gangs anymore, so I haven't kept up with Campos's people. It does seem unlikely that Campos's men would travel to Utah. Oklahoma is much closer to St. Louis. Why not attack there? And shooting out a tire is definitely not their MO. Having said that, you're right. The chances of a stray bullet hitting a tire in a place like that? I'm looking at the satellite image, and I simply can't come up with a logical way that would happen accidentally."

He was quiet again, and when she couldn't stand it another minute, she said, "So, you're saying...?"

"That I need to look into it. You have the accident investigator's name and number?"

She pulled the business card from her jeans pocket and read the information to Falk.

"I'll look into it."

"Do you think I should bring Zoë here? Should I assume—?"

"It feels unlikely that Campos knows where your son vacations but doesn't know where you live. I think that, if you or your kids were targets, Campos and his men would have gone to Oklahoma. I can only guess, but I doubt this was Campos's people. Just sit tight. I'll get back to you."

She stared at the phone after he hung up, willing her heart to stop pounding. Falk hadn't assured her as she'd hoped, but he was a conscientious man. He wouldn't blow off her concerns. He was looking into it. That was his job.

She wouldn't panic.

She had to be strong.

For four years, she'd told herself she had to be strong.

If only she could fall into Daniel's arms, let him be the strong one. She was so tired. Almost no sleep the night before, all the trauma of the day, now the conversation with Falk. She couldn't do it.

She couldn't.

"Camilla?" Marcy's voice came from down the hall.

Camilla pulled a deep breath through her nose, pushed it out her mouth, and turned.

Her sister's eyes were wide. "Evan's really hurting. They're considering exploratory surgery to find out what's causing it."

Camilla crossed the space and took Marcy in her arms.

Marcy collapsed against her and held on. "If they could just figure it out, they could fix it. But the scans aren't showing anything."

"He's going to be okay," Camilla said, and then she prayed while her sister wept on her shoulder.

Whether Camilla felt she could do this again or not, here she was. She wasn't going to fall apart or run away. She was going to stay by her son's side, support her sister and brother-in-law and, if necessary, protect her family from evil. She had no choice.

CHAPTER NINE

DEAR CAMILLA,

I had no intention of returning to church.

The following weekend, a bunch of my friends and I found an off-campus party, and I did my best to get into the mood. I had a beer, but it was flat and tasteless and turned my stomach like bad fish. I talked to a few girls, but without the benefit of alcohol, I saw beyond their makeup and too-revealing clothes to the human beings beneath. They weren't playthings. They were daughters, sisters, friends, and someday they'd likely be wives and mothers.

It's a lot harder to fall into bed with a girl when you see her like that. And once you see her like that, it's hard to make those images go away. I'm embarrassed to say I tried.

I just wanted things to go back to the way they'd been before. But the fun was gone.

I went to bed early—and alone—and intended to catch up on my sleep Sunday morning. But I awoke at eight o'clock, the words *time for church* ringing like bells in an old-fashioned steeple.

As soon as I entered the auditorium, the professor caught

my eye and waved me over. I slid into the row and sat beside him, then met the people on his other side—his wife and teen children. I enjoyed the service, and if I looked more than once for your dark hair, who could blame me? I needed to know where you were if I was going to avoid you.

You weren't there, not that Sunday, not the next two.

I started attending every Sunday and going to the professor's small group of college kids every Wednesday night. On weekends, I hung out with my new church friends and blew off the frat parties and keggers that had been my entertainment for a year. By Thanksgiving, God had set me on a new course, a course that changed my life.

I still didn't get how the course I had been on would have ruined my future, but I knew my God, and I trusted Him. "In repentance and rest is your salvation. In quietness and trust is your strength."

I told you once about that scripture in Isaiah and how much it meant to me. You painted the words on a canvas and hung it in our home. Do you know what that meant to me?

Camilla, you make everything more beautiful.

I didn't know that yet. What I knew was that God's kindness brought me to repentance. I was on the right track—to Him, and ultimately, to you.

Yours always,

Daniel

CHAPTER TEN

CAMILLA'S STOMACH GROWLED. She needed to eat something besides cheese sticks and yogurt, but she didn't want to leave Jeremy. Marcy and Kevin were at Evan's side, and she didn't have the heart to ask one of them to stay with her son so she could scrounge up dinner. Every so often, the sound of Evan's cries of pain would reach her, and she would squeeze her eyes closed and pray for him.

Jeremy was blessedly unconscious. He'd be in pain when he awoke. Three broken ribs would be bad enough, never mind the lungs, the wrist, and the thumb. She silently thanked God that her son was sleeping through it and asked the Lord to keep his blood pressure up so the doctors wouldn't have to wake him.

The phone on the wall rang, and Nathan snatched it. He covered the mouthpiece and turned to her. "There's someone here to see you, says he's your friend—a Paul Harrington?"

Paul? She'd been texting back and forth with him all day, and he hadn't told her he was coming. Suspicion rose in her belly, but she squelched it. Whoever it was had to have shown his ID, same as she had when she'd arrived.

"Camilla?" Nathan prompted.

"Yes. He can come in."

Nathan spoke into the phone, then hung up and said, "Just so you know, only one outside visitor at a time. If you don't mind, we prefer if you walk to the entrance and bring him in. We don't like guests wandering around by themselves."

"Of course." She hurried to the ICU door to find Paul standing at the entrance, an oversize shopping bag in one hand. When he saw her, he dropped the bag and held his arms wide.

She stepped into them. "What are you doing here?"

He stroked her hair. "Where else would I be?"

She stood back and looked up at him. He was shorter than Daniel's six-two and had brown eyes and brown hair with just a hint of gray at the temples. She usually saw him in casual clothes, but he wore a suit and tie now.

"I can't believe you flew out," she said. "Why didn't you tell me?"

"Crazy day. I had court this morning, and then I had to get an extension for a hearing tomorrow. And then there was weather in Oklahoma City, and I was afraid the flight wouldn't take off. I didn't want to get your hopes up." He picked up his bag in one hand and took hers with his other. "How's Jeremy?"

Though she wouldn't say they were dating, they held hands often. She was thankful for the warmth he offered her. The support. "Come on." She updated him on her son's condition while they walked the maze to Jeremy's room.

When they arrived, Paul peeked in, then turned to her, eyes wide. He seemed almost too surprised to speak. Finally, he managed, "I knew it was bad, but..." He didn't seem to know how to finish the sentence.

"You can go in if you want."

He dropped her hand and glimpsed Nathan. "Paul Harrington."

Nathan stood and shook his hand. "You live here?"

"Oklahoma. Just came out to offer my support."

"Nice." He turned to Camilla. "Just so you're not surprised, I want to tell you my replacement should be here soon."

He wasn't staying? Of course not—the man needed to sleep. But she'd grown accustomed to Nathan's confident presence in the room.

He must've seen the concern on her face because he said, "She's good. Don't worry. We'll all take care of him."

"I know." Camilla couldn't help a small thank-you smile. "You already are."

Paul stepped to Jeremy's bedside. Like she had when she'd first arrived, he struggled to find a place to touch him. Finally, he laid his hand on Jeremy's forehead. "Hey, bud. It's Paul. Just came to tell you I'm praying for you."

Jeremy, of course, didn't respond, and Paul stood back and faced her. "Can he hear anything?"

Nathan said, "Doubtful."

Camilla stood at Paul's side. "He hasn't responded to me."

"Is that normal?" Paul asked.

"We're keeping him sedated," Nathan said. "It's pretty uncomfortable to be intubated."

They stood looking at Jeremy a few moments, and then Paul held out the bag he'd carried in. "I stopped at the store on my way to the airport and got a few things."

She looked in the bag to find bottles of water, a container of granola, apples and oranges, a little package of cleansing wipes—in case she couldn't get a shower, she assumed—and three magazines.

"I had no idea what you'd need," he said. "So I just grabbed a bunch of random stuff. Now that I'm here, though, I can pick up whatever you want."

She swallowed the tears that tried to rise. "This was so kind of you." She opened the granola. "I'm starving, actually, and I've had as much yogurt as I can stand." She took a handful and munched. Delicious.

He gently took the package from her hand. "Why don't we go get something to eat?"

She looked at her son. "I can't leave him."

His eyes narrowed slightly, and then his lips pulled up at the corners in a closed-lipped smile. "Okay. I can get something and bring it back."

"I hate to ask—"

"I came to support you." He focused on Nathan. "Where do you recommend?"

Thirty minutes later, Paul returned with a big salad, two burgers, french fries, and two drinks. They set the food on the little adjustable table meant for the patient and shared their dinners.

They were halfway through when she said, "How long are you planning to stay?"

Paul set his burger down and leaned toward her. "As long as you need me."

She mulled the words as she finished the meal. Did she need him? Maybe. Probably. It was certainly nice to have him nearby, to have someone to get her food, someone to talk to while she sat at Jeremy's bedside.

But she'd worked hard to keep their friendship casual. Non-romantic. His being here put their relationship on a new level. That he was willing to drop everything and fly to Salt Lake said a lot about how he felt about her.

Did it change how she felt about him?

CHAPTER ELEVEN

CAMILLA SHIFTED on the chair-turned-cot by her son's side. It resembled a bed in that when it was stretched out, it was flat and there was a little padding beneath the Naugahyde cover. Those were the only resemblances, though. The night nurse, Kelsey, had given Camilla two sheets, a blanket, and a little plastic bag containing an eye mask and ear plugs. She'd shut off the light around ten, just minutes after Paul left. She'd changed into her yoga pants and an oversize T-shirt, brushed her teeth, and attempted to sleep.

Except the bed could have doubled as a torture device and her son was fighting for his life. If those weren't enough reasons to keep her from sleeping, the nurse's constant presence on the far side of the room added extra tension. Even with the earplugs, the hospital sounds—faraway dings, people moving around, occasional conversations had by the nurses at the station right outside the door—pulled her from sleep whenever she got close.

Camilla needed sleep desperately and told herself to trust the nurse and doctors, who never seemed far away. Eye mask in place, she turned toward the wall and silently recited from memory scriptures she'd known for years.

Sleep came in snatches. Whenever anyone stepped into the room, her eyes popped open. She'd lift the eye mask, stand to look at Jeremy, then lie back down.

Unfortunately, that happened often.

Something was going on. She didn't know what, but this much activity in the middle of the night didn't seem normal.

When, once again, she heard someone step out, she sat up and looked at the nurse. "What's wrong?"

Kelsey said, "We're pushing fluids to try to bring his blood pressure up."

Camilla slipped on her sweat jacket and zipped it before she stood. She looked at the numbers on the monitor. The top number had fallen by fifteen...what? Degrees, points? She couldn't think. Sixty-two on top—that was low. Way too low.

Two men in green scrubs stepped in. One was thin and wore a white lab coat. He approached her, hand outstretched, and introduced himself as if it were three in the afternoon, not three in the morning. "Dr. Reynolds. Alan."

Behind him, the other doctor said, "Sorry we woke you." She'd met him—a resident who looked barely older than Zoë. She couldn't think of his name.

"Jeremy's blood pressure is dropping," Alan said. "We've been pushing fluids, but it's not doing tonight what it did last night. Hen told me you thought he'd behave if we took him off the sedative. Is that right?"

She was so tired that she couldn't think.

"We can restrain him if you're not sure." The doctor squinted, studying her. "Often, patients will try to rip out the tube, which can do serious damage. Do you think he'll do what we say?"

"He will. He's a good kid."

Alan turned to the resident. "Let's do it."

The younger doctor spoke to the nurse, who made an adjustment to the machine. Then, they all watched Jeremy for a moment.

"How long before he wakes up?" Camilla asked.

Alan said, "Probably an hour or so. We'll be close by if you need us." After the doctors left, Marcy stepped in and slipped her hand into Camilla's. "I saw the activity. What's going on?"

She gave her sister an update, and Marcy prayed aloud that Jeremy would be calm when he woke up, that his blood pressure would rise, and that this would be just one more positive step in Jeremy's recovery.

Camilla could only add a silent *please, please, please* to Marcy's prayer. When her sister was done, Camilla said, "Go back to sleep. I'll wake you if anything happens."

"You sure?"

"Seems silly for all three of us to stand here and stare at him."

The nurse across the room smiled. "We've got it."

Marcy stepped toward the door, then paused and looked back. "Paul seems nice."

Camilla had introduced Marcy and Kevin to Paul when she walked him out the night before. "I was shocked when he showed up."

Marcy cocked her head. "Are you glad he's here?"

She was glad to have a friend to sit with her, but she didn't know how to feel about what this would do to their relationship. All too complex to discuss in the middle of the night, so she said, "Sure. How's Evan?"

"In pain." Marcy's lips tightened. "They need to figure out what's going on."

After Camilla prayed with her sister for Evan and his doctors, Marcy returned to Evan's room. Camilla made her cot back into a chair, grabbed her toiletries, and went to the restroom, where she readied herself for the day ahead. Back in Jeremy's room, she shoved all her stuff inside her suitcase and closed it. It wasn't easy trying to live in a glass-fronted room where a nurse kept constant vigil. She shoved the torture chair into the corner and chose the higher rolling chair, which she moved to where she could see both Jeremy's face and the monitor. She pulled out her laptop and typed notes to her clients to tell them what had happened and, in some cases, ask for deadline extensions. She'd been working as a freelance graphic designer for years, and she prided herself on never missing a deadline. She wasn't sorry to break her streak.

Every few seconds, she glanced at Jeremy's face, waiting for some flicker, some movement.

On the far side of the bed, the nurse also watched.

When Camilla couldn't focus on work anymore, she slid her laptop back into its bag.

The nurse nodded toward the door where Marcy had disappeared. "You two are close."

"Always have been," Camilla said.

"You're lucky. And the boys are?"

"Best friends, even though they haven't lived near each other for a long time. Kevin, my brother-in-law, did his post-doctorate work in St. Louis when we lived there. The boys lived down the street from each other for about seven years. They've stayed close."

"You're from St. Louis?"

"Marcy and I grew up in Joplin. My husband and I lived in St. Louis for most of the kids' childhood. We relocated to Oklahoma a few years ago." She didn't say what city. The fear she'd lived with since Daniel's death had faded, but Camilla was still cautious. They'd moved. She'd contemplated changing her name, but Agent Falk had assured her that, with Daniel out of the way, Campos's people would leave her and the kids alone. He'd been right. Four years had passed uneventfully. But now...

"Your boyfriend...he lives in Oklahoma, too?"

"He's just a friend." Camilla said the words, realizing how silly they sounded. She and Paul had held hands, had eaten together. The man had flown a thousand miles to support her. Did that make him her boyfriend?

The word felt wrong.

"Oh. I just assumed..." Kelsey's gaze slid to the monitors for a moment. "Do you suppose he knows that?"

Camilla laughed to cover her worry. "Definitely something for me to deal with."

"I'm afraid that might be true." Before Camilla could respond, Kelsey asked, "Do you have other kids?"

"A daughter, Zoë. She's twenty-one."

Camilla asked the woman about her family, where she went to school, how she liked her job. The overhead light was still off. Beyond the window behind Jeremy's bed, the sky was black. But Camilla wasn't going back to sleep, not if there was a chance she'd miss her son's eyes opening.

While they talked, they watched Jeremy's blood pressure inch back up. "It's working," Kelsey said.

More than an hour passed before his eyelids fluttered.

Camilla jumped up and rested her hand on his shoulder. "Hey, baby. It's me."

His eyes drifted closed. She continued to murmur words and pray silently until, finally, his eyes opened and met hers.

She smiled despite the tears streaming down her face. "There you are."

"I'll let the doctor know." Kelsey grabbed the phone's handset and stepped out.

Jeremy's gaze flicked around the room. He reached for the tube in his mouth, but Camilla took his wrist, careful of the needles. "You have to leave that in. I know it's uncomfortable, but you need it to breathe."

He dropped his hand but didn't look happy about it.

"You were in a car accident. Do you remember?"

His eyes narrowed as he studied her. After a moment, he nodded, a slight movement thanks to the neck brace.

"Do you remember what happened?"

The head shook, and then his eyes widened in terror.

"Evan's okay," she said. "He's in the next room."

Jeremy moved as if he might get up. He'd barely shifted before he fell back against the bed, his hand flying to his side.

"You've got some broken ribs. Do they hurt?"

He looked at her, the words *stupid question* clear in the set of his lips.

She heard footsteps and turned to see Alan stepping in. "There's our patient." He stopped at the side of the bed. "I'm Dr. Reynolds. Just call me Alan."

Jeremy glared, but Alan only smiled. "I guess you can't call me anything out loud yet, but you will. How do you feel?"

He made a thumbs-down gesture.

"That good, huh? Are you in pain?"

Jeremy touched his ribs.

"Yeah, you cracked three of them. On a scale of one to ten, where would you put the pain right now?"

He held up four fingers, dropped one, and waffled his hand.

"It's hard to know because you just woke up," Alan said. "Is it bearable?"

Thumbs-up.

"Good. You let us know if it gets worse. We'll do our best to manage it. What else?"

Jeremy tried to lift the plaster cast, and his eyebrows rose.

"Broken wrist and thumb," Alan said. "We're going to deal with those today."

Jeremy's gaze turned to Camilla, who said, "I spoke to the orthopedic surgeon, and he assured me they're clean breaks. You're going to have surgery later."

Jeremy nodded, then gestured to the neck brace.

"That's annoying, I know," Alan said. "We can't take it off until we can determine if you have damage to your neck. And we can't know that until you can talk. And you can't talk while you're intubated."

Jeremy squinted, seeming confused. Amazing how much Camilla could guess just from his facial expressions.

"That's what we call it when we have a machine helping you breathe," Alan said. "The tube down your throat —in*tu*bated."

Jeremy tried to nod, then turned to her as if expecting her to answer his unspoken question.

What did he want to know?

The nurse stepped in and stood by the doctor. When Jeremy saw the pretty brunette, his eyes widened.

She said, "I'm Kelsey. Your nurse."

He winked, and everybody laughed.

Alan looked at Camilla. "Quite a ladies' man you have there."

Camilla wiped the tears that seemed to perpetually fall. "Under all those bandages and all that equipment, he's very handsome."

Jeremy rolled his eyes, but his face turned serious, and he focused on Camilla again. He curled his fingers and pointed his thumb down. Half a heart. She knew what that meant.

She kissed his forehead. "I love you too."

When she backed up, she saw tears in his eyes.

"Hey, you're okay," she said.

He shook his head, closed his eyes.

"What is it?"

He took her hand and started writing on it.

She picked up an S, then an O. Then two Rs.

"Sorry?"

He nodded, and tears escaped his eyes.

"The accident wasn't your fault." She wouldn't mention the gunshots. Maybe he remembered, maybe not, but now wasn't the time to try to unpack that mess. "The tire blew out. You lost control of the car. It was an accident."

He tapped his chest, shook his head.

"It wasn't your fault," she said.

He looked to the other side of the bed, and Alan patted his leg. "I know we just woke you up, but get some sleep. It's the middle of the night. We'll be back to check on you later."

He stepped out, and the nurse followed him.

Jeremy stared at her.

"What?"

He took her hand again and wrote. E...V...A...

"Evan is right next door. He's going to be fine." She prayed that was true.

The nurse stepped back in, but Jeremy paid her no attention. He started writing on Camilla's hand again. A...U...N...T

"Aunt Marcy and Uncle Kevin are here. You want to talk to them?"

He nodded.

"I'll see if they're awake. You'll be okay with Kelsey?"

Even with all the bandages and the tube in his mouth, he managed to give her an *I'm seventeen, Mom. I'm not a baby* look. She was glad to see her son was in there.

She hurried to Evan's room. Kevin was stretched out on the torture bed, snoring. Marcy was seated at Evan's bedside. Evan's eyes were closed.

Camilla whispered, "Hey."

Marcy stood and met her by the nurse's station.

"Jeremy's awake."

"Oh, good. How is he?"

"His blood pressure is going up. He wants to see you. I can stay with Evan."

"He's sound asleep, and Kevin's there." She walked to Jeremy's room and stepped in. "Hey, buddy. How you feeling?"

He reached toward her, and she lifted her hand to meet his. He flipped it over and wrote on her palm.

A moment later, she said, "He's all right. He's dealing with some pain, and they're trying to figure out what's causing it, but he's in a lot better shape than you are."

He squinted as if he didn't believe her.

"I promise, he's all right," Marcy said. "He's right next door."

Jeremy seemed to accept that. He started writing on her hand again. After a moment, she grabbed his hand to stop him and leaned close. "It wasn't your fault. You have nothing to apologize for."

He tapped his chest, then wrote on her hand again.

"No," she said. "The accident investigator said you were doing nothing wrong. It was an accident. Accidents happen."

He dropped his hand, looking irritated, though Camilla couldn't imagine why.

Marcy kissed his forehead. "I'm going to go stay with Evan, but Uncle Kevin and I are here if you need us."

He made the half-heart sign, and she patted her own chest. "I love you too."

After she left, Camilla stood at Jeremy's side. She wanted to ask him what they'd been doing in the desert, but now wasn't the time. "Try to sleep."

He reached for her hand and wrote on it. M...Y...F...A...U...L...T

"It wasn't. It was [illegible]"

His slashing motion across his throat shut her up. He patted his chest, wrote again on her hand.

D...A...D.

Dad?

That didn't make sense at all. Surely, he hadn't forgotten his father was dead. It had been four years. He was watching her for a reaction as if he knew he made no sense.

"Baby, your dad's gone. Remember?"

He continued to study her. After a moment, he took her hand once more and wrote CONFUSED.

Confused. That might make sense.

Except he didn't seem confused about anything else.

She'd ask the doctor about it the next day. Because if Jeremy thought his father was still alive, there was something seriously wrong.

CHAPTER TWELVE

DEAR CAMILLA,

Two years passed. Two whole years and I never saw you.

I'd given up looking for you at church, figuring your attendance that day had been as random and unplanned as my own. I never told you this, but I always had an eye out for you. Whenever I saw a woman with your hair color on campus, I'd look closer. I started to think you'd left school. Or maybe you'd never been a student at all.

I did run into Lynne a few times around campus, but whenever she saw me, she averted her gaze. I didn't want to talk to her, either, so I let her pretend. Easier that way. But you were never with her.

I know it was God who'd saved me from the path I'd been on, but somewhere in my mind, I credited you and your disapproving eyes.

I was on a date with a girl I'd met at church. Blonde, pretty, smart, and Christian. Exactly the kind of girl I should have been attracted to. It was our third time out together, and I'd chosen a Thai place off campus. We shared a noodle dish. Sherri's idea.

The meals were huge, but I had a metabolism that burned calories like brittle leaves in a forest fire.

I'd asked Sherri out because people told me I should and because the rest of the girls my age at church were already paired up—mostly with my friends. By the winter of my senior year, all of my Christian friends were in serious relationships, many of their girlfriends sporting engagement rings. I'd gone from being every guy's buddy to being every couple's third wheel.

Sherri was studying accounting. Who made a career out of adding and subtracting?

I must have let my feelings on her major slip because she spent half the meal explaining to me how important a good accountant was to the working of the American economy.

The whole time she was talking, I was thinking, *Check, please.*

Don't worry, Cammie. I was polite. I paid the bill, helped her on with her coat like a gentleman, and then led her past the tables and out of the restaurant.

We were walking toward the parking lot down the street when I heard a man's voice.

"Get in the car."

"Only if you let me drive." This from a woman.

When Sherri and I stepped off the sidewalk to cross a narrow alley, I got a glimpse of the couple. The man was standing beside his open passenger door. The woman stood a few feet behind the car, her back to me, shoulders straight.

"I'm fine to drive." His words were loud and angry.

I asked Sherri to wait there and call 911 if anything happened. Then, I crept into the alley. I didn't want to make a scene, but I wasn't about to let a woman be bullied if I could help.

"I'm sure you are," the woman said, calm as could be,

though I detected a hint of fear in the words. "Still, I'd feel better—"

"I don't give a flying..." There was a word there. I won't repeat it. "Get in the car."

She stepped away, wisely not turning her back to him. "I'll call my roommate. We'll talk tomorrow."

The man slammed the door and stalked her direction. "I said—"

"Leave her be." I don't remember exactly what I said after that, but it was something like, "She doesn't want to go with you tonight, man. Just let it go."

When he turned to me, his face was red with rage. Even in the dim light, I could see that his eyes were dilated. Could be from alcohol, but I suspected something stronger.

Without looking her direction, I told the woman to join my date and go inside.

I couldn't see her reaction, but I did hear the click-click of her heels on the asphalt.

The man let out a stream of curses and charged.

I side-stepped, and he missed me and landed with an *oomph* on the street.

"I don't want to fight you. Just go home, sleep it off, and call your girlfriend tomorrow. Getting your butt kicked isn't going to ingratiate you with her."

I probably should have edited that last sentence. He took it not as a warning but as a challenge and charged me again. This time, I spun away and elbowed him in the nose.

He kept to his feet and prepared to charge again.

From the mouth of the alley, Sherri shouted, "I called the police. They're on their way."

The man's head swung toward her, then back to me. He studied me through slitted eyes, growled, and bolted to his car.

The car disappeared around the corner at the far end of the

alley. I stood there a few moments, breathing in and out. Processing what had just happened. When I felt calmer, I turned and saw Sherri standing beside the woman. In the dark, I could hardly make out her features.

I spoke to Sherri first. "Are the police on their way?"

"She asked me not to call." Sherri nodded toward the woman, so I turned my focus to her.

"You don't think we should…?"

That's when the light from the shop on the other side of the alley illuminated your face. I was speechless.

The way your eyebrows lifted, you were too.

Sherri sighed. "It's freezing. Can we go now?" Do you remember what she said? "You can get a ride, right?"

"Of course, yes." Your voice quavered when you thanked me. "I've never seen him like that before. In the restaurant, he told me I could drive, but when we got to the car…"

"Why don't we give you a lift?" I asked.

Your eyebrows rose. Were you surprised or afraid?

"We'll drop you off first. I promise, you'll be safe with us."

I thought Sherri scoffed but decided I must've heard wrong.

We made the fifteen-minute drive to campus mostly in silence. I figured Sherri would talk to you, make you feel comfortable. But she didn't. For my part, my adrenaline was draining, and I couldn't seem to formulate a question.

Did I really get into an alley fight? I had no cuts or bruises to prove it, but only because the guy had been too wasted to aim properly. If he'd been a little less chemically altered, he'd have beaten me into next week.

From the backseat, you gave me directions to your apartment. I was surprised to find you still lived in the same building.

I stopped at the curb.

"I don't know what would have happened if you hadn't

come," you said. "I never thought of him as violent, but..." You shook your head, forced a smile. "Thank you for stepping in."

"My pleasure."

Did you recognize me?

You hadn't mentioned our earlier meeting. Maybe you couldn't place me, or maybe you were shocked to find that the man who'd nearly had a one-night stand with your roommate was more than a random, creepy guy.

You closed the door, and I waited until you were safely inside your building before I drove away. I don't remember the exact conversation that happened next, but this is pretty close.

"Well, that was interesting."

I chuckled and pulled onto the quiet street. "Seriously."

"And utterly unnecessary."

The clipped way Sherri said the words had me turning to face her. "Is there a problem?"

"Did you have to drive her home? Bad enough you went all hero-rescues-the-damsel-in-distress when you were on a date with another woman, but—"

"Are you really angry at me for helping her?"

"She didn't need your help. All she had to do was scream, and a dozen people from that restaurant would've been there to help her. And anyway, the guy probably wouldn't have hurt her. They were on a *date*."

"Women get hurt on dates all the time. Hurt, raped, murdered."

"We were on a date too. You're such a man. Such a...a Neanderthal."

For helping a stranger in need, I was a caveman? A word popped into my head, but it couldn't be true. "Are you jealous?"

The scoffing noise she made didn't convince me.

"You're jealous that I paid attention to another girl on our date."

"I'm just saying, no woman needs any man to step in and save her. Women are just as capable as men."

"Right. But not as strong."

"Here we go. Let's talk about how women are weak."

It was probably the surreal events of the evening, the lethargy left after the adrenaline drained, and maybe the utter lunacy of what Sherri was saying that made me do it. I chuckled.

"Are you laughing at me?"

I forced myself to shut up and kept driving.

"How dare you!"

I turned onto her street and parked in front of her sorority house. After putting the car into park, I faced her.

I should have just said good night. There was no reason for me to argue. But I was young and arrogant—and pretty sure I was right. "A woman was being bullied in an alley by a man a good fifty pounds heavier. I stepped in, and you're angry. It's irrational."

"Irrational!" She literally shrieked the word, Cammie. If you'd been there, you'd have laughed too. "Just like a woman, right?"

"Not most women. Just you." I nodded to her building. "I'd open your door, but that would be a Neanderthal move. Although I do note that your feminist ideals stop you short of paying your own way." She had no response to that. "I'd offer to walk you in, but you obviously don't need my protection. I'll see you around."

You wouldn't have believed the transformation. From angry to apologetic in an instant. "Look, I didn't mean—"

"This"—I gestured between us—"isn't going to work. I don't know if you're jealous or if you really believe all that junk you just spouted. Either way, you and I are too different. Good night, Sherri."

A long moment passed before she opened her door and stepped out. She said nothing before she slammed it and stalked to the door.

I felt... relieved.

I know you always wondered what happened between her and me. Now you know.

As I drove home, all I could think about was you.

Yours always,

Daniel

CHAPTER THIRTEEN

IT WASN'T QUITE five a.m. when a group of people—doctors and nurses—stopped outside Jeremy's room. He'd fallen asleep, and Camilla had been dozing in the chair in the corner but woke when they walked in. A woman pushing a big machine said, "Good morning."

Camilla stood. "What's that?"

"We need to do a chest X-ray. I understand our patient is no longer sedated?"

Beside her, Jeremy lifted a hand in greeting.

"Hey, dude." The woman lowered the bed so he was lying flat, then put down the rail. "How you feeling?"

Jeremy waffled his hand.

"I bet. I'm sure Kelsey's keeping you comfortable."

His eyes found the nurse, and he nodded.

"We're just gonna get a quick X-ray, and then we'll let you go back to sleep."

Camilla watched as they lifted her son, slid something beneath his back, and got their images. The whole process took about ten minutes. Outside the door, they studied the screen, and Camilla went to see what they were looking at.

Those were Jeremy's lungs? She'd seen images of lungs, of course, but what she saw on the screen didn't match her memory. Shouldn't they be bigger? These weren't the right shape, and one seemed about half the size of the other.

A young doctor in green scrubs said, "It's improving."

"Is it?" She pointed to the misshapen organ. "Why is that one like that?"

"It collapsed and folded in on itself," he said. "It's still working to open back up."

Folded? Like an empty balloon?

"This one"—the doctor indicated the other lung—"didn't have as much damage, but it's still not as expanded as it should be."

"But you said it's better?"

The man said cheerfully, "You should have seen it yesterday."

Why didn't that make her feel better? "Any idea how much longer before he's back to normal?"

The man's smile slipped. "It's going to take time."

"What about getting the tube out?"

He shrugged. "I think Hen plans to talk about that later. Maybe tomorrow."

That was good news. She chose to ignore the *maybe* part. She wanted her son back, she wanted to hear his voice. *Let it be tomorrow, Lord.*

By the time they wheeled the machine away, Jeremy was sleeping again. Kelsey sat at the desk on the other side of the room.

Camilla voiced the fear that had hummed below the surface since the X-ray techs had stepped in. "They must be worried something's wrong to come by so early."

"Actually," Kelsey said, "this is their normal time."

"Seriously?"

Kelsey's smile made her even more attractive. The drugs Jeremy was on must've knocked him out. He'd certainly not choose to sleep when there was such a beautiful woman in the room. "There's not much difference between daytime and nighttime in the ICU. We just turn down the lights and try to talk quieter."

That tracked with the way the night had gone. Which meant Camilla wasn't likely to get much sleep. She wished someone would give her a hint as to how long Jeremy would be there, but nobody would assure her that he was going to get better. Whenever she asked, they hedged.

We just have to keep watching it.

We're doing everything we can.

Your son's a fighter.

Nobody would say the words she longed to hear. Nobody would promise her it was going to be all right, that he would have a full recovery. That he would walk out of there and resume a normal life.

She returned to her chair in the corner, pulled the blanket over her, and closed her eyes. She tried to pray but found rational words wouldn't come.

If only Daniel were there. She longed for him as she hadn't in years. She could imagine how different this would be if he were by her side. He'd be asking intelligent questions, explaining all the things she didn't understand. More than that, he'd be the solid presence that kept her sane. One of his strong arms would hold her up. The other hand would be touching Jeremy, tending him, calming him.

If Daniel were there, he'd know how to pray. Unlike the gibberish she was lifting to the Lord—*please, Jesus, please*—Daniel's prayers would be technical, detailed, yet still heartfelt and sincere. His prayers would calm her. She'd stand by his side and mutter her agreement. Daniel's prayers would reach the throne of God.

The Lord whispered to her heart, *Yours do too.*

She knew that. She knew He heard her and filled in all her blanks. But she needed her husband, needed him as she never had before.

If only she could go back, she'd do everything differently. She knew now that the problems they'd been having in their marriage were temporary, related to schedules and time management. Silly problems they'd have worked out, if only she'd kept her mouth shut that day. If only they hadn't argued. If only she hadn't been so selfish.

Lord, forgive me.

He had. She knew that. Still, the regret lingered. She'd never been able to rid herself of it, and she never would. Because of her selfishness, Daniel was gone. Her children were fatherless. Her son... had he forgotten, or was their trip to the desert somehow related to his need for his father? It didn't make sense.

She longed to understand, and yet she knew that when she did, the regret, the guilt, would flare again. She would never recover from it—not that she deserved to—because her children would never get over Daniel's loss. Neither would she.

CHAPTER FOURTEEN

THE SUN HAD BARELY RISEN over the mountains to the east of the hospital when a second group of people gathered outside Jeremy's door. Some stood in front of computers on rolling stands they'd brought with them. Mostly doctors, but Nathan, who'd returned a few minutes earlier, joined them too.

Kevin caught her eye through the glass and waved her out. "They're doing rounds. Now's a good time to ask questions."

She joined the crowd in the corridor and saw Hen, who said, "Is it okay if your brother-in-law stays? He was here yesterday, but now that—"

"Of course."

Kevin stood beside Camilla in the circle, and they listened to the doctors. Most of what they said was gibberish to her, but Kevin was nodding along.

The doctors focused mostly on the lungs and how they were improving. Nathan gave them an update on the chest tubes and what had drained. Someone else tapped a screen and said something about the X-ray. One doctor said, "The plan for anesthesia today?" and another answered with the names of drugs, she assumed.

Everyone seemed on board with... whatever it was they'd decided. Finally, Hen turned to Camilla. "Questions?"

Since they probably didn't have time to take her through med-school basics, she said, "He's still having surgery?"

Another doctor said, "We'll come get him about eleven."

"How long will it take?" Camilla asked.

"A couple of hours."

"When do you think the tube'll come out?"

Hen answered. "Maybe tomorrow. We'll just have to see how he does today."

Again, they waited while Camilla tried to think of other questions. When she couldn't, she said, "Thank you."

The doctors moved along, and she and Kevin stepped into the room. "How's he doing?" Kevin asked.

"He was awake some last night, but mostly he slept."

Kevin looked at the monitors. "His blood pressure looks good. I hate that he has to be awake with that tube down his throat. He did okay?"

She shrugged. "I don't have anything to compare it to, but he wasn't angry or upset. A little frustrated."

"He's a great kid. You should plan to get out of here for a little while when he's in surgery. Go for a walk, get a shower."

She stepped away. "Is it that bad?"

He laughed. "For your sake, not ours."

She returned the laugh with a smile. "But shouldn't I be with him?"

"They're not going to let you into surgery." His smile was patient. "You might as well take a break."

Paul showed up around nine thirty bearing steaming cups of coffee. "Sorry I'm so late," he said. "I meant to be here an hour ago, but I got a call from a client."

"Not a problem at all." She sipped the brew and explained what had happened overnight while they walked from the ICU entrance to Jeremy's room, finishing with, "He woke up about thirty minutes ago."

Paul slowed. "He's awake now?"

"Awake and active, actually."

Paul's eyebrows lowered. "Does he know I'm here?"

"I haven't mentioned it. Why?"

Paul looked toward the glass doors of Jeremy's room. They'd stopped a few feet out of his view. "Do you think he'll mind?"

"Why would he? I'm sure he'll be happy to see a familiar face."

Paul's closed lips told her he wasn't sure that was true, but he forced a smile. "Let's hope you're right."

But when they stepped into the room, Jeremy had closed his eyes. Now that Paul had mentioned it, she wondered if Jeremy would be unhappy Paul was there. Jeremy had always liked him, but as an old friend of his dad and Camilla. Had Jeremy thought of Paul as a suitor? Paul's being here made it clear to everyone—even the nurse had picked up on it—that he was hoping for more than friendship.

How would Jeremy feel about that?

How did she? If she were to marry again, Paul would make an excellent choice. He was kind and generous and attentive. He was everything she wanted in a man.

Except he wasn't Daniel.

They stepped into the room, and Camilla sat in the rolling chair while Paul took the leather chair in the corner—behind where Jeremy was facing. She wondered if he sat there so that, if Jeremy's eyes opened, he wouldn't see him.

Which didn't make a lot of sense. Why fly all the way to Salt Lake if he didn't want Jeremy to see him? Part of her wanted to ask, but most of her couldn't be bothered. She had too many things to worry about to let any possible romance between herself and Paul intrude.

While they chatted, Paul checked his emails. "I hope you don't mind. So much going on at the office this week, I have to keep abreast of it."

"I understand completely." That was one of the things that had always worked between them. If Camilla had to cancel plans to complete a project, Paul always understood. If something came up and Paul couldn't make one of their dinners, she didn't fault him for it. She appreciated a man who took work seriously.

Why hadn't she learned to appreciate that about Daniel instead of acting as if his work were a mistress or an addiction? The man had loved his job, and he'd loved her. Why hadn't that been enough?

She understood now what she hadn't then. If she ever married again, she'd be more flexible, less demanding, less critical.

From the corner, Paul blew out a long sigh.

"Something wrong?"

He stood. "I have to jump onto a conference call."

"Now?"

"Sorry. I'll come back when it's finished."

"I might not be here. Jeremy's surgery is—"

"I forgot." He snapped his laptop closed. "What terrible timing. You can finally get out of here, and I have to go. I'll call when I'm done and come find you."

"Sounds good."

She walked him back to the ICU entrance, and he kissed her cheek before he left. "Call if anything happens."

She watched the door close behind him, touching the spot he'd kissed. He'd done that before a couple of times after they'd enjoyed dinner together. A nice, friendly kiss.

She wished he'd been able to stay longer. Marcy and Kevin were sitting with Evan. Even though they were next door, she couldn't spend much time with them. Paul offered company, normalcy.

But what would Jeremy think about Paul's presence? Would it upset him or make him angry? The last thing Jeremy needed in his life was more to worry about.

CHAPTER FIFTEEN

THE DOCTORS CAME a little after eleven. Jeremy was awake and, though he couldn't talk, managed to make everybody smile with his hand gestures and facial expressions. The amount of work they had to do to move him overwhelmed her. Machines had to be taken off their stands and connected to his bed. They disconnected the ventilator and used a balloon-like thing to manually push air into his lungs. Jeremy took the balloon and did the squeezing himself, which made the group laugh.

Camilla followed them, taking a video because she knew Jeremy would want to see it when he was better. They rolled along a maze of hallways, through secure doors, and to another part of the hospital. They pushed him into another glass-fronted room.

A woman with a computer on a stand met her there. "You're Mrs. Wright?"

Camilla forced her gaze away from Jeremy and the doctors. "Yes."

The woman rattled off Camilla's cell number. "You can be reached on that?"

She confirmed it, kissed Jeremy goodbye, and found the

Ronald McDonald room on the ICU floor, where she showered. Just that one act made her feel normal again, or as normal as someone could feel after so little sleep.

She rolled her suitcase back to Jeremy's room and then found Marcy and Kevin with Evan. "How's he doing?"

Marcy's eyes were bloodshot, and Kevin didn't look much better. "Still in pain," Marcy said.

"What can I do?"

"Just keep praying." Marcy joined her at the door. "Jeremy's in surgery?"

"Yeah, I'm going to get something to eat. Want anything?"

With requests from both of them, Camilla found the skybridge to the next building. A different hospital altogether. Just when she was sure she'd gotten hopelessly lost, she reached the cafeteria and ordered her meal and the ones for Marcy and Kevin. She found a seat alone by the back windows and wished Paul were with her—or Marcy or Kevin.

Or Daniel.

She'd learned to live without him, but since the accident, thoughts of him were never far away.

She was halfway through the chef salad when a man approached her table. He was tall, slim, and had the blackest skin she'd ever seen. He looked at least a decade younger than she was and wore a crisp white button-down shirt and a blue tie. His smile was broad. One of his top teeth was a little crooked, but that didn't detract from the kindness she saw in his expression.

"Do you mind if I join you for a moment?"

He spoke in a rich baritone with an accent she couldn't identify. His English was perfect.

Hadn't she just wished she weren't alone? Yet now, she wanted to send this man away. Her feelings were all jumbled, confused. She wasn't accustomed to eating lunch with strangers.

She opened her mouth to politely decline, but there was something about this man. And he had promised it would be only a moment. "Sure."

He didn't have any food, just a cup with a straw sticking out, which he set on the table between them as he sat. "I am Bachir Hari. I don't often join strangers to eat, but I saw you and knew I needed to speak to you."

She set her fork down. "Why?"

"What is your name?"

"Camilla."

He held out his hand, and she shook it. "It is a pleasure to meet you, Camilla." He let her hand go and nodded to her food. "I have just finished my lunch. Please, eat."

She took a bite of lettuce and tomato. "I'll eat if you tell me why you wanted to talk to me."

"A fair exchange. It is nothing serious, only that I can see in you a strong spirit."

She sat back. Was he some sort of spiritualist or new age guru? Maybe he was going to try to sell her something.

He nodded to indicate her meal. "You enjoy your lunch."

She was starving, so whatever this guy wanted, he'd have to talk while she ate.

"You think I am crazy. But I think you know the same Spirit God that I know, the only Sovereign King. Yes?"

"I'm a Christian."

"When you walked in, I could see the Spirit of Christ on you."

Her fork stilled halfway to her mouth. Was he serious?

"You are filled with Him. Am I wrong?"

Was he wrong? Camilla had a strong faith, read her Bible daily. She'd been praying constantly. But did that mean she was filled with the Spirit? She thought of the scriptures she'd memorized, the chapters and chapters she'd read. Even when she felt far from God, He was with her. "You're not wrong."

"You do not work here, right? You are here because of a loved one?"

"My son." She gave him the short version of what had happened, strangely eager to tell the story. She finished with, "He's in surgery now, which is why I'm here instead of with him."

Bachir said, "And he is going to be all right?"

"The doctors won't make any promises."

"I see. Do you mind if I pray for him?" Before she could answer, he didn't close his eyes or bow his head but simply spoke to God as if He were sitting in the empty chair. She set down her fork and closed her eyes and let this man's deep voice calm her. His prayer was short and simple but powerful. When he finished, he said, "Eat, eat. God is with your son. You must care for yourself so you can care for him."

She forked a bite of grilled chicken. "Where are you from?"

"I was stolen from my village in Sudan when I was a boy and given a gun and told to fight, but the Lord delivered me from that life before I was in a single battle. I escaped and was found by an English couple, who took me to a mission. These English people raised me, taught me to read. Their mission sent me to college, and then I received a scholarship to go to medical school."

"You're a doctor?"

"I am in university now."

"And your parents?"

"Dead. Killed in the raid when I was taken."

"I'm sorry. I'm sure they'd be very proud of you."

He looked toward the ceiling. "I think perhaps they would be, but I am only here by the grace of God and the kindness of His people. He has gifted me and led me. I look forward to when I finish my studies and can return home to help my people."

She regarded him. "You've already overcome so much. I believe you will make an enormous difference."

He dipped his head. "You, too, have overcome much."

"You see that in my spirit, too?" She smiled, teasing.

But he didn't return the expression. "All of us have mountains to climb. Do you not think so?"

She wasn't sure what he meant but nodded anyway.

"Some people look at the mountain and think, I cannot do it," he said. "They sit at the bottom and ask God to change the mountain. He is a God who moves mountains, but more often, I believe that He wants us to climb. Some people, though, they refuse."

Her phone dinged with an incoming text. She glanced at it. Paul. She nodded for Bachir to continue.

He said, "Others will start up the mountain confidently, but when the way becomes steep or treacherous, they, too, sit. They complain that the mountain is too difficult and ask God to make it easier. They decide not to go farther."

Camilla sipped her iced tea. This man's voice was mesmerizing, his story interesting.

"Others, though, see the mountain and scale it. When the way becomes steep and treacherous, they rely on God to help them, and they keep going. When it becomes impossible, God makes it possible. These people, they do not stop until they've reached the summit. They discover that God has indeed given them the feet of mountain animals."

She thought of the passage in Habakkuk. *He has made my feet like hinds' feet and makes me walk on my high places.*

"From there," Bachir said, "they can see not only the difficult journey behind them but the future on the other side. You, Miss Camilla, have the spirit of one who has reached the summit. A faith like yours can only be attained in such a way."

"You don't know anything about me."

He tapped his heart. "Only what the Spirit tells me. I am wrong?"

"Completely. I'm a mess." Tears stung her eyes, but she tipped her gaze to the ceiling and forced them back. "I have no idea what I'm doing most of the time." She lowered her gaze to the man across from her. "And now my son is fighting for his life. I'm not special or unique. I'm just trying to figure it out."

"That is because you are climbing another mountain. The way is difficult, but you press on."

"I have no choice."

He smiled at her. "That is where you are wrong. You could curl into a ball and refuse to face it. You could sink into despair or lash out in anger. You could lift your fist to the Lord as Job's wife suggested he should do. 'Curse God and die,' she advised. But Job refused. As you refuse."

Her heart was pounding, though she couldn't explain why. Everything in her pulsed at this man's words.

"You, Miss Camilla, are a strong woman, not because you wield your own strength but because you know the One who strengthens you."

He stood and rested his hand on her shoulder. "I must go, but I will be praying for you and your son. I hope I will see you again."

As she finished her salad, she replayed the strange conversation. Had she reached a summit? Hardly.

But...maybe, in a way. Daniel's death could have destroyed her. The grief, the guilt, the regret. But she'd survived. She'd had to. Her kids had needed her. She'd pressed into her faith. She'd relocated her family. She'd built her business and found a way to support them. She'd created a new life for herself. And—Bachir was right—she'd attained a greater faith.

A summit? She'd never seen it that way before.

Though her heartbeat returned to normal, she didn't feel the same. She checked her text—Paul was headed back to Jeremy's room. As she walked that direction, she whispered, "Was that You, Lord?"

Though He didn't speak, she knew the answer. With her next exhale, she breathed a prayer of thanks for His encouragement. *You will get me through this. Just, please, get Jeremy through too.*

CHAPTER SIXTEEN

DEAR CAMILLA,

I never told you this, but that night, after I dropped Sherri off, I drove back by your apartment. I wanted to have a real conversation with you. But it was after eleven, and I wasn't dumb enough to knock on your door.

A crowd of college students gathered on the far sidewalk, but otherwise the street was quiet. Your brick building had a few windows lit up. I remembered your apartment was on the third floor. There were four windows there, one lit from within.

Were you seated in front of your easel? Did you see me out there, looking for you?

You probably would have thought I was a stalker.

I worried that your boyfriend would show up and considered calling the police to report what had happened. But you'd asked us not to, and I wanted to honor your wishes. Even then, I knew you were an intelligent woman. I trusted your judgment.

I prayed for you as I left that night.

The next day after class, I returned. I stopped at the door and studied the intercom. There were names beside the buttons, but none of them was yours. Or Lynne's, assuming you two still lived together.

Somehow, I doubted it.

The apartments weren't numbered according to floor, making it impossible to guess.

The door opened, and a guy held the door open. I was tempted to lecture him about security—what if I'd been your boyfriend?—but instead I slipped into the building and up the stairs.

On the third floor, I thought back to that drunken night my sophomore year and remembered the layout of the apartment that had been yours. I whispered a quick prayer for wisdom and words and...success, I guess, and knocked.

A moment later, I heard, "Who is it?"

"It's Daniel Wright. The guy from the restaurant last night. I just wanted to make sure you're all right."

The door opened, and there you were.

You wore a green sweater and faded jeans tucked into short boots. Your sable hair shimmered in the pale hallway light, and your eyebrows hiked over blue eyes. "How did you know which apartment was mine?"

"You don't remember me, do you?"

Your curious expression—eyes narrowed, head tilted slightly to the side—is familiar to me now. Back then, I thought, how does she keep getting more beautiful?

"I knew you looked familiar," you said, "but I can't place you."

"It's been a couple of years."

Apparently, that was all the memory-jarring you needed because you stepped back. "You and Lynne..."

"It was a long time ago."

You nodded slowly.

I had the distinct impression you were about to close the

door in my face. "I saw you at church that Sunday, and..." And what? *I've been looking for you ever since?* The goal was *not* to come off as a stalker. I stuck out my hand. "Daniel Wright."

You glanced at my outstretched peace offering. I was sure you'd reject it. Reject me. But you're so kind. You slid your hand into mine and squeezed. "Camilla Brown."

"I'm afraid I didn't make a very good first impression."

"You salvaged it."

"Anyone would have stepped in last night."

"I mean you salvaged it when you didn't stay with Lynne. She was way too drunk to make good decisions."

"I wasn't exactly a paragon of good decisions myself back then."

That made you smile.

"I remember seeing you at church," you said.

"That was the first time I'd been in a while. Since then, I've attended regularly. Haven't seen you there again."

"I'm there every Sunday." You leaned on the doorjamb. Such a casual, trusting move. "I go to the early service."

"Early, as in...eight thirty?" I'd known, intellectually, that there was a service before the one I attended, but it had never been real to me. Like the Serengeti, the planet Mars, and quantum physics. Things I'd heard of but never considered in any real way. The eight-thirty service was for the elderly and parents with toddlers. It was for people who needed to get home in time for mid-morning naps.

The early service wasn't for college girls with the most beautiful blue eyes I'd ever seen. Eyes that were laughing at me.

"It's a thing," you said. "There are people there, and the worship team, and the pastor, all behaving as if it's totally sane."

I shook my head. "I don't believe it."

"Maybe you need to check it out sometime."

Was that an invite? "If I do, will you walk me through it? Be my support system?"

"Like a safety buddy?"

I loved that you played along. "Yeah, that. Keep me from drowning."

Do you remember what happened next? You laughed. Such a simple sound, but it settled inside me. It became something I wanted to hear a lot more of.

Maybe that seems stupid. I'd been thinking about you for years. You didn't know me, barely remembered me, but I never forgot you.

"I suppose," you said, "seeing as how you saved me and all..." The words stole the smile from your lips.

"I was worried your date might come over last night."

"He did. Mashed my intercom until I called the police."

"I'm sorry. I know you didn't want to do that."

One shoulder lifted and fell. "His choices are not my responsibility."

You always were wise.

Silence settled between us, and I realized I had no good reason to be standing at your door.

I said, "Anyway—"

"—As you can see..."

We spoke at the same time. I nodded for you to continue.

"I'm fine. I'm glad I saw his true colors before I let myself get attached."

"So he wasn't a longtime boyfriend?"

"We'd been out a few times. He'd never had a drink on our dates, but something told me to order a glass of wine last night, even though I don't usually. When I did, he got a beer and then ordered a couple more. I was surprised at how quickly he went from sober to drunk."

"I think maybe he took something else."

Your pretty eyes widened.

"I mean, if he only had a few drinks," I clarified. "He was far from sober, and his pupils were dilated, which is an indication."

"Of what exactly?"

"Lots of things." I shrugged. "I wouldn't try to guess. The point is, you were smart to refuse to get in the car with him."

Your smile was slight. "That's me. Wise and boring."

I thought back on the years since I'd rededicated my life to Christ. Sure, I'd given up partying, and there'd been no serious girlfriends, but I'd gained so much. A life of service to others, greater knowledge of the Bible, a deeper relationship with Jesus. "There's nothing boring about being wise. I think the most exciting lives are the ones dedicated to the Lord."

You crossed your arms, and that little line appeared between your eyebrows. "How does a guy who was seconds away from a one-night stand—"

"I'm not that man anymore. I'd love to prove it to you, if you'd let me."

"How exactly?"

I shrugged as if this were oh-so-casual, but somehow, I felt my life balancing on the edge of a pin. "Go to lunch with me?"

"What would Sherri think about that?"

"Sherri and I won't be seeing each other again."

You pushed yourself from the doorjamb. "I hope I'm not to blame."

I brushed away your words. I didn't want to talk about her. "She and I weren't meant to be. So...lunch?"

I held your eye contact while you considered it.

I was sure you were going to turn me down. But then, you said, "Well, Mr.... Wright." My name tugged the corners of your lips up. "I suppose it won't hurt. But let's make it breakfast after church on Sunday. I'll meet you in the lobby at eight-thirty."

I agreed. We exchanged phone numbers, just in case. I was

so surprised you didn't turn me down that I didn't even flinch at the idea of rousing myself for the early service.

You were worth waking up early for. You were worth sacrificing everything for. I'm sorry I forgot that.

Yours always,

Daniel

CHAPTER SEVENTEEN

THURSDAY BEGAN MUCH like Wednesday had, with the invasion of the X-ray machine and the little crowd that followed it.

The afternoon before had been uneventful. Jeremy had still been sedated after his surgery and was quiet.

When he woke, he'd been happy to discover that the plaster cast was gone, replaced with a splint that looked flimsy. Nathan had assured Camilla a better cast would be put on before Jeremy was released.

She loved that word—*released.* It would happen. At least Nathan thought so.

When Jeremy saw Paul, he'd squinted as if he were confused. Camilla explained that Paul had come to see him, and Jeremy had smiled behind the tubes.

Buoyed by Jeremy's acceptance—or at least non-rejection—Paul had talked with Jeremy for an hour, catching him up on the March Madness tournament. When he ran out of things to say, he asked Nathan if they could turn on the TV.

Together, Jeremy and Paul—and Nathan, when he wasn't busy—watched basketball while Camilla logged on to her laptop, checked in with her clients, and updated her friends and family about the boys' conditions. She chatted with Zoë, who seemed to be holding up fairly well, though she still insisted she wanted to fly out. Camilla put her off. When they hung up, she answered texts, checked Facebook, and read all the kind messages and promises to pray. Mostly, she listened to the men chatter and saw Jeremy's smiles behind the tubes.

It all felt so...normal.

She could get used to this—Paul being a bigger part of their lives, becoming a father figure to Jeremy and Zoë. A husband, though?

She couldn't think about that, not yet. Even though four years had passed, she wouldn't consider remarrying. It was too soon.

That night, after Paul left and Jeremy fell back asleep, she brushed her teeth and crawled onto the horrible cot. It was not quite ten, but she figured she'd be interrupted often during the night. Her exhaustion overcame the discomfort and fear, and she slept, only waking a few times to check on Jeremy. She probably got no more than five hours of sleep, but that was more than she'd gotten the previous two nights combined.

It was about four thirty when Camilla pulled on her sweatshirt as the X-ray techs came in. She stood at Jeremy's head. His eyes were open, but he didn't make any effort to communicate as the people did their work.

The doctors and techs chatted with Jeremy and the night nurse. This one, with her gorgeous long blond hair, beautiful smile, and sweet bedside manner, made the nurse from the night before look average.

When they were finished, Camilla looked at the image on the screen. "It doesn't look better."

The resident said, "I see improvement."

If that were true, then... "Yesterday, they said the tube might come out today."

"Maybe tomorrow."

Was that the doctors' standard answer? Was Jeremy's recovery never going to happen today? Always tomorrow? Was that what they told parents when they didn't want to tell the truth?

That recovery wasn't assured?

That the tube might never come out?

The doctor must have seen the worry on her face because he added, "He's doing really well. It just takes time."

Stupid tears filled her eyes. "If you say so."

After the X-ray was wheeled away and Jeremy drifted back to sleep, Camilla walked to Evan's room. Marcy was lying on the cot at her son's bedside. Camilla was about to walk away when her sister waved, stood up, and stepped out.

"I hope I didn't wake you," Camilla said.

"He's been in pain all night. He's asleep now, but the painkillers only work for a little while before he starts hurting."

"Any more guesses about what's wrong?"

"They're going to take him for surgery in an hour."

An hour? The sun hadn't even come up yet. Her surprise must have shown on her face because Marcy added, "They don't want to wait any longer. We were on the fence before, but the pain is only getting worse."

Surgery. And not a simple orthopedic procedure, but surgery that opened her nephew up and dug around. The thought of it had Camilla's stomach lurching. "I'm sorry this is happening."

"It's not your fault."

She wanted that to be true, needed it to be true. Agent Falk hadn't called her back. Did it mean she was worrying for nothing?

Marcy crossed her arms, holding herself together. "What's scary is that they don't know what they're looking for. Something in his bowels—a twist or a kink maybe."

"Will Kevin be back in time?" He'd rented a room in a nearby hotel the night before. He and Marcy planned to take turns going for the night.

"I called him after the doctor came by. He'll be here. You should come with me to sleep tonight, assuming the boys are okay."

The thought of sleeping at a hotel, in a real bed, was tempting. "I can't leave Jeremy."

"Kevin will be here."

Camilla glanced at her son's room. "I know he could manage it, but I don't think Jeremy would like being alone, and Evan's going to need his father."

Marcy yawned. "Sleep is overrated."

"Must be."

"Did you know there's a Ronald McDonald House nearby?" Marcy asked.

Camilla tried and failed to suppress a yawn. "I showered there yesterday."

"Not the rooms in the hospital. It's like a hotel, and it's about five minutes from here. Kevin and I live too close to take advantage of it, but you could get a room there."

Five minutes away, except not really. Not when one didn't have a car and would have to rely on Uber. Not when it took five minutes to get from the front door to the ICU. "Maybe when he's better."

"You need to sleep, Cammie."

The only people who called her that were Marcy and Daniel.

Now, just Marcy.

"Last night was better," Camilla said. "I'll be okay."

She cleaned up in the bathroom, made coffee in the break room, settled back at Jeremy's bedside, and checked her phone. It was too early to respond to the texts she'd gotten late last night, but she typed an update in a private Facebook message to her friends and family. When she finished, she checked her missed calls.

Still nothing from Agent Falk. Why hadn't he gotten back to her?

CHAPTER EIGHTEEN

CAMILLA WAS PRAYING FOR EVAN, who was in surgery, when Nathan stepped into the room to relieve Ashton, the night nurse. Before she could update him on how Jeremy's night had gone, Nathan turned to Camilla. "There's someone here for you. Name's Falk. You want to see him?"

The bottom fell out of her stomach.

Nathan must've seen the fear because he stepped around the bed and gripped her arm. "You all right?"

No. She wasn't all right. She couldn't go through this again.

She closed her eyes, imagined a rocky incline. Feet like a mountain goat's. She could face this. She had no choice.

"I can tell him to leave," Nathan said. "It's up to you."

"No, no. I need to see him." She glanced at her sleeping son. Her kids had seen a lot of Agent Falk four years earlier. Seeing him now would only upset him. "Not here, though. Will you let me know if anything changes?"

Nathan looked at the whiteboard. Her phone number was written there. "I'll call you."

She thanked the nurses and hurried to the ICU entrance.

Special Agent Lincoln Falk leaned against the counter,

arms crossed. He looked much like he had years earlier, except his short hair was more gray than black, as was his goatee. She couldn't help but compare his chocolate brown skin with the coal-black skin of the man she'd met the day before in the cafeteria. She guessed Falk was in his midsixties. She knew he was married because of the gold band on his left hand, though he'd never spoken of his family. He wore a suit and tie, as usual. No matter how frazzled she felt, how out-of-control things had seemed after Daniel had disappeared, Falk never took off his coat, never loosened his tie.

Behind him, the lady who manned the desk was trying to pretend she wasn't watching him.

When Falk saw Camilla, he pushed off the counter. "Mrs. Wright. Sorry to just show up like this." They shook hands. As much time as they'd spent together four years earlier, they'd never become friendly.

"It doesn't feel like this can be good news."

He looked around. "Where can we talk?"

"Mind if we go down to the cafeteria? I haven't eaten, and I'd rather everybody in ICU not know my business. Plus, Jeremy might wake up, and he doesn't need to see you."

"That'll work."

She pushed the button to open the door. As they stepped out, a woman in a sharp business suit turned their way.

"Mrs. Wright," Falk said, "this is Agent Siple. She's going to be in charge of your protection while you're here at the hospital."

Siple extended her hand. "Ma'am."

Camilla's heartbeat raced, but she managed a quick "Hi" as they shook hands, casting a glance at the agent.

"I'll explain." He started down the corridor, and she walked beside him.

Except for the agent behind them, the corridor was empty. "Why are you here?"

"I flew to St. Louis after your call the other day and met with the gang task force there."

"You're not based in St. Louis anymore?"

"Atlanta. I needed to get up to speed on the Vipers. I flew here yesterday. I apologize for not calling you back. I was tied up in a meeting."

Despite the fear that was building in her stomach, she kept her voice steady. "Long meeting."

A beat passed. "I didn't want to worry you until I had more information."

Meaning, now that he did have more information, he wasn't concerned about worrying her.

They took the escalator to the first floor and entered the cafeteria. This one was much smaller than the one in the other hospital, but it was also less busy. She ordered a breakfast sandwich and coffee, he ordered coffee, and they found a table far from other patrons.

Siple stood near the entrance.

"She doesn't want anything?" Camilla asked.

"She's on duty. Eat," he said. "You look like you need it."

"Tell me what you've learned."

"Eat first."

She took a bite of the sandwich, barely tasting it. She set it down, but he only sat back and sipped his coffee. Fine, then. She took another bite, then a third, before she pushed the food away. "You don't think I'm just being paranoid?" She couldn't help the hope that infused her voice, despite the fact that his presence, and the bodyguard's, made the answer obvious.

His lips flattened. "Unfortunately, I do not."

She steeled herself. "Go ahead."

"First, let me update you on what the local investigator

found. The tire was shot out, which caused the blowout that caused the accident."

"But that's not their style, right? They're not exactly subtle."

"It is odd and makes me wonder what the endgame is. If they wanted your son dead, he'd be dead."

She crossed her arms, needing to hold herself together.

"I wonder if he was only trying to disable the car," Agent Falk said.

"Why?"

His lips pressed closed, the pressure paling them. "We could only guess."

"So, guess."

He held her gaze. "Perhaps he hoped to take Jeremy hostage."

She closed her eyes to absorb the information. Hostage? Should she be thankful he was in ICU fighting for his life instead of in the hands of some gangster?

"The investigators found rifle shells on the ridge about a hundred twenty-five yards from the accident site. There were no fingerprints on the shells. There were boot prints. So far, it seems both the boots and the rifle are pretty common.

"Tracks from a dirt bike came from a spot about fifty yards south of the shooter's position. Witnesses say the man who reached the accident site first—the 911 caller—drove off on a dirt bike. The distance between the tracks and the shooter confirms that the 911 caller wasn't the shooter. They still haven't found the caller."

"It's all so weird," she said. "Is it possible it was a coincidence? The guy on the dirt bike was just out for a ride. The shooter was hunting. The boys were...unlucky?" Her voice faltered on the last word. She knew how foolish she sounded. Still, she hoped.

The gentle smile Falk gave her hardly softened the blow.

"Francis Campos has a brother, Robert. They call him 'Little Brother' because of his relation to Francis, but he's anything but little." He pulled his cell phone from his breast pocket and turned it to face her.

She wanted to squeeze her eyes closed.

Hinds' feet for high places.

She didn't want goat feet. She didn't want to scale mountains. She wanted a lush valley with tall grass and a pretty, meandering stream where she and her children would be safe. Was that too much to ask?

She took a deep breath and looked at the image.

It was a mugshot. The man on the screen stood over six feet tall, according to the ruler on the wall behind him. Dark hair so short, it looked as if it had been recently shaved. His mustache and beard were trimmed like parentheses around his mouth. He had a thick head, no neck, and arms as wide as tree trunks. He was built like an NFL linebacker. The flat expression in his cold black eyes sent a shiver down her spine.

He looked like a bigger, uglier, meaner version of his brother. Where Francis had been passionate, Robert looked calculating and unfeeling.

"He's six-three, three hundred pounds." Falk's voice was calm as ever. "He was twenty when Francis was sentenced, a small player in a big gang. The gang is leaner now, and Robert had risen in the ranks. Until last summer, he was one of the top guys in the Vipers."

"What happened last summer?"

The downturn of Falk's lips told her he didn't want to say. But he'd always been straight with her. She just waited.

"Last July, Robert Campos went to the home of a rival gang leader. Their gangs had been in a war for weeks after the murder of one of Campos's men. Campos and a bunch of his thugs broke into the man's house. He rounded up the man's wife and four children, bound and gagged them, and then shot each one in the head. He made the man watch as his family was killed. Then, Robert killed him."

Camilla too easily imagined the scene. The room started to spin slowly, and she gripped the table as if that would make it stop.

Falk continued. "One of the thugs was arrested and told the police what happened, apparently haunted by what they'd done. It's one thing to kill a man. To kill an innocent child..." He shook his head. "Robert found out about the betrayal and arranged for the guy's murder. Unfortunately for Robert, we have enough evidence to convict even without the other gang member's testimony—assuming we ever find him."

She somehow found her voice. "You don't know where he is?"

Falk's gaze slipped, and he looked past her before meeting her eyes again. "Nothing solid. Nothing definite. But there've been sightings in Las Vegas."

Las Vegas. That wasn't very far from Utah. But that didn't mean Campos was here.

Unfortunately, based on the look on Agent Falk's face, he thought it did.

"I don't understand," she said. "It's been four years. Why would he all of a sudden come after Jeremy?"

"I posed that question to the agent in charge of the search. He had some theories. It doesn't seem as if Campos has made much of a name for himself in the Vegas branch of the Vipers. The special agent in charge thinks maybe Campos is just bored. He also wonders if killing his rival fed his bloodlust, and he's looking for an excuse to do something similar."

Similar. An image of herself and her children, bound and gagged, and murdered...

The three bites of sandwich churned in her stomach.

"I don't think that's what it is," Falk was quick to say. "If he wanted to do that, he'd have gone to Oklahoma, to your home. Remember what I said—if he knows your son's vacation plans, then he knows where you live."

"You really know how to put a girl's mind at ease."

A muscle ticked in his cheek. "Four years ago, I promised you I'd always be straight with you."

He'd kept that promise.

But then what he said registered. This guy knew where they lived. And he was after them. "Zoë! She's alone. I've got to—"

"She's safe for now. I have someone watching her." When Camilla started to question him further, he added, "You know you can trust me."

She did trust him. What happened to Daniel hadn't been Agent Falk's fault.

"There must be something we're missing." He rubbed his jaw, looking beyond her. Then, he shook his head. "We'll keep digging. We'll figure it out. Your husband made the ultimate sacrifice to take a murderer off the streets. When we arrested Francis Campos, a void was left at the top of the organization, and that void helped the local police get a man on the inside, which led to the takedown of most of the gang's leaders. The reason the Sons of Vipers are smaller today is because of Daniel's sacrifice. We owe your family a great debt, and we take your safety very seriously."

Her gaze found Siple, who hadn't relaxed her vigil. But old bitterness rose. "Not seriously enough for witness protection."

"You know if it'd been up to me... I could probably get it approved now. After Daniel's death, we were all sure the gang would leave you alone. And for four years, they have. We just don't know what's going on. Which is why"—he nodded toward the guard nearby—"we have Siple here. She will coordinate efforts to protect you. She's already discussed the situation with hospital security, and they assure us that, as long as you're in the ward, you'll be safe. So Siple or another member of her team will be stationed outside the ICU doors. Whenever you or anyone you're with leaves—your sister, brother-in-law, Paul—the security team will accompany them."

It didn't even surprise her that he knew about Paul.

"What that means is," he said, "if one person is gone, another can't leave the ward."

"Okay."

"If you want to leave the hospital for any reason, you must let us know in advance so we can plan your security. No rushing out of the ward or out of the hospital without someone with you."

What Daniel had done had mattered. She knew that. Still, she couldn't help the anger that rose when she thought of the sacrifice they'd made. The gang still operated. There were still drugs in St. Louis, and violence. Maybe Francis Campos was off the street, but nothing had really changed. Not for the city, not for the country.

Everything had changed for her family. She wanted her husband back. She wanted her family safe. She wanted none of this to be happening. "We can't go anywhere until Jeremy is healthy again anyway. What's your plan for Zoë?"

"I called the local police department and told them what was going on. They're stepping up patrols near your house and at her school. I have a friend who used to work for the Bureau who lives in OKC. He's keeping tabs on her. She's in class right now."

"You're thorough." Camilla wasn't surprised. "But I need to get her on a plane."

"I think that's the best course of action," he said. "This hospital is secure, the ICU especially. They have your son and your nephew in the system under false names."

Silly names. Kevin had explained that they did that to protect the boys' privacy since the accident had made the news. Photographs of the crumpled car had circulated on the internet, photographs that churned nausea whenever she saw them. The false names had been used to protect the boys' identity. Between that and the security needed to get into ICU, it did feel like a safe place.

Falk pulled a business card from his breast pocket and handed it to her. He'd written on the back of it. "Here are the best flights. My friend is willing to get her safely to the airport until she's through security. I'll have someone here meet her at the gate and bring her to the hospital. Text me which flight you choose when you book it."

He'd gone above and beyond to protect her and her family. He'd been just as conscientious when he'd worked with her before.

She pulled out her phone to call the airline. "Thank you for this."

Falk stood. "I'll keep you—"

"Wait." She stood as well. "I just remembered something. When Jeremy woke up, he said the accident was his fault."

"I thought he had a tube down his throat."

"He does. He writes on my palm. When I asked him why he thought that, he spelled 'dad' into my hand."

Falk's eyes narrowed, but he said nothing.

"When I pressed, he said he was confused. I don't know if that has anything to do with anything, but I thought I should mention it."

Falk looked over her head, continuing to stare as she dialed the airline and waited through on-hold music.

Finally, he looked back at her. "Is he up for being questioned?"

"Oh." She hadn't considered he'd want to talk to Jeremy. "If you think it's necessary."

"What about your nephew? Evan, right?"

"He's in surgery." The reminder sent fresh anxiety to her stomach, and she lifted a quick prayer for him, feeling guilty she hadn't been praying this whole time.

Too much to worry about, think about, and pray about.

"It makes me wonder if someone used his dad to lure him to the desert," Falk said. "Is your son on social media?"

She almost laughed. After Daniel's death, she'd tried keeping her kids off social media, but they'd begged and pleaded. After they'd been in Oklahoma for a couple of years, after no threats from Campos's people, she'd begun to feel safe and let them join with the caveat that they never share their location. Knowing what had happened to their dad, they'd agreed and, as far as she could tell, had always abided by her rules.

Maybe it was a mistake, but she hadn't wanted to raise her kids to fear. She'd hoped they could feel confident and safe in their new lives.

More than that, she'd wanted them to *be* safe in their new lives. Now she felt like a fool having to admit it. "Jeremy's not only on social media but he's got a good-sized following. And by good-sized, I mean a couple hundred thousand followers."

Unlike most people, Falk didn't even raise an eyebrow at the number. "I may need his login information, but I'll see what we can find out without involving him."

"I know his passwords," she said. "I'll dig into all of his accounts too."

The agent at the airline came on the line.

"One sec." Camilla spoke to Agent Falk. "Thank you for not discounting my worries, for taking me seriously."

"Be safe. I'll be in touch."

CHAPTER NINETEEN

DEAR CAMILLA,

I just reread my last letter. I think my memories make me seem more confident than I was. I was just a dumb kid who happened to get a few things right.

I remember you so clearly. Your words, your facial expressions.

That Sunday, though I'd suspected maybe it was all some cosmic joke played on late-sleepers, there were actually people in the church lobby when I arrived. And they weren't all old or carrying toddlers. There were young people, even some who looked like students. Outside, the low clouds promised snow, and the temperature had dipped into the twenties. Yet here were all these dedicated churchgoers wearing puffy coats and scarves and smiles.

When you stepped into the lobby and scanned the faces, my heart thudded and raced.

I was starting to worry I had a medical condition.

I caught your eye, and you grinned. "You made it." You sounded genuinely shocked.

"Didn't think I would?"

"You seemed rather skeptical."

Inside the sanctuary, a lot of the seats were blocked off, so the congregants were herded to the front sections. You chose seats in the third row. I'd always been more of a back-row kind of guy, but I didn't say that as I slid in beside you.

I tried to pay attention, but my focus was on you.

Had I really thought you looked dowdy at our first meeting?

Not only were you gorgeous but also kind and pure. I watched you while you worshipped. Good thing your eyes were closed or you'd have seen me staring.

You were absolutely radiant.

You still are, by the way.

All these years later, when we're worshipping together, I have to close my eyes, too, or I'll focus more on you than on God.

That morning, we hadn't even made it to the offering before I knew I was in deep trouble. Or I was right where I was supposed to be.

I'd heard about the place I chose for brunch from friends. I'd never been there because it was twenty minutes from campus. I'd never had a date I wanted to extend my time with like I did you. We got lucky with that seat by the window. I wasn't sure about the place—a Victorian house-turned-restaurant?—but you seemed to like it, and it sure smelled good.

I remember you called it charming. "Do you bring all your dates here?"

"Only the ones I go to eight-thirty church with." I added a wink, immediately regretting it and praying I didn't come off as smarmy.

But you smiled at me.

After our coffees were delivered—you remember how delicious it was—we ordered omelets. While we waited, something out the window had your breath catching. "Look, it's snowing."

I gave the outside a cursory glance. Sure enough, tiny snowflakes gently danced across our view as if they were showing off.

"I love snow. Don't you?" You were mesmerized by the sight of it.

I was mesmerized by the sight of you. "I grew up on a big property with a long driveway and a walkway that needed to be shoveled. My brothers and I made it fun for the first few snowstorms of the year, but by March, we were over it."

"How many brothers?"

"Five. I'm the oldest."

"Any sisters?"

"Nope."

Your eyebrows hiked. "That's a lot of testosterone. Where'd you grow up?"

"Maine. How about you?"

You studied me over the lid of your cup. "Near Joplin. We got snow, but not so much that it was a nuisance, at least not for me. Snow meant no school and sledding on the hill behind our house."

"Brothers and sisters?" I asked.

"One sister. Marcy. She's two years older than I am. Are you still in school?"

I told you my plan to go to medical school, taking sips of strong and utterly unnecessary coffee. I felt like I hadn't been that awake, that alive, in years. How could such a simple, seemingly banal conversation be so energizing?

That was how I felt about you then, like you were my energy.

I'm sorry I forgot that.

"Why a doctor?" you asked.

"My father's a general practitioner. I think it's in my blood. How about you? What do you want to be when you grow up?"

My question made you smile. Before you answered, I remembered what you'd been doing the first time I saw you. "Let me guess. An artist?" I thought back to what I'd seen two years earlier and the little glimpse I'd had two days before. "The canvases on your walls—are those yours? They're beautiful."

You brushed your dark hair behind your ear and dipped your chin. "I would love to try to make a living at art, but it's not very practical."

"Practical is overrated. You should do what you love, what makes your heart sing."

Leaning slightly forward, you held my gaze. There was something so earnest, so honest, in your eyes. "Will practicing medicine make your heart sing?"

You made my heart sing. "I think so."

That was the first lie I told you. Because I didn't *think* it, I knew it. The Lord had created me to be a doctor, to help people, heal people. I'd worked with Dad a few times on medical mission trips as a kid, running errands and doing odd jobs. I'd seen enough of his life to know it was what I was meant to do. Obviously, I knew there were other things that came first—loving God, loving my family. But as a profession, I couldn't imagine doing anything else.

The purity in your eyes prompted me to amend my half-truth. "I'm sure it will."

"I love that certainty."

The server delivered our omelets. Before you could take your fork, I reached for your hand. "Mind if I pray?"

"Not sure anybody's ever prayed with me on a date before."

"I like to stand out." I bowed my head before I could add another smarmy wink and asked for a blessing over our food.

After we tried our eggs, I asked something like, "If you could do anything you wanted in the world, if money were no object, what would you do?"

You remember what you said?

"Paint. Maybe become an interior designer."

"So you're studying...?"

"Marketing."

I set down my fork. "Why?"

You shrugged. "I can use my artistic side to design websites, advertisements, stuff like that. Nothing wrong with applied arts."

"You think that'll make your heart sing?"

"A singing heart doesn't pay the bills."

"Ah, sweet Camilla. You need to learn to trust the Lord."

You sat back, and by the look on your face, you were offended. "What makes you think I don't? What makes you think the Lord didn't lead me to study marketing?"

"Did He?"

I can still see your halfhearted shrug.

And hear my arrogant questions.

"Why would God give you the heart of an artist and then shove you into a business role? Not that you won't be able to do it, but shouldn't you do what brings you joy? What brings Him glory?"

You took your time swallowing a bite and then sipped your coffee. You gazed out the window at the falling snow. "I didn't consult Him when I chose marketing, and now I'm almost finished with it. If I could go back, I'd choose a different school and a different major."

A different major? Definitely. But if you'd chosen a different school, then we never would have met. Even then, that thought did something to me.

You tore your gaze away from the winter scene. "I graduate in May, and then I'll need to get a job."

"You're, what, twenty-two? That's not exactly retirement age."

You aimed your fork my way. "You're messing with my head. Yesterday, I was excited about my future. An hour with you and I'm questioning everything."

"Life's too short to settle. God's plan is too good to miss. Not that I go around telling beautiful women what to do, but if I were you, I'd spend some time with Him over the next couple of months, see where He wants you to go from here. His plan may be very different from yours."

The conversation moved on to other topics. While we talked, the snow accumulated out the window. You gave it an occasional glance, which softened your already beautiful features into an expression of wonder. Watching you was more enchanting than anything that could be going on outside.

Two hours passed before I paid the check. I wasn't ready to deliver you home and hoped you felt the same. But I had studying to do, and you had a life to live.

My little sedan was lighter than the SUV I'd driven in high school. I never told you this, but I was nervous on the trip back to campus. You were precious cargo. I went slowly enough that, if we slid off the road, you'd hardly be bruised.

Beside me, you were quiet. I guessed you were scared, too, until I caught you staring not out the front window with clenched fists but out the side, relaxed as could be. You trusted me.

How I wish I'd never ruined that.

Finally, I delivered you to your apartment building and walked you to the door. Inside the foyer, you faced me. "Thank you for brunch."

I took your hands and looked down at your lovely upturned face. "Is it okay if I kiss you?"

"You're asking? That's a first."

"I told you, I like to stand out."

"You definitely do that." Your gaze flicked to my lips.

I took that as a yes and kissed you. It was powerful. So powerful I ended it only seconds after it began.

Slowly, you backed away, gaze on mine.

"Okay, then," I said like an idiot.

"Okay."

"Dinner this week?"

"Yes, please." You swallowed, and your cheeks turned an adorable shade of pink.

It was the first time I'd made you blush, and the feeling was heady.

"I mean," you added, "that sounds great."

"I'll call you."

That afternoon, our conversation about your future was at the forefront of my mind. The more time we spent together, the more I wondered... Did God's plan for you include a certain wannabe doctor headed to med school?

I hoped so.

It still amazes me how quickly I fell for you.

And that you fell for me at all.

Yours always,

Daniel

CHAPTER TWENTY

THAT AFTERNOON, Camilla and Paul stood outside Jeremy's room while the doctors removed one of his chest tubes. That he was getting it out was good news, excellent news. Still, as she watched the procedure, she hugged herself and prayed. All those doctors with their covered faces and serious eyes. It was terrifying, despite Hen's reassurance that all was well.

Paul's arm was snaked around Camilla's back. "He's going to be okay."

She wanted to snap at him—*you can't promise that*—but her lips were pressed closed. She couldn't seem to open them to make words come out.

They'd numbed the area, but it was clear by the way Jeremy's hands were curled into fists that he was experiencing more than the "mild discomfort" they'd promised. Fortunately, the procedure took only a few minutes.

When they finished, the resident—Mark, she remembered—stepped out of Jeremy's room. "He's all set."

"No problems?"

"Nope. Looks good."

Camilla hated to ask, but the words popped out anyway. "Any idea when you'll take the tube out?"

The doctor shrugged. "Maybe tomorrow."

"What are you waiting for?" Paul asked.

The doctor gave Camilla a quick look.

"I'd like to know," she said.

"We need to see Jeremy's lungs working better. We've adjusted the ventilator a couple of times, but his lungs aren't picking up the slack."

"Why not?" Her heart raced. "Is something wrong?"

"The trauma was extreme. I know it's frustrating to hear, but it takes time. He *is* healing. He's strong, he's young and healthy. Don't be discouraged that it's taking so long. Be encouraged that he improves every day."

Paul said, "Getting the chest tube out today, that's a good sign, right?"

The man smiled. "One step in the process. We keep taking a step every day, and soon enough, he'll be back to normal."

Paul squeezed her waist. "We just have to be patient."

We. It was good to be part of a *we* again.

She thanked the doctor and stepped into the room and took Jeremy's hand. "How's it feel?"

He gave a thumbs-down.

Nathan stood at his side. "Where's your pain level?"

He lifted five fingers, then lifted two more. Nathan checked the screen above his head and frowned. "Okay, let's see what we can do about that."

He gave Camilla a look, then stepped out of the room.

Paul started to follow, but she shook him off and followed Nathan to where he stood out of sight of Jeremy.

"What's wrong?"

His calming smile didn't slip, but his eyebrows scrunched a bit. "He's complaining of pain." He kept his voice low. "If it was that bad, his blood pressure and pulse would show it. They don't."

Her own blood pressure spiked, and her words lowered to a vehement whisper. "Are you saying he's lying?"

"No, no." He shook his head to emphasize the point. "I'm saying I think what he's feeling is anxiety, not pain, especially after that procedure. It's common and nothing to worry about. Rather than give him more painkillers, I think I'll ask the doctor about giving him something to help with anxiety. I just wanted you to know."

"Oh." She felt silly for getting upset. "I'm sorry. I shouldn't have—"

"You're fine." He squeezed her upper arm. "You're handling this all very well."

Why did people keep saying that? She felt like she was trying to climb that mountain Bachir had mentioned, only wearing a blindfold and in a blizzard.

Nathan stepped away to talk to the doctor, and she glanced at her phone. Zoë should be here by now.

Camilla should have gone to the airport herself. What if Campos caught wind of Zoë's flight plans? What if he'd found her?

She reread the text she'd received from her daughter just ten minutes before. The standard,

On my way!

But what if Campos had sent the text? Camilla had wanted to call her daughter, but Jeremy had been in the middle of his procedure.

Jeremy didn't know his sister was coming. Zoë had insisted Camilla keep the secret. Despite all the fear and uncertainty Zoë had to be dealing with—because of course Zoë knew about the FBI agent, knew there was more to the accident—Zoë was thinking of how to lift her brother's spirits.

Camilla was just about to dial her daughter when she heard, "Look who I found wandering around."

She turned just in time to catch Zoë as she flew into her arms.

Behind her, Kevin smiled as he pulled Zoë's suitcase into Jeremy's room. He must have been waiting for her as he'd waited for Camilla on Tuesday.

When he stepped back into the corridor, Camilla mouthed, *thank you.*

He nodded and returned to Evan's room.

Camilla held her daughter close, savoring the feel of her, the smell of her, in her arms and safe. "I'm so glad you're here."

Zoë backed up, tears dripping from her eyes. "I'm glad to be here. I didn't want you to pick me up at the airport, but being with those FBI agents freaked me out."

Camilla wiped her daughter's moist cheeks. "Agent Falk didn't want me to leave the hospital and promised me you'd be safe."

"Will you tell me what's going on now? And don't tell me it's just a precaution, either. FBI agents don't act like chauffeurs for fun."

Camilla needed Zoë to know just enough to be cautious, but no more. "There's a chance the boys were lured to the desert. Their tire was shot out, and—"

"Shot, like, with a gun?" Zoë's brown eyes widened.

"It might've just been an accident, a hunter who didn't see them." Though nobody believed that anymore. Poor Zoë had dealt with nightmares for more than a year after her father's murder. They all had. It was bad enough for Camilla to scale this mountain again. The last thing she wanted was for her daughter to scale it too.

Zoë crossed her arms. "But you don't think so, or else you wouldn't have brought me here. And the FBI doesn't think so, or else they wouldn't have acted as my escort."

"We're just being careful."

"Tell me the truth."

Camilla kissed her daughter's forehead. "The truth is that we're all here, and we're safe, and we're going to let the FBI worry about all that while we focus on getting your brother well."

Lips closed and eyes squinted, Zoë studied her face. After a moment, she said, "Okay, for now. But eventually, you're going to have to tell me everything."

Her daughter was right. But not yet. Not until Camilla had more facts and fewer guesses. "Fair enough. Until we know more, don't say anything to Jeremy. He needs to heal."

"I get it." Anger forgotten, Zoë hooked her arm in Camilla's. "Where is he?"

Camilla led her daughter to Jeremy's room. She'd sent photos so Zoë wouldn't be shocked at the sight of him. Still, Zoë hesitated before stepping in.

Camilla watched from the door. Paul was at Jeremy's bedside. When Zoë appeared, he smiled, though Camilla doubted she even noticed. Her gaze was on her brother.

Jeremy's eyes brightened. He angled his bed higher, and Zoë leaned in for a hug. "I left you alone for one week!"

Jeremy rolled his eyes, but tears dripped.

Zoë sat in the rolling chair. "Tell me everything."

Behind the tape and the tube, his cheeks lifted and eyes crinkled. A smile.

Zoë laughed. "I guess I'll have to wait for the rundown until you get that stupid tube out of your mouth."

Jeremy reached for her, and she gave him her hand. He

flipped it over and began to write. She said the letters out loud as he spelled, *Glad ur here. Am I dying?*

Zoë blanched. "That's not even funny!"

Camilla stepped into the room. "Zoë just needed to see for herself that you're doing well. She thought I was sugarcoating it."

His eyes narrowed, and he looked from Camilla to his sister. Zoë had never had much of a poker face, and even Camilla could see the fear there. Hopefully, Jeremy would interpret it as fear for his health and nothing more.

"She was worried about you, man," Paul said. "It's what women do."

Jeremy studied Paul's casual expression, then turned back to his sister.

Zoë laughed, and it almost sounded natural. "Mostly, it was a great excuse to get out of school and work for a couple of days."

The fear slid off Jeremy's face.

Paul came around the bed and gave her a quick side hug. "How was the flight?"

After a glance at Camilla, she said, "Uneventful."

Camilla let herself breathe in the relief.

"Mom, why don't you and Paul get out of here for a little while?" Zoë said. "I can hang out with Jeremy."

"If you don't mind," Camilla said. "Just remember"—she gave Zoë a stern look—"he needs to rest, so don't excite him."

Zoë's eyebrows lowered as she glared. "I got it, Mom." In other words, *Duh, I'm not gonna tell him anything.*

Camilla hoped that was true as she walked out.

She'd told Paul about Agent Falk's visit, but she hadn't told Marcy and Kevin anything more than that Zoë was coming. Now that Evan was out of surgery and recovering, she needed to share everything she'd learned.

She stopped before they reached Evan's room and faced Paul. "I need to talk to them privately. Do you want to meet me in the cafeteria downstairs for dinner?"

"Why don't we go out and get something? There's a bakery just—"

"I don't want to leave the hospital. The cafeteria will be fine."

Only the slightest hesitation, and then, "Whatever you need. But let's go to the one in the other building. They have a better selection. I'll wait for you by the escalator."

It would only add about twenty minutes to the time she was away. She could do that.

Marcy was sitting in the rolling chair watching Evan when Camilla stopped outside his room. Kevin was reclined in the shorter one, typing on his laptop. They both looked up when Camilla stepped in. "How is he?"

"Sleeping off the drugs." Marcy had a real smile on her face for the first time since Camilla had arrived two days earlier.

"Good news?"

"The surgeon was here a little while ago. A segment of Evan's intestines was damaged badly in the accident, thanks to the seatbelt. They cut it out and sewed the rest back together. They didn't see anything else to worry about."

Kevin snapped his laptop closed. "The surgery should do it. If all goes well, they're going to move him out of ICU tomorrow."

"Oh, good." She infused her voice with enthusiasm, though her first—very selfish—thought was that she liked having them close by.

"He's going to neuro," Kevin said, "wherever that is."

The nurse sitting at her desk said, "Go down the hall past Jeremy's room. Follow it to the right, and boom, you're there."

Marcy's smile brightened further as she stood and stretched. "That's perfect."

"Why neuro?" Camilla asked.

"The concussion," Kevin said. "Once they've done all their tests, I think they'll send us home, maybe Saturday."

In two days? Just like that? "That's such good news." Camilla tamped down her selfishness again. She wanted Evan to recover. She just wanted Jeremy to recover too. "I'm glad."

Marcy approached the door. "I need to say hi to Zoë. I just wanted to give her a minute with her brother."

"First, can I talk to you two? I need to tell you something."

Marcy's joyful expression faltered. "Is something wrong with Jeremy? What is it?"

"No change there, but..." She glanced at Kevin. "Somewhere private, if you don't mind."

Kevin and Marcy followed Camilla to the empty hallway past Jeremy's room.

She faced them, swallowing a sudden lump of fear. They loved her. They'd forgive her for almost getting their son killed. Right? She should have gone over this in her head first.

"What is it?" Kevin said.

"Turns out..." She took a breath. "I called the special agent we worked with when Daniel..."

"Agent Falk, right?" Marcy said. "You talked a lot about him back then."

"I figured I'd better let him know what happened, just in case it was related. I was sure it wasn't, but—"

"It was?" Kevin's back stiffened. "Are you saying somebody targeted them?"

"Maybe." She watched the color seep from Marcy's face. Kevin's darkened.

Camilla told her sister and brother-in-law what Falk had

told her. Halfway through her story, Marcy gripped Kevin's arm.

By the time Camilla was done, tears were dripping from her sister's eyes. Camilla took a tissue from her pocket and handed it to her. "I'm so sorry Evan got involved in this. I can't even..." She tried to temper the emotion in her voice. "I would never do anything to harm your son. If I'd known, I swear, I would have—"

"It's not your fault." Marcy pulled Camilla into a hug, and Kevin wrapped his free arm around her back.

"You couldn't have known." His voice was stiff.

She backed up to face him. "I wouldn't blame you if you were angry with me."

"Not you." The words were low. "That monster... It wasn't enough that he killed Daniel, but now to go after his son, our son." The low tone vibrated with fury. "What kind of a man targets children?"

"They're going to figure out what's going on. Falk is here."

"Here?" Marcy asked. "As in, in Salt Lake? Doesn't he work in St. Louis?"

"Atlanta now. When I called, he flew out."

"This is serious," she said.

"Of course it's serious!" Kevin snapped. "They tried to kill our sons." His voice cracked at the end, and he swallowed. "Do you think Marcy's in danger?"

"There's an FBI agent outside the ward. If you go anywhere, she'll go, too. Her name is Agent Siple. Just introduce yourselves when you leave. The thing is, we have to stay here or stay together, since there's just one agent assigned to protect us."

"Just one?" Kevin said. "They should send—"

"Call Agent Falk and see what he says. He's the one to talk to about it." She pulled the business card he'd given her from her pocket and handed it to him. "He doesn't sugarcoat anything."

"Good." He turned to Marcy. "You have to be careful. If this agent person isn't there when you walk out, then you don't go." He turned to Camilla. "Same goes for you."

"I know the drill," Camilla said. "I've lived it before."

Marcy was shaking her head. "I doubt anybody would be after us."

Kevin took his wife's hands. "You're her sister. If someone took you, how far do you think Camilla would go to rescue you?"

Marcy's jaw dropped. "Oh. Right."

Kevin continued. "The news reported where the boys were taken. If someone's after Camilla then they might be after anyone she loves. They'll know where to find you. Until this guy is caught, we all have to assume we're targets."

CHAPTER TWENTY-ONE

THE SUN HAD long since set by the time Camilla kissed Jeremy's forehead and turned to Zoë. "You'll call me if anything happens?"

"I promise."

Nurse Ashton was back tonight. Camilla spoke to her. "They tell me it's only five minutes from here."

Ashton said, "I promise to call you if we need you. Go, sleep."

She needed to, desperately. Still, she hesitated.

Jeremy grabbed her hand and started writing. *Please.* He pointed to her, mimed turning a steering wheel, pointed to himself, and then circled his finger near the side of his head.

She was driving him crazy.

She laughed. "Wow. That's the thanks I get."

He smiled and squeezed her hand. She saw the teasing in his eyes.

He would be all right.

Zoë pulled her mom to the door, then deposited her suitcase beside her. "Sleep, please. You need it."

The very thought of it had Camilla yawning. She hugged

her daughter. "I'm so glad you're here." Then she whispered, "Please don't tell him anything. He needs to rest."

Zoë stepped out of the hug. "Still not an idiot, Mom."

"I know. Sorry. And don't forget you have to—"

"Not go anywhere without protection."

Kevin stood, arms folded, in the hallway. The scowl that had appeared on his face when she'd told him the bad news hadn't faded at all.

She hoped he'd been honest when he'd said he wasn't angry with her. She'd hate to be the recipient of all that fury.

Beside him, Paul leaned against the wall, casual as could be. Even after a long day in the hospital, he looked handsome in his jeans and sweater.

The two men hadn't had much time to get to know each other, but she had caught them talking earlier, mostly about the boys and sports. They might become friends eventually.

Paul pushed himself off the wall. "Ready?"

She swallowed a wave of panic. Could she leave her son? Was she crazy to leave the safety of the hospital with a killer out there?

Paul approached and rubbed her upper arms. "What is it?"

She needed to sleep, which meant she had to trust the FBI agent with her safety and her kids' even as she trusted the hospital staff with Jeremy's health.

"I'm fine."

Paul pulled her suitcase, and they made it to the ICU exit, where Agent Siple waited. Once they stepped into the hallway, Paul shifted from friendly to vigilant. It was as if he'd slipped into full-on fight mode. He'd spent time in the military and had served in Iraq, so he was no stranger to war. She hated that her battle had become his—and Marcy's and her family's.

The FBI had been at the Ronald McDonald House earlier to ensure the place was secure. They'd seemed happy with what they learned. After Siple got Camilla inside, she'd drive Paul to his hotel. They weren't as worried about his safety, and he'd refused protection, but he had wanted to accompany Camilla.

They arrived at the property ten minutes after they left Jeremy's room. Siple walked with them to the door, buzzed the receptionist, and got them inside.

"Good security," Paul said.

Once they were safely in the lobby, Camilla turned to him. "I'm safe now. You don't have to hang around."

Before he could respond, Agent Siple jumped in. "We'll wait until you have your key."

Camilla filled out paperwork and handed it to the receptionist.

She glanced at the papers and set them aside. "Your background check turned up nothing to be concerned about."

"Background check?"

"We do them for everyone who checks in."

Paul seemed to relax. "That makes me feel better about leaving you."

Siple stood by the door silently.

The clerk handed her the key. "I'll just show you around, and then you can get to your room."

Siple pushed off from the wall. "The tour is required?"

"Yes. We like our residents to know—"

"We'll go, too."

The woman's gaze flicked behind her as if someone might give her permission for that.

"My office called today." Siple handed the woman a business card. "I stay with her until she's in her room."

The three of them followed the woman around the building. Laundry room, exercise room, TV room. Most impressive was the enormous, fully stocked kitchen. Camilla wouldn't be taking advantage of most of the house's amenities, but what a blessing for parents whose kids were undergoing long-term treatment.

Finally, the tour was finished, and Agent Siple and Paul walked Camilla to her room on the third floor. After Siple did a quick walk-through, she wandered to the end of the hallway to wait.

Standing outside her room, Paul took Camilla's hands. "You call me when you're ready to come back. I'll Uber over here and ride with you to the hospital."

"You don't need to—"

"I won't sleep if I think you're in danger. My hotel's only a few minutes away, so call before you're ready, and I'll be here as quickly as I can. Okay?"

"If Jeremy needs me, if there's an emergency—"

"Then you'll let me know, and I'll meet you at the hospital. But if not… Please?"

She squeezed Paul's hands. "I'll call you."

He folded her in his arms, and she melted against his chest. His jacket was open, and she pressed her cheek against his soft cashmere sweater. His embrace was warm and comfortable. It was good to have someone to rely on, to not have to do this alone.

Paul rubbed her back, kissed her head.

She backed away from the embrace. "I'll see you in the morning."

He leaned down and kissed her cheek. "Sleep well."

CHAPTER TWENTY-TWO

DEAR CAMILLA,

That spring break, we both went home and told our families about the other, and both of us received *don't rush into anything* lectures. Since we respected our parents, we took their advice.

Sort of.

I couldn't believe it when you took that job in Chicago.

I started medical school at Northwestern, and you worked an entry-level job as a graphic designer. Despite my very arrogant lecture on our first date, you loved your job. Did it make your soul sing? I don't know, but you found satisfaction in the work.

We rented apartments not far from each other and moved in with roommates we'd never met before and spent every available moment together. There weren't many of those, though. Med school was harder than anything I'd ever done, and your job wasn't exactly eight-to-five. We met for quick lunches a few times a week, ate dinner at your apartment or mine on the evenings we were both free, and attended church together on Sundays.

Between the pressures of school and work, the difficulty of

living with people we barely knew, and the challenges of trying to remain pure when nobody was watching, it was a hard year. Hard, but we made it. We were dedicated to our different vocations, but we were dedicated to Christ first and each other second.

Those days seemed so challenging to me at the time. I look back on them with fresh eyes. It was a joy to be studying what I loved. Not just medicine but the woman who would become my wife. The way you took to Chicago, to the work, to the different environment... You were amazing.

I fell in love with you more every single day.

I was so nervous on that spring break trip to Joplin to visit your parents. When I surprised you by taking you to the restaurant where we had our first date, you were too happy to be there to notice my shaking hands.

I'd called ahead and arranged for us to sit at the same table. If I could have arranged a snowstorm outside the window, I would have, but God blessed us with a sunny spring day instead. Birds singing, a gentle breeze—the works. After we ate our omelets and drank our coffee, in front of total strangers and with the restaurant manager surreptitiously filming from the corner, I got down on one knee and asked you to be my bride.

And you said yes.

I can still see the happiness in your expression. I can still remember how amazed I was that the most beautiful woman in the world would choose to spend her life with me.

I ruined it. I ruined us. I know that. Oh, sweet Cammie, I'd do anything to go back to that restaurant and punch that stupid man in the face. I'd tell him to remember that moment, the love that overflowed in your tears—and mine.

I'm sorry, Cammie. I'm so sorry.

I forgot how precious you are. I forgot to cherish you. I

forgot to keep God first and my marriage second and my children third and my work a distant straggler.

You made your share of mistakes. Don't worry—I'm not seeing the past through tinted lenses. But I was the head of our family. I was the one who set the tone.

There's nothing like the cold hint of death to encourage a man to be honest.

At what will probably be the end of my life, I can admit what I denied for so long.

What happened to our marriage was all my fault.

I hope you can forgive me.

Yours always,

Daniel

CHAPTER TWENTY-THREE

IT WAS STILL DARK when Camilla's eyes popped open. She'd fallen asleep within minutes of arriving in the large hotel-like room. She glanced at her phone. It was a quarter past three. There were no messages from Zoë or the nurse, which meant Camilla could assume Jeremy was doing well.

There were messages—a bunch of messages—from Daniel's brothers. They'd texted the night before, but she hadn't had the energy to read and respond. Camilla had let Roger and Peggy know about the possible connection to the man who'd wanted Daniel dead. Maybe she shouldn't have worried them, but they were prayer warriors, and she'd take all the prayers she could get.

Grant, a former bodyguard, was more of a take-action kind of guy.

I can have a team there ASAP.

Sam added:

I'll pay for it.

And Bryan chimed in.

You don't get all the glory, bro. I'll help.

Followed by Derrick's...

Me too.

Only Michael hadn't responded yet. He was traveling a lot these days. Maybe he didn't have service. As the brother nearest to Daniel in age—only five years younger—he'd been the closest to Daniel over the years. When he heard what happened, he'd want to help too.

But a team of bodyguards? Just what she needed, to be surrounded by hulking men wherever she went. Although, if they could protect her children...

But Falk believed the hospital security and the FBI agent assigned to protect them were enough. For now, she agreed.

We're okay until Jeremy gets released. At that point, maybe. Thanks for the offer.

She'd try to go back to sleep, but her mind was churning—Jeremy, Evan, Campos, Paul.

And Daniel, though she tried hard not to think about him. Four years he'd been gone, but she yearned for him now as if it'd been four days.

In the dark room, she opened the Bible app on her phone and read the eighty-fourth Psalm, praying for the ability to make this valley of suffering a place of springs. She asked God to show her the pools of refreshment. *Lord, help me go from strength to strength until I reach the end of this battle.* Maybe the Valley of Baca was like the mountain Bachir had spoken of the other day. Every mountain had a summit. Every wilderness road led to a place of bounty. She would reach the end of this trial.

She set the phone aside, turned on the bedside lamp, and picked up Daniel's letters. Until this trip, she hadn't reread them in months. Now, she opened the next in the stack—the one that recounted Daniel's proposal—and skimmed her fingers over the handwritten words, feeling the indentations in the paper as she read. She could still remember the joy that had risen in her heart when he asked her to marry him. She could still hear the applause of the strangers when she said yes.

A lot had happened since then, but if she had it to do all over again, she'd still say yes.

Despite all the difficulties, all the trials—despite losing him far too soon—she would never regret marrying Daniel Wright.

She tucked the letter back in its envelope and slid it to the bottom of the stack.

A glance at the clock told her Jeremy would have his X-ray soon. She should be there for that, find out if he was better.

She showered, dressed in clean clothes, and then climbed back into bed with her phone. Here, where Zoë wouldn't be looking over her shoulder and asking a bunch of questions, she opened TikTok, logged into Jeremy's account, and scrolled posts. It didn't take long before she found the one where he'd told his fans where he was going for spring break.

What part of *don't share your whereabouts* did Jeremy not understand?

They'd have that conversation later. She scrolled the comments, looking for anything suspicious. She found nothing worrisome. Well, she found a few things worrisome—all those girls who thought her son was *so cute!* Girls who'd love to meet him in person.

How her son kept his humility with all those adoring fans, she had no idea.

She moved on to his private messages and scrolled. Lots from girls, their comments more forward than the public ones. Jeremy was kind but didn't get into serious conversations with any of them. Wise boy.

Camilla was running out of time if she wanted to make it back for Jeremy's X-ray. She sent Paul a quick text, and he responded immediately.

Be there by 4:30—unless you need me to rush.

Four-thirty—only twenty-five minutes from now. She responded,

Perfect. See you then.

She texted the number Agent Siple had given her and received an immediate reply.

I'll be at your room by 4:25.

After she filled a small shopping bag with the things she'd need, planning to leave her suitcase in the room, she continued scrolling through Jeremy's TikTok messages.

And then she found one dated a week earlier from someone named Roger.

Roger was Daniel's middle name and his father's first. It wasn't exactly the most common name among teens.

As she read the most recent message, her hands started to shake. Written by Roger, it read, *Monday night, 7 pm, old copper mine off 36*. A map was attached.

She scrolled to the start of the conversation. Roger had initiated it with a striking message.

You have to promise me you won't tell anybody, especially your mom and sister. I have information about your father.

Jeremy had responded, *Who are you?*

A friend, Roger said. *Do you promise? I don't want them to get their hopes up.*

The next message, dated a day later, read, *Fine. I promise. What about my father?*

I'm your father. I'm alive.

She stared at the words, and her blood ran cold.

No, no, no! Who would say such a thing? Who would *do* such a thing?

A knock on her door made her jump. She opened it, and Agent Siple stood in the hallway. "You ready?"

With trembling hands, Camilla slid her phone into her pocket and grabbed her bag. She forced a casual tone despite her pounding heart. "Did you get any sleep?"

"I'll sleep later."

"You didn't see anything suspicious?"

Siple shook her head. "Hospital is secure. This place is too." Her words were crisp, her voice strong. She didn't show a lot of emotion, but Camilla figured that, beneath the fitted suit and the sidearm, she had plenty of personality. "You're safe here," Siple added. "The most dangerous time is when we're on the road. I'm glad we're getting back to the hospital early."

Paul was standing outside, shivering, when they stepped from the building. The agent's car was idling in the drive.

Paul kissed Camilla's cheek, and they climbed into the backseat. "How'd you sleep?"

"Fine. Thanks for coming." She couldn't do small talk right now, though. All she could think about were the messages she'd just discovered. She focused on the phone.

Jeremy had ignored the crazy message, but Roger hadn't given up.

I want to see you.

The next day, *Please, Jeremy. I miss you so much. I need to see you, and then I'll disappear again.*

Jeremy's answer was, *Stop messaging me.*

The man had responded immediately, *I can prove it.* He sent an attachment.

She tapped the tiny image on her phone, and it expanded.

It was a photograph. Blue skies. Sandy ground. Thatched roofs over huts made of sticks. A crowd of people. Most had skin as dark as Bachir's. In the foreground, a man was tending a wound on the arm of a small boy, who sat on a table in the sun.

Behind him, others were working. Two middle-aged women talked to another woman, who held a toddler. A white elderly couple was handing out water bottles. Beside them—

She gasped.

"You all right?" Paul glanced at her phone. "What are you doing?"

"I'm fine." She angled it away from him, staring at the image.

The man was crouched in front of a little girl seated on a bench. He was probably unaware the photo was being taken.

He had graying hair and a full beard. His skin was tan, and he wore black-rimmed glasses. But past the beard and glasses...

Daniel.

No.

It looked like him, but it couldn't be him. It couldn't.

Besides, this man was too old to be Daniel.

Except Daniel would have aged since—

No!

Daniel was dead.

Angry, frustrated tears pricked her eyes. Who would do this? Who would lead Jeremy to believe...

The car stopped at a stop sign. The roads were deserted, the landscape dark.

"Are you all right?" Paul asked. "What are you looking at?"

She didn't want to tell him. Couldn't even form the words. "It's just… I'm not sure yet."

The car glided forward.

"Maybe I can help," Paul said.

"I just need to look at this real quick." She made sure he couldn't see the image. She knew what he'd say, what everyone would say. Daniel was dead.

Everybody knew Daniel was dead.

Jeremy knew it too. Her poor baby. What hope had led him to that deserted road?

She took a screenshot of the photo, then kept scrolling. *I can't come to Oklahoma,* Roger had written. *They'll be looking for me there. But when you're in Utah…*

The messages continued, and Jeremy finally agreed to meet.

Had he told Zoë? Surely, she would have told Camilla if she'd known.

What despair Jeremy must feel now to realize he'd been fooled. Had he known at the time of the accident that he'd been shot at? That whoever had tricked him into going there had caused his accident?

Or did he believe he'd ruined his chance to see his father? No wonder he hadn't wanted to tell her the truth. No wonder Evan hadn't told her.

No wonder Jeremy blamed himself.

Did they think it had been a practical joke? After what happened, why hadn't they been honest?

The car came to a stop, and she looked up to see they were at the hospital. Siple opened Camilla's door, and she stepped out. They walked into the glass-fronted entrance. Beside her, Paul said, "If you want me to go back to my hotel…"

"No, no. I'm sorry." She slid the phone into her purse. "I was going through Jeremy's messages, and I think..." She wasn't ready to tell him. "I'll explain when I know more. But of course, you're welcome."

He nodded, no smile. "I'm going to grab a coffee. You want one?"

"Sure."

Paul headed for the cafeteria, but Siple kept a quick pace to the escalator. Only when they reached the ICU doorway did the woman stop.

"Thanks," Camilla said.

"My replacement will be here in a couple of hours. We'll text you his photo before he comes so you'll know who to trust."

"Okay, thanks."

Inside the ICU, she turned away from the boys' rooms. She needed to call Falk now, and she didn't need anybody listening in on the conversation.

He answered, voice groggy. She told him what she'd learned and promised to send screenshots of the conversation. His voice went from gruff to interested in seconds. "Send them now, please. And I'll need your son's login information, too."

When they hung up, she tried to send what he'd asked for, but nausea gurgled in her stomach. Before she could finish the task, she hurried to the nearest bathroom and threw up.

When she'd emptied what little was in her stomach, she sat back on her haunches, trembling.

Lord, this mountain is too steep. I can't climb it.

Not again.

CHAPTER TWENTY-FOUR

WHEN CAMILLA finally pulled herself together, she texted Falk the photos and information he'd requested, then headed for Jeremy's room, where the X-ray techs were just about to roll their machine to the next patient. Camilla hurried past the nurse's station to meet them. "Can I see it?"

The doctor tapped a few buttons and stepped away from the screen, and Camilla peered at the image. The lungs looked larger, lighter. "They're better, right?"

"We're still seeing some build-up of fluid in the right chest cavity." He pointed, but Camilla had no idea what to look for. It seemed like the rest of the non-lung space to her.

"That's where he got the tube out, right?" Camilla said.

"Yeah. We'll watch it today. We turned the vent down earlier, and your son's lungs are doing their part."

Camilla let the worries from the messages she'd seen slide away for a moment. "He's breathing on his own?"

"Not yet." His smile was indulgent. "But he's getting there. We're seeing improvement, and that's a good sign."

Camilla told herself not to ask, knew asking would only lead to disappointment, but still she said, "Any idea when you'll extubate."

"Maybe later today."

Today? The *maybe* was still there, but... "I didn't think *today* was ever going to be an option."

The man looked through the glass at Jeremy a long moment. When he turned back to Camilla, his expression shifted to something more serious. "When he first came in, I didn't think so either."

The words were so honest, so scary. Jeremy truly had been on the brink of death. But now he wasn't.

The doctor patted her shoulder. "You've got every reason to hope."

After the doctor and X-ray techs walked away, Camilla stepped into Jeremy's room. He was awake, and at the sight of her, his expression shifted from tense to relaxed. She kissed his forehead.

He took her hand and wrote *glad ur here.*

"Me, too."

Zoë was sound asleep on the torture cot in the corner.

"Did your sister sleep all night?" She'd hoped Zoë would tend to her brother's needs, keep him company if he woke.

He shook his head.

"I should have stayed. I didn't want you to be alone, but if she slept—"

Jeremy cut his finger across his throat—*stop talking.* He took her hand. *I slept. I'm fine.*

She took a breath. "Good. Sorry for worrying."

Her phone dinged, and her stomach lurched. She looked at the screen. Not Falk but Paul. She shouldn't have called him this morning. She didn't want to visit. She didn't want to tell him what she'd discovered about Jeremy's trip to the desert, but she didn't think she could pretend all was well.

But she hadn't sent him away, and she wouldn't be unkind. She stood. "Paul's here."

Jeremy's eyes narrowed.

She wondered what put that look on his face but didn't ask. "He brought coffee. It seems rude to send him away after waking him up at four o'clock."

Jeremy took her hand. Wrote *Did he...*

And then he stopped.

"Did he what?"

He shook his head, but she could see frustration in his expression. Maybe anger.

"Jeremy, what? What's wrong?"

He took her hand again. *Tired.* And then he closed his eyes.

She watched him, wondering what he'd wanted to ask. What he'd been afraid to ask about Paul.

Did Paul... what?

Stay with her?

She'd bet anything that was the question. Or maybe he'd been trying to find a more subtle way to ask. Too hard without the use of a voice.

"Jeremy?"

His eyes popped open. He looked irritated.

"Just so you know, I stayed at the Ronald McDonald House. Paul has a hotel room. He stayed there."

He snatched her hand, angry. *Don't owe me*—

"We're not dating. We're just friends."

He gave her a *whatever* look and closed his eyes again.

She waited, unsure what to do. Maybe there was more to her relationship with Paul than friendship, but not anything near what Jeremy was thinking. At least what she guessed Jeremy was thinking. Communicating with a teenage boy was hard enough without adding the inability of that boy to speak.

After a few minutes, the anger faded from Jeremy's face. Drugs and exhaustion won, and he slept.

Lord, what do I do? I don't want to hurt Paul. I don't want to hurt my children. I need Your wisdom.

She had no idea how to handle this, but Paul was waiting at the ward door, and she'd left him long enough. She hurried to walk him in.

When Paul saw her, he pushed off the desk and handed her a cup of coffee. His customary smile was missing. "You seemed upset in the car. Anything I can do?"

She didn't want to tell him. She didn't want to share the news with anybody. But maybe she needed to. Maybe she needed to talk it out in order to make sense of it. Normally, Marcy would be her sounding board, but she and Kevin had enough to deal with.

She'd noticed an empty conference room behind the nurse's station the day before when a group of people had gathered in there. She spoke to the nurse. "Can we go in that room and talk for a minute?"

"Sure." She pushed open the door and flipped on the light. "Nobody needs it for hours. Take your time."

They stepped in, and Paul closed the door behind him. It looked like any conference room in any office building in the country. Long room, long table in the center surrounded by comfortable chairs. No windows. Camilla sat, and Paul took the chair beside her. "Bad news?"

She set her coffee cup on the table, opened her phone to the app, and showed him the messages. "The first one came about a month ago."

Paul read the messages, his expression shifting as he scrolled from curiosity to confusion to anger. "What kind of sick jerk...?"

Camilla gazed at the screen as he read. The tension in the

room seemed to tighten with each new message. When Paul got to the photo, he clicked to enlarge it, then studied the image.

"It kind of looks like him, but..." He shook his head. "I wonder how they did it. Maybe got an image of Daniel's face and ran it through one of those age progression things."

Obviously, the photo was doctored. Why hadn't that occurred to her? She lowered her gaze, feeling foolish. Feeling the hope seep out of her like air from a leaky balloon.

She stared at the table's smooth dark wood, willing her emotions to settle. Some horrible person had played a sick joke on her family. But what if...?

"Camilla?"

She looked up, blinking away the crazy thoughts.

"You know it's not him, right?"

"Of course." But her voice betrayed her. In the two little words, she heard hope, longing.

And Paul didn't miss it. His lips turned down at the corners, and his eyes softened. "Sweetheart, Daniel is gone."

"I know that."

"If he were alive, he'd have gotten in touch with you."

"I know. Obviously." Unless he'd been trying to keep her and the kids safe. Unless he'd—

"Camilla, don't do this to yourself. Daniel is gone."

She pushed back in the chair and stood. "I'm aware of that, Paul." The anger in her voice bounced off the walls. "You don't need to tell me he's gone. I've lived without him for four years."

Slowly, Paul set the phone facedown. "I just don't want you to get your hopes up. Daniel wouldn't want you to—"

"Don't do that," she snapped. "Don't tell me what my husband would or wouldn't want."

"Your *late* husband." He stood and took a step toward her.

She backed up. She didn't want to hear this. Didn't want to

hear all of Paul's logical reasons why Daniel was dead. She knew already. She knew.

And she didn't want him to comfort her. She didn't want comfort. She wanted... she wanted...

To hope.

Was it so awful to hope?

"I sat with you, night after night, as you grieved him. We grieved him together."

"He wasn't your—"

"I know." Paul's voice was low and soothing. "I lost a friend. You lost a husband. I know it's not the same. I'm just saying, it was agony watching you come to terms with it, watching you grieve, watching the kids try to deal with the fact that their father had done what he was sure was the right thing, and he'd died anyway. I just don't want to see you go through it again."

He took another step toward her, arms reaching toward her, but she backed up, her thoughts focused on one part of what he'd said. "What do you mean by 'what he was sure was the right thing'? Do you think he was wrong to testify?"

Paul froze in place, and his arms dropped to his sides. "I wouldn't have made that choice," he said. "I'm not saying it was wrong. Just...I wouldn't have done it." Emotions played across his face, tightened his jawline. She saw the stubble there and realized she'd never seen him unshaven. It was...intimate, somehow.

She didn't know what to think of that thought.

"I only know that, if I were ever lucky enough to be your husband, nothing could compel me to leave you or to put you in danger. Nothing."

Oh.

That wasn't what she needed to hear.

She needed to think.

She didn't know where to focus her thoughts. On Paul's

judgment of Daniel or on that last part. *Husband?* She knew Paul wanted to be more than her friend, but *husband?*

Why did the word throw her? She knew. She'd known for a long time how he felt about her. But to say it, out loud, here, in this conversation...

It was too much.

"I'm sorry." Paul returned to his chair, his awkward movements far from the relaxed attitude he usually had around her. "I'm sorry," he said again, "but I can't watch you go through this again. I won't."

"I'm not doing anything. I'm just... It's a shock, that's all."

Paul pulled out her chair. "Please sit."

She did, swiveling to face him, unsure what to do now.

After a deep breath, Paul said, "Daniel was murdered, Camilla. His car was found covered in blood. *His* blood."

The images burned into her mind four years ago filled her vision. Blood on the steering wheel, the floorboard, the windows. She covered her face with her hands. "I know—"

"His car was found in an alley behind a funeral home with a cremation chamber. The back door lock had been jimmied, the building broken into. Your husband's blood was found—"

"I know what happened." She pushed away from the table.

"A drop of his blood was found on the floor near the door, another on the wall by the chamber. The furnace had been lit."

"I know!" The shout bounced off the walls, which were closing in. She forced her voice to a normal volume. "I know he's dead."

Paul stood and held out his arms. "I don't want to hurt you or cause you pain. You know I'd never..." He swallowed. "I'm afraid you're going back to that place you were four years ago. It was a dark place, Cammie."

"Don't call me that." She stepped back, breath heaving as if she'd been in a race.

He didn't move, and his arms didn't lower. "Camilla." The single word held such defeat, she nearly cried. "I'm sorry. I'm sorry about Daniel. I'm sorry about Jeremy. I'm sorry about this crazy guy who... I'm sorry about all of it. I wish I could fix it for you."

But it wasn't fixable. It felt like it never would be.

Still, Paul stood there, arms wide, waiting. Tenderness in his gaze. And fear... Fear for her, for her heart and mind. Fear that she'd go back to the dark days after Daniel's death. Days of depression and loneliness, of wondering if life could ever be good again. She'd moved to Oklahoma, and within a year, Paul had moved there too. Because, after his divorce, his kids had moved away, and he had no reason to stay in St. Louis. And because she'd needed a friend. He'd cared for her, even then.

He cared for her now.

She stepped into his arms, and he wrapped them around her.

He kissed the top of her head. "It's going to be all right. Whatever happens, I'll be with you."

But she thought of Jeremy's reaction to Paul's presence. Jeremy liked Paul. If they were together, Jeremy would get used to the idea.

Zoë would be in favor of a relationship with Paul. At least Camilla thought so.

And then she remembered her own wish that very morning, the wish that she'd sent him away. What was wrong with her? She had this amazing, tenderhearted man, a man so devoted to her that he'd dropped everything to be with her. A man who'd picked up his life, moved his business, all to be close to her. A man who...

Loved her.

She stepped away. "I'm sorry. I just..."

She needed Paul. She cared for him. She enjoyed his company. But did she love him?

Could she, eventually?

Thoughts of Daniel were too thick in the room, in her head. She needed space. When they were home, when things returned to normal, she'd think about it. Not now.

"I need to get back."

"Whatever you need, I'll be here for you." He took his coffee cup and she took hers. He opened the door and held out his hand toward her.

She slipped hers into it, and they walked to Jeremy's room.

She told herself to be thankful for his presence, to be thankful that she had such a wonderful man who cared for her, but in the back of her mind, all she could think was...

Daniel.

CHAPTER TWENTY-FIVE

DEAR CAMILLA,

When we first moved into that tiny, dingy apartment in Chicago, I hated it. Even though you said it was fine, I planned to find us something better. Once I finished med school, we had the money, but you surprised me, Camilla. You wanted to stay. It was well situated between my hospital and your ad agency. It was in a safe neighborhood, and we'd come to know our neighbors.

You were right, of course.

We both worked too many hours, but yours were a lot more reasonable than mine. While you worked forty to fifty hours a week, my residency demanded closer to eighty. You knew what you'd signed up for and hardly complained. On the few occasions you did, I appeased you with the promise that it wouldn't be forever.

While I was busy doing what I loved, you were home alone or going to church alone or driving to Joplin to visit your family alone. You scrubbed and painted our apartment. You found that used dining room set and refinished it. You learned to reupholster furniture by practicing on a little chair you'd seen on the sidewalk one day.

You were sure it would be gone by the time I grabbed it, but I wasn't about to take furniture off the street in broad daylight.

What did you call it? A slipper chair? Who makes a chair just for putting on slippers?

You shopped sales and painted canvases. All by yourself, you transformed that little apartment into a home. I noticed. I know you don't think I did. I should have told you how much I appreciated you, and not just because of what you did with our home. You supported me. You made it possible for me to achieve my dream.

Finally, five years after we married, we moved back to St. Louis. I know you weren't thrilled with the hospital where I'd accepted a job, always worried about its location in the city. But at least we were closer to your family. We'd saved enough money, mostly thanks to your good salary and frugal choices, that with a little help from our parents we were able to buy a house.

You were three months pregnant the day you took me to see the one you wanted, a fixer-upper in McKinley Heights.

I wasn't impressed.

Built in 1910, it had been updated in the fifties (when pink bathroom tile was fashionable) and again in the seventies (orange-and-avocado linoleum?). Nobody had touched it since. No humans, anyway, though more than a few rodents made their home there. All I saw was work, everywhere I looked.

"You really think we can take this on?" Translation: *Please don't make me do this.*

You gave me that look—eyebrows raised, lips turned down at the corners—that told me I'd said something stupid. "Who is this *we*?" Before I could clarify—and, knowing I was in trouble,

I took my time—you added, "You and I both know that whatever *we* do to this house will be done by me."

I stopped myself before I reminded you that my job would fund it. Instead, I patted your still-flat belly. "You have the baby to think about, sweetheart."

You kissed my cheek. "I'll have it livable before the little one arrives. After that, we can take our time."

True to your word, you worked like crazy for months. We moved in two weeks before the due date.

A week later, I was in the middle of an overnight shift, taking a much-needed break, when my cell phone vibrated in my pocket. After ten on a weeknight. I connected the call, expecting to hear your voice, but it wasn't you on the other end. It was our neighbor.

"Camilla's in labor."

My first thought—why had you called her and not me?

I put the phone on speaker. While she gave me the specifics, I looked at my call history.

Turned out, you'd called me multiple times. There'd been a wreck on the interstate, and I'd been so focused on the trauma patients that I hadn't noticed.

My daughter hadn't even made it into the world yet, and I was already a lousy father. The good news was, I could only improve. That was what I told myself, anyway.

Our neighbor brought you to the hospital while I found someone to take over my shift. An hour after you arrived in a flurry of chaos, of rolling you to a delivery room, of the doctor's instructions—*Don't push yet...hold on one more second*—Zoë entered the world.

I'll never forget the sight of you holding our newborn daughter. Your hair was sweat-soaked and plastered to your pale face. Your eyes were red-rimmed and puffy. But when you gazed down at the perfect little bundle in your arms, the most precious child who'd ever lived, I'd never felt more in love.

My amazing, beautiful, talented treasure had given me the greatest gift a woman could give a man. You'd carried our child, nurtured her, protected her for nine months. The love in your eyes as you gazed at Zoë's chubby little face made my heart nearly explode with affection and tenderness and all those feelings I'd never been good at sharing.

You stared at Zoë. I stared at you. You two were my whole world. All I wanted was to be there for you, to take care of you, to protect you.

I had one goal. One small but vastly important goal.

And I blew it.

I'm sorry.

Yours always,

Daniel

CHAPTER TWENTY-SIX

PAUL AND ZOË had just left to pick up lunch when a new doctor stepped into the room. Camilla had seen him the day of Jeremy's surgery—had that only been two days before? But he'd been too busy to chat.

He had dark skin and straight black hair and introduced himself to Jeremy with a long name she'd never remember. "Call me Kavi," he said with a thick Indian accent.

Jeremy held out his hand, and Kavi shook it. "I am a pulmonologist, which means I specialize in the respiratory system, which is what makes you breathe."

Jeremy gave him a look that clearly communicated *Duh*.

Kavi smiled. "I am guessing you knew that already. I am accustomed to working with children, but you are clearly no child."

Jeremy's irritation slid away.

"I have been consulting on your case," Kavi said.

Camilla tried to ignore the shot of adrenaline that had set her pulse racing the moment the doctor walked in. "Is something wrong?"

He glanced at the ventilator's screen. "Quite the opposite." To Jeremy, he said. "We have good news today."

She loved the way this doctor—all the doctors—spoke to Jeremy, took him seriously. She'd watched as Jeremy had spelled out things on their hands. Everyone had patiently waited, answering his questions and remarking on what a great kid he was. Between his facial expressions and his hand motions, his personality shone through, despite his lack of a voice.

"We adjusted the vent this morning, and your lungs have done what they hadn't done prior to this. They have picked up the slack."

Jeremy pointed to the tube in his mouth, then made a yanking motion, eyes wide with hope.

"I believe so, yes. We are going to adjust the vent once again, and if all goes well, then we will extubate you today."

Jeremy's arms—even the one in the cast—lifted in triumph.

Hot tears filled Camilla's eyes. Jeremy was going to be all right. *Thank You, Jesus.*

She squeezed his shoulder but focused on the doctor. "Any idea what time?"

"First, we wait, watch, and be sure. The last thing we want is to remove it too soon." He made an adjustment to the machine. "I will come back in an hour or so. You just relax and let your lungs do the work. I hope that, when I return, we will take that thing out."

Jeremy reached out again, and Kavi shook his hand. Though Jeremy couldn't voice the thank-you, Kavi must have seen the words in Jeremy's expression, because he said, "You are very welcome."

After Kavi left, Jeremy held out his palm. Camilla slid hers in it, but he shook her off, held his fist to his ear, and then held it out again.

Ah. He didn't want to hold her hand. He wanted her phone.

She handed it to him, wishing he had his own. It hadn't been found at the accident site. She'd have to get him a new one, eventually.

He pressed a few buttons, and music started to play. Within a few seconds, he was taking a video of himself.

She chuckled and stepped out. "Be right back."

He gave her a thumbs-up, and she walked to Evan's room. Her nephew was sitting up, eating lunch. Kevin was beside him.

Marcy was gathering up their belongings and putting them in her duffel bag.

"Guess what!" Camilla said.

They all looked at her. "Good news?" Evan's voice was filled with hope.

"They might extubate him today."

"Yes!" Evan punched the air. "Can I go see him?"

Marcy said, "Uh..."

But the nurse stood. "We can arrange that." She looked at Marcy. "If it's all right with you."

"Of course. We'd love it."

After the nurse stepped out of the room, Camilla approached the bed. Evan's color was back to normal. The whites of his eyes were still blood red, but he'd assured her they didn't hurt. She pushed his shaggy brown hair off his forehead. "You look like a new man."

"Feel like it, too. We're moving today, and I think we're gonna go home tomorrow."

"That's fantastic news."

"What's Jeremy doing?"

"Making videos."

Evan laughed. "Figures."

Paul popped his head in. "Got lunch." He handed two containers to Marcy, who said, "Thanks so much."

Zoë stepped in. "I thought I'd eat with you guys if you don't mind."

"Course not!" Marcy slid the chair toward her. "You sit here. I'm sure Evan would like company besides me and his dad."

"Definitely," Evan said.

Camilla and Paul returned to Jeremy's room, where music still played—the kind of music he forced her to listen to in the car whenever they rode together. She used to complain about it, wishing for quiet, or at least something less offensive. Ever since Jeremy had gotten his driver's license, they hardly ever rode together anymore. She missed him and his music. Right now, she missed his voice.

Nathan was singing along.

Paul said, "Feels like a celebration."

She shared the good news, and Paul high-fived Jeremy. Whatever irritation Jeremy had felt that morning had dissipated.

Zoë flew into the room, eyes bright. "Evan just told me—they're taking it out?"

Jeremy lifted his arms and danced from the hips up.

"That's awesome!" Zoë said. "I'm eating with Evan, but I'll be back soon." She danced her way past the glass doors.

All that energy proved Jeremy was getting enough oxygen. His breathing seemed normal.

This was good. Very good.

Kavi returned less than an hour after he'd left, stopped inside the door, and said, "Kanye West?"

Jeremy nodded, impressed, if the look on his face was any indication.

When the doctor approached the vent, the music shut off.

They all watched him as if he held the fate of mankind in his gloved hands.

He studied the machine, turned to Jeremy, and said, "You ready to get that thing out?"

Camilla and Paul stepped out of the room to give the doctor and the nurses space to work.

"Get Zoë, would you?" Camilla said.

Paul walked away and returned with Zoë seconds later. Marcy came, too.

They peered through the glass in silence, though there were so many people around the bed, they could only see Jeremy's legs.

Kavi walked Jeremy through the process, then, a minute or so later, said, "I need you to cough now."

And then, just like that, the tube was out.

When the doctors and nurses were done, Camilla moved to Jeremy's side. He had a clear oxygen tube across his nostrils. But his mouth was free. The dirty tape that had spanned from one side to the other was gone, as was the neck brace. She could see his face. His beautiful face.

Camilla took her son's hand. He looked so much like Daniel, her heart constricted at the sight of him. "How do you feel?"

Jeremy smiled, swallowed. "I love you, Mom."

CHAPTER TWENTY-SEVEN

MINUTES AFTER JEREMY WAS EXTUBATED, a nurse rolled Evan into the room and stopped the wheelchair beside Jeremy's bed. Evan held out his hand, and Jeremy gripped it. It seemed neither knew what to say.

Or maybe neither could speak.

Finally, Evan said, "I thought you were dead. Or in much worse shape. All this time... I mean, I knew they wouldn't lie to me"—he glanced at his parents, who hovered near the door, then at Camilla—"but I was so scared they didn't want to tell me the truth."

Jeremy cleared his throat. "I thought the same thing. I kept asking, and they kept saying, 'Evan's fine.' But now that I see you... Dude, what happened to your eyes?"

Evan laughed. "Creepy, right? Dad says they're just bruised, only there's no skin to hide the red."

"You look good. I mean, like Satan, but otherwise..."

Evan turned to his parents. "Any chance you could, you know..." He nodded toward the door.

Camilla took Paul's arm. "Let's let the guys talk for a little while."

Even Nathan followed, though he leaned against the glass outside the door.

Marcy said, "Come on. I'll show you our new room."

Camilla, Paul, and Zoë followed Marcy and Kevin down the abandoned hallway where they'd had so many private conversations, turned at the corner, and came to a couple of rooms. Marcy stopped at the first one. "I think they gave us this because it's closest to Jeremy's."

Camilla stepped inside. It looked like a normal hospital room—except larger. There was a couch that, she presumed, pulled out into a bed. It faced a wall of counters and cabinets.

Zoë immediately plopped herself on the couch. "Comfy."

"I don't trust your judgment," Camilla said. "You thought that torture device in Jeremy's room was comfortable. You could sleep anywhere."

Zoë stretched out. "It's a gift."

Camilla loved having her daughter here. The worry that had kept Zoë's smile away the day before was gone now. "You even have a door—and it's not made of glass," Camilla said to Marcy. "A little privacy."

"It's probably just for tonight." Kevin leaned against the doorjamb. "Unless something goes wrong, they're going to release him tomorrow."

Marcy's lips bunched together.

"Are you all right with that?" Camilla asked.

She shrugged. "They know what they're doing. It's just scary going home. He's on lots of meds, and there's so much to watch for. It's easier to be here where the nurses are keeping track of everything."

Camilla could understand how her sister felt. As terrified as she'd been these last few days, at least there'd been a professional in charge. How could she care for Jeremy on her own?

Kevin hugged his wife's shoulders. "It'll be fine. We can do this."

The difference was in that one little word. *We.*

Camilla didn't have a *we.* Zoë would help, but when they returned home, she'd resume school, go back to work, and be gone more often than not.

Beside her, Paul slipped his hand into Camilla's and squeezed, as if he knew exactly what she was thinking.

He was so sweet to offer his support. She hated herself for wishing it was a different man beside her.

Her phone rang. She saw who it was and stepped out of the room. When she was far enough away that nobody would overhear, she slid the call to connect. "Agent Falk?"

"I'm on my way up the escalator. Can you meet me outside ICU? We need to talk."

She'd walked farther into the neuro floor and turned in time to watch her family and Paul head back toward ICU. None of them noticed her.

"I'll be right there." She typed a quick text to Paul.

Be right back. Text if you need me.

He responded with,

Anything wrong?

Nope. Stay with Jeremy, please.

She managed to get through ICU without any of them seeing her, stepped out of the unit, and found Falk leaning against the far wall, a computer bag slung over his shoulder. "Cafeteria?"

A fountain drink sounded good, but... "I don't have my wallet."

He started walking. "I'll buy."

With the protective agent ahead, they made it to the cafeteria, where they both got drinks and found a table in the corner. She sipped her soda and tried to settle her nerves.

Falk pulled a laptop out of his bag, opened it, and tapped the keyboard. "Here's what we've learned." He turned the laptop so she could see the screen, which showed the image of Daniel—*not* Daniel.

"Our specialists say the picture hasn't been doctored. It was taken by a photographer who was working with a magazine doing a story on Christian medical missions in Sudan. This photo wasn't used in the magazine, so the photographer put it on one of those online sites where people buy pictures. The rights aren't exclusive, so that means multiple people can buy and use it. And many have. It's been mostly distributed by an organization seeking donations to stop world hunger. It's been distributed widely, used in Facebook ads among other things."

He glanced at her, so she said, "Okay."

"We spoke to the photographer this morning, and he told us the name of the mission where the photo was taken. I called them and asked for the name of the man who looks like Daniel."

She swallowed the hope trying to rise.

"His name is Elias Lunden. He's a Swedish doctor who practices just outside of Stockholm. He makes multiple mission trips to Sudan every year." Falk tapped on the computer, and she waited until the website loaded.

There was Lunden. His hair was graying, and he had a beard, just like in the photo she'd seen that morning. But his face was too wide, his eyes the wrong color.

It wasn't Daniel.

She'd known that. Of course it wasn't Daniel. Daniel was dead.

Still, her heart broke all over again.

That was what she got for hoping.

"I'm following up," Falk said. "I've left a message for him to call me back, just to confirm what we know."

"What do you think happened?" She tried to ignore the not-Daniel image on the screen.

"Campos's people obviously thought Daniel was dead four years ago, or else they'd have come after you. So now maybe Robert Campos saw that image and thought it was Daniel. Maybe he figured that, if he kidnapped Jeremy, he could draw him out."

She closed her eyes to absorb the blow. "Which means he won't stop. If he thinks Daniel's alive..."

"Another option is that someone saw the image and decided to use it somehow. Maybe someone who has it out for your son."

"Jeremy has no enemies."

Falk snapped the laptop closed. "I wasn't so sure. With so many followers on social media, we thought he might've made someone mad along the way. We combed all his messages and posts for the last year. No threats, nothing concerning at all. What about you?"

"Me? I'm a graphic designer. I can't imagine that anyone would do this to me." She lifted her drink, then set it down again without taking a sip. "What do we do now?"

"Once we confirm this doctor's information, we may reach out to someone in the Vegas Vipers and show them what we learned. They could potentially tell Robert that the man in the photo isn't Daniel. Assuming he's working with them."

"You don't know?"

"The people looking for Robert think that's what he's doing in Vegas, but nobody has been able to confirm yet."

"Even if you could get the message to him, why would he believe you? Maybe if you could convince Francis Campos, he could get his brother to back off."

Falk's head dipped to the side. "You haven't heard?"

She tensed, afraid of what he was about to say.

"Francis Campos is dead. He was murdered by a fellow inmate last month."

Dead?

The murderer Daniel had risked his life to put in prison was dead?

"Someone from the gang task force was supposed to call you. I offered to do it, but I guess..."

She heard Falk's voice, but her mind couldn't comprehend it.

He was dead.

The man who'd ruined her family was dead.

Finally, she forced words out. "You're saying someone's trying to kill Jeremy to pay Daniel back for sending a man to prison, a man who's not even alive anymore?" Her voice rose, nearly shrill. She took a breath and started again. "Do you think that's why this is happening now? Is his death related?"

"Maybe Campos just wants revenge on the family of the man who put his brother in prison."

"Do you think he went looking for someone who looked like Daniel to draw Jeremy out?"

Falk shrugged. "We don't have enough information at this point to know. I can tell you that nobody else in the Vipers seemed too upset that Francis was murdered. The St. Louis task force thinks the new leader of the Vipers arranged it. So nobody is out to avenge Francis's death or imprisonment except Robert. When we find him, your family will be safe."

A tiny speck of good news in a sea of despair.

Falk sighed, the sound dimming that hope. "I don't see the point in trying to convince Robert Campos of anything. He won't trust the FBI, which is why, when Jeremy is better..." He took a breath, and Camilla's stomach tightened.

She was afraid of what was coming next. Afraid because Falk, who'd always been straight with her, seemed reluctant to say it.

"I've spoken to the US Marshals," he finally said, "and they agree. I think we need to consider WITSEC."

She sat back against the cold cafeteria chair.

The federal witness protection program.

She and Daniel had been willing to go before, but they'd been turned down. The powers-that-be had decided that Francis Campos wasn't a big enough fish to make it worth the cost of protecting Daniel and his family in exchange for his testimony. Then, after Daniel was murdered, they decided Camilla and her children weren't in danger. And for four years, that had been true. But now...

She swallowed, swallowed again. The world narrowed, dimmed.

Witness protection meant they were in danger.

Witness protection meant... it meant losing everything. Her job, her home, her friends, her sister.

It meant her kids losing everything. Zoë's school, her plans.

Jeremy's social media following, his dreams.

It meant losing their names.

It meant losing themselves.

Lord, please...

They'd already lost so much. How could they do this? How could she ask her kids to do this?

A warm hand on her forearm pulled her back from the darkness, though it hovered just beyond her vision, ready to yank her under.

Would they never be free?

Agent Falk leaned closer, spoke low. "Listen to me."

She tried to focus. When she'd quieted the fear in her mind, she nodded.

"Only until we find Campos. When we find him—"

"*If*," she said. "*If* you find him, then..." By then, all would be lost. How would they resume their normal lives at that point?

How would this ever be made right?

"Mrs. Wright."

She heard the words as if from the bottom of a deep hole. She tried to climb out. But...witness protection. How would she tell her children? How could she keep them safe?

"Camilla."

It was Agent Falk's use of her first name that snapped her out of it. She drew in a long breath. Focused on what was good, right, true, noble...

Jeremy was recovering.

Zoë was safe.

They were together.

They could do this. *Lord, please help us.*

Falk said, "We're going to find him. We've got people searching. In fact..." He sat back, glanced around, and leaned forward again. This time, his voice was even lower. "I debated telling you this."

"You need to tell me everything." Because she'd handled it all so well so far. Still, despite her emotional reactions, she needed to know.

"A patrol officer picked up Campos's license plate in Ogden yesterday. We know he's here, and he's driving his own car. There's an APB out for him. Someone will spot it and grab him. He doesn't know we're onto him, and he's an arrogant son of a... gun. We'll find him."

"If you don't?"

"I promise, Camilla. Either way, we'll keep you and your family safe."

CHAPTER TWENTY-EIGHT

ALL THE WORRIES about her family's future and safety huddled in the background of Camilla's mind as she stood by her son's bedside. It was two in the morning. She hadn't slept a moment, and neither had Jeremy.

Maybe he'd just overdone it. So many people around. The videos he'd made that afternoon, the upper-body dancing, the jokes, the laughter. Maybe it was too much on the day he was extubated.

His eyes were squeezed shut, his healthy hand clenched the bar on the far side of the bed in a white-knuckled grip.

The nurse who'd just stepped out returned. "We're going to try a different pain med." She injected something into Jeremy's IV.

"Why is he hurting so much? It was under control before."

"It can feel like two steps forward, one step back." This was a new nurse, one they hadn't met before. Young like the others, attractive and kind. "Jeremy leapt forward today, so maybe..." She shrugged.

A tear dripped from Jeremy's eye. Camilla wiped it away, praying softly.

Jeremy had his voice back, but he said nothing. It seemed he couldn't make his mouth form words. His injured hand pressed against his chest.

"That should kick in here in a second," the nurse said.

Camilla wished Nathan were there. He'd figure out what was going on.

The nurse watched Jeremy a moment, but by the expression on her face, she wasn't satisfied by what she saw. "Be right back." She disappeared out the door.

She returned right away and, two minutes later, a doctor stepped in. Mark, the resident Camilla had met the first day. He stood at Jeremy's bedside. "What hurts."

Jeremy patted his chest. "Breathing." The word came out on a grunt of pain.

"Okay. We're going to figure out what's going on." Mark muttered something to the nurse, then checked the container on his side of the bed, the one collecting whatever came through the chest tube on that side.

Not the side Jeremy was holding.

Mark said, "Sit tight," and left.

Sit tight? Sit tight!

She wanted to scream at him to fix this. Her baby couldn't breathe, and they seemed to feel no sense of urgency at all.

An hour before, the nurse had laid a cloth on Jeremy's head. Camilla took it now, ran it under the cold water at the sink, and returned it to his forehead. "Does that help at all?"

He nodded.

"What can I do?" she asked.

"Nothing. There's nothing..." His body tensed, his eyes closed. She took his hand, but he wrenched it away and gripped the bed rail.

Jesus, please, please. Save him.

Minutes passed. He inhaled and exhaled, the agony on his face making her stomach churn.

And then, a crowd of people...and the X-ray machine.

She whispered to Jeremy, "I'll be right here," and faded behind the bed so they could work.

When they turned Jeremy to slide the board beneath him, he cried out in pain.

Nausea rolled in her stomach, she leaned on the chair for support.

"I know it hurts," the tech said. "This'll just take a sec."

They finished the X-ray, and Camilla followed them out of the room to look at the screen. She stood behind the doctor to see what he was seeing.

The right lung looked much better. The other one—where they'd taken out the chest tube—looked smaller.

And...the color was the wrong shade of gray.

The doctor muttered, "What were they thinking?"

"What's wrong?"

He turned, eyes wide. "I didn't realize you were there."

Obviously.

"What's wrong?" she said again.

"We need to put that chest tube back in. I don't want to intubate him again. I'm going to talk to them about a tracheotomy instead. That's where—"

"I know what it is." Her words were shrill. "Why?"

"We can only keep a patient intubated so long before it starts to do damage. This way, he could talk some, and—"

"What are you saying?"

The doctor glanced at Jeremy, who was clutching his chest.

"Let me call Hen, see what she thinks."

So many doctors involved. Hen seemed to be in charge, but Kavi had made the decision to extubate. Mark was here tonight

—but he was a resident. Others had been in and out. Did they know what they were doing?

Camilla felt helpless and hopeless as she returned to Jeremy's side. "You okay?"

"No."

She ignored the anger in his tone.

Thank heavens she'd sent Zoë to the Ronald McDonald House.

An hour of pain, of fear, of frustration passed before Hen stepped into the room, curly hair wet as if she'd just stepped out of the shower. She spoke to Jeremy. "I hear you're having a rough night."

"It kills. I can't breathe."

"Heard that too." Hen's smile was tight when she looked at Camilla. "We're going to have to put the chest tube back in."

"You took it out too soon?"

Hen looked back at Jeremy. "Your lung looked good. Now, not so much. There are no hard-and-fast rules about these things. The tube wasn't pulling anything from the chest cavity, the lung had expanded. Now, the pneumothorax is back, and we have to deal with it."

"Will it make this pain go away?" he asked.

"It will." Hen sounded confident, but the tone didn't calm Camilla's fears.

"Is it gonna hurt?" he asked.

"Not you." She winked. "You'll be drugged. Your mama, though..." She glanced at Camilla. "I think Mama's gonna have to step out."

"You're going to do it here?" When the tubes had gone in Monday night, she'd still been in Oklahoma.

"It's a quick procedure. You don't have to leave, just step out the door."

As Hen spoke, people streamed in. Residents, nurses. Hen called out instructions, and they bustled around.

They were doing this now? As in, *right now*? At three a.m., in the room?

Camilla felt sick. "How long will it take?"

Hen looked up from Jeremy's bedside. "Ten, fifteen minutes. Don't worry. We've got it."

Feigning a calm she didn't feel, Camilla kissed Jeremy's forehead. "This will make it better." She prayed her words were true. "I'll be right outside the door."

She started to walk away, but Jeremy grabbed her hand. "I love you."

Tears stung her eyes, but she blinked them back. "I love you too. You're going to be fine."

She stepped beyond the glass and watched. Dazed.

She wore her yoga pants and T-shirt, no bra. She'd pulled on her sweatshirt but wore only socks on her feet. It was the middle of the night.

Her son couldn't breathe.

The doctors and nurses buzzed all around him. It wasn't long before Jeremy was talking in a relaxed tone, though she couldn't make out the words. He must've been saying something funny because everyone around his bed laughed.

He wasn't unconscious. Why hadn't they sedated him?

His blood pressure? Maybe they were worried about it dropping again. Maybe it was too dangerous. Maybe this could kill him.

Don't think about it. They know what they're doing.

Except they hadn't known what they were doing when they took out the chest tube in the first place.

No. These were good doctors. This was an excellent hospital, one of the highest rated in the country. They were doing their best. And they were, after all, *practicing* medicine. What had Hen said? *No hard-and-fast rules.* Two steps forward, one step back still meant forward progress.

She kept up the stream of encouraging words in her heart, but behind them always were prayers.

Jesus, please, please.

If Daniel were there, he'd tell her what the doctors and nurses were doing. He'd wrap his arms around her from behind, and she'd lean back into him, let his warmth and confidence calm her. They'd watch, but she wouldn't be afraid. Daniel's presence would make it better.

Everything seemed to be going well. Jeremy was babbling. Hen was talking.

And then, something started to beep.

Hen, so casual a moment before, shouted, "Get him down, get him down!"

The bed lowered, and Hen crawled up behind his head.

She gave orders.

Someone bolted out of the room.

Nobody was laughing now.

Jeremy was not talking.

Camilla crossed her arms, hugged herself. She had no idea what was happening.

The beeping continued.

Please, Jesus. Please...

The woman who'd run out returned. The doctors and nurses worked.

What would Daniel be doing if he were there? She could imagine his arms tightening, his fists clenching. He'd want to be in there. He'd be demanding to know what was going on.

Or he would know. Would that be better?

He wouldn't be calm, because the doctors weren't calm.

Please, Jesus, save my baby.

And then, just like that, the mood in the room shifted.

Hen climbed down from her spot by Jeremy's head.

Everyone seemed to take a collective breath.

Camilla backed up, leaned against the wall. Wiped her tears with the sleeve of her sweatshirt.

Through the glass, Hen met her eyes. She said something to the doctor beside her and stepped out. "How you holding up?"

"What just happened?"

"Because of your son's low blood pressure, we used ketamine to anesthetize him. It doesn't put patients to sleep or lower blood pressure, but it keeps them from feeling anything. I've used it hundreds of times, and I've never had that happen. He had a little seizure. Nothing to worry about. Fortunately, it happened after we got the tube in."

"So..."

"He's fine." Hen gripped Camilla's forearms and stood in front of her. "He's fine. Ketamine works fast. Your son's hallucinating now, which is completely normal. In just a few minutes, he'll be back to his old self."

"Will there be any long-term issues because of...of..." She waved toward the room, unable to vocalize her worries.

"No. None. He's fine."

Camilla swallowed, took a deep breath. "And the chest tube?"

"It's working. Your son should get some relief soon." She squeezed Camilla's arm. "You did very well. You're a strong woman."

Apparently, Hen hadn't seen Camilla bawling outside the door.

"Will you need to intubate again?"

"I don't think so. We'll check back in a couple of hours."

"Mark said something about a trach?"

"If the tube does what it's meant to do, then we won't need to intubate or perform a tracheotomy."

Within ten minutes, all the extra personnel had left Jeremy's room. Camilla sat by her son's bedside, telling herself all was well and listening to Jeremy's constant stream of conversation. He was making no sense, and she would have laughed at his silliness under normal circumstances. She would have laughed if this were the aftereffects of him having had his wisdom teeth removed or his tonsils out. But they'd put in a chest tube so his lung could expand. So he could breathe.

There was nothing funny about it.

CHAPTER TWENTY-NINE

DEAR CAMILLA,

I loved my job. You already know this, but I'm not sure I've ever articulated it before.

Working in the ER, I treated everything from flu symptoms to gunshot wounds. The frenetic pace, the energy, the ever-changing cases—I loved everything about it.

And the people. All of them. The stooped and clear-eyed elderly, the eager and innocent children, the hard-working and harried adults. I even loved the ones who'd taken wrong turns, who'd become addicted to drugs or gotten pulled into gangs or became pregnant too young. I loved the fatherless ones who looked at me as if I could save them.

I couldn't.

I knew that.

But I also knew the One who could, and I told my patients and their families about the Jesus I knew. Did it cause me trouble sometimes? Sure. Not everybody wants a sermon. "Just patch up the bullet hole, Doc, and I'll be on my way." But I've found that there's nothing like a near-death experience to send a gaze upward, a soul inward, and a life on a new path.

Ever since the moment I walked in on Campos in that hospital room, I've felt like my time was running short. As the date of the trial nears, I can almost hear the ticking of a timer, counting down. Knowing every day might be my last, that truth is more real to me than ever.

I loved being a father and a husband, but I let you do most of the heavy lifting at home. You were good at motherhood. I was good at being a doctor. We had the whole division-of-labor thing down.

Remember when we started trying for another baby? Zoë was only six months old, but we'd always wanted a houseful.

But months went by, then a year, and you didn't get pregnant. We knew you were fertile. Little Zoë's great big presence in our home proved that. There was no reason to believe another child wouldn't come in God's timing.

His timing wasn't the same as yours.

I grew up in a big family, and I loved it. But Zoë was a handful. She took up a lot of space in our lives, so much that I couldn't imagine another child nudging her aside. I knew in my head that that wasn't how it worked, but I was content with Zoë.

I know what you're thinking, and you're right. I was simply too busy to worry about it. While you were at home with our only child, I was at work.

I'd promised that my schedule would improve after residency, but my new job took more time than I thought it would. Over and over, I vowed to cut back on the hours.

But I didn't.

Can I tell you the truth? Now that it's almost over, now that my time is running out?

They needed me at the hospital. Solid ER doctors were hard to find and harder to keep as the neighborhood became more and more dangerous. I was valued at work. I made a difference there.

You didn't need me. You managed our home with ease. You raised our daughter and kept meals on the table, all the while fixing up our house. By Zoë's second birthday, it was a masterpiece, fit for a feature in one of those decorator magazines.

At home, my job was to provide a paycheck and occasionally call a repairman, but even that was rare. When the dining room chandelier quit working, I was ready to buy a new one. You replaced the switch, and it worked again.

I knew how to do that. I'd helped build our family "camp" in Maine, after all. I'd laid tile and installed light fixtures and sanded drywall.

I'd hated every minute of it. To me, the benefit of making good money was that I wouldn't have to do home improvement projects anymore. So, I didn't.

When a toilet broke, you repaired it.

When a picture needed hanging, you hung it.

I'd promised to be in charge of lawn maintenance, but after our first summer in the house, you hired that job out, freeing me up so we could spend more time together.

I filled those hours with work.

This morning, I looked at photographs of Zoë during the first few years of her life, and I thought, *Did I pay any attention to you back then? Did I know you?*

Did you know me?

Despite my constant busyness, you made sure we had family time. My hours were strange, different every week. No matter which days I had off, you treated them like a weekend. You'd plan a day trip or an event for the three of us. Or you'd line up a babysitter so you and I could go out. Our marriage, despite my many hours away from home, was good.

And if you longed for another child, you didn't mention it to me, not very often anyway. I thought you were content.

We went to the lake for the weekend, leaving three-year-old Zoë with your parents for the first time.

I awoke on Sunday morning to find the bed next to me empty. You weren't in the kitchen or the living room of the small secluded house we'd rented. I found you on the back deck, watching the sun rise over the treetops on the far side of the water.

I stood inside the sliding glass door and watched you, my lovely bride. It was fall, and everything seemed tinged with a golden hue. You wore nothing but a silky bathrobe, standing at the railing with one hand raised to the heavens. Praising God. It was a breathtaking sight.

Until your shoulders heaved, and your arm dropped. You settled in a chair, bent over, and wept.

I was scared, Camilla.

Remembering that moment, tears prickle my eyes even now.

What would bring you to weeping? Were you not happy? Had I failed?

I slid open the door and stepped onto the deck. "Sweetheart?"

You turned to me, wiping your tears. And you smiled. You pulled something small and white out of your bathrobe pocket and held it out to me.

I studied the plastic thing, the little windows. The two lines.

"We're pregnant?"

You nodded, and more tears fell.

I wanted to whoop and lift you up and spin you around and shout to the world.

I guess I'd wanted another child more than I'd known.

But I didn't do any of those things because your smile faltered.

I wrapped you in my arms, and you cried against my shoulder. You wept like I'd never seen you weep. I didn't know what to say, to think. Did you not want another baby? Were you disappointed?

That didn't make sense, but then neither did your tears.

I didn't ask. Worry kept my lips sealed. Maybe you weren't happy. Maybe you wanted out of the marriage, and another child would keep you tethered to me for that much longer.

After all, you'd complained about my long hours. You'd suggested many times that our daughter needed to see her daddy more than she did.

Deep down, I knew you weren't happy.

But I wasn't ready to change. My work was too important. *I* was too important—at the hospital.

How arrogant I was.

I held you and whispered loving words in your ear and prayed that my fears were way off, that you still loved me, that our family was okay.

Finally, you brushed your tears away and leaned back to face me. Still, you didn't speak.

I couldn't stand it anymore. "I thought you wanted another one."

"More than anything."

"Then why are you crying?" I realized I was too. I didn't know what was wrong, but something was, and it was my fault.

More tears filled your eyes, which you dried with the sleeve of your bathrobe. "I'd given up hope. I've been praying for another baby, trying to get pregnant for so long. I'd resigned myself to having an only child."

"So those were tears of...joy?"

You nodded, but I wasn't convinced. "Didn't look that joyful to me."

You sighed and faced the lake again.

I stood beside you and waited, my insides burning with fear.

"You can say it, Cammie. Whatever it is. You don't have to be afraid of me."

You looked at me then, your eyes red and watery. "I was angry with God because I couldn't get pregnant. And I've been a little..."

You didn't finish, but I guessed. "Angry at me?"

You faced the lake again. "I know you love your job."

I waited until you looked at me again. "Not more than I love you."

An expression crossed your face. Disbelief. Maybe scorn. It was there and gone so fast, only by God's grace did I see it.

You doubted my love for you.

I did love you and Zoë—and this new little one growing in your womb—more than I loved my job.

Didn't I?

But I'd just admitted that I wasn't ready to change. Hadn't I just told myself I was too important to take a step back?

All the lives I saved, all the people I told about Christ, yet the most important person in my world doubted my love.

Did Zoë, too? Would she be like one of the many girls and young women I treated—for teen pregnancy, for addiction, for wounds inflicted by hateful men. Girls whose fathers had been either physically or emotionally absent?

That one glimpse into your heart blew through my being like a nuclear blast. Melting my lies. My selfishness. My greed.

"Oh, sweetheart." I pulled you against my chest and held you and cried. "I'm so sorry. I'm so sorry you ever doubted my love for you. I promise, things will be different from now on. I'll cut back. I'll be home more." I held you away from me so I could see your face. "Do you believe me?"

God bless you, my loving, trusting wife. You did.

Yours always,

Daniel

CHAPTER THIRTY

AFTER THE KETAMINE WORE OFF, Jeremy slept. Even though the nurse assured Camilla that he was doing well, she sat by his bed and watched him, occasionally checking the container that collected what was being drained by the chest tube. Blood, other fluids, air. Looked like a lot to her, but it was coming off now. Jeremy was breathing easier. He was sleeping soundly, so the pain had abated.

But the nurse hovered. And Camilla couldn't help but think that something was wrong.

Maybe that was a result of not having slept. Maybe the disturbing procedure—and Jeremy's adverse reaction—were still too fresh on her mind. Whatever the reason, she couldn't force herself to close her eyes.

All was not well.

And when her mind did drift away from Jeremy's health, she thought about Agent Falk's news.

Witness protection.

How would she tell her children? Would they get to go home, or would WITSEC take them straight from here? Where would they be taken? Would she have a choice? She couldn't remember much about the process from four years past when they'd first discussed this, back when she'd hoped and prayed Daniel would change his mind about testifying. She'd hardly paid attention because it had never felt real.

After everything her kids had been through, how could she do this to them now?

How could Daniel have done this to them?

She grabbed her things and went to the restroom to clean up for the day. It was after seven, and she needed to do something to stem the flow of her thoughts.

She yanked a brush through her hair and dabbed on some makeup to try to hide the dark circles under her eyes. It did little good. Marcy would notice. Paul would notice.

Paul.

Another worry niggling at the edges of her consciousness.

He'd questioned her about where she'd gone the previous evening after they'd seen Evan's new room, and she'd admitted she'd met with Agent Falk.

Though he hadn't said anything, Paul's frustration had been obvious. She'd seen it in the tightness at the corners of his lips, the twitch in his jaw. Because Marcy had been nearby, and because everyone had still been celebrating Jeremy's newfound voice, he hadn't said anything. He'd never had the opportunity to question her about it further before he'd ridden with Agent Siple to deliver Zoë to the Ronald McDonald House. He hadn't texted to tell Camilla good night.

She couldn't exactly be angry about that, though. She hadn't texted him either.

After gathering her things, she found Marcy standing outside Jeremy's room, a wide smile on her face. A smile that faded as Camilla neared.

"What happened?" Marcy asked.

Apparently, the makeup hadn't covered everything.

"Rough night." Camilla updated her sister on the events of the morning.

Marcy touched Camilla's arm. "Did you sleep at all?"

She shifted to look at Jeremy through the glass. "The pain started at eleven, so..."

Marcy slid her arm around Camilla's back and squeezed. "You must be exhausted. Maybe you can get a nap today after Zoë gets here."

She shrugged. Sleep sounded good.

She remembered her sister's smile. "How about Evan? Good news?"

"They're going to release him."

"Does that make you nervous?"

"It did, but he slept all through the night and woke up hungry. He has a little pain from the surgery, but he says it's nothing compared to how it hurt before. At this point, the biggest issue is the head injury. He's going to need therapy over the next few months. But they assure us that he'll eventually be back to normal."

"That's such good news." Camilla turned away so her sister wouldn't see her tears. She was thrilled for Marcy and her family, thrilled Evan was going home. But she was so tired, the other emotions—sadness, fear, loneliness—spilled from her eyes.

"I can stay here with you," Marcy said. "Kevin can handle him."

"You need to be with your family. I have Zoë. And Paul."

Marcy took Camilla's hand and walked her down the corridor. "Any more news from Falk?"

Camilla had told her sister and Paul most of what she'd learned from the FBI agent the day before.

But she hadn't told them about the possibility of witness protection. And she wasn't going to now.

"We're just hoping they catch him soon."

"What about Paul?"

"What about him?"

Marcy's eyebrows hiked, the unspoken question obvious. When Camilla didn't say anything, she said, "I like him. And he seems very devoted to you and your family."

"Very."

"But?"

Camilla sighed and stared at the floor. "But... But when I saw that photograph of Daniel yesterday..."

Gently, Marcy said, "Not Daniel."

"I know. I know. But..." There was no *but*. Paul was a wonderful man who cared about her. The kids liked him. Jeremy had been annoyed when he'd thought they'd stayed in the same room, but after she'd cleared that up, he'd been as welcoming to Paul as he had everyone else. Paul was caring and kind and...

And she was being given a second chance at love. She should take it. Assuming, of course, that Robert Campos was caught. But if he wasn't, if they had to go into WITSEC...?

She'd have to leave Paul behind. Only family would be taken, and he wasn't. The only solution to that would be marriage.

"I can't make decisions about anything right now," Camilla said.

"Of course. You're smart not to." Marcy squeezed her hand and returned to Jeremy's room, and Camilla followed. A new nurse was there—one she hadn't seen before—getting briefed by the night nurse on everything that had happened. Camilla longed for Nathan, who'd become a comforting presence, but he'd warned her he wouldn't be back until Monday.

Marcy said, "Camilla and I are going for breakfast. Be back in a few."

"Wait," Camilla said. "I can't just—"

“Go.” The older woman with frizzy hair looked at the phone number on the whiteboard. “I’ll call if anything happens.”

Marcy took Camilla’s hand and pulled. “Jeremy is asleep. Evan’s on his dad’s computer playing games. They’ll survive without us for a little while.”

Camilla didn’t have the energy to argue. And her stomach was growling. They were halfway across the skybridge, Agent Siple just feet behind, when Camilla realized… “It’s snowing.”

“Your keen senses astound me.”

Camilla chuckled. She couldn't remember the last time she'd laughed. She'd been too busy watching her son breathe to look out the window. Now, she saw a world covered in a blanket of fluffy, sparkling white. The image reminded her of one years before when the snow fell outside the window of that charming restaurant while she fell in love inside. On their first date. Ridiculous. But even then, she'd known Daniel would be the one. Even before she'd believed there would be a *the one* for her. She'd never wanted to marry. Never met a man who'd moved her to even consider such a thing. Until Daniel.

In the cafeteria, they ordered their meals and found a table.

Marcy sipped a glass of orange juice. “Let's talk about Daniel.”

“What about him?”

“I loved him. Everybody loved him.”

Camilla buttered her toast and took a bite, waiting for her sister to finish.

“We admired his courage when he testified against that guy.”

Ire rising, Camilla set down the toast and salted her eggs. She had no idea where Marcy was going with this, but she didn't like the direction she'd taken.

“But he took *one* gangster off the street ”

“More than one.” Camilla sounded defensive, but she

couldn't help it. "After Francis Campos was put away, the organization splintered. The task force got a man on the inside. Daniel's sacrifice took a lot of gangsters off the street."

"But it wasn't just Daniel's sacrifice." Marcy's words came slowly, softly. "It was yours and your kids' sacrifice too."

"You think I don't know that?"

"I'm just..." She looked past Camilla. After a moment, she met her eyes again. "I love your loyalty. It's one of your best qualities. But Daniel's been gone for four years. What keeps you tethered to him?"

"He's my husband."

"Was."

This was too similar to the conversation she'd had with Paul the morning before. "Technically, he still is. He's never been declared dead."

"You know what I mean."

Camilla sat back and crossed her arms. "What do you want me to say?"

"I want you to tell me why you feel so guilty."

Was it that obvious? Camilla had never told her sister—told anybody—about what had happened that day four years before. She couldn't then. She couldn't now.

"I've never pried," Marcy said. "And I don't want to pry now. But there's more to this story, and I think you need to share it."

Camilla's hands shook as she stabbed a bite of eggs. Frustrated as she was, angry as she was, she needed to eat.

"Cammie, whatever it is, you need to let it go. Only when you're free of it will you be able to move forward with your life. I'm not saying that should be with Paul or with another man or with no man. But whatever this is—"

"It was my fault." Camilla resisted the urge to slap her hand over her mouth. Her sister was right. Maybe, if she told someone the truth about that horrible day, she could finally find freedom from the shame.

She waited for Marcy to argue with her, but her sister just nodded for her to continue.

"We argued. All that stuff you said earlier... I loved Daniel's heart. He was always fighting for patients—with administration, with insurance companies. He'd come home with stories about people he'd shared his faith with, some of them gang members who'd been brought in with stab wounds or bullet wounds. In his *spare time*"—she clenched her fists to keep from adding air quotes around those last two words—"he volunteered at the free clinic. He was always giving himself to everybody...except us.

"He came back to the safe house the day he testified and declared that we'd have to go into hiding. I'd known it was coming, but..." Camilla looked out the window at the swirling snowflakes. Just as they neared the ground, the wind would pick up, toss them back into the storm.

"I lost it." Camilla forced her gaze away from the windows and back to her sister. "I was furious. Yes, Campos needed to be stopped, but did Daniel have to be the one to do it? I just...all along, I'd been sure..."

Four years had passed, and Camilla could still hear the words hurling from her mouth like stones from a slingshot. "I can't believe you actually did it."

They'd been standing in the kitchen of the tiny house where the FBI had hidden them.

The agent who acted as their guard said, "I'll just..." and stepped outside.

Daniel'd said, "Cammie, please under—"

"You put our lives in danger, and for what? To take out one guy, one bad guy who'll be replaced by someone else"—she'd snapped her fingers—"just like that. It won't make a lick of difference to the gangs, to the drugs in this city, to anything!"

Daniel hadn't responded to her anger with anger, though. Instead, he'd closed the space between them and taken her in his arms. "I know you're scared. I'm scared too. But I couldn't have lived with myself if I hadn't testified."

"You and your overactive conscience!" She'd pushed him away.

She could still see the pain, the hurt in his eyes, but that hadn't stopped her fury. "How is that conscience going to feel when Jeremy and Zoë end up dead?"

He flinched. "I'm not going to let that—"

"How is it going to feel when you have to explain to them that, once again, you chose your pathological desire to save the world over us?"

"Cammie, I did this *for* us."

"You just ruined our lives."

His face had turned red then, his hands clenched into fists. "What kind of world do you want them to grow up in? The kind where good men do nothing to stop evil? That's not the example I want to set."

Her voice lowered, calm but vibrating with fury. "You're not a good example. Fathers who love their kids more than their work—they're good examples. Fathers who protect their families, don't put them in danger—they're good examples. You... you're an example of what not to do." And as an afterthought, in case she hadn't quite wounded him enough, she'd added, "We'd be better off without you."

Camilla didn't share the conversation word for word, but she told Marcy enough to cause the blood to drain from her sister's face.

"Daniel stared at me across the island in that kitchen. His face, his handsome, kind face, shifted into something I'd never seen before. Not angry. Defeated. It...it silenced me. I regretted immediately what I'd said. I knew the words would always hover between us. I apologized. I said I didn't mean it. He just snatched his keys and walked out." Camilla could still see his retreating back, hear the door slam.

"I ran after him. He wasn't supposed to leave without an agent. He wasn't supposed to leave without permission, but..."

Camilla watched the snow fall through the windows, unable to face her sister. She'd been hauling the heavy burden of her sin, and all she'd done by speaking it aloud was add to Marcy's burden.

Marcy's hand slid over hers. "Look at me, Cammie."

Cammie forced herself to meet her sister's eyes, and Marcy leaned forward. "What happened to Daniel wasn't your fault. You shouldn't have said those things to him, and he shouldn't have left. But the blame for his death lies only with the man who murdered him and the man who arranged for that murder. They are responsible for Daniel's death. Not you. Not Daniel."

"If I hadn't—"

"If you hadn't yelled, if Daniel hadn't left... But there's a lot more to the story. If Daniel hadn't testified—"

"He had to. It's who he is. Was. It was wrong of me to expect him to make a different choice. The thing that compelled him to testify was the very thing I loved most about him."

"Let me finish." Marcy's tone was low and serious. "The reason Daniel testified was because he witnessed a murder. If Francis Campos hadn't killed that man, none of it would have happened. The blame for all of it—*all of it*—lies at the feet of Francis Campos. Not you. Not Daniel."

"I know, but—"

"You've carried the burden long enough." Marcy pushed the food out of the way and took both of Camilla's hands. "It's time to let it go. It's time to forgive yourself for your fear, your anger, and your very human reaction to what was happening in your life. You've been paying for that day long enough. It's time to give it to God."

Could it be that simple? *Lord?*

He didn't speak, but truth entered her heart. Jesus had carried her sins to the cross. She was meant to leave them there.

She took her hands back to brush away her tears and smiled at her sister. A tenuous smile, she knew, but a smile nonetheless. "You're right."

Marcy winked. "Obviously. I am the *wiser* sister."

"Ha!" The laugh barked out too loud. "Older doesn't always mean wiser." But in this case, her older, wiser sister had spoken truth.

CHAPTER THIRTY-ONE

CAMILLA STEPPED into Jeremy's room to find the frizzy-haired nurse hovering over her sleeping son.

"Everything okay?" She expected the nurse to reassure her, but this woman's look was anything but casual. Her eyebrows were lowered and drawn together. "His temperature is concerning us. The doctor prescribed—"

"The doctor came and you didn't call me?"

The woman's lips pressed together. "You know you can trust me, right?"

Camilla's heartbeat raced, but she swallowed the anger that wanted to come out in her voice. "What's your name?"

She held out her hand. "I should have introduced myself before. I'm Delia."

Camilla took the woman's hand and held it. "Delia, I need you to call me if anything happens with my son."

The nurse's smile was tight. "Hen stopped by to check on him, I told her about Jeremy's temperature, and she prescribed an antibiotic. Then she left. You didn't miss anything."

Camilla glanced at the screen and saw that Jeremy's temperature was nearing a hundred and one.

"What does that mean?"

"An infection."

"From the chest tube?"

"It's impossible to know for sure where he got it. It's possible one of the spores he inhaled during the accident has festered all this time and is just making itself known."

Spores? She didn't know exactly what the woman meant, but the words frightened her anyway. "But he's going to be okay, right?"

"It's a setback, nothing more."

A setback. Two steps forward and one back was still forward.

Marcy had gone to check on Evan after breakfast. Now, she entered Jeremy's room. "They're doing the paperwork, so we're leaving soon." She walked up to the bed and gazed down at Jeremy. "How is he?"

Camilla told her sister the bad news, and Marcy's lips twisted. "I'm going to tell Kevin I need to stay with you. I can't go while—"

"You absolutely can," Camilla said. "Your son needs you. Go home and take care of him."

"But you—"

"I'm fine." Camilla pulled her sister out the door so they wouldn't wake Jeremy. "Paul and Zoë will be here soon. I've got"—she waved toward the nurse—"Delia. We're okay, I promise. And I know you're dying to get home and put your feet up."

"I'm sure you are, too," Marcy said.

"Yeah, well..." Camilla and her kids might never go home.

"I feel guilty leaving," Marcy said.

Camilla hugged her tight. "I could never have gotten through this without you. There's nobody I'd rather have in my worst nightmare than you."

"Gee, thanks." Marcy chuckled as she pulled out of the hug.

"I feel the same way, though. I hated that we had to go through it, but I'm glad we went through it together." Her eyes narrowed. "Except you're still in it."

"Don't worry about me."

A few minutes after Marcy left, the doctors stopped outside the door on their rounds. Camilla listened in.

When Hen nodded to Kavi, the pulmonologist, he said in his thick Indian accent, "If the infection isn't under control by evening, I recommend a tracheotomy."

Camilla gasped. She squeezed her eyes shut to absorb the blow.

"Mrs. Wright?"

She opened them to find Kavi looking at her.

"It would be only temporary," he said. "We don't want Jeremy to have to work to breathe. We want him to rest and recover, and this may be the best way to accomplish that."

Despair lodged in her throat like a solid mass. She tried to swallow it down so she could speak, but it wouldn't budge.

Compassion filled Hen's eyes. "Jeremy is young and strong. There's no reason to believe this is anything more than a minor setback."

Camilla tried to believe the words. But it had been six days since the accident. Six days, and Evan was going home. But Jeremy was still fighting for his life. After the celebration the day before, she'd foolishly believed he was nearly recovered. Now...

"Do you have any questions?" Hen asked.

What was there to ask? She shook her head and returned to Jeremy's bedside.

~

Zoë hurried into Jeremy's room a little after ten, her hair in a ponytail. She wore a long sweatshirt over leggings and no makeup. "I overslept. I'm so sorry. I'm such an..." She saw Jeremy, still sleeping, and lowered her voice. "Is he okay?"

Paul stood in the doorway behind her. He'd texted earlier, wishing he were at the hospital, but he'd promised to ride with Zoë and the FBI agent, as he'd done with Camilla. He carried two coffee cups, one of which he held out to Camilla. She took it with a quick "thanks."

"What's going on?" he asked.

Outside the room, Camilla gave them a rundown on what happened overnight and the current fever.

By the time she was done, Paul's arm had slid around her back. She leaned against him, thankful for the support.

Zoë's hand covered her mouth, and she spoke through her fingers. "Is he going to be all right?"

Camilla pulled away from Paul to comfort her daughter. "The doctors seem really confident that this infection is just a setback."

"But?"

"There's no *but*. He's strong. He's got good antibiotics and an excellent team of professionals watching over him. He's going to be fine." *Please, Jesus, let it be true.*

Seeming satisfied, at least for now, Zoë went into Jeremy's room and sat in the rolling chair by his bed. She pulled out her phone and was focused on it in seconds.

"Can we talk?" Paul asked.

She'd been dreading this conversation since the evening before. "Sure." She got Zoë's attention. "We're gonna go for a walk. You need anything?"

"Could you get me one of those oatmeals?" Zoë asked. "Apple cinnamon, if they have it."

"Sure." Camilla walked beside Paul out of the ICU. She

nodded to the agent standing there, this one a man. He followed them down the hall and to the small Ronald McDonald room. The agent waited in the hallway.

She found the oatmeal and started a cup of water in the microwave.

The room was, mercifully, empty.

Paul sat on the sofa and patted the space next to him.

She sat and waited for him to begin, since he'd requested this...meeting, for lack of a better word.

"I was ticked at you last night." At least he wasn't going to waste time.

"I picked up on that. I'm not sure why, though."

That muscle in his jaw tightened. "No guesses?"

As if she had nothing better to do than to analyze his feelings. "I'm a bit tired. It'd sure be easier if you'd just tell me." Despite the fact that she'd tried to hide her frustration, she heard it in her words.

"When you met with Falk the other day, I wasn't here. You had to do it alone, and I hated that. But I was five feet from you when he called you yesterday, and still, you met with him alone. I'm here to support you, but you won't let me."

"You've been a great support. I don't think I could have done any of this without you." She stood, avoiding his eye contact, and looked in the fridge for milk. "What's going on with Falk and Campos... That's my stuff to deal with. It's private and—"

"Private?" The tone of his voice had her turning to him. His eyebrows rose halfway to his hairline. "As if I don't know everything? I was there, remember? I was Daniel's attorney. From the time he witnessed the murder, I've been involved. What's the big secret?"

She set the milk on the counter and leaned against it. A lit candle on the end table wafted the scent of vanilla into the room. The homey scent did nothing to cut the tension. "There's no secret."

He lowered his head to the couch behind him, eyes closed. A moment later, they popped open. "Witness protection. He wants you to go into..." He stood, crossed the small room, and gripped her hands. "That's it, isn't it? You don't want to tell me because he wants you to disappear."

The microwave dinged, and she pulled away from him to grab the cereal. And to escape.

"Camilla?"

The truth was, it hadn't occurred to her to involve Paul in her conversation with Falk. She hadn't thought Falk would appreciate him tagging along, and it felt private.

With her back to Paul, she stirred the dry oats into the hot water. "My mother used to make oatmeal and cinnamon toast on cold mornings," she said. "This always reminds me of her."

Paul said nothing.

When it was mixed, Camilla took a fortifying breath and turned. "When we worked with Falk before, he always wanted us to keep our conversations private. I've told you more than he'd want me to."

He stood. "Am I right about witness protection? Does he want—?"

"We talked about it."

Paul regarded her a long moment, then stepped closer. "I love you. You know that, right?"

He'd never declared his feelings before. She wished he hadn't now.

"I've loved you since...I don't know. Not long after Daniel died. I've been trying not to push you." He ran a hand over his head, messing up his usually neat hair. "It's been four years. I enjoy our friendship and the time we spend together, but it's not enough for me."

Her heart raced, but she couldn't identify what she was feeling. Tenderness toward this man, definitely. But the tenderness was tempered by...fear.

"If you have to go into witness protection—"

"Only if they don't find Campos." She didn't want him to say what she saw in his eyes. "Agent Falk is confident—"

"If you have to go..." He dipped low to study her face. "I know you don't return my feelings yet. I know you're still struggling with Daniel's death. But we're good together. We could be happy."

She couldn't think about this right now. She couldn't consider anything but Jeremy's health and the danger hanging over their heads.

"I'm still married. Daniel hasn't been officially declared dead, so even if I wanted to—"

"I could petition the court on Monday. There's plenty of evidence. If you'd let me do that years ago, you'd have gotten his life insurance money, and you'd—"

"I don't care about the money."

"—be free to remarry."

Free.

Was that what she'd be?

Why did the idea of it churn acid in her stomach?

The question had barely presented itself before she admitted the answer in the privacy of her mind.

All these years, she'd hoped. If she let go of her hope, slim as it was, that Daniel was still out there, would she feel free?

Did she want to be free of her first marriage? Of the only man she'd ever truly loved?

"Daniel is gone." Paul's voice was flat. "I'm here, and I love you. I want to take care of you. He'd want—"

"Don't tell me what he'd want," she snapped. "What he would want doesn't matter."

"That's right, it doesn't." Paul stepped back, breath suddenly coming fast. "What Daniel wants doesn't matter because he's dead. He drained your savings account—"

"Because we were running. We were going to disappear."

"So where's the money?" Paul asked. "That never made sense to me. He stormed out of the house on a whim but took all that cash? Why?"

Daniel hadn't carried it with him. He'd taken nothing when he left that day. She didn't know what had happened to the money. He'd put it somewhere. He'd...he'd had a plan. He would have explained that plan. If he'd survived, it would have made perfect sense.

"He left you penniless."

"He died, Paul. He wasn't leaving me or the kids. He was murdered."

"I know that. I'm just saying... You weren't Daniel's priority. You were never his priority. And yet, four years after his death, you still can't let him go. It's not healthy. Camilla." His Adam's apple bobbed. She could feel him trying to pull his temper under control. "You will always be my priority. Always." Paul reached for her.

She folded her arms.

He blew out a long breath and stepped back. "We're running out of time. If they don't find the guy—"

"I know!" Her voice was too loud in the small room. "I know what the stakes are."

He ran his fingers down her hair, then pressed his palm against her cheek.

His touch was tender, filled with love. She needed that, needed him.

"I don't want to lose you," she said.

"I don't want to lose you either."

He closed the distance between them and set his hands on her hips.

Something she hadn't felt for years rose in her body, tingled across her skin. To be touched by someone who loved her.

Desire.

She hardly remembered the feeling.

He angled his head toward her, watching her eyes. Giving her all the opportunity she needed to step back.

But she didn't. Because this man had been her rock. He'd been her shoulder to cry on, her sounding board when she needed advice. He'd been her friend, her very dearest friend.

She did feel something for him. And that something went deeper than friendship.

He covered her lips with his.

Her arms slid around his neck, and she pulled him closer.

But the desire she'd felt only moments before dissipated. These weren't Daniel's lips. Those weren't Daniel's hands.

Daniel was dead. She knew that. But...

She pushed Paul away and swiveled to the counter. After a couple of deep breaths, she added a packet of sugar and a splash of milk to the oatmeal with shaking hands. Holding the bowl and spoon against her chest like a shield, she turned back to him. "Could you get the door?"

"Camilla—"

"I can't do this right now. It's not fair for you to ask me to."

"Not fair?" His skin flushed, and he fisted his hands at his sides. "After everything... I'm here, Cammie. Daniel's not. He put you and your family in danger and then left you to fend for yourself."

"He was murdered."

"I know!" His shout bounced off the walls in the small room. He reared back as if his tone had surprised him. "I know what happened. I'm just saying...I love you."

She needed to get out of that room. She glanced at the door, then back at Paul. Tears blurred her eyes, and she blinked them back. "Please?"

Reluctantly, Paul pulled the door open, and she hurried back to ICU.

CHAPTER THIRTY-TWO

DEAR CAMILLA,

We were fighting more and more. When the call from the ER came in, I knew what you were going to say.

The same old tired argument we had all the time.

"There's a gang war going on." My voice, my words, sounded so reasonable. "The ER's overrun."

"They'll survive without you for one night," you said. "You're not the only doctor. You're not on call."

"I don't know if you heard that"—I gestured to my cell phone lying on the bathroom counter—"but that was a call."

You glared at it like you might a hated enemy. I had a flashing fear that you'd snatch it up and flush it down the toilet. But then you'd have to fix the toilet, and God forbid anything go wrong in your perfect little home.

I'm embarrassed to admit what I was thinking.

I knew. Even then, I knew I justified my poor choices by focusing on yours. I stuffed the truth away and finished shaving.

It was Friday evening, and we'd planned to attend Jeremy's baseball game and then go to dinner together as a family. Zoë had even turned down an invitation to spend the night at her friend's house.

The first few years after the conversation at the lake had been the best of our marriage. I'd made good on my commitment to spend more time at home, and I'd forged strong relationships with our children. In the previous few months, though, things had begun to change. One of the doctors I worked with had resigned, which left a hole in our staff. We'd hired another, but he was young and inexperienced. Eventually, he'd do a fine job, but for now, he needed looking after.

Meanwhile, tension brewed between two of the largest gangs in the city. We'd seen more gang-related violence in the last six months than we'd seen the previous year, and it was only getting worse.

I'd spent more time at the hospital than normal, but it wasn't as if I had a choice.

Or so I told myself.

In the mirror, you glared at me. The afternoon sun streamed through the windows, highlighting the anger on your face.

"It's the last game of the season," you said. "You've only been to two. You've hardly seen him play."

"He doesn't even like baseball," I snapped. "I doubt he'll play again next year."

"He plays because he's trying to connect with you."

I remember thinking, is that true?

Your arms were crossed, your eyebrows lowered.

"That doesn't even make sense," I said. "I never encouraged him to play."

"You used to play ball with him."

"That was about us being together, not about baseball."

"Hmm. And I wonder why he'd gravitate toward something that you used to do together." You tapped your nose as if deep in thought. "It's a mystery."

"Sarcasm doesn't become you." I splashed water on my face to wash away the shaving cream and started the shower.

"Seriously?" You sounded genuinely surprised. "You're not coming to the game? The game you yourself admitted might be Jeremy's last."

I yanked the T-shirt off over my head and dropped it on the floor, mostly to irritate you. "I. Have. To. Work."

We stared at each other. I wasn't about to back down, and you weren't either.

Finally, you spun and stalked out of the bathroom, slamming the door behind you.

I finished getting ready, silently arguing with you, defending myself and my decision. There'd be plenty of time for games and meals with my family. Right now, the hospital needed me. Lives were on the line. You might not have cared about those lives, but I did.

That was how I felt at the time. Justified.

I see the truth in retrospect. Yes, the hospital needed me. But so did you and Zoë and Jeremy. Why did I always put work first?

After apologizing to Jeremy for missing his game and to Zoë for missing our family night, I headed to work. I'll admit I wasn't sorry to miss the evening with you.

All thoughts of our argument evaporated when I arrived at the hospital. That day's violence had started with a midafternoon drive-by shooting. A gang member—a sixteen-year-old boy—was dead, his seven-year-old sister critically injured.

They'd been playing with a new puppy in their front yard.

The gang that had been attacked retaliated. The police were still trying to get it under control.

I treated a mom who'd gone to her neighborhood park to get her kids home after the shooting started. She was crossing the street when a car careened around a corner. The woman pushed her kids ahead of her to keep them out of harm's way, but she didn't move fast enough.

According to a witness, the car didn't even slow down after it clipped her.

She wasn't seriously injured. But if she'd been a step back, she could have been killed.

The thought of you and our kids preparing to go out into that violence made my blood run cold. The baseball field was nowhere near where these street gangs operated, but still.

The city wasn't safe.

"Everything okay?" You answered the phone with no irritation in your tone. I appreciated you for that, appreciated that, despite our disagreements, we loved each other first and always. We didn't hold grudges.

Just hearing your voice made me feel better. "The streets aren't safe. Please, don't go to the game."

"Daniel." I picked up your irritation. "We'll be fine. Jeremy's looking forward to it."

I leaned against the corridor wall and tapped my head against it. I should have stayed with you. Instead, I'd come to the hospital to care for strangers and left my family unprotected.

I felt it, Cammie. I felt the weight of regret then. I know you wonder if I ever did.

I did. Often. That night, especially.

"Please." I was reduced to begging over the phone.

"We'll be careful," you said. "We'll get straight on the interstate and avoid surface roads. We'll have dinner by the ballpark, not in town. Okay?"

Not okay. Not even a little. But I wasn't there, and I wasn't the kind of guy to pull the "I'm the man of the family so do as I say" card. You were a grown woman, intelligent and savvy. I trusted you.

But you didn't know what I knew. You didn't see the effects of the violence like I did.

"Do me a favor?" I asked. "Call Paul and see if he'll go with you?" Paul and I had met at church. He was my lawyer and my only friend outside the hospital. His kids were grown, and he and his wife had recently separated. Apparently, while he'd been growing closer to Christ, his wife had been growing closer to a man at work. Paul was heartbroken and lonely. I figured he'd jump at the chance to have something to do.

There was a long pause on the other end of the phone. You thought I was being unreasonable. But then, you hadn't just patched up a woman your age who'd had the audacity to try to protect her children.

"I'm serious, Cammie. There's a war going on out there."

"Fine. I'll call him."

Twenty minutes later, I got a text from Paul saying he was taking you to the game and promising to keep you safe.

If jealousy crept up my spine, it was my own fault. I should have stayed with you and the kids. Why did I think I was the only capable doctor? Why did I think the world would fall apart without me?

While I tended to strangers, Paul enjoyed family night.

That was my fault. I know that. It still hurt.

Yours always,

Daniel

CHAPTER THIRTY-THREE

JEREMY HAD BARELY OPENED his eyes all morning. Camilla, Zoë, and Paul sat in the room, mostly in silence. Zoë was on her phone, Paul on his laptop. Camilla had tried to work but hadn't been able to concentrate on her latest client's new fliers. Instead, she updated her friends on Jeremy's health and then opened a novel. It should have been a lovely escape from reality, but there were too many worries drawing away her focus.

Every few minutes, she felt Paul's eyes on her. They'd not spoken privately since they'd returned with Zoë's oatmeal.

Her reaction had been ridiculous. She wasn't married. Daniel wasn't coming home. She cared for Paul more than she'd ever admitted before. Their kiss, before she'd ruined it, had stirred up in her feelings she hadn't had since...

She had to stop thinking about Daniel. She had to stop comparing Paul to Daniel. Wishing for Daniel. He was gone.

Paul was here, and he loved her. Maybe, if she could overcome her guilt regarding Daniel's death, if she could quit hoping that he'd walk through the door as if nothing had happened, she could truly open her heart to Paul.

Lord, I need Your wisdom. I don't know what to do, and I hate the ticking clock on my decision. If we have to disappear, what should I do about Paul?

The very fact that he was willing to go with her said everything about his feelings.

But what of *her* feelings? They were so jumbled up with shame and guilt and desire and...

Please, Lord. Tell me what to do.

Though His voice had been clear other times this week, clearer than it had in years, He didn't respond now.

She added to her prayer. *You know the issues. You know the deadline on this decision, assuming they don't catch Campos.*

Please, let them catch Campos.

I trust You to make my path clear when the time is right.

She did trust Him. She kept reminding herself of that.

Finally, after lunch, Jeremy woke and raised his bed.

Camilla stood beside him. "How do you feel?"

He inhaled and blew the air out. "Doesn't hurt as much."

"Good news." Except that he was on some pretty heavy painkillers.

Zoë stood beside her. "Mom said you were hilarious when you were on those drugs this morning. Wish I'd been here."

Jeremy smiled at his sister. "Me, too. You'd have taken a video." He looked at his mom, eyes bright. "Any chance you—?"

"Didn't even occur to me." She'd been too busy praying he'd survive.

Jeremy's countenance fell, and it seemed more than just the lack of video evidence of his ketamine experience.

The nurse asked him a few questions, checked his numbers, and then returned to her seat.

Jeremy's gaze flicked to Paul, who was seated in a chair he'd brought in from another room. He lowered his voice and spoke to Camilla. "I need to tell you something."

Something private, apparently. Camilla said, "Delia? Would you mind giving us some privacy?"

She smiled. "I'll be at the nurse's station. Let me know if you leave."

When Jeremy cut his gaze to Paul, he stood and stretched. "I need some caffeine. Anybody else?"

"I'll take a Diet Coke," Camilla said.

"You want me to leave, too?" Zoë asked Jeremy. When he shook his head, she looked at Paul. "Dr Pepper?"

Paul gave Jeremy a questioning look.

"Delia will bring me a drink if I want one. Thanks, though."

After Paul left, Zoë rounded the bed to stand on Jeremy's other side. "What's up?"

Jeremy looked at Camilla and swallowed hard. "We did go skiing."

She nodded but said nothing.

"But after... The reason we were out in the desert... I got a message from a guy who claimed to be Dad."

Zoë gasped.

After reaching across the bed to take her daughter's hand, Camilla rested her other palm on Jeremy's shoulder. "Okay."

Jeremy's eyes narrowed. "Why don't you seem surprised?"

"It's a long story. Why don't you finish yours first?"

After a moment of watching her, he took a deep breath—such a beautiful sound. "This guy messaged me a month or so ago. He told me he had information about Dad and made me promise not to tell you guys."

Zoë said, "I can't believe you didn't even—"

"Let him finish," Camilla said.

Zoë dropped her mother's hand and crossed her arms.

Jeremy said to Camilla, "I'm assuming you saw the messages?"

She nodded.

His lips pressed together. "So you know everything."

"I don't know anything," Zoë said.

Jeremy gave his sister a quick rundown of the messages he got from the man who called himself Roger.

"I can't believe you didn't tell me." Zoë's accusation was directed at her brother and then at Camilla.

"He told me he didn't want you guys to get your hopes up," Jeremy said, "that he wanted to see me, and then he was going to disappear again. I figured it was just some...some hoax, but the photograph—" His gaze snapped to his mother. "Did you see it?"

As gently as she could, Camilla said, "It's not your dad."

Jeremy's eyes filled, and he tilted his head back to keep them from falling. "How can you be sure?"

"Part of that long story I'm going to tell you."

Zoë wasn't as successful at keeping her tears at bay. They dripped down her cheeks, and she dabbed at them with the sleeve of her sweatshirt.

"We'll never know because I got in that stupid accident," Jeremy said. "I checked the app on your phone to see if he messaged again, but he didn't. Not even to ask why I didn't show up."

Camilla looked at her daughter. "Would you sit down, please? I need to tell you both what's going on."

Zoë glared, but the anger didn't fully mask the fear behind it as she pulled the nurse's chair close and sat.

Focusing her attention on her son, Camilla said, "It wasn't an accident. Somebody shot out your tire."

"He was shot at?" Zoë's voice was too loud.

Jeremy blinked. "You're serious?"

Camilla slid the sliding glass door closed for the first time since they'd been there. "Unfortunately." Hating that she had to do this, Camilla filled her children in on what she'd learned in the last few days. Zoë had known the FBI was involved but hadn't known about the photograph of Daniel. Jeremy'd known about the photograph but hadn't heard about the FBI.

Neither asked questions as Camilla related what she knew, though both shed more tears when she explained why they were certain the photograph hadn't been of Daniel.

"The thing is, we think the man responsible for this believes it was your father. He thinks your dad's still alive. We don't know what his endgame is here. Probably to punish us since he can't get to Dad, but—"

"What does this mean?" Zoë stood, the words angry. "Does this mean... I thought we were safe in Oklahoma." Her gaze flicked from Jeremy to her. "Are we...? We are going home, right?"

Covering her heart with her free hand to try to soothe the physical pain there, Camilla said, "I don't know. I think—"

"Wait!" Jeremy tried to sit himself up, then winced. "What are you saying? We can't go home?"

Camilla swallowed the sob that wanted release. She'd worked hard to create a home for them. It was unthinkable that they'd have to leave it.

It wasn't an expensive home. It wasn't a particularly unique home. Just a three-bedroom in a neighborhood of similar houses. But they'd made it theirs. Zoë's room with its pale-blue walls and chocolate-brown comforter. The white shelves that displayed the artwork she'd done through the years. Jeremy's khaki-colored walls and red-and-blue checkered bedspread. His new shelves, the painting she'd done. Those rooms reflected her children. That house symbolized their life. Their safety. They'd started fresh without Daniel. Could they do it again?

Her children watched her, waited. She couldn't stop the tears that fell when she said, "We can't go home until they find this guy."

"I'm not going into witness protection," Zoë said. "Forget it."

Camilla reached out for her, but Zoë backed away.

"Sweetheart, it'll only be until they find him."

"If they were sure they were going to find him"—Zoë's words were hard, angry—"then they wouldn't be talking about sending us away forever. Witness protection is for people they think will never be safe."

Unfortunately, her daughter was not wrong. "Agent Falk seems confident."

"Not *that* confident," Zoë said.

"I'm not going either," Jeremy said.

Camilla couldn't have this battle right now. To Jeremy, she said, "You're underage. You'll do as I say."

"Until August," he snapped. "And then I can do what I want."

The kids were angry. She knew how they felt. "Let's not borrow trouble. Let's just pray the FBI finds him quickly."

Jeremy's anger seeped away. He reached out and touched Camilla's arm. "I'm sorry, Mom. This is all my fault."

"None of this is your fault. If you hadn't come to Utah, he'd have come to Oklahoma."

"But I told him where I was going to be. You had one rule—"

"He already knew where we lived. Remember, he said he couldn't come to Oklahoma, that people would be looking for him there."

"Oh, yeah," Jeremy said.

Zoë grabbed her brother's hand. "I would have done the same thing," Zoë said. "If he'd reached out to me, I'd have done anything to see Dad." She swiped her fingers beneath her eyes.

"We're going to make it through this." Camilla filled her voice with confidence she hoped, one day, she'd feel.

"We are." Zoë glared across the bed. "But I'm serious. I'm not going into witness protection. Ever."

~

Camilla loved the relationship her kids had with each other, so when she felt they wanted to talk about all they'd learned—without her—she was happy to let them. She needed a moment to process.

As soon as she stepped out of the room, though, she saw Paul talking to one of the other parents in the ICU. The nurses at the door had gotten used to him, so they no longer called her to come walk him in. They saw him as part of her family.

She should have too. After all this time, after all he'd done for her.

Feeling guilty, she turned the other direction and wandered down the hall toward Evan's room. Maybe her sister was still there. Maybe they could have one last conversation. But Evan's room was empty.

Camilla had nowhere to go.

She continued deeper into the neuro ward to a window that faced the city. The haze of pollution—inversion, they called it—that usually hung over the valley was gone. The snow had cleared it away.

She wanted to go outside and stand in it, feel the cold against her skin. She wanted the snowflakes to wash away her fears and doubts, to wash away the danger that surrounded her family. To cover her and hide her.

She wanted to run away from all of it.

She hadn't stepped outside since she'd returned from the Ronald McDonald House—had it only been the morning before?—and that had barely counted. If only everything could go back to the way it had been before Jeremy's accident. If only they could go home as if none of this had ever happened.

If only Daniel hadn't testified.

She closed her eyes, absorbed that last thought. She needed

to forgive herself for the words she'd hurled at him before he died. She needed to forgive Daniel for putting her family in danger—and for leaving her.

Maybe, if she did, she could move on. She could allow herself to fall in love with Paul. She could have a normal life again.

Assuming, of course, that Robert Campos was caught.

Lord, help.

She leaned her forehead against the cold glass and closed her eyes, straining to hear God's voice.

"Miss Camilla?"

She turned to find Bachir behind her, his coal-black eyes sharp.

"I thought that was you." His voice was low and filled with concern, just as it had been the other day when he'd approached her in the lunch room. "Has your son been moved to this ward?"

"No. I was just...hiding."

He stepped beside her and looked out the window. "I never saw snow until I came to the United States. It is beautiful."

"As long as you don't have to drive in it."

He smiled at her. "Sometimes, it is worth it to endure a little danger in order to experience beauty. Do you not think so?"

All she wanted were safety and security. She'd had enough danger to last a lifetime.

"I have learned to ski," he continued. "It is quite frightening to strap slippery boards to your feet and hurtle down a mountain. But exhilarating. Do you ski?"

"Used to, when my husband was alive. He loved it. I spent all my time worrying one of my kids was going to crash into a tree and be paralyzed."

"That is no way to live."

If she'd known then what she knew now, she'd have let

herself enjoy the freedom of the slopes. Skiing seemed tame compared to what she was dealing with today.

"Your son is not better?"

She gave Bachir a quick rundown on Jeremy's health.

"The infection is under control?"

"His temperature is lower. But..." She shrugged. "What are you doing here?"

"I am working with a doctor in this department. He asked me to meet him here, but he is with a patient, so I wait. And you are here because...?"

She waved toward the hallway that led to ICU. "Because it's close to Jeremy but...away."

"You need to rest."

"I will. When Jeremy is better. When everything is..." But she didn't finish the thought.

Bachir leaned his shoulder against the window and faced her. "It is very difficult, this mountain you climb. But I believe you are near the top."

If only that were true.

Bachir laid a hand on her head, and his warmth flowed past her hair and into her scalp. He spoke words over her, words she didn't understand. A prayer? Something else? For all she knew, it was a curse.

Except, it wasn't. Because with the warmth came peace.

When he opened his eyes, he said, "You are nearing the summit. On the other side, you will find freedom from your fears. You must only keep going a little while longer."

"How can you be so sure?"

He dropped his hand. "I am not, but my God, He tells me things sometimes. You, I see on the top of the mountain with your family. You are safe." He winked. "You are not wearing skis."

She chuckled at that, wiped fresh tears. "I love your confidence."

"It is not me." He pointed toward the ceiling. The heavens. "He sees you, Camilla. He is with you." Bachir looked over her head. "Now, I must meet the doctor. I will continue to pray for you and your family."

After he left, Camilla turned her gaze to the city again. Everything was covered in a blanket of fresh snow. Like a new start.

Would that her family could clean the slate so easily.

CHAPTER THIRTY-FOUR

AFTER PAUL and Zoë left Saturday night, Camilla crawled onto the horrible cot and slept until the X-ray techs arrived. Long, blessed sleep.

Jeremy's lungs looked better. Even the doctor seemed pleased.

The overnight nurse assured her that Jeremy's temperature had stayed down.

Now, in the dark and quiet room, Jeremy's eyes were open. He'd seemed sad since their conversation the day before. She knew how he felt. They'd known Daniel was dead, yet they'd all held out hope. Foolish hope.

The night before, they'd borrowed a movie from the selection near the ICU's entrance. There'd been plenty to choose from, and they'd all agreed on *The Secret Life of Walter Mitty*, the recent one, not the old one. Zoë and Jeremy had enjoyed it. Paul had seemed engaged, though she caught him watching her more than once.

Camilla hadn't been able to focus. On the screen, Walter fantasized about adventure, but all Camilla wanted was her life back. Her normal, boring life.

If only the night before had been a typical Saturday night. Zoë working, Jeremy out with his friends. If only this were a typical Sunday morning. She'd meet Paul at church, where they'd worship together and then go to lunch.

She and Paul had been going to church together for years.

He was a good man. A kind man. A man who loved her. And she was a fool for not returning his feelings.

When the day nurse came on duty, she told Jeremy it was time to start him eating again. The whole time he'd been in the hospital, they hadn't fed him, not even through a tube. She'd worried, but he hadn't been hungry, and the nurses had assured her he'd be fed when he needed to be.

Now, his eyes lit up.

"Something soft," Delia said. "Yogurt, or—"

"Ice cream?"

"How about a milkshake?"

Thirty minutes later, Jeremy took a sip of a chocolate milkshake and groaned with pleasure. "Seriously, the best thing I've ever tasted."

He looked better. His color was nearly back to normal, his bruises fading, his eyes bright. He was talking and breathing on his own, though the clear narrow tube was still delivering oxygen into his nose.

During rounds, the doctors seemed optimistic. After the rest of the crowd moved along, Hen stepped into the room and spoke to Jeremy. "If your temperature holds steady, we're going to move you out of ICU today."

Jeremy lifted his hand in triumph. "That's awesome news."

Hen grabbed his shoulder and squeezed. "You're a tough kid. You're gonna be back to your old self again before long."

Thank God. He was recovering. After everything, Jeremy would get through this. Still, Camilla worried. She followed

Hen out of Jeremy's room. "You're sure he's ready for that? Just yesterday, his temperature spiked."

"The antibiotics took care of the infection. His oxygen levels are good. When he's been off the oxygen for a day, we'll send him home."

Home?

Would they be able to go home?

Jeremy was still celebrating when Camilla's phone buzzed with a text. Agent Falk was there. Even though Jeremy knew what was going on, she didn't want Falk coming to the room. She wanted Jeremy to enjoy his good news, not be pulled down by bad.

In her experience, Falk's news was always bad.

"I'm going to go for a walk," she told Jeremy. "Your sister and Paul should be here soon. You'll be okay here by yourself?"

"Sure." He clicked on the TV. "Take your time."

She grabbed her jacket and met Agent Falk in the hallway. "Mind if we step outside?"

One eyebrow hitched. "I'm sort of attached to my toes."

"I'm getting cabin fever."

As soon as the door opened, the cold air hit her, and she shivered but didn't stop until she'd reached the treed area beyond the drive. She didn't step into it, though. The ground was covered with a couple inches of snow. Her sneakers wouldn't keep the moisture out, and Falk was wearing leather shoes. She turned to face him. "What's up?"

He crossed his arms and looked around. "Not sure I'm dressed for this."

"I haven't been outside the hospital in over forty-eight hours. I need fresh air."

The protection agent's gaze darted around the area. He didn't look happy.

"How's Jeremy?" Falk asked.

She suppressed a shudder. It was freezing. Though the snow had stopped, the skies hadn't cleared. Would it snow again? She should check the weather.

Not that it mattered to her. Not for a couple of days anyway. "They think they're going to move him out of ICU today."

"That's great news." But he didn't smile.

"What's going on?"

He looked around, huffed a breath. "I don't like this. We're too exposed."

She almost smiled. "Exposed to the cold, you mean? In St. Louis, you could handle a little chilly weather."

He wasn't amused. "Can we please go inside?"

She wanted to argue as a point of pride, but she was freezing. She followed him into the lobby. The protection agent brought up the rear. Falk walked past the gift shop and the cafeteria, which was packed this morning. He stopped halfway to the hospital's rear door. "Do you remember who Alfredo Punta is?"

She squeezed her eyes closed, and images she'd never seen in real life flicked across her brain like a slideshow. Blood everywhere, all over Daniel's car.

She forced her eyes open. She hadn't heard the name in a long time. Hadn't wanted to think about him. Before she could answer, Falk continued.

"He's the hitman we believe killed your husband. We couldn't prove it, still can't."

"What about him?" She heard the flat tone of her own voice, covering up a world of fear beneath.

"His body turned up in Phoenix this morning."

Fear rose like nausea. She swallowed it back and leaned against the wall, needing the support.

"Murdered?" she asked. Though the answer was obvious. Falk hadn't come to tell her the man had died of natural causes.

"We think Robert Campos took him out. Punta has been dead at least a week, so the working theory is that Campos killed him, dumped his body in the desert, and then made his way here."

She covered her face with her hands, absorbing the news. How did it feel to know the man who'd taken Daniel's life was dead? If someone had asked her the day before how she'd feel, she'd have guessed she'd feel...vindicated. He'd gotten what he deserved, hadn't he?

All she felt was sad.

When that man's mother had held her baby for the first time, she'd seen beauty in his eyes. She'd seen the fingerprints of God.

That woman had to bury the son who'd drifted far away from the plan God had intended for him. Maybe Punta'd had a wife and kids who would now live without him, just like she'd had to learn to live without Daniel.

Tragedy upon tragedy.

"What does this mean for us?" she asked.

"Nothing, really. I got a call from that Swedish doctor last evening confirming what we'd learned from the refugee camp in Sudan."

Confirmation that Daniel was dead, as if she hadn't known.

Why did the news keep hitting her like it did now, sending the shakes to her hands and pain to her chest?

"Any update on Campos?"

Falk shook his head. "When your son is released, we're going to move you to a safe house nearby. We'll figure out what to do from there."

"My daughter tells me she's not going into witness protection."

His lips pressed together. "You need to make her aware of the danger."

"You think I haven't tried?"

"When you get to the safe house, I'll talk to them both. Hopefully, I can convince them—"

"But... I mean, you think you're going to find Campos, right?"

"We have to plan for every contingency. When you leave the hospital, you'll need to be somewhere safe."

Safe. It had always only been an illusion. "Daniel's brothers have offered to get us bodyguards. Maybe I should take them up on it?"

Falk shook his head. "You're safe in the hospital."

"But when Jeremy's released—"

"We'll protect you."

Like they protected Daniel? But that wasn't fair. Daniel took off, left the safe house. That was on him.

And her.

"The more people involved," Falk said, "the more opportunity for leaks. Sorry, but you're going to have to trust us."

She wasn't surprised by his answer. Grant and the brothers wouldn't be happy about it, but she did trust Falk. "Any more information for me?"

"I wish I could deliver good news one of these days."

They were halfway back to the ICU when she asked, "You know about Paul. We've been friends since—"

"Daniel's lawyer. I remember him."

"We've become close. If we go into witness protection...?" She let the question hang, mostly because she wasn't sure how to finish it.

"If you're not married, he can't come with you. You'll have to cut off all ties to him."

"He wants to get married. But Daniel's not officially dead."

"We could help with that," he said. "We can hurry that along in court."

"But I'd have to marry him before. Right away." She continued down the long hallway. "And, if I don't... What if I leave him in Oklahoma and then change my mind? What if I—?"

"Mrs. Wright." Agent Falk stopped and faced her. "I can't help you with this decision. If you're not married, then he can't join you, and you'll have to cut off your ties to him. There won't be any going back. Unless you decide to leave the program, of course. But as long as Campos is out there, that wouldn't end well." He tilted his head to the side, his lips pressed flat. After a moment he said, "I'm no expert on romance, but if you're not sure, maybe that's your answer."

CHAPTER THIRTY-FIVE

DEAR CAMILLA,

I never told you about Alfredo Punta. I tried my very best to keep my work life and my home life separate, especially when it came to the ugliness I encountered daily.

I failed. How spectacularly I failed.

I was no expert on the local gangs, but I'd learned to recognize some of their tattoos. The snake inked on the back of Alfredo's hand told me he was a member of the Sons of Vipers.

When I met him, Alfredo was a fifteen-year-old kid. Brown eyes and head nearly shaved, he had the long, lean look of a boy who'd had a recent growth spurt without the accompanying weight gain. A few days after the gang war erupted, he strutted from the waiting room, tough as nails, lifting his chin in greeting at a fellow gang member as he passed him in the corridor.

But I saw the scared child.

In the exam room, I asked him to take off his shirt, but he was too injured to make it happen. The nurse cut it off him, revealing pale skin stretched over his ribcage covered in red welts. "What happened?"

Alfredo had been friends with one of the early victims. He

and his friends had raged into their enemy's neighborhood, intending to take out their fury on everyone they met. But revenge wasn't sweet—or easy. Alfredo got separated from his buddies and was caught in an alley alone.

His voice hitched as he told the story. The tough exterior crumbled. His friend had been murdered because he'd gotten caught up in something bigger than himself. Something more evil than he ever could have imagined.

And Alfredo could have been killed. Rival gang members had been in the process of beating him soundly when a pair of police officers broke up the fight.

"They just ran into the alley, guns drawn, like a couple of super-freaking-heroes," Alfredo said. "And them Crips, they done run. One of 'em got caught, though. I got that guy good, stabbed him in the thigh, and he couldn't get away."

His wicked smile had me wanting to step back.

Was there still an innocent kid in there? Or had the innocence been pounded out of him by hate and drugs and violence?

I patched his wounds and ordered an X-ray for what I suspected was a broken arm. Though the emergency room was overrun, I sent the nurse out and sat and faced my young patient. "Do you think you were lucky tonight?"

"Yeah, I was! Them cops aren't all good for nothin'."

"I don't think you were lucky. I think you have a God who loves you, and He sent those police officers to save your life."

Alfredo rolled his eyes. "You sound like my *abuelo* and all them people at church, always with the God-loves-you stuff. But there ain't no God where I live."

I patted Alfredo's uninjured arm. "There is, and He was there for you tonight. What would have happened if He hadn't sent those police officers to rescue you?"

Alfredo looked away.

"He saved you tonight. Maybe you should try to figure out

why. Maybe He has a better plan for you than the one you're living."

Alfredo didn't scoff again. He turned back to me and held eye contact for a long time. "You think so?"

"I know so. Walking with God isn't easy, but there's peace in knowing, even if you're in a war, you're on the side of good."

"Hey, them Crips started it."

"And you think you can finish it? Other boys just like your friend died tonight, boys with moms and dads and grandparents and siblings who loved them. Human beings created by God. You were a part of that, of the evil and hate. But you can be free of all of it. Free and forgiven in Jesus."

Before he could respond, the nurse knocked and stepped inside, pushing a wheelchair. "We're moving you to X-ray."

Alfredo hopped off the bed and into the chair. "I could get used to this. Riding in style."

I settled my hand on his shoulder. "Think about what I said. If you ever want to talk about it or about anything, just come in and ask for me. I'll make time for you."

I remember the conversation vividly. Even though I talked to a lot of guys about Jesus, that boy's face stuck with me. I watched until he was rolled around the corner and out of sight, lifting a prayer for his soul, for God's mercy on him and on all the poor deluded children who'd been dragged into gangs.

It all seemed so futile, Cammie. That night, it all seemed so useless.

What was I doing there, trying to save kids who didn't want to be saved? Trying to make a difference in the hospital when my family was alone.

God called me to that life. I know He did. But He also blessed me with you and Zoë and Jeremy. I had to find a way to balance it all better.

The violence raged. I needed to make changes, but the

hospital relied on me, and it was easier to be there than at home, facing your disappointment.

So, I changed nothing.

The next two years were hard. The kids didn't seem to miss having me around. As I'd predicted, Jeremy had given up baseball, instead pouring all his energy into skateboarding. I'd seen enough skateboarding injuries to know how dangerous the sport was. I lectured him often about wearing his helmet and, as far as I knew, he did. But how would I know? It wasn't as if I ever saw him on his board.

Am I arrogant to believe Zoë got some of her personality from me? Not just with her good grades, but the way she volunteered regularly at the food bank. Like me, she had a heart for the downtrodden and wanted to fix all the world's ills. Also like me, she tended toward workaholism. I lectured her as often about her need to rest as I did Jeremy about skating safety. My warnings tended to fall on deaf ears, though.

Do as I say, not as I do.

I was glad when you got involved with local charities. Galas, food drives, and the annual home show, you found ways to use your artistic talents to serve the community.

Do you have any idea how proud I was of you? How proud I still am?

Sometimes I had to don a tux and accompany you to fancy dinners and listen to the most boring speakers on the planet. Sorry for all the complaining about that. At least the balls were more about dancing than talking, and having you in my arms on the dance floor made enduring the monkey suit worth it.

It was a dull Tuesday afternoon at work. I was told the man in the exam room was suffering from flu symptoms. After I knocked, I stepped in to find an older man lying on the exam table, pale and trembling.

Beside him, Alfredo Punta held his hand. When he saw me,

his face broke into a smile. At first, he seemed just like the skinny kid I'd treated two years earlier. But that impression didn't last.

After a nod to Alfredo, I turned my attention to the old man and extended a hand to shake. "Dr. Wright."

"Diego Punta," he said.

"This is the doc I told ya 'bout," Alfredo said. "The Jesus dude."

"I've been called worse."

Mr. Punta chuckled, but it turned into a cough. For the next few minutes, I examined him while he insisted he was fine. "Nothing to worry about. My grandson thinks I'm so old that I can't fight off a cold."

"Let's just prove Alfredo wrong."

"You remember my name?" Alfredo seemed surprised.

"I always remember my favorites." Truth was, I remembered the ones the Lord brought to mind, and he'd brought Alfredo to mind many times over the years.

Mr. Punta spoke in Spanish to his grandson, his words laced with kindness.

While I examined him, I considered the changes in Alfredo. Where he'd once been skin and bones, he now sported thick muscles that rippled below the sleeves of his T-shirt. More tattoos marred his pale skin, three smaller snakes surrounding the large one he'd had before. Another gang member had told me those small snakes represented kills, but I couldn't believe that.

Surely this kid hadn't killed three people.

Maybe he only wanted people to believe he had. I hoped and prayed that was the case.

The way he was watching his grandfather convinced me that Alfredo wasn't the hardened gang member he wanted others to believe. From what I'd experienced, when they were alone and injured or sick, all of them seemed vulnerable. Human.

But there was something lurking behind Alfredo's eyes, something I wanted to shrink from. Something...evil.

His grandfather was dealing with more than a cold, more than the flu or even a respiratory infection. I suspected pneumonia and ordered an X-ray.

The next day, I was there when the pulmonologist gave Mr. Punta and his grandson the diagnosis. Lung cancer.

Mr. Punta took the news with the grace of a faith-filled man.

Alfredo's hardened eyes filled with tears, then fury. Once again, I tried to tell Alfredo about the Lord, focusing on the God who heals, but he was less open to Christ now than he'd been the first time I met him.

Before they left, Mr. Punta took my hands and thanked me for my thoroughness. "I have a chance to survive because of you."

"Because of God," I said, and Mr. Punta smiled. We both knew something Alfredo didn't.

Alfredo didn't seem to care.

Gangs were ripping families apart. But so were drugs and disease. It felt like the world was unraveling all around me. Not just at work, where I saw people at their worst, but in our family as well.

You and I weren't happy. I knew that. I knew you filled your time with activities because you were lonely. And I knew that was my fault. But I didn't know how to fix it.

Patching up wounds was easy. Patching up our marriage wasn't only hard, it was terrifying. But I thought I'd have time.

Today, I can feel death circling like a chill on my feet. It keeps getting closer, colder. And I watch you, still warm, still protected from the evil I brought into our lives. It hurts to know how badly I failed you—and to know I'm not going to have the chance to make things right.

All these words, my ramblings, my memories. I doubt they'll help you at all. What you need, what you've always needed, is your husband at your side.

I couldn't give you that before because I was afraid. I was competent at being a doctor. I've never felt competent at being a husband. I always kept myself distant from you, safe. As if you were a threat.

Is it too late, Cammie? If I can fix our marriage, then what? I can't walk away from what I saw. I can't.

And they won't let me live with telling the truth.

You and our children will pay the price.

The chill is climbing up my legs. The end is coming. I know I sound like a madman, but I can feel it closing in.

Forgive me for what I've done to us. I love you. I'll love you until my heart stops beating. And then I'll love you more.

Yours always,

Daniel

CHAPTER THIRTY-SIX

MONDAY MORNING WAS a whirlwind of activity—doctors signing off, nurses preparing. Finally, Camilla walked beside Jeremy's bed, along with Zoë, Paul, and Jeremy's favorite nurse, Nathan, as orderlies pushed him out of ICU. Agent Siple accompanied them as well. They wound around a whole new maze of corridors to the new room. A large hospital room with a solid door and a couch and privacy and the very real hope of recovery.

Once Jeremy was settled, the FBI agent left to stand outside the ward.

Nathan shook Jeremy's hand. "They'll take good care of you here." He winked at the sixty-something female nurse who stood in the doorway. "Miss Annie's the best."

Annie said, "Yes, sir, I am."

After Nathan left, Zoë went to see if this ward had any good movies while Jeremy made a video showing his new room.

When Zoë returned, Camilla caught Paul's eye. He'd been leaning against the window, arms crossed. "Want to go for a walk," she asked, "and get the lay of the land?"

Paul pushed off the windowsill and started for the door.

"Be back in a minute," she said to the kids. The curious looks on their faces told her they hadn't missed the tension stretching between herself and Paul.

She led him past a number of rooms and came to a window at the end of the corridor. It was relatively quiet there, and nobody lurked nearby. She looked out at the snow-covered foothills, feeling Paul's presence beside her. Feeling the strain.

He stared out the window too. After a moment, he said, "You're not ready."

She turned and took his hand, but he didn't face her. "My mother always said, 'When in doubt, don't.'"

The muscle in his jaw ticked. "After all this time, you still have doubts about me. I think that tells me all I need to know."

"Not about you, Paul."

He turned to her, his eyebrows lifted.

"I know it's stupid. I know Daniel's gone and he's never coming home. I know that, but I just... I can't accept it. I can't let him go."

"I think you could." He pulled his hand away and crossed his arms. "When the right man comes along. I thought I could be that man."

"You know I care for you."

His gaze was over her head as he nodded. "It's not enough for me anymore. Our friendship, the time we spend together... It's been wonderful, but..."

"When we get home—"

"If you get home," he said.

She breathed through that terrible truth. "If we go home, I hope you and I can—"

"No." He took a step back. "I moved to Oklahoma because I love you. I came here because I love you. Because I love your kids. I came because...because I thought that you'd realize you love me too. I thought, if I supported you through this, you'd understand my feelings. You'd realize you shared them. But you don't." His eyes closed briefly before he added, "You don't share my feelings."

She didn't, but... "It's not fair for you to expect me to make this decision right now."

"If your life weren't in danger, I wouldn't have asked you to."

"I know."

Paul looked back out the window. The snow had stopped, but the sky was still cloudy. Maybe the storm was only taking a break. Maybe all of life was just one storm after another with a few breaks in between.

"I thought coming here would bring us together," he said.

He'd been like a father to her children. He'd been her plus-one to every event for four years. He'd been her closest friend.

He'd been everything they'd needed. And she did care for him, as more than just a friend.

How could she do this? How could she reject this kind, wonderful man?

But how could she not when she doubted she'd ever return his feelings? She'd prayed, agonizing over what to do. The truth was, for Paul's sake, she wanted to say yes to a future with him.

She wanted to say yes to Paul for her own sake as well. Because she couldn't imagine life without him. She didn't want to go to church solo. She didn't want to eat all her meals by herself, to never have a companion, to never have a date. When Jeremy left for college, she didn't want to be alone.

But Paul wasn't the companion she craved.

And he deserved a woman who adored him. He deserved so much more than she could offer.

How selfish she'd been to string him along. After four years, he needed to move on, to move past her. And she needed to trust that God knew what He was doing.

She took his hand again. "I wish things were different."

He swallowed hard and kissed her cheek. "Tell the kids I said goodbye."

She nodded but couldn't speak for the lump in her throat.

"I'll keep praying for you."

Before she could respond, he walked away, around the corner and out of sight.

CHAPTER THIRTY-SEVEN

CAMILLA SAT in an empty stairwell until her tears ran dry. After she splashed cold water on her face in the bathroom, she returned to face her children.

They'd been watching a movie. When Jeremy caught sight of her, he said, "What happened?"

Zoë paused the movie, and they both stared at her, clearly seeing what the cold water hadn't washed away.

She stood by Jeremy's bed and gripped the cold bed rail for support.

"What is it, Mom?" Zoë stood. "Did something happen with that Campos guy?" Her gaze cut to her brother. "Is it Jeremy?"

"No, no. Nothing like that."

Zoë crossed the room and took her hand. Her voice squeaked when she said, "Paul?"

Her daughter's guess surprised her. Zoë was more insightful than Camilla had realized.

She nodded, and the tears started again. "I know you two love him."

Jeremy slid his hand over Camilla's on the bed rail.

The sweet gesture only made the tears fall faster.

"We love *you*, Mom." Zoë squeezed her hand. "Paul has been good to us. And if you two had stayed together, it would have been fine."

"But he's not Dad," Jeremy said. "As much as he tried to take Dad's place..."

She started to respond, but he hurried to continue.

"Not that he was trying to do that. Not that he was doing anything wrong. He's been nice to us."

"We want you to be happy," Zoë added.

Jeremy let go of her hand. "I can't believe he did this now, though." Anger infused his voice. "Why now?"

Before Camilla could formulate an answer, Zoë said, "Witness protection, obviously." She turned to Camilla. "Did he break it off because he doesn't want to go into hiding?"

"No." Camilla took a breath. "I broke it off because I'm not ready. We'd have to be married."

"Ah." Jeremy sat back. "Again, all my fault."

Camilla squared her shoulders and faced Jeremy. "Not everything is about you."

"I just meant—"

"I know what you meant. The accident wasn't your fault. Your being here isn't your fault. And my relationship with Paul has nothing to do with you."

Jeremy's uninjured hand rose, palm out. "I didn't mean anything by it."

"You need to stop doing that," Camilla said. "None of this is your fault. You were the victim here."

"If I hadn't—"

"Give it a rest, bro." Zoë turned to Camilla. "If you'd gotten that message, wouldn't you have wanted to find out?"

"I'd have gone anywhere." She swallowed a lump in her throat. "I'd have done anything, risked anything, to see your father again."

Zoë's eyes filled, and she squeezed Camilla's hand. "Me, too." She faced her brother. "So knock it off. That guy targeted you because he knew you'd be in Utah. If you hadn't come out here, he'd have come to Oklahoma. To our home, where our friends live. Maybe it's selfish, but I'm glad we're here and not there. So quit acting like this is all about you. It's not."

Jeremy stared at the door, away from them. "Whatever." The single word was angry, but something else buzzed beneath the anger. Fear, maybe.

No. Sadness.

Camilla wiped Jeremy's too-long hair back from his forehead. "This is just..."

"It sucks," Zoë said. "This is all just..."

"Bull...crap," Jeremy supplied.

Camilla guessed what her son had almost said. "Nice save."

Jeremy nearly smiled.

Camilla agreed with her kids, though. "We've worked so hard to get past the grief, to move on. This has brought it all back. It really highlights how far we've come, though, don't you think?" She pulled up a chair and motioned for Zoë to do the same. When they were settled, Camilla continued. "Think about where we were four years ago, after Dad's memorial. We were so..."

"Lost," Jeremy said.

"Sad," Zoë added.

"Such small words for such big feelings." Camilla fought the tears that wanted to fall. "Those small words defined us for a long time. Everything we did—selling the house, moving to Oklahoma, getting you two into a new school. My work, your skateboarding"—she patted Jeremy's knee, then ran her hand down Zoë's ponytail—"your art, it was all overshadowed by those two feelings—lost and sad."

Camilla's kids were crying now. Would they ever feel

normal again? Find joy again? The joy of the Lord was supposed to be her strength. She didn't feel joyful, and she didn't feel strong.

"That first year was... awful. But we survived it. With God, we overcame." She shot a look to Zoë, who was nodding along. Her daughter didn't attend church anymore. She didn't like to talk about God. But she still believed. She would return to Him.

"Four years later," Camilla continued, "our lives are full. We've built a great home, made friends, gone after dreams. Are those feelings still there? Do we still feel lost and sad sometimes? Of course. Your father..." She paused to get ahold of her emotions. "Your father is worth our tears. He's worth our sadness. It's okay that we still feel lost without him sometimes. But we are a family." She looked her son in the eyes, then her daughter. "The three of us, we are a family, and we've overcome terrible tragedy. We will do it again."

Zoë said, "But, if they don't find Campos—"

"We'll do what we have to do." Camilla took her daughter's hand. "As a family. Together."

Jeremy touched his sister's shoulder. "We have to stay together. Mom's right. We need each other."

Zoë looked from him to Camilla. "I don't want to lose everything again."

"You'll still have us," Camilla said. "You'll still have God."

Zoë didn't speak, but her slight nod gave Camilla hope. Her family could survive—if they stayed together.

CHAPTER THIRTY-EIGHT

THE DAY GOT BETTER after Paul's departure and the conversation with the kids. They watched a movie, and then the physical therapist came by. First, they helped Jeremy dress in some old sweatpants and his favorite T-shirt. Just that little thing—getting him out of the hospital gown—made a huge difference in his attitude.

Jeremy looked like himself again.

Though he wasn't moving like himself. He was moving like a ninety-year-old man recovering from a broken hip.

The physical therapist walked by Jeremy's side, arm wrapped around his back, as they slowly made their way down the hallway.

Camilla walked backward in front of him, hands outstretched, just in case.

Zoë followed, pushing an empty wheelchair the therapist had given her. Her eyes were wide, her lips pressed together as she regarded her brother's wobbly progress.

Camilla knew how she felt.

One hand was pressed to his ribs, the other holding the PT's hand in a death grip.

With help, he'd walked to the restroom and back a couple of times while they were in the ICU, but this therapist was aiming higher.

"All the way to the window." Her voice was perky, which probably would've annoyed Jeremy if she weren't so pretty.

It wasn't that far, but the way he winced with every move, it might as well have been a mile.

Camilla said, "Are you sure? That's a long way."

"I can do this, Mom." His voice was strained and tight, and he didn't look up from the floor.

"That's why we've got the wheelchair," the therapist said.

Ella? Emma? No, Emily. Camilla had met so many doctors and nurses and therapists that she couldn't keep them straight.

"He can sit and rest whenever he wants. You need a rest, Jeremy?"

"No." The word was ground out through a wall of pain that was clear on his face.

Camilla's stomach roiled as if she were the one in pain. She'd never understood that reaction when she'd been young. Her best friend growing up would feel sick if anybody else got hurt. Even talking about an injury would have the girl's hand covering her stomach. Camilla had always thought her friend was faking that, but now she understood. There was no greater agony than watching her kids suffer.

Or thinking of her husband's suffering.

Finally, Camilla bumped against the floor-to-ceiling window. She stepped out of the way, and Jeremy reached it.

Emily said, "You need to sit?" Then to Zoë, "Roll that up—"

"I'm fine." Jeremy stared out at the snow-covered foothills. His legs were trembling with the strain. "Look at that," he said. "There's a whole world outside of this hospital."

Nobody responded. They just watched him take it in.

"A world I almost never saw again." The words were so quiet that Camilla barely caught them.

She rubbed his back. "You're here. God protected you."

He tipped, and she grabbed his elbow.

Emily, on his other side, eased her arm around him. "Let's get you into the wheelchair."

Zoë had already placed it behind him, and Jeremy sat, slowly. He looked at the therapist. "I can't believe this is so hard."

"You just walked twenty-five feet." Her eyebrows rose. "Did you do that in the ICU?"

"Not even close."

"Tomorrow, I bet you'll walk twice that, and by Wednesday, we'll be working on your balance." She pushed the wheelchair back to his room. "And then we'll be talking about sending you home."

Jeremy looked at his mom, a sad smile on his face. Would they go home?

"Do you have stairs in your house?" the therapist asked.

Jeremy quickly said, "Nope."

"That makes it easier." They reached the room, and the therapist helped him into his bed and placed the oxygen tube back over his face. "You did great. How do you feel?"

"Tired."

"Think of it, though," she said. "The last time you walked, you probably had to drag your IV tower and oxygen."

His smile was slight. "True."

"This was all you," she added.

"And you, and Mom, and the wheelchair."

"I helped," Zoë said. "Don't forget about me."

He smirked at his sister. "I'm ready to not need anybody's help."

The therapist squeezed his arm. "You'll get there. From

what I heard about your accident, you're lucky you're moving at all."

"Not luck." Jeremy pointed up. "God."

She smiled. "I think you're right."

After the therapist left and Zoë and Jeremy were settled, Camilla said, "I'm going to make a call." She wanted to let Falk know they'd need a safe house with one level.

Camilla returned to the stairwell where she'd had her cry earlier and dialed the agent.

He answered on the first ring with, "Everything okay?"

"When we get out of here, we're going to need to go someplace with no stairs if you can arrange it."

"We figured." That he'd thought of it already comforted her.

"Any news on Campos?"

"Unfortunately, no."

"Maybe he left town?"

"I don't think so."

The way he said the words made her ask, "What do you think he's doing?"

A long pause, and then, "He's planning something."

She'd always appreciated how honest Falk was with her, but sometimes, a little sugarcoating would have been nice. "Any idea what?"

"Nope. Honestly, the man looks like a thug. You saw his photo. But he's a schemer. I mean, think of the planning it took to pull this thing off with Jeremy. He's smart, and he's patient. Whatever he's planning..." The words trailed off, and probably not because Falk didn't know how to finish the sentence.

"What? What do you think it is?"

"I wish I knew. I do know it won't be pretty. Which is why we have to catch him. Soon."

~

Camilla spent Monday night at the hospital, sending Zoë to the Ronald McDonald House. Tuesday night, Zoë stayed, and Camilla left the hospital for the first time in days. Jeremy was recovering quickly now, so she wasn't even nervous about leaving him.

His physical therapy had been going well. As Emily had predicted, he'd walked farther every day. The day before, Emily had taken Jeremy into an exercise room, and they'd worked on balance while Zoë and Camilla stood against the wall and watched. When Emily finished, Jeremy had stayed another fifteen minutes to shoot baskets into the child-sized hoop with a little girl, who seemed to take great delight in Jeremy's antics. He might've looked like an adult, but sometimes, the boy she remembered came out.

The storm had cleared the day before, but more clouds had moved in by that evening. The weather felt irrelevant though, and that night, as Camilla slipped between the sheets of a real bed, she praised God for her son's health, for all the things He'd done for them, for the ways He'd protected them. She fell asleep confident that God would continue to protect them.

Camilla arrived at the hospital Wednesday morning to find Jeremy sitting in a chair eating breakfast with his sister. When she walked in, he stood and held out his arms for a hug.

She stepped into them. "How was your night?"

"Fine. Slept well." He squeezed her tight, but she didn't squeeze back, afraid to hurt him.

He backed out of the hug. "I'm gonna take a shower today."

"Good news!"

"Yeah. I feel disgusting. The nurse is going to come back with a thing to cover my splint. Oh, and she said I'm going to get a real cast today, too." He settled back in the chair and focused on his breakfast.

Camilla sat beside Zoë on the couch, trying to take it all in. They were preparing Jeremy to go home. She'd known it was coming—they'd told her probably Thursday, and by the looks of things, they were sticking to that schedule.

This was good news. But where would they go? The pulmonologist had told them not to put Jeremy on a plane until the following Monday because of the trauma to his lungs. If not for Campos, they'd stay with Marcy and Kevin for a few days.

But that wasn't an option with Campos out there, planning something.

Fear nipped at her as they went through the day. Jeremy's shower had to be put off because ortho collected him to put on his cast. After lunch, they took him to physical therapy, and then a doctor came by to discuss Jeremy's care after they left the hospital.

By the time Jeremy got his shower, it was midafternoon. Still moving slowly, he walked into the bathroom, a nurse at his side giving instructions.

When he had the shower running, Zoë said, "I might as well go take a shower too."

"Don't go anywhere without the FBI agent."

Zoë's look carried a definite *duh*.

"Sorry. I worry."

Zoë grabbed her things and kissed Camilla's cheek. "I know."

As her daughter disappeared out the door, Camilla told herself Zoë would be safe with Agent Siple. But worry dogged her anyway. Campos was out there, plotting something. His last attack had failed. Would they survive the next one?

CHAPTER THIRTY-NINE

DEAR CAMILLA,

We used to dream. You remember how we'd lean close, heads nearly touching, and plan our future?

And then we were living it. Our life together wasn't a disappointment, but it wasn't the idyllic existence we'd imagined. It was life, with all its highs and lows, triumphs and trials. The thing was, triumphs and trials were rare. Mostly, life for you and me became predictable.

Maybe that was one reason I spent so much time at the hospital.

Am I making excuses? Probably.

I loved the frenetic activity and the constant challenges. It sounds stupid to say so now, but I even relished the hint of danger. There I was, a doctor who, thanks to your contacts, rubbed elbows with the city's elite. The rich, the famous, the influential. The mayor himself had called to ask me to recommend a heart surgeon for his mother.

At work, I dealt with the other extreme. The poor, the underserved, the disenfranchised.

The mayor knew my name. So did local gang members.

I took pride in that. I took pride in the way I served the poor, the way I shared my faith.

Our home was restful—thanks to you—and I loved it. I loved being with our kids. When they were home—which was less and less as they grew older—I spent time with them. We watched movies and played games. I took them each to lunch or dinner at least once a month. I made a point to attend church with you all every week. But most of the time, I found our home life rather...dull.

I'm sorry.

You no longer nagged me about my long hours. You'd learned to live without me, filling your time with the kids and charity events. The rare evenings we went out, just the two of us, we talked about Zoë and Jeremy or our various activities. We talked about sports. We talked about politics.

We didn't dream together anymore.

But I still believed there'd be time for that. We were in the crazy years—busy kids, both of us doing what we loved. There'd be time to rekindle our romance, to rediscover our intimacy. Despite the difficulties, I loved you, and I believed you loved me. As long as we had that, we'd be okay.

Okay.

What a lofty goal. As if the Lord called us to a life of "okay."

As I imagine the wrong end of the gun barrel that will probably take my life, my mistakes flash by in Technicolor.

I'd give anything for another chance. I'm writing all these letters to tell you things I've been so bad at saying these last few years. I love you. I appreciate the life you created for our family. You make me a better man.

I can't imagine life without you.

Of course, my life won't go on without you.

You'll have to live without me.

Remember that Friday night? Late March, and I had news I

couldn't wait to tell you. I texted an hour before the end of my shift.

"Let's go to dinner tonight, just you and me."

You responded with a thumbs-up and the little salsa dancer emoji, followed by a question mark.

I hadn't taken you dancing, just the two of us, in years. I didn't even know where to go. But the idea of holding my gorgeous wife in my arms, swaying to the music, had me responding with, "It's a date. Put on your dancing shoes."

When I arrived home, you were in the bathroom applying mascara. You'd curled your long brown hair. The dress you planned to wear—my favorite because it showed off your figure—hung from a hanger propped on the closet door. You only wore a silky robe.

"Hey, handsome." You met my eyes in the mirror.

You didn't mention that I was thirty minutes late. That, once again, you'd be waiting while I washed off the memories of the day.

I slid my arms around you and rested my hands on your stomach, gazing at you in the mirror. How easy it would be to skip dinner and dancing and get to the fun part of the evening. I could see in the way your eyes sparkled that you were thinking the same thing.

But the anticipation was half the fun. I gently moved your hair aside, kissed the skin behind your ear, and whispered, "Try to be patient, Mrs. Wright."

You giggled as I shed my clothes and climbed into the shower.

An hour later, we were seated by a tuxedo-clad maître d' at a fancy steakhouse we'd never been to. As he poured water into our glasses, you pressed your lips together in that way that told me you were amused but trying to look serious.

When the stuffy man walked away, you said, “Fancy place, mister. What’s the occasion?”

“I have some news.”

Your eyebrows rose. “Interesting. So do I.”

A fun twist. Though I didn’t say so aloud, I guessed what your news was. Zoë had taken the PSAT, and her scores were due. I wouldn’t be a bit surprised if she was a National Merit finalist. I had been, after all, and Zoë worked a lot harder in school than I ever did.

I didn’t press you, just enjoyed watching you with your secret.

We chatted about nothing until the waiter brought our bottle of wine. He opened it at the table, poured me a splash, and then nodded for me to sample it.

What I knew about wine you could fit in a thimble, but I’d seen what people did on TV. I lifted the glass, swirled the dark red liquid, then sniffed.

Smelled like wine.

You were watching me with that suppressed grin on your face. I wanted to see a real grin, so I downed the liquid like a shot of whiskey.

You laughed.

The twenty-something server said, “Uh, so is it okay?”

Which made us both laugh harder.

I’d have to tip well, but it was worth it.

He poured us each a glass and, after taking our dinner orders, scurried away.

“You’re so refined,” you said.

“I know, right? Me’n you got some celebratin’ to do.”

Your giggle had me wishing I hadn’t promised dancing. The sooner I could take you home, the better.

I held my glass over the table. “To us.”

You clinked—“To us”—and sipped.

The wine really was exceptional. I'd texted Paul from the hospital and asked him to look at the wine list and tell me what to order. I'd have to thank him later.

"So," I said, "do you want to go first, or shall I?"

"You first."

"Dr. Burman is retiring."

I can still see the expression on your face morphing from amused and eager to something else entirely. "I take it you already know who's replacing him."

"They told me today."

I thought you'd be happy.

I don't know why I thought that. In retrospect, your reaction was predictable.

You sat back. "Head of the department. Congratulations." Your tone was flat.

I set my glass down maybe a little too hard. "What's wrong?"

You adjusted your napkin in your lap. You didn't look at me.

"This is what I've been working for," I said.

"I know."

"So what's the problem?"

Finally, you met my eyes. "You and I both know what this means. Longer hours, more time at the hospital, more time away from home."

"I can finally make the changes I've been suggesting for years. I can upgrade our equipment, improve our processes, make us more efficient. We can serve more—"

"Don't worry." For an instant, I imagined you pushing back and walking away. But you didn't. You leaned forward, voice low and humming with disdain. "I know how important you are. How important your job is."

"I'm the only man I know who gets in trouble for getting a promotion." Irritation, anger, defensiveness. They swelled like an injury, filled with poison. Poison that needed out. "This means more prestige. That's important to you, isn't it? All your fancy friends will be so impressed." I don't know where the words came from. I didn't even know I felt them until they came out of my mouth. "This means more money for you to donate and decorate and...whatever else you do."

"You think I care about that?" Your voice, high and shrill, had the couple at the next table turning our direction. You leaned close. "We don't need more money, Daniel. Our kids need their father. I need my husband."

"You don't need me. You don't need me for anything. You have my money to pay for the house. You have Paul when you need help with the kids."

Paul, my best friend, had stepped in more than once when I couldn't be with my family. Every time, a little more jealousy trickled through my veins like drugs in an IV.

"Thank God for Paul. If not for him—"

"Yeah, I know how wonderful he is. I know all about perfect Paul."

You slouched in your chair and covered your face with your hands.

And I felt about two inches tall.

I was angry that you weren't happy for me. But you didn't deserve the things I'd said. If Paul was too much in our lives, it was my fault, not yours. I'd started it. I'd asked him to keep an eye out for you and the kids more than once. I'd created his place in our family by not being available when you needed me.

If I sometimes saw a glimmer in my best friend's eyes, something more than friendship for you, I couldn't blame you for that. It wasn't your fault Paul saw you for what you were—and still are. A gorgeous, generous, gentle soul. A soul I'd neglected and taken advantage of for most of our twenty years together.

Did I realize all that at dinner? Probably not. I'm being

kinder to myself in hindsight than I deserve. Either way, any confession or apology I would have made was frozen in my mouth when you dropped your hands and looked up.

"I'm going back to work," you said. "That's my news. Not that you asked. Not that you cared."

To my credit, I didn't say what I was thinking. Though why you would even consider it was beyond me. You had the house to take care of, the kids to look after, all your charity work. And we didn't need the money.

We'd managed our lives with a carefully planned division of labor. I made the money, you took care of everything else. I didn't interfere with your part, and you didn't interfere with mine.

Except now, it seemed you'd decided to dip your toe into my end of the pool.

You watched me, eyes narrowed, frown in place. I'd hardly noticed the lines like parentheses around your mouth, but they were deep now as if etched there by years of discontentment.

Finally, I managed a simple, "Why?"

"Because I want to. Because the kids don't need me like they used to. Zoë's busy with school and all her activities. Jeremy's hardly ever home anymore, always off with his friends, doing his own thing."

"But you have all your charities."

"Two, Daniel. I volunteer with two charities. A couple of meetings a month. They're not that time-consuming."

I'd thought it was more—more charities, more time-consuming, more fulfilling—but I didn't tell you that.

I should have known. I should have paid better attention.

"An old friend called and asked if I'd be interested in doing some work for her agency in Chicago, and I—"

"Chicago?" The wine swirled in my gut, made my insides

churn. Were you leaving me? Was this your way of telling me you were moving out, taking the kids?

Were you that unhappy?

"I'll work from home," you clarified. "Part-time."

I sat back, relief flowing through me. But what did it say that I'd thought it? Deep down, I knew how unhappy you were. Deep down, I dreaded the day you would give up on our marriage.

You studied me across the table as if trying to discern my thoughts. I was thankful you couldn't read my insecurity and fear.

I should have confessed it all that day, how sorry I was, how wrong I'd been, how I'd been seeking worth in my job. Not that you didn't already know that last part.

I'll admit it. I felt more like a guest at our dinner table than a member of the family. I feared answering our kids' requests, knowing most of the time I got the answers wrong. More often than not, I responded with, "I don't know. Ask your mother."

You didn't need me.

Maybe that was the root of all of it. You didn't need me. The kids didn't need me. They did just fine on their own.

My patients needed me.

Now, my department needed me.

"How are you going to juggle it?" I asked. "Work and taking care of our home."

You huffed. "I thought my husband would support me, even help out."

"It's not that I'm against you going back to work eventually, but with the kids still in school, maybe now's not the time. It feels like we should talk about it."

"Like we talked about your promotion?"

"I've been talking about that for years. You knew I wanted to head the ER."

"Today, when they told you the promotion was yours, I assume you told them you'd need to go home and discuss it with your wife, right? Is that what this"—you flicked your hand at our table—"is all about? So we can discuss it?"

I sipped my wine, but it soured in my mouth. Obviously, I'd accepted the position.

"I didn't think so."

"I thought you'd be happy for me."

You leaned forward and lowered your voice. I'll never forget the words you said. "I accepted my job despite the fact that I knew you wouldn't be happy for me."

"What's that supposed to mean?"

"I am speaking English. It's not so complex that the brilliant Daniel Wright can't figure it out." Fury hummed in your words like power in a wire.

I wanted to fix it, Cammie. I did. I wanted to pull us back from that dangerous place. But I didn't know how. "I'm happy that you were given the opportunity. Happy to see you use your talents. I'm just saying—"

"That my dreams can wait. That my job is to make your life easier."

"No, but—"

"That what matters to me is secondary to what matters to you."

"I didn't say that."

"Then what are you saying?"

What was I saying? I prayed for wisdom, but God was silent.

The waiter approached with our salads. Oblivious to the tension, he set the plates in front of us. We both declined the cracked pepper and the Parmesan cheese, and he left us alone again.

I took a few bites of my Caesar. Crisp lettuce, creamy dressing, but the combination, mixed with wine and fear, didn't settle well. I snatched a roll from the basket, buttered it, and took a bite.

You didn't eat.

I set my bread down. "I didn't know you wanted to go back to work."

The expression on your face...

I could have handled anger or frustration. Even disdain, which I'd seen often enough. But what I saw there was a deep, profound sadness.

"How could you have? Despite the fact that I've been talking about it for years, you don't hear me. You don't see me."

"I always thought you'd wait until after the kids were in college."

"When this opportunity came up, I realized how much I missed it. How much I missed...mattering."

"You matter." How could you doubt it? "To Zoë and Jeremy and me, you matter."

"I know that." You picked at your salad, mostly rearranging the bits of lettuce and croutons. "When they graduate, they're going to leave me, and I'll be all alone."

"You'll have me."

"Will I?" When you looked up, the look on your face—all my own fear reflected back at me—broke my heart. "You'll have the hospital. Your patients, your department. I'll have nothing."

Those weren't the last words you and I spoke that evening, but they're the ones that resonated after I paid the check and drove home, neither of us in the mood to dance. Those words lingered that night when you left me in front of the TV and went to bed alone.

Those words resonate in my heart still. You believed our marriage was nothing.

I'd allowed you to believe that.

No matter what I said to you, my actions told the truth. You didn't have me. The kids didn't have me. My work had me, and I wasn't about to let it go.

Replaying that night, I see all my sins, all the lies I let myself believe. If I could do it all again, I'd do it differently. But there won't be a second chance for me. Or for our family. As little as it means, it'll always be true...

Yours always,

Daniel

CHAPTER FORTY

AFTER HIS SHOWER THAT AFTERNOON, Jeremy had crawled into bed and fallen asleep.

Zoë still wasn't back. Obviously, she was taking her time getting cleaned up.

Camilla relished the time alone. She had a plan now. When Jeremy was released, they'd go to a safe house until he was well enough to fly—Monday, the doctors had told her. If Campos wasn't found by then, they'd go into witness protection.

They'd have to leave everything they'd brought with them from St. Louis and everything they'd accumulated since then. Most of the stuff didn't matter to her. But Daniel's class ring, the painting she'd done of him and Jeremy, the rest of her artwork... Not to mention all the kids' mementos of him and of their lives.

All gone.

Worth it to secure their safety, but still, the weight of loss pressed down on her. How could they be here again? Why hadn't the government protected them before and after the trial? Now, *now* they were worth protecting. Now that it was too late for Daniel. Now that Zoë was in college, Jeremy close enough. This would have been much easier four years earlier.

She shook off the regret. There was no going back. Jeremy was alive. Zoë was safe. And Camilla would do anything to keep her family together. If that meant starting over—again—then that was what they'd do. They'd survive this.

No matter where they went, God would be there. He'd pull them through.

Choosing to quiet the maudlin thoughts, she checked her emails, trying to figure out how she was going to get all her projects completed on time after nearly two weeks away. She'd already been over-scheduled. If they had to go into witness protection, at least she wouldn't have to catch up on work.

A very, very thin silver lining.

Her phone rang. She grabbed it and saw Zoë's name. She kept her voice low so as not to wake Jeremy. "Hey, sweetie."

"Ma'am? Hello?" A man's voice, high-pitched with worry.

She stepped out of the room. "Who is this? Where's my daughter?"

"I think she fell or something. She's unconscious."

"What do you mean? Where are you?" Camilla hurried toward the ward's exit.

The man said, "I'm in the second-floor Ronald McDonald room. I just came in, and she was lying here. Her phone was unlocked, and I found the number for Mom."

"You're in a hospital!" She shouted the words. "Get help!"

"Oh. Right."

Camilla was almost to the ward's exit. She needed security. Agent Siple was with...

"There should be a woman in a suit outside the door. Get her. She can help you."

"There was nobody," the man said. "Just—"

"Look again!" Camilla burst into the corridor half expecting to see Siple, but her FBI protector wasn't at this door, either.

Camilla sprinted down the hall. Had Campos gotten

to Zoë?

She needed to call Falk. She would, as soon as she knew what was going on.

She careened around a corner, almost crashing into someone. She pushed past him. Finally, she saw the entrance to the Ronald McDonald room. No FBI agent.

Camilla glanced at her phone. The man had disconnected. Maybe Siple was tending Zoë right now. Maybe all was well. She reached the door, fumbled for the card that would unlock it, which hung from the lanyard around her neck. Before she got it out, the door opened. A man was there and stepped out of her way. She barely glanced at his face.

When she got into the room, Zoë wasn't there.

The man handed her a cell phone. Zoë's cell phone. Camilla recognized the blue-and-purple paisley case.

The man said, "Talk."

The door closed behind him, and he stood in front of it, blocking her exit.

Every nerve felt strung tight. Something was very wrong, but her brain couldn't process what was happening. "Where's my daughter?" Maybe Zoë was in the bathroom. Maybe she was better. Camilla walked down the hallway toward the shower, looking at the cell phone. A call was in progress.

Whatever was happening...

She reached the bathroom door. It was open. The lingering scent of her daughter's favorite body wash hung in the air with the moisture from the shower. Drops of water dotted the tile. A towel had been dropped onto the floor beside the clothes Zoë had been wearing. Not her shoes, though. They were gone. Her overnight bag was open on the long counter.

This was all wrong. That man...

She turned. The man was standing in the bathroom doorway. He nodded to Zoë's phone. "Talk."

Hands trembling, she lifted the phone to her ear. "Where's my daughter?"

"Safe, for now." The voice was deep. The three words had her knees buckling.

The guy in front of her grabbed her and kept her from falling.

She shoved him away.

He stepped back and gestured toward the exit.

She spoke into the phone. "What do you want?"

"You will turn off your phone and your daughter's and hide them in one of the cabinets. Then, you will take the phone my friend has for you. You won't tell anyone anything. You won't try to signal anyone. You'll do exactly what I say, and maybe, if you do, your pretty little girl will survive this. We will talk again when you've done it." The line went dead.

Camilla stared at the two cell phones in her hand. Links to her loved ones. Links to help.

The man walked back to the front room and waited by the exit while she powered off her phone and Zoë's and hid them in the back of a cabinet below the coffee machine. When she turned, he held out another phone. Again, a call was in progress.

She looked more closely at him. White, about five-nine, clean-shaven, early twenties. Brown eyes, brown hair. Narrow face and strong chin. She could draw his likeness if she ever got the chance.

His smile was condescending. Apparently, he wasn't worried.

She took the phone and lifted it to her ear. "Now what?"

"You and my friend will go for a walk. You'll keep the connection open. If you try to warn anyone, he will see, and your daughter will die. If you break this connection, your daughter will die. If you don't follow my instructions, your daughter will die."

For days she'd worried her son would die. Now...Zoë.

Her sweet, sweet girl.

Panic welled up, but she forced it back down. This mountain was too steep, too treacherous, but she would climb. She had no choice but to climb.

She followed the man out of the room. Silently, they rode the escalator, then crossed the sky bridge into the adjoining hospital.

They were just passing the cafeteria when she caught sight of Bachir coming out. He saw her and smiled. He must've seen something in her face, because the expression faded.

His head tilted to the side.

She averted her gaze. She didn't need rescue. She needed Zoë. She'd go wherever, do whatever, to protect her daughter.

Bachir turned away, probably assuming she was being rude.

Camilla and her escort wound through another maze of corridors. They reached the exterior door and stepped into the cold. Snowflakes swirled in the wind and settled, dusting the black asphalt in a layer of powder.

The man led her to the driver's side of a black SUV. "Get in."

She did as he said.

He leaned across her, and she pressed against the seat to avoid his touch as he dropped the keys into the center console. As he backed out of the car, he said, "Start it."

She pressed the ignition, and the engine roared to life.

Through the speakers, a man said, "You're in the SUV. Good."

She jumped at the sound of Campos's voice. It had to be him, the brother of the man Daniel had sent to prison.

The man who'd tried to kill Jeremy.

She turned down the volume, then set the cell phone on the console near the keys.

"Do you see the map?" Campos asked.

The car had a navigation system. "I see it."

The guy standing at her side slammed the door and walked away.

He wasn't getting in? They were leaving her alone?

"Follow the directions exactly," Campos said. "There is a camera mounted. Do you see it?"

A tiny black something was attached with Velcro on the top of the dashboard. "I see it."

"Wave to me, so I know."

She lifted a trembling hand toward the camera.

"You can do better than that. Give me a good wave."

She did, shifting her hand back and forth as if she'd just spotted a good friend across the room.

"There it is," he said. "Nice to see you up close, Camilla."

She swallowed at the use of her name.

"I can see everything you do. It is a fisheye lens, so I can see all of you—your face, your hands. If you try to get anyone's attention, I will see you. If you get out of the car, I will see you. This protects us both. If we get disconnected, then you will pull over, put your hands on the steering wheel, and wait for me to call you back. That way, I'll know you're doing nothing wrong. You understand?"

"Yes."

"Good. Drive."

She drove away from the hospital, from Jeremy. "Why are you doing this?"

"Your husband evaded me once. He will not do so again."

"My husband is dead." She was surprised by the confidence in her tone. "Your man killed him four years ago."

"I saw him with my own eyes. Did you know he was alive? Or did he lie to you too?" Robert Campos sounded reasonable and intelligent. She'd expected...something else. As Falk had said, he looked like a thug. But he didn't speak like a thug. He had a normal, midwestern accent. He didn't use slang or foul language. He seemed...educated.

The FBI had been searching for him for months, and he'd never been caught. He was too clever to get caught.

"My husband is dead," Camilla said. "The man in that photo is—"

"It's him."

"Even the FBI thinks—"

"You think they'd tell you the truth?" The volume in Campos's voice rose, sending a jolt of fresh fear down her spine. "They cannot be trusted. *You* cannot be trusted."

"And you can? I want to talk to my daughter."

She expected him to tell her no, but only silence followed.

Camilla followed the map through downtown Salt Lake City.

Cars all around, but she couldn't signal any of them. She couldn't do anything that would risk Zoë's life. It was just after four thirty. She imagined mothers all over the city carting their kids home from after-school activities. Fathers leaving offices. Children huddled over homework. Little ones having snowball fights and building snowmen and sledding.

Camilla didn't care about any of that. She didn't care if anything was ever *normal* again. She only wanted her daughter back, safe and sound. She'd give anything, give her life, her future, to protect Zoë. And Jeremy, too. Thank God he was safe in the hospital. He was probably awake and wondering where she was. Would he contact the FBI? She should have given him Agent Falk's number, not that they could do anything now. But at least Falk would know what was going on. *Lord, help.* There were no words. But God knew. He saw her. He was with her even now.

Campos was so quiet that she worried that she'd lost the

connection. She glanced at the phone's screen and saw that he was still connected.

She kept her words steady when she said, "I would like to talk to my daughter, please."

"When you are on the highway," he said, "I will let you."

"Thank you." Her baby was still alive. Of course she was. She had to be. Camilla couldn't face a world without her children.

She followed the directions and turned onto I-15 South. "I'm on the highway now."

A moment later, he said, "Talk to your daughter."

"Zoë?" Her heart raced. "Baby, are you okay?"

"Mom? I'm scared." The words were teary and terrified.

"Zoë!" Tears streamed down her face. "Are you all right? Did he—?"

"Now you have talked to her."

Not enough, though. "Please, don't hurt her. She didn't... She was only a child then. Don't blame her for what Daniel did."

"I don't want to hurt her, Camilla. So do what I say."

"I will. I promise." Everything in her wanted to beg for her daughter's life, to plead. She remembered the story Falk had told her about Campos, about how he'd killed his rival's entire family before shooting the man himself. Campos was a cold-blooded murderer. Though she knew the words would have no effect, she said, "Please don't hurt my little girl."

"We will see."

He said nothing more, and neither did she. At the bottom of the navigation screen, she saw that her expected time of arrival wasn't for another hour. She couldn't see where she was going and didn't want to touch the screen and screw it up. What did it matter, anyway? She would go where this man told her to go and do what he said. She would do whatever it took to save Zoë.

CHAPTER FORTY-ONE

NEARLY AN HOUR HAD PASSED since Camilla left the hospital. The gray afternoon light was fading, and she checked to be sure the headlights were on. She'd followed the directions on the screen, but she wasn't making progress as quickly as the navigation system seemed to think she would. Apparently, the map didn't realize it was snowing.

More than snowing now. She was driving through a blizzard. She hadn't checked the weather app in days and didn't have any idea when the snow would stop. Not soon, if her guess was correct.

Add the weather to the normal rush-hour chaos, and she'd been in stop-and-go traffic on I-15 for many of the twenty miles she'd been on the interstate.

She finally exited on a street called Thanksgiving Way.

Thanksgiving.

She thought of things to be thankful for. The time she'd had with Daniel before his death.

The four years she'd had with Zoë and Jeremy since.

Jeremy's miraculous survival and recovery.

But it wasn't enough. She wanted more. She wanted to see

her children marry. She wanted to rock her grandchildren. She wanted to live in freedom, in peace.

More than all of that, she wanted Zoë to get out of this alive.

Swallowing a sob, she prayed aloud, not caring what Campos thought of it. "Thank You, Lord, for delivering us. Thank You for your protection. I trust You."

Through the car's speaker, she heard, "God can't help you now."

It was the first time Campos had spoken in thirty minutes, and his deep voice sent a charge of fury through her. How dare he?

He laughed, the sound rich and filled with scorn. "You look upset, Camilla. Something I said?"

She swiped at angry tears and tamped down the anger she wanted to hurl his way. When she'd pulled herself together, she said, "You don't know my God."

"Your God didn't protect your husband."

"You seem to think He did."

Silence.

"You have this bizarre idea that Daniel is still alive, so maybe God did protect him from you. Maybe He'll protect us all."

"Don't waste your time worrying about God," Campos said. "I'm the one you should be worried about. God is irrelevant."

She thought of the Psalms, of David's cries for help, appealing to God to protect His own name. She wished she knew some of those verses, but she understood the sense of them. *Save us, Lord, for our sake and for the sake of Your glory. We are Your children. Protect us. Vindicate us. Be magnified in this situation. Don't let this...this blasphemer, this evil, violent man, win.*

A wave of peace washed over her. Whatever happened,

God was here. Whether He saved them or not, she would worship Him.

She rounded a corner, and the SUV fishtailed on the slick road. She managed to straighten it out, barely.

"Be careful." Campos's words were harsh. "If you wreck the car, my plans will be ruined. I'll have no reason to keep your daughter alive."

"I'm doing my best," she snapped. "In case you haven't noticed, it's a blizzard out here."

There was a long pause before he said, "Take your time. Just don't wreck."

He needed her there...wherever *there* was. Why, she had no idea. What he hoped to accomplish, she couldn't possibly understand.

The longer she drove, the more sparse the cars and buildings became. She'd passed a few neighborhoods and even a golf course a while back, but now it seemed she was driving into nowhere. The darkness that had fallen didn't help that feeling.

An inch or more of snow had accumulated on the road. Fortunately, the SUV was big and heavy, and except that one time, the tires held.

Behind her were a single car's headlights, but it was a hundred yards back at least. Aside from the occasional vehicle coming toward her, she was alone. Even the streetlights had faded in the rearview mirror. She watched the snow swirl in the beam of her headlights and lift over the SUV's roof.

Suddenly, a decade slipped away. Her kids were eight and four, and the family was making the long drive from St. Louis to Colorado to go skiing. Daniel was driving. Camilla was trying to calm Jeremy in the back seat, who was getting stir-crazy after sitting in his booster all day long. They'd known snow was coming, but the weathermen had predicted it would start later that night. When the blizzard hit around four in the afternoon, they were in the middle of Kansas with no place to stop for miles.

Daniel hadn't worried at first. He knew how to navigate snowy roads. As time passed and snow accumulated, Camilla's anxiety rose. Jeremy picked up on her worry and became even fussier until he was outright bawling to get out of the car.

Daniel's calm disintegrated. Fists clenched on the steering wheel, he said in his scary Dad voice, "Jeremy, stop." When their son quieted his crying to sniffles, Daniel said, "Cammie, look for a place to shelter. A restaurant, a gas station, anything. We've got to get off the road."

Daniel's sudden worry fueled her fear. A few minutes later, she spotted a blue sign telling them about the restaurants off the next exit. Daniel stopped at the first one he came to, a Kentucky Fried Chicken.

Cranky, tired, irritable, they went inside and ate. While they did, the snow waned. The hotel where they'd planned to stay was only another thirty miles or so, and they could make it, but the thought of getting back in the car didn't appeal to any of them.

The SUV was parked at the edge of the parking lot in front of what was probably a grassy area beneath all that snow. After dinner, Daniel jogged ahead to unlock the doors, or so she thought. She and the kids were almost there when the first snowball flew and bounced off Zoë's behind. She turned, ready to be angry, but saw her daddy's wide smile. She made a snowball of her own and hurled it. Daniel angled into its path so she wouldn't miss. "Oh." He held his hands to his chest. "You got me."

Jeremy kneeled down in the snow and made his own snowball, which flew seconds later. For a four-year-old, he had a great arm.

Cammie had been cold and tired and eager to get to the

hotel and get the kids to bed. "Daniel, we really need to—" Her words were cut off by a snowball to the head.

And that was it. She joined the fray, and within minutes, they were having what would forever be known as the Epic Wright Snowball Fight. For years after, debate continued about who'd won and who'd lost.

Truth was, they'd all won.

Camilla glanced at the navigation system. Her time of arrival had adjusted to her speed. She should be wherever she was going in another twenty minutes.

She was distancing herself from civilization. What if she lost cell service? What if she already had? "Are you still there?"

"You're getting close," he said.

His voice through the speakers comforted her. He was her only link to Zoë. "How's my daughter?"

"Eager for you to get here." She picked up a touch of humanity in his voice. As if, beneath the violence and hatred, he cared that he'd kidnapped an innocent child.

Young woman, Camilla reminded herself, but to her, Zoë was still a child. *Her* child to protect and comfort.

"Can I talk to her again?"

"Just drive." The compassion she'd heard—or maybe imagined—was gone.

She glanced in the rearview mirror. She was driving very carefully. The car behind her was going just as slowly. It hadn't closed the distance at all.

Maybe... maybe somebody had seen her leave. Maybe she was being followed. Maybe Falk was tracking her even now.

But how could that have happened? Siple hadn't been there to sound the alarm. What had Campos done to the FBI agent? Had she lost her life trying to protect Zoë? Camilla thought back to the state of the Ronald McDonald room. Nothing had been out of place. There'd been no indication that a fight had taken place. Even the bathroom had seemed normal. How could Campos have gotten Zoë out of the hospital without being seen? What had he done with Siple?

She almost asked. But she didn't want to know. She didn't want to know that the pretty young FBI agent had tried to protect Zoë with her life—and had failed. She didn't want to think about how Campos had forced her daughter out of the hospital, past doctors, nurses, family, and security. Had she been drugged? Unconscious? Threatened?

Camilla didn't want to know. Not yet. When she held her daughter in her arms, then she'd learn the details. Right now, she had to focus.

Thoughts demanded her attention, thoughts she'd been trying to keep at bay since she'd climbed in the car. Longer than that—since Daniel had witnessed that murder. If Daniel were here, would he think it had been worth it? If he'd known what would happen—to Jeremy and Zoë and herself—would he have still testified? He'd been willing to risk his own life to put Francis Campos away. But had he truly understood how he'd also risked theirs?

She didn't think so. She thought, if Daniel were sitting beside her right now, that he'd be sorry he'd done it. He'd be begging her forgiveness.

And what would she say to him? That she forgave him? Did he need her forgiveness? Maybe.

Maybe not.

The man on the other side of her telephone, Robert Campos, was a brutal murderer. Just like his brother. If Francis Campos had gotten away with murder in the hospital in St. Louis, there'd have been more. More murders, more death. Armed robbery, drug smuggling, human trafficking. How many people would have died if Daniel had chosen his family over doing what was right?

Even if only one person was saved by Daniel's sacrifice, was it worth it?

During those months in the safe house, Daniel had quoted Edmund Burke more than once—*the only thing necessary for the triumph of evil is for good men to do nothing.*

Daniel had refused to do nothing.

He'd refused to let evil triumph. Maybe his sacrifice hadn't saved millions. That had never been the point for Daniel.

She thought back to the night Daniel had come home and told her what he'd seen. He'd already called the police, already identified Francis Campos as the killer. They were already packing their bags, preparing to go to the safe house. The kids, not entirely sure what was going on, were packing in their own rooms.

Camilla had looked around at the house she'd loved, the decor she'd carefully chosen to make the space their home. "Will we ever come back?" she'd asked.

Daniel had paused on his side of the bed and regarded her over their open suitcases. "I don't know."

She'd left her clothes and gone to her nightstand, where her favorite photos were displayed.

Daniel had joined her, wrapping his arms around her from behind, and looked over her shoulder at their framed wedding photo. Her in her puffy white dress, him in his black tux. They were on the dance floor, alone. The customary first dance. He'd just spun her, then pulled her close—not to hold her but because she'd nearly tripped in her too-high heels.

Her head was tipped back. His gaze was on her. They were both laughing.

"I love that picture," he said. "You're so beautiful. So happy."

She'd tried to blink back the tears, but they fell anyway.

"I know it's hard," he said. "I know it's not what you want."

"I love our lives here."

She leaned back against him. "Do you have to...?" She'd tossed the question over her shoulder in hopes that he'd consider, just consider, not testifying.

He turned her to face him, his expression as serious as she'd ever seen it. "When the Nazis were hauling away Jews, most of the Germans did nothing. Most just closed their doors. Their eyes. Their hearts. They did it to protect their families. Even after the rumors were rampant. Even after they knew, *they knew*, what would happen to their Jewish friends, neighbors, and business associates, they did nothing."

"This isn't Nazi Germany, Daniel. This isn't—"

"I will not stand by and let a murderer walk free. I will not." He backed away. His brown eyes, usually so tender, hardened. "And I know, if you were in the same position, you wouldn't either. We have a God, and He is our foundation." He lifted his arms to indicate the room, the house. The life. "This is not our security, Camilla. I'm not your security, and you're not mine. We have a God, and He is good. And this is what He asks of us. Are you going to turn your back on Him? Would you choose to cling to your stuff"—he pointed to the photograph—"your trinkets?"

"That's not a trinket. It's—"

"A photograph reminding us of who we are. But the photograph is meaningless. The marriage, the family, the faith—those are the things that matter." He stepped near, and she rested her cheek against his chest, heard his heartbeat. His beautiful, steady heartbeat. "We can do this. You and me, Camilla. We've got this. Whatever happens."

At that moment, Camilla had been with him. She'd understood his desire to do the right thing, despite the risks. But, as time went on, as the trial neared, fear had taken over.

Fear and...greed.

She'd wanted her house, her friends, her life. She'd wanted to cling to what they'd had rather than dive blindly into the unknown. She'd become focused on the security of her home, her job, their friends and family... And she'd forgotten her faith.

She'd hurled angry words at her husband, words that had, ultimately, led to his death.

What she wouldn't do to have those words back. To have her husband back.

Now, as she drove toward this uncertain future, possibly her own death, she understood the courage Daniel had had four years earlier. Only Daniel hadn't risked his life to save his daughter. He'd risked it to save strangers.

Everyone Daniel had saved by testifying that day... They were all somebody's daughter or son or parent or sibling or spouse. They all mattered.

If only Daniel were here. If only she could tell him how wrong she'd been. If only they'd relocated together all those years ago, they'd have built a good life because they'd have had each other. The house, the stuff... None of it mattered.

Lord, forgive me for my foolishness and my fear. Help me see Daniel's sacrifice through Your eyes. You never promised Your followers that life would be easy, only that You would be with us. Help me be wise now. Help me be courageous.

Help me save my daughter.

CHAPTER FORTY-TWO

DEAR CAMILLA,

The next time I saw Alfredo, I'd been heading the department for a few months. It'd been a smooth transition at work, less so at home. Your new job required more hours than you'd thought it would. To your credit, despite the time you spent in front of your computer, you managed the household as well as you ever had. The issue came when you needed to go to Chicago for a few days and expected me to take time off work.

Of course, they needed me at the hospital. If there'd been another way, I'd have found it.

Instead, the kids stayed with your parents.

You weren't happy, but then, when were you ever those days? Maybe with the kids, maybe with your friends, maybe with your work, but never with me.

If home had been a less hostile environment, I'd have wanted to spend more time there.

Or so I tell myself now.

The night I saw Alfredo, I should have been at home. My shift had ended hours before, but thanks to an eruption of gang violence, the ER was overrun. I stayed to help out and ended up treating a gunshot victim, who I shuffled up to surgery.

When I walked toward the group that had brought in my patient, Alfredo was the first to stand.

The small crowd of people around him—muscled and tattooed men and teenage boys, skinny girls wearing too much makeup and too little clothing—followed his lead.

He was nineteen or twenty at that point, a natural leader. I approached him, hand outstretched. "Alfredo, it's good to see you. I was sorry to hear about your grandfather's passing."

Grief crossed his features, gone before I could be sure. When I'd heard Diego Punta lost his battle with cancer, I'd sent a card to the address we had for the old man. I didn't know if Alfredo got it.

A few of the others in the room looked at him with raised eyebrows, seeming to wait for the tough guy to say something tender.

Alfredo only scoffed. "Don't matter."

A girl of maybe seventeen stood beside him, a dark-haired baby in her arms. "How is Robbie? Is he going to be okay?"

I shifted my attention to her, grateful to have someone to focus on besides Alfredo. "Is his family here?"

"I'm his sister. Mama's on her way."

The baby angled for Alfredo. "Papa, papa."

The girl shifted the child into his arms, and the little boy hugged Alfredo's tattooed neck.

Papa?

I wanted to ask, but the worry in the girl's expression kept me focused.

I itched to put my hand on her shoulder, not that she needed any more weight there. Seemed the weight of the world was already pressing down on her. "He's been sent up for surgery. They're doing everything they can." I didn't add that the prognosis wasn't good. I didn't add that she'd likely be burying her brother in the days to come. God could do a miracle, and I prayed He would. "Somebody will be by to let you know how it went, but it'll be a few hours." I told her where she could wait and hoped this whole crowd wouldn't wait with her. The last thing the other families of surgical patients needed were these rough-looking characters crowding them out. But the hospital was there to serve the whole community, even the scariest sorts.

When Alfredo held the baby against his shoulder and pulled the young woman close, I got a glimpse of the tattoos covering his arm. A quick count told me there were nine snakes.

Nine kills.

Can you imagine that, Cammie? A twenty-year-old kid had killed nine times? I was past pretending I didn't know what the tattoos meant. I knew. He was a murderer. He was also God's creation. It was an effort to see him that way.

I wanted to pull him aside and ask about the baby. See how he was doing. See if I could help. But I chickened out. Despite the tenderness he showed the baby and his mother, Alfredo exuded anger. Gone was the boy sporting a man's tattoos, the kid who'd come in frightened and teary a few years before. Gone was the concerned young man who'd insisted his *abuelo* go to the hospital and then held the old man's hand through the tests and, ultimately, the cancer diagnosis. The Alfredo I faced now looked at me with such coldness, such hatred, I wondered if that boy was still in there at all or if the violence and anger had killed him off completely.

I was afraid of him. I was afraid of the evil that had engulfed him. And frankly, I knew pulling him aside would do no good. He was surrounded by his people. He would do nothing to risk his standing in his gang.

If the child in his arms hadn't changed him, nothing I said would.

How could I be in the presence of a murderer, of a gang of murderers, and then go home to you? Wickedness doesn't wash off in the shower like sweat from the day.

You spent your life creating beauty while I patched up evil.

I longed for you that day, Cammie. I longed to go home and wrap you in my arms and never let go. But you were in Chicago, building a life without me.

I'd never felt more alone. My fault, I know.

Yours always,

Daniel

CHAPTER FORTY-THREE

CAMILLA TOOK A STEEP TURN. Beneath the SUV's tires, the road felt rougher. It might have been dirt, though it was hard to tell with the snow covering the surface. She inched forward slowly, wishing she could see farther than her high beams allowed.

In the rearview mirror, she saw the car that had been following her for miles and miles pass by. It had never been a rescuer. She knew that. Still, the sight stabbed as her last link to help drove by without a care in the world.

She felt more than saw that her SUV was moving upward. There was a mountain or two—maybe they'd call it a range—between Salt Lake City and her sister's home near Tooele. When they drove out to Marcy's, they drove north of the mountains, south of the great lake for which the city was named. This time, she'd headed south. And now she was driving into those mountains.

And then it occurred to her... The boys' accident had been near here, hadn't it? Okay, maybe not *near,* per se, but they'd been driving south of Tooele and east of the highway. Hadn't that police detective told her there'd been a ridge on one side of the road? A ridge could only mean a mountain.

The boys hadn't been on a dirt road, though.

Why even try to figure it out? All she had were the tiny map on the screen and her own sense of direction—on a dark and snowy night. She navigated the switchbacks, winding ever higher. Her anxiety ramped with each turn of the wheels beneath her. She had no idea what to expect. Where was Campos hiding out? Was Zoë safe? Was she warm? Was she injured or sick?

"The next road is hard to see." Campos's voice startled her, and she jerked the wheel. "Be careful!" he snapped. "I don't want to wait for you if you have to walk in this."

"Your concern for my well-being is touching."

She drove another mile and navigated the SUV around a bend and stopped. This was where the navigation ended. The headlights illuminated the road, which continued up a slope. Everything else was dark.

"Shut off the car and walk to your right," Campos said.

She looked that direction but saw nothing. "Where am I going?"

"Now."

When she killed the engine, the headlights stayed on. She pulled in a deep breath and prayed for courage and help and safety. And wisdom. With that thought, she snatched the phone and the SUV's keys and slid them into her jeans pocket. Maybe he wouldn't think to check.

She stepped out of the car. It was freezing, and she didn't have a coat. She wore only jeans, a T-shirt, and a zipper sweatshirt. Had Zoë been out in the elements all this time? Her coat was in Jeremy's room. Jeans, a sweater, her canvas shoes and thin socks—those wouldn't keep her warm.

Camilla tried to ignore the chill and the flakes blowing in

the storm as she walked around the back of the SUV. Her tennis shoes kicked up the featherlight snow. She took her time, careful of where she was stepping.

Behind her, the SUV's high beams clicked off. She froze to wait for her eyes to adjust. She made out a faint glow. It drew her forward. The outline of a hillside loomed ahead, though the ground was flat beneath her. She crossed ten yards, twenty, and reached the rocky face. The glow was coming from a cave. The opening was low, not as high as she was tall, and she couldn't see inside, couldn't see what awaited her.

"You made it."

She gasped and spun, hand over her heart. There, hidden in the shadows, she barely made out the outline of a man. A giant of a man.

"Go on in," he said.

Everything in her trembled at the sight of him, the sound of his voice so close. And the sound of...nothing else. It was too quiet. No distant car engines. No skittering animals. Even the wind seemed to have lost its breath.

She had the sudden impulse to run, to race back to the SUV and take off as fast as she could.

The last thing she wanted in the world was to be there. To go into a cave in the middle of nowhere with a murderer.

She thought of Zoë, and she ducked down and passed through the cave opening.

It wasn't a very big space—maybe eleven feet deep, seven feet wide. The arched stone ceiling was high enough that she could stand upright. Daniel could have, too. In the center of the space, a kerosene heater glowed, warming it.

There was nobody there.

She spun to the cave opening, where Robert Campos's over-large body blocked the exit. "Where's Zoë?"

Campos's teeth glowed in the reflection of the heater's

flames, some expression between a smile and a smirk. "She didn't make it."

What? What did he mean? It couldn't be...

She didn't make it.

Camilla's knees hit the stone floor as the words bounced against the cave's walls and reverberated in her brain.

She. Didn't. Make. It.

Zoë. Her sweet, sweet baby.

How could she be gone?

How could the planet continue to spin without Zoë in it? How could the snow fall? How could the wind blow as if nothing had changed?

A wail rose from deep in Camilla's body, drowning those four words in fury and distress. She felt raw pain in her throat, but she didn't care. It didn't matter. Nothing mattered now.

For days she'd been praying for Jeremy's health, his recovery. And now she'd lost her daughter. Her little girl.

Oh, Daniel, I'm sorry. I didn't protect her. After everything, I didn't protect her.

She forced herself to lift her gaze to the evil man who watched. His amused expression...

That was what did it.

That was what stole her last link to sanity. She charged. No plan, no idea what she would do when she reached him, only that she had to hurt him, hurt him like he'd hurt her.

But he blocked her effortlessly, hurled her against the wall. Her head hit the rock, and she fell to the cave's floor.

There should have been pain, enough pain to dull the agony his words had caused. But nothing could soften the blow.

Zoë. Oh, Zoë. Gone.

How could she be gone?

Camilla had done everything, everything he'd asked. She'd

followed all his instructions. She'd obeyed every last one. And still, he'd killed her innocent daughter.

She didn't ask, didn't speak. Campos was a monster, and monsters couldn't explain their monstrous tendencies.

Thank God Jeremy was safe in the hospital. Thank God at least he would survive this. But only if Campos was stopped. Otherwise, what would keep him from going after Jeremy, too?

Oh, God. Please protect my son.

She wanted to trust Him. But He hadn't protected Daniel. He hadn't protected Jeremy and Evan. And now Zoë... She couldn't even think the words. *I can't live through this again, God. I can't.*

God was silent, or maybe His voice couldn't be heard above her own internal wails. Maybe the monster who held her captive in this cave had been right. Maybe God wasn't there or wasn't listening. Maybe it was truly just her and Campos.

She had no idea why he'd lured her here, but she was certain of one thing. She wasn't getting out alive.

CHAPTER FORTY-FOUR

CAMILLA DIDN'T KNOW how long she lay on the cold cave floor before she came back to her senses.

Zoë was gone, but Camilla had to survive. For Jeremy's sake, she had to survive.

But how?

Campos was sitting with his back to the wall near the cave entrance, staring straight ahead. Calm as could be. Except for the quiet hum of the kerosene heater, the cave was silent.

She still had the phone. She shifted so her back was to him and tried to get it out of her pocket.

"What are you doing?"

"My back is cold." Not true. The lantern had warmed the space nicely.

"Turn around."

She stilled. "I'd rather just—"

"I said, turn around!"

Heart pounding, she sat up and pressed her back against the wall. "Better?"

He squinted at her as if trying to solve a puzzle.

She studied him right back. He'd looked like a thug in the

photo Falk had shown her. But he'd let his hair grow out a little, and he'd shaved the thin mustache and beard. Now, he just looked like a guy. Sure, he was huge. What had Falk said? Six-three, three hundred pounds? But there were a lot of perfectly normal men his size. Men who lived lives free of crime and hate. Under different circumstances, Campos could've been a football player, a wrestler. He could've been a normal person with a normal job. Not a gangster. Not a killer.

But he hadn't chosen that route. He'd chosen evil. Murder.

Oh, Zoë.

She squeezed back the tears. She had to get out of there, but with him watching her so closely, there was no chance she'd be able to make a phone call or even send a text. Assuming she could get service on the mountain in this cave.

He'd had service, though. And she had all the way up.

She let her gaze roam the space. Stone all around. Above, wooden beams had been wedged against the ceiling, perhaps to gird it up. For what purpose?

On the opposite end from the entrance, there was a curve and, from her vantage point, she could just make out horizontal and vertical lines. A grate? It was tiny, just large enough for a small person to crawl through. Where did it lead? Was that another way out?

"What is this place?" The sound of her own voice surprised her. But maybe, if she could get Campos talking... What? He'd decide he liked her too much to kill her?

"There's an old copper mine farther up the road," he said. "I think maybe this cave used to be one way to get in it—or maybe an escape if it collapsed."

An escape? Maybe if she—

"You could always try." He followed her gaze. He couldn't see the grate from where he was sitting, but he obviously knew it was there. "But I'd have you before you got your skinny behind through that hole, assuming you could get that grate open. I couldn't."

She turned back to face him. There was no amusement on his face now. No smirk. Just dead calm.

"What do you want from me?"

"You're doing it. You're the bait."

"Bait for what?" she asked. "Who do you expect to—?"

"Your husband, of course." The confidence in his words had her stomach sinking. Because he was so sure Daniel was alive. But he was wrong.

"My husband was murdered four years ago."

Campos's lips twitched, his eyes slits. "I'm trying to figure you out. You're either a very good liar or your husband has deceived you too."

"He's dead!" Her shout reverberated off the cave walls and made her head pound. She pressed her fingertips to her forehead and covered her eyes with her palms until the wave of pain passed.

"I didn't plan to hurt you," he said. "You come at me again, and you'll get a lot worse than a bump on your skull."

She dropped her hands. "Daniel is dead. That man in the photograph... He's a Swedish doctor. Lunden... Elias Lunden. Google him. He looks like Daniel, but he's not."

Campos stood and poked his head out of the cave.

He was insane. They would wait here forever because Daniel would never come. What would Campos do when he realized his plan to summon a dead man had failed?

She reached into her pocket, yanked the cell phone out, and just as Campos was turning back around, shoved it in her sweatshirt pocket. She just had to be patient. Dial 911. Mute the phone so Campos wouldn't realize what she'd done.

He stalked toward the heater and warmed his hands. "He should be here by now."

"He's not coming."

He turned and loomed over her, closer now than he'd been before. "I saw him."

"I told you, that photograph—"

"I saw him last week." He crouched down in front of her, blocking the light so that all she could see was his giant silhouette. "I never meant for your kid to flip the car. I shot out the tire and figured he'd pull over. I planned to take Jeremy hostage, leave the other boy to fend for himself.

"When the accident happened, I was going to grab him and bring him..." He looked around. "I figured Wright would do anything to save his son. And I was right, because as I was running to the accident site, he was there, riding a dirt bike toward the car. I didn't line up my shots. I just hoped by firing, he'd stop and take cover. Then I could grab Jeremy, and Wright would come. But he didn't take cover. He risked being shot to save his kid. Would a stranger do that?"

"A good man—"

"You're delusional." Campos waved off her words. "If I'd hit him, this would all be over."

"But it wasn't—"

"It was him!" He screamed the words. "It was him! I'd have had him, but other cars started showing up. Cops had to be on the way. I had to get out of there."

"How did you know it was Daniel?" Camilla kept her voice level. "The investigators told us the man who saved the boys was fifty yards from you. And you'd have only seen his back as he rode toward the boys. How could you be so sure?"

"Because he was *there.*"

"What does that—?"

"You don't understand anything. He was there. And he'll be here."

Campos circled the heater, hands clenched into fists. He

had made up this crazy scenario in his head, and when that stranger had run to help the boys, Campos had decided it was Daniel. He hadn't seen his face. He hadn't known who that stranger was. He'd fired at the man who'd saved the boys' lives.

She wouldn't argue with Campos. Eventually, he'd realize the truth. When Daniel never showed, maybe he'd realize he'd been wrong about it all. Until then, Camilla had to figure a way to escape.

Maybe, if Campos stepped outside, she could go through the grate. When he looked away, she glanced toward the only possible exit. All she'd have to do was get out of his reach. No way he could follow her into the tiny hole.

If only she could figure a way to get through that...

Something moved.

On the other side of the grate, she saw...something.

Campos paced around the fire. When his back was to her, she looked again. It could've been a bat. The thought should've had her shuddering, but frankly, nothing was as scary as the crazy man who held her captive.

She hadn't heard anything that indicated there were bats.

A rodent, then?

Campos seemed to be calming down. He settled again near the cave entrance.

"I need to go to the bathroom," she said.

He scoffed. "There's one just down the hall to the left."

She attempted a smile. "Maybe I could just..." She nodded toward the back of the cave. "I know it's gross, but I really need to go."

"Go ahead."

"Would you turn around?"

His eyes narrowed. "What do you think?"

She sighed loudly. "Where do you think I'm going to go? You're standing at the entrance."

He stalked across the space, grabbed the grate, and yanked. It held fast.

She stared at the unguarded entrance. If only...

"Don't even think about it."

She turned to see Campos standing over her, a handgun aimed her way.

She flinched, covered her head with her arms, as if that could protect her. As if anything would stop a bullet. She tried to shrink into the wall behind her. "Please don't—"

"You try it, you'll be dead before you get there."

"I'm not going to. I was just thinking maybe I could go outside instead. Otherwise, it's going to stink in here."

"I've smelled worse."

She crawled toward the back of the cave and around the slight bend. Hardly enough space to hide. She did need to empty her bladder, but mostly she wanted to see what was beyond that grate. She squatted—in case Campos turned around—and peered through the hole.

Saw two white...

Eyes!

They blinked.

A hand came through for an instant, and she touched warm fingers.

Two whispered words carried in the silence, barely audible. "Sit tight."

She wasn't alone! She wasn't—

"Hey! What are you doing?"

"Nothing. I just... I changed my mind. I can't make myself..."

She hurried back to her spot near the fire. "I'll probably pee my pants, but I just can't bring myself to go here."

He crouched near the cave's entrance. "It won't matter. Your husband should be along any minute."

CHAPTER FORTY-FIVE

DEAR CAMILLA,

I've replayed the incident so many times that the images are burned into my brain.

Snow had fallen all day, bringing with it a rash of minor car accidents to add to our typical cases. I'd treated a young man, an assault victim, patching a couple of wounds and ordering an X-ray on what was clearly a broken wrist. He belonged to a different gang, one that had been growing. My understanding was that this new gang—I didn't even know the name of it—was challenging the Vipers for control of the drug trade in the city.

None of that was on my mind when I headed to the man's room to tell him the news. His wrist was crushed, and he'd need to see an orthopedic surgeon as soon as possible. I'd found one who could see him the following day. I knocked an instant before I stepped inside.

And froze at the threshold.

A man was standing over my patient, his back to me. He had a pillow pressed against my patient's face.

My patient's arms reached blindly for help. His feet dug

into the mattress, trying to push himself away with his one good arm, but the killer was too strong.

And then my patient stopped moving.

In that instant, my life flashed.

You, Zoë, Jeremy.

I love you.

I love you more than my job, more than all the accolades. You are my life.

I'd been such a fool.

Should I have stepped out, closed the door, and pretended I'd seen nothing? Should I have let that man kill my patient? Two gang members, one no better than the other. Both lost. Both filled with hate. Both fighting for the opportunity to destroy more lives with the drugs they flooded onto the streets. For them, I would sacrifice everything?

Again, hindsight is kinder to me than I deserve.

The truth is, the cost of what I did next didn't occur to me. I simply did what seemed right—and was right. I know that.

I do.

Still.

I screamed, "Security!" and barreled forward. I grabbed the would-be killer and shoved him aside.

He stumbled, smashed against the wall, but righted himself before he fell.

The man looked at me with murder in his eyes. It was only an instant, but I saw the warning there before he shouldered past me and out the door.

He didn't make it far.

Hospital security guards grabbed him.

His name was Francis Campos. Viper Gang leader. Murderer.

Despite my attempts to resuscitate my patient, it was too late.

I'd risked my life, all our lives, to save a drug dealer, and I'd failed.

I couldn't let Francis Campos walk free. Even though it put us all at risk, justice matters.

Doesn't it?

I don't know anymore. I only know that I love you, and I'd give anything for this nightmare to be over.

Yours always,

Daniel

CHAPTER FORTY-SIX

ANOTHER HALF HOUR passed before the silence threatened to drive Camilla mad. Her back and bottom were nearly numb against the hard stone, but her face was warm in the glow of the heater. Her head ached, her heart hurt.

Thoughts of Zoë nearly drove her mad. This man, this evil, insane man, had killed her daughter.

The more she thought of it, the more she wanted to attack him again. Who cared if he hurt her? At least the pain would distract her from this agonizing grief, this agonizing captivity.

She didn't bother with the cell phone. The man on the far side of the grate had told her to sit tight. But in the long, torturous minutes since she'd returned to her spot on the cave wall, she'd begun to wonder if she'd conjured those eyes, those whispered words.

Maybe she was alone. Maybe nobody was coming. Maybe she would die here. And if that was the case, then she had to understand. "Is it that important to punish Daniel for putting your brother in prison?"

He turned cold eyes on her. "Your husband ruined my life." He still held the gun, though it was resting casually across his bent knee. "Francis was gonna make me his number two. Other leaders were ticked about it, but hey, I was his brother. When he was out of the picture, everything fell apart. Guys got caught and sent to prison. I was in charge, but half the gang wanted me out. They blamed me for everything that went down. They finally figured a way to get rid of me. They told the cops I killed this guy in another gang and his whole family. I didn't do it, but one of my guys"—he slammed a hand against his chest—"*my friend* lied, said I murdered those people. Children! I been on the run ever since." He aimed the gun at Camilla. "It all started with your husband. Now, nobody trusts me. I can't get in anywhere. I'm on the FBI's short list, and I didn't even do it. I wasn't even there. I'm not a cold-blooded killer."

She thought of Zoë. Her sweet, sweet girl, gone at this insane man's hands.

Campos's eye contact slipped, and he stared at the heater.

Camilla worked to keep her voice level. "Why not just turn yourself in and tell the police what happened? You must have an alibi."

He barked a laugh that held no amusement. "My *alibi* was in on it. I'm screwed."

"Seems like your beef is with them, not with Daniel."

"Your husband started this, and he's gonna finish it."

"How is he going to do that?"

"I'm not an idiot. I'm not getting out of this alive. But as long as Daniel Wright ends up dead, too, that's fine with me." He pushed to his feet. "Where is he? He should be here by now." He crossed the space and yanked her from the floor, then pushed her toward the cave's entrance. "I'm done. I know what he's doing. He's waiting for the cops to show up. Well, screw that. He and I are gonna have it out now." With Camilla's arm in his meaty grip, he pushed her through the narrow gap and outside.

The frigid air shocked her, and she sucked in a breath.

Campos yanked her a few feet from the entrance, hand squeezing her upper arm. She stumbled, but he kept her upright. He put her in front of him and screamed, "Where are you, you coward! Come out now, or she dies."

The barrel of his handgun pressed against her head.

Tremors slithered through her, panic sending adrenaline to her veins, freezing her breath in her lungs. She would have screamed if she'd been able to draw air. She wanted to wrench away from him, to bolt, but found herself too afraid to move, to even breathe.

"Come on, Wright! Show yourself!"

The gun barrel lifted from her head.

A gunshot cracked in the silence.

She jerked, gasped, pulling air in, unable to push it out.

The barrel was back against her head, hot now after firing.

"You have until the count of three," Campos shouted. "One. Two. Th—"

"I'm here." The man's voice was rich and deep and seemed oddly familiar.

Not Daniel.

In the back of her mind, she'd hoped, foolishly hoped, that maybe Campos was right. Maybe Daniel was alive. But she'd recognize her husband's voice, and that wasn't it.

"Show yourself, Wright!"

"I am not Daniel Wright," the man said. "I'm just a friend of Camilla's."

The man clearly had an accent. Either Campos thought it was an affectation or was so deluded that he didn't hear it.

"Liar! Show yourself or she dies!"

It was dark, so dark. But the snow reflected faint moonlight coming through thin clouds, and she saw a man step from behind a short bush. He was on a rise across from them. She couldn't tell the distance in the dark—maybe a hundred feet. She could hardly see him, though she caught the glimmer of a gun pointed their direction.

The man walked closer. "You do not have to hurt her. Hurting her will not help you."

His voice...the accent.

The stranger stopped when he was partially hidden behind the SUV. The gun in his hand... It wasn't a run-of-the-mill rifle. It looked like one of those big scary things soldiers carried. It was pointed at Campos's head.

"Where's Wright?"

"I don't know anything about him," the man said. "I am only a friend."

It was Bachir. The man from the hospital. The medical student. The one who'd prayed for her and Jeremy. The one she'd seen when she'd been forced out of the hospital. Had he followed?

How?

If so, why hadn't he called the police?

And where had he gotten the rifle—and why?

It made no sense. Had it been his voice in the cave? Must have.

Too many questions. No answers.

The only thing she knew, the only solid thing right now, was the gun pushing against her temple.

Bachir met her eyes. Trying to tell her what? What could she do?

She considered Campos's handgun. It was pressed high on her head. If she fell, maybe it would slip. Maybe, if he fired, his bullet would miss.

Maybe.

She'd only need a second, and then Bachir could fire. She remembered what he'd said—that he'd been stolen from a village, given a gun, and told to fight. He'd been rescued before he'd had to, but maybe before that, he'd learned to shoot. Maybe, he could save her.

And not get killed in the process.

"The police are on their way," Bachir said. "Your only hope is to surrender."

Campos's words were cold and measured. "Where. Is. Wright?"

"I am sorry, my friend. I do not know."

"You're lying!" His shout was swallowed up in the darkness.

They couldn't do this much longer before Campos lost his temper and shot her. If she didn't do something fast, she would die.

Please, God, let Bachir stop him. Only then will Jeremy be safe.

Camilla might not survive. She wanted to live. She did. But death would mean release from the regret and grief she'd carried for four years. Death would mean seeing Daniel again. Seeing Zoë again.

But Jeremy needed her.

In the cold of the cave, Camilla had thought about what would happen to Jeremy if she didn't survive. Her sister would take him in. Jeremy would learn to be happy with them. He and Evan were practically brothers already. Marcy and Kevin would love Jeremy like their own. They'd care for him. They'd watch him graduate from high school. They'd be with him on his first day of college. Marcy would fix him chicken fried steak for his birthday and kiss his cheek even when he pretended he didn't want to be touched. Kevin would teach him how to be a man.

They could do it.

And then Camilla would be free.

But the cold steel against her temple brought it all into perfect clarity.

She wanted to live. She wanted to be there for Jeremy, despite the pain and grief and hardship. She wanted to see her son grow up and make a life for himself. She wanted to see her baby's babies someday.

And she needed to be the one to tell him about his sister's death. She needed to spare him from her own.

She needed to survive. *Please, Jesus, protect me. Jeremy needs me.*

"Daniel Wright!" Campos shouted. "I am going to kill your wife."

Bachir continued to hold her gaze. Without moving her head, she looked down, slowly, and then back up.

Campos was still screaming. "And then I'm going to find your son, and I'm going to put a bullet through his skull."

Bachir's gaze slipped, landed somewhere to her right. What did that mean?

"One!" Campos pressed the gun so hard into her temple it hurt.

Bachir came back to meet her eyes. Blinked twice. What did that mean? Go ahead, or...

"Two!"

She let her legs fall out from under her.

A gunshot rang out. She felt the whisper of a bullet lift her hair an instant before she hit the cold snow.

CHAPTER FORTY-SEVEN

DEAR CAMILLA,

I really believed I was doing the right thing for our family. The world our children live in will be safer if more people stand up to evil.

As we were shuffled away from our home, the home you'd poured your heart and soul into, I told myself all would be well.

As we settled in the safe house, I allowed myself to believe we could still reclaim all I'd cost us.

As I sat on that witness stand and related what I'd seen, Campos's threatening glare never leaving me, I assured myself that you and the kids would be safe.

But Campos was out for revenge, and he had plenty of loyal followers on the outside.

If I'd known what was going to happen, would I have done it? Or would I have done what so many others chose to do—pretend I hadn't seen anything? Close my eyes and hope somebody else would do the right thing.

If I'd known all it would cost me, would I have made a different choice?

I hope not.

I hope so.

I don't know what I hope. I only know that every decision I made has led us here.

Could a man whose wife doubted his love be good? Could a father whose children craved his attention be good? Did saving lives and fighting for justice make me good?

Maybe this is the end I deserve for all my bad choices.

But it's not the end you deserve, Cammie.

If I could do it over again, I wouldn't be at the hospital in the first place. If I could do it over again, I'd be home with you in my arms. Where I belong.

But once I saw what I saw, there was no undoing it.

Justice matters. When we choose selfishness over justice, we're lost as a community, as a society. Ultimately, I know my God is a God of justice. To deny justice is to deny Him.

But if I could do it all over again, I would value what is most valuable. The choices I made before the day I witnessed the murder were just as important as the ones I made after it. Those were the choices I'd change. What they say is true. As the chill of death surrounds me, I'm not wishing I'd spent more time at work.

I want you, Cammie. I want our children. I want the life we should have had.

I spent my whole life believing it was my job to save everyone. I ended up putting the people I love the most in danger.

Now, the beautiful future you and I could've had together slips away like water through my fingers. It's all gone. I know that. I know there's no escaping the end that's coming.

If this is my last chance to talk to you, there are a few things I need you to know.

I love Zoë. I love Jeremy. And I love you. I love the three of you more than my life. I will give anything, do anything, to be sure you're safe.

Don't live with regret. I know you're angry and scared. I also know you love me. You have always been so much better at love than I have.

Forgive me. When I'm gone, may the Lord protect you and our children. Have an amazing life, my love, and cling to God. He's our only hope now.

Yours always,

Daniel

CHAPTER FORTY-EIGHT

CAMILLA WATCHED BACHIR JOG FORWARD, gun raised. He was speaking, though she couldn't hear the words.

Her ears were ringing.

She shook her head to try to clear them, but the movement throbbed. She closed her eyes and curled in on herself. Curled against something warm and comforting.

Another gunshot rang out.

The warm thing held her.

What was happening?

A voice came from closer. She couldn't make it out at first, and then, as the ringing subsided, the words registered.

"Cammie. Are you hurt? Are you hit?"

That voice... The way he said her name.

Was she dead? She blinked, felt the chill of the air, the snow melting through her jeans. She wasn't dead.

Heaven wouldn't be this cold.

The man slid into view. He had a thick beard and a mustache. Black-rimmed glasses. But those eyes... Soft brown, filled with love.

They roamed her face. "Did he hurt you?"

She breathed in. Breathed in again.

He backed away, his gaze skimming her body, but she couldn't move. Couldn't exhale.

"You're okay." His palms found her cheeks, and he held her there and looked into her eyes. "Are you okay? Breathe, sweetie. Exhale. It's okay."

She tried. For that voice, that face, that man...

Daniel.

She'd do anything to make the vision real.

She couldn't stop looking at him, at the beloved face she'd longed for.

Maybe she'd been shot and she was in a coma. Maybe she was hallucinating.

She touched his whiskers. Her Daniel had never gone a day without shaving. If they had evening plans, he'd shave a second time. He hated the feeling of hair on his face, complaining that it itched. This beard wasn't scratchy but soft against her fingertips.

His lips were moving. He was talking, and though she loved the sound of his voice, she couldn't understand him. None of this made sense.

From the corner of her eye, she saw Bachir bent over Campos. She wanted to yell at him to be careful. Campos was dangerous. Crazy.

"Cammie." The bearded man who couldn't be Daniel was staring into her eyes. "Cammie. Are you with me?"

Still, she couldn't speak.

"She needs a blanket." His voice was calm and gentle in the silent night. He unzipped his jacket and pressed her to his warm chest. "She's in shock."

Bachir stood and ran.

Leaving Campos alone. Panic rose, and she tried to move, to escape and hide before he hurt her.

"Hey, you're okay," the man said.

"He's going to kill us. We have to—"

"He's dead, Cammie. He's dead."

She wanted to look, to make sure, but she couldn't drag her gaze away from the man who couldn't be Daniel.

But was Daniel.

Daniel was here, and Campos was dead. Could it be true?

Her husband held her close. "I'm so sorry. I'm so sorry."

She didn't know if this was real or imagined, but she savored the moment.

His warm breath whispered across her forehead. His arms held her close.

She wanted this to never end. To never return to reality, to that terrible, cold world.

Thoughts of that world niggled. There was something...

No. She didn't want to think about it. If she let herself think about it, then Daniel would disappear. This fantasy would melt away like spring snow, and she'd have to face life without him. Again. And without...

A scream started in her belly. She felt it rising, tried to close her mouth, but the truth...the truth couldn't be tamped down.

Zoë.

She screamed. Screamed and screamed.

He held her tighter. "You're okay. You're safe."

She couldn't make herself form the words. But she had to. She had to let go of this fantasy and embrace reality. Daniel was gone. Zoë was gone. But Jeremy needed her.

"She's gone. My baby is gone."

A blanket came over her shoulders. "We should get her back into the cave." Bachir dropped a backpack on the ground beside them. "She needs—"

"No." She tried to wrench away from this not-Daniel

person, but he didn't loosen his grip. "Don't take me back in there. Please."

"Okay." Daniel-not-Daniel said. "Do you know where the keys are to that SUV?"

She shoved trembling fingers into her jeans pocket and pulled them out. Bachir took them. A moment later, the engine roared to life.

The man lifted her as if she weighed no more than a child. Daniel had been strong, but not that strong. This man wasn't Daniel.

Daniel was with Zoë. They were together now.

He set Camilla on the backseat, slid in beside her, and pulled her onto his lap. He settled the blanket over her. "The police are on the way. We were trying to wait until they got here, but he didn't give us any choice."

She couldn't focus on his words. She was slipping again, back into the fantasy. Daniel's voice, Daniel's arms.

He held her against his chest. "I'm so sorry. I never wanted to leave you. I just wanted you to be safe. I needed you to be safe."

"Stop it. You're not Daniel. Daniel is gone."

The man flicked on the overhead light, took her shoulders, and moved her away from him so he could see her face. "Cammie, look at me."

His warm brown eyes held her gaze.

"Look past the beard and mustache. Look past the gray hair. Don't you know me?"

"You can't be alive." Her words were pitched too high. "If you're alive...I'm afraid."

"I had a contingency plan. The hitman, Alfredo Punta. I'd treated him at the hospital. I knew him. I'd known him for years. When he found me that night, I offered him money, told him my plan. He helped me fake my death."

She watched his mouth form the words. Tried to understand what he was saying. He'd planned it?

He'd left her—on purpose?

"I'm so sorry." Tears dripped from his eyes. "I didn't want to do it. I wanted us to disappear together. But when he found me… It was either that or he would've killed me. I was trying to protect you and the kids. I hated leaving you. From the very beginning, I hated it. I wanted to undo it. To fix it. But it was too late. To keep you guys safe, I had to stay away."

Daniel.

It was really him. He'd left her…left her to raise their children alone. She wanted to be angry with him, to be furious. But all she could think of, all she'd ever think about for the rest of her life, was Zoë.

Despite all Daniel had done, despite all Camilla had done, their daughter was dead.

Between the heat blowing through the vents and the heat of her husband's arms, she was warming up. Her mind was defrosting. She was thinking clearly.

She had to tell him the truth, to make him understand.

She pressed her hands to his chest, felt the heartbeat through his scratchy sweater. Said what she'd always longed to say to him. If this fantasy ended, at least she could pretend she'd had the opportunity. "I'm sorry for what I said that night. I didn't mean it. I shouldn't have argued and made you feel like—"

"I know, sweet—"

"Let me finish. When I finish, you'll hate me." Fresh tears filled her eyes, and she could hardly force the words out. But Daniel needed to know what he was coming home to. "I tried to protect them. But…she's dead. It's my fault. Zoë…" She could hardly speak through the thickness in her throat, which ached with the truth. "Campos took her. He killed her."

"No, sweetie." Daniel tried to pull her close, but she fought him.

He needed to understand.

"Listen to me." Daniel held her eye contact. "She's safe."

"He took her, he stole her. She's not here, so she has to be dead. He said—"

"She's at the hospital. She never left the hospital."

"No. He said—"

"He lied to you." Daniel pressed his palms to her cheeks. "Bachir was there. He told hospital security right away that you'd been taken. They found Zoë and an FBI agent bound and gagged. They'd been sedated. Zoë and Jeremy are both safe."

Bound and gagged?

But alive?

"I don't understand." But even as she said the words, she did. Hadn't she wondered how Campos had gotten Zoë out of the hospital? Hadn't she wondered what had happened to Agent Siple? She hadn't had time to consider it or look for them. The man had been there, and she'd left. Just like that. Without confirming. Except—

"I talked to her," she said. "He let me talk to her."

"He couldn't have," Daniel said. "Zoë is alive."

Camilla was afraid to believe. Afraid to hope.

Daniel rolled down the window and called, "Bachir? Can you come here for a second?"

Bachir had been inside the cave. He jogged out, past Campos's body and the blood that stained the snow, and stopped at their open window.

Daniel said, "Campos told Cammie that he'd kidnapped and killed our daughter. Can you tell her what you told me?"

Bachir ducked to meet her eyes across the seat. "The last I saw your daughter, she was sitting at Jeremy's bedside. They were holding hands and praying for your safety. She is well."

Cammie's breath hitched. She grasped at the hope the man's words offered.

Jeremy was alive.

Zoë was alive.

Daniel was alive.

And Campos...

Campos was dead.

CHAPTER FORTY-NINE

THE AUTHORITIES ARRIVED WITHIN MINUTES, bathing the small, flat area in light. A black sedan led the way, and Camilla wasn't surprised to see Agent Falk when he bolted toward their SUV.

Paramedics streamed from an ambulance toward Campos's body.

Camilla slid off her husband's lap, but she stayed right beside him, hip to hip. There were too many emotions to catalog. Anger that he'd left her.

Relief that he was alive.

Terror that he'd leave her again.

"Can you stand? We should get out."

He opened the door, and they slid from the backseat.

Agent Falk stopped a foot from them. He stared at Daniel a moment, then gripped his shoulder. "It's good to see you."

"You too."

Falk didn't look surprised.

"You knew!" Fury rose at the very thought that this man had known all along—

"Not until today. The Swedish doctor... On a hunch, I had

Interpol do some digging. The doctor existed, and everything about him checked out—except for that image on the website." Falk's gaze found Daniel. "How'd you meet him?"

"I worked at a Christian mission in Sudan," Daniel said. "He came a lot to volunteer. We became friends. When my photo hit the web, I reached out to him, and he agreed to help me."

"It was a good idea. If Campos had done the digging I did, he'd have found the website. Chances were good he'd never have discovered what the real Elias Lunden looked like." Falk's lips pressed together. "I was fighting to get you in WITSEC back then. You just needed to be patient. You didn't have to—"

"Punta found me," Daniel said. "It was either fake my death or take a bullet to the skull. I had no choice."

Camilla looked up into her husband's face. "I'm sorry for everything I said that day. I've never forgiven myself for—"

"I forgave you the moment you said it." He kissed her forehead. "I knew you didn't mean them. My only regret was that the argument was our last conversation."

"Why didn't you contact me?" Her words were high and teary. "We could have come to you."

"I couldn't take the risk Campos was watching you. You went on without me, Cammie. You survived."

"We needed you."

He pulled her into an embrace. "I know. I'd give anything not to have lost those years with you and the kids. I'd give anything."

She backed up so she could meet his eyes. It wasn't okay. But he was there. "Are you staying now?"

"If you want me."

Very little made sense to her at the moment, but she could put the fear in his eyes to rest. "We'll work through it together." She swallowed a sob and faced Falk. "My daughter is—?"

"Safe and sound."

"I'm an idiot."

Daniel said, "No, sweetie."

"You're a mom," Falk added. "You did what any mother would do. You risked your life to save your daughter. That makes you a hero."

Her short burst of laughter surprised her. A hero? Far from it.

She and Daniel sat shoulder-to-shoulder, thigh-to-thigh, in the backseat of Falk's sedan for the ride back to the hospital.

Bachir had gotten a ride with a police officer to his car, which was apparently parked down the road.

She wanted to understand everything that had happened, but she didn't have the energy to ask the questions. Later, she'd figure out how they found her. Who Bachir was. Right now, all she cared about was the man whose arm was wrapped around her. The man she'd fallen in love with when she was too naive to understand what love cost.

Every few seconds, he kissed her—her temple, her hair, her cheek.

They hardly spoke. She didn't even know where to begin.

More than an hour later, Falk parked his car in the circle drive in front of the hospital and walked them to the glass doors. "Go on up and see your kids. I'll be up in about an hour to go over everything that happened."

"Tonight?" Daniel asked. "Is that necessary?"

"A man is dead," Falk said. "You came back from the grave. We have some questions."

"But my family—"

"Will have you for the rest of your lives."

The rest of their lives. Beautiful words.

The hospital lobby was bright and cheerful, belying the dark night. She glanced at a clock on the wall. Only ten thirty? It felt like days had gone by since she'd last been here, but only about six hours had passed since she'd walked out of the hospital with that—

"The man who escorted me to the car," Camilla said to Falk. "I can describe him, even draw you—"

"He's in custody. I'll explain everything."

She led Daniel up the escalator, around the maze of hallways, and to the doorway that led to Jeremy's ward. He stopped her before she pressed the button to ask for admittance.

"You should warn the kids about me," Daniel said. "I don't want to shock them like I shocked you."

"That was..." Amazing.

Also, terrifying. But probably more because of the gunshots and the killer who'd fallen dead beside her.

Daniel rubbed his beard. "I don't look the same. I'm not the same, and neither are they. They—all of you—have every right to be angry with me. I need them to know it's okay. Their feelings... If they hate me, if they—"

"Stop." She pressed her finger against his lips. "They're going to be thrilled."

"Maybe. But if they're not..."

"They will be. Like I am."

His lips quirked up at the corner, an almost smile that told her he knew better. "You might be thrilled," Daniel said, "but you're also..."

He let his sentence trail, offering her the opportunity to tell the truth.

"Furious. Hurt. Confused." She stepped close and wrapped her arms around him.

He was thinner than he'd been. Also, harder, as if he'd spent the last four years in the gym. But he smelled like Daniel. He felt like Daniel.

"Happy," she added. "Hopeful."

He kissed the top of her head. "I'm sorry. I'm so sorry."

She backed up and smiled at him. "We'll figure it all out. We'll get past it." She looked at the closed doors and remembered what he'd asked. "I'll warn them, if you want."

He gave her a quick once-over. "We need to get you cleaned up."

In the ward, Camilla led Daniel to a bathroom. They stepped inside together and locked the door, and she got a look at herself in the mirror.

"Oh." She touched her head. The paramedics had treated the cut on her scalp on the mountain, but dried blood stained her forehead.

Daniel wet some paper towels and dabbed the wound.

Emotion clogged her throat. In the bright bathroom, she was able to see her husband's new wrinkles, the gray in his hair. The kindness in his eyes. So much had changed, but her Daniel was still there. The only man she'd ever loved.

She couldn't take her eyes off him.

He ran his fingers over her hair, her cheeks. Seeing her gray roots and her wrinkles. When his eyes met hers, tears filled them. "Thank God. When Bachir called to tell me Campos had taken you... I've never been so scared."

"How do you know Bachir?"

He kissed her forehead. "I promise to tell you everything. But first..."

"The kids." She backed from his embrace and looked in the mirror. Her hair was a mess, but the blood was gone.

Also gone was the widow who'd stared back at her for four years. Gone was the grief in her eyes. She was Cammie again. Or would be, when this was all a memory. Someday, she'd be herself again, fun-loving. Happy. She smiled at herself and at Daniel, who was watching her reflection.

She leaned back against him, and his arms came around her and pulled her close. A feeling she'd imagined a million times.

He kissed her head. "You're the most beautiful sight I've ever seen."

She knew how he felt. This man with his beard and mustache and geeky glasses—he made her heart soar.

She turned in his arms. "You ready to see your kids?"

He let her go, his nod quick and determined.

She took his hand. "You have nothing to fear, my love. They'll be as happy as I am."

CHAPTER FIFTY

CAMILLA LEFT Daniel around the corner and hurried to Jeremy's room. The door was closed, and a man stood outside. Based on the suit and tie and straight posture, this was an FBI agent. He nodded and stepped aside when he saw her, and she opened the door.

Zoë was seated at her brother's bedside dressed in a sweatshirt and jeans.

Jeremy's bed was raised.

They were holding hands and looked up when she walked in.

Zoë launched herself into Camilla's arms. "Mom, thank God. Thank God you're okay."

Camilla hugged her daughter. She was alive. Camilla had known it, but to touch her...

Camilla reached for Jeremy's outstretched hand and squeezed.

Tears streamed down his face.

Camilla gently pushed her daughter away so she could see her face. "Are you all right? What did he do to you?"

"He didn't hurt me. Scared me, but didn't hurt me. I guess he drugged me because I went to sleep."

Cammie didn't want to think of that man anywhere near her daughter. But it hadn't been Campos, it had been the other man. The one now in custody. "Thank God you're all right." She turned to Jeremy. "Are you okay?"

"Just worried about you. What happened? Is that guy—?"

"Campos is dead."

"Oh." Jeremy took that in. "Did the Feds rescue you? What happened?"

"Someone else rescued me. It's a very long story, and I promise to tell you everything, but first, there's something more important I need to tell you." She nodded to the chair. "Would you sit?"

Zoë did, eyes wide.

Jeremy, too, looked more frightened than curious.

"What is it?" Zoë asked.

"It's good news. The very best news." She stood beside her children and held their hands. She was excited to tell them, and suddenly as nervous as Daniel had been. "I don't know how to tell you this. I found out tonight… I was rescued by…" This was hard, harder than she'd imagined it would be. "I need you to know…"

Behind her, a rush of air told her someone had pushed open the door. A nurse?

But Jeremy's jaw dropped.

Zoë gasped.

Camilla stepped away as Daniel entered the room. Tears streamed from his face.

Zoë stood. Jeremy leaned forward.

Daniel took Camilla's place. Seemed unable to speak.

Zoë said, "Daddy?"

He opened his arms, and she fell into them.

He held her close, then leaned down to Jeremy, pressing his lips against his temple before grasping his hand. "Son."

Jeremy's eyes never left his father's face. "I don't understand."

"I was trying to protect you. All I wanted was to protect you three. I left to—"

"You faked your death?" Zoë said.

"My greatest fear was that, in doing the right thing, I'd lose one of you." He rubbed the arm of his sweater across his wet eyes. "But..." He looked around the hospital room and shook his head. "All I did was put you in greater danger. I'm so sorry. I hope someday you'll forgive me."

Jeremy lifted his father's hand and pressed his face against it.

Zoë wrapped her arms around Daniel's middle as if she might never let go.

"There's nothing..." Zoë couldn't seem to make the words come out.

"We're all safe," Camilla said. "It's over."

Jeremy's eyes squeezed closed, pushing new tears out. "You're home now. All that matters is that you're home."

CHAPTER FIFTY-ONE

THE KIDS HAD SO many questions. Camilla did too, but Daniel deflected them all, staring at them, focusing on them. Asking about their lives. Telling them how proud he was of them and the people they'd become.

Camilla watched, happy tears washing her face, joyful praises flitting through her mind.

Daniel was alive. He was really and truly here. She could hardly wrap her mind around it.

Too soon, Agent Falk knocked on the door and stepped into the hospital room. He approached the bed and held out his hand. "Jeremy. Wow, you've grown up."

They shook hands, and then Falk greeted Zoë. "Glad you're safe. Sorry about what you went through. Agent Siple—"

"Is she all right?" Zoë asked, then added quickly, "It wasn't her fault."

"Don't worry about her." Falk's smile was kind. "Wounded pride more than anything."

"I'm glad." Though she was focused on the FBI agent, Zoë didn't budge from her father's side.

Falk turned his gaze to include Camilla and Daniel. "I've

got a room down the hall for us to go over what happened. If you two will—"

"Wait." Zoë's single word was too loud. "Jeremy and I are coming. We need to know."

Daniel said, "I don't think you guys need to hear this."

Zoë looked past her father to Camilla, brows lifted, eyes wide.

Daniel wanted to protect them, and Camilla appreciated that. When he'd last been here, they'd been children, seventeen and thirteen. They'd been naive and innocent. Now, Zoë was an adult, and though Jeremy wasn't quite, the years and the tragedy they'd overcome had matured him.

"They've lived this nightmare, too," Camilla said. "They deserve to hear how it ended."

Daniel watched her a long moment, frown in place.

He was going to have to trust her, and it seemed he realized that. His lips pressed together, not in anger but in grief.

They'd grown up, and he'd missed it.

"You're right." He squeezed Jeremy's shoulder. "Let me get you a wheelchair." He paused on his way to the door and turned back, focus on Camilla. "When was the last time you ate?"

"Oh. Uh..." She thought back to the lunch she and the kids had eaten a million years ago. "Noon?"

"A salad, probably," Daniel guessed. At her shrug, he shifted to Agent Falk. "Can you—?"

"I'll see what I can do." Falk stepped out of the room.

A few minutes later, they gathered in the same conference room where she and Paul had spoken a few days earlier.

Paul.

She wasn't going to think about him.

Falk sat on the far side, a thick file folder in front of him.

Daniel slid one of the chairs away and rolled Jeremy up to

the table. Leaving a chair for himself, he pulled out one for Zoë on his other side.

Camilla took the chair beside her daughter. They'd barely gotten settled when a nurse pushed the door open. "They're right here," she said.

Bachir stepped in, smiling.

Daniel stood and embraced him. "I didn't know you were coming."

When Daniel stepped back, Bachir squeezed Camilla's shoulder. "You are well, yes?"

She nodded, patting his hand, though words wouldn't come.

Bachir didn't seem to mind. He brought with him his peaceful, joyful countenance. To Daniel, he said, "Agent Falk asked me to join you."

"I'm glad." Daniel introduced him to the kids. "This is Bachir Hari, a dear friend of mine."

Bachir sat beside Agent Falk, who cleared his throat and began.

"Let's start with today and work backward." Beneath the bright lights, Falk's exhaustion was obvious in the smudges beneath his eyes and the red streaks in them. "Agent Siple was standing guard outside the bathroom door while Zoë showered. She said a man came in and fixed himself a cup of coffee. He was scrolling on his cell phone, and then, according to Siple, he collapsed. She went to see if she could offer aid, and that's the last thing she remembers. Her blood test revealed he'd injected her with a drug called"—he opened the file and glanced at the paper—"midazolam."

Daniel sucked air through his teeth. "Fast-acting sedative. She wouldn't have gone right out, but she'd have been too weak to protect herself."

"That's what the docs here told us. He dragged her into one

of the bedrooms and bound and gagged her. Then, he broke into the bathroom."

Camilla grabbed Zoë's hand.

Daniel scooted her closer and wrapped his arm around her shoulders.

Zoë leaned into him, face pale.

Falk nodded to her. "Do you want to tell us what happened—?"

"Not really."

Falk continued. "He broke into the bathroom and told Zoë to get out of the shower."

Zoë's face paled, but Daniel's cheeks flushed. "I'm sorry, baby." His voice was tight with suppressed anger.

"I'm okay." The words came out high-pitched and shaky.

"We understand," Falk said, "that he was, uh, respectful of Zoë's privacy. That he—"

"He handed me a towel through the shower curtain and told me to dry off and get dressed. He didn't watch or anything."

Thank God. Camilla had tried very hard not to think about that part.

Daniel nodded. He didn't seem able to speak.

Camilla couldn't imagine how terrified her daughter must've been. It was one thing to be threatened, but in the shower? Horrifying.

But Zoë was holding up. This young, beautiful woman, handling it all like the heroine of her own story. How had she grown up to be so courageous?

A rush of affection had Camilla squeezing her hand. "I'm so proud of you."

"I didn't do anything."

"You're doing it now," Camilla said. "Surviving. Being strong. A lot of women would be lying in a puddle of fear. But you, you're..." She couldn't finish for the tears clogging her throat.

"I take after my mother."

Oh. She and her daughter shared a look. They'd endured so much. Too much. But it was over now. They were on the mountaintop, studying the cliff they'd just scaled.

Soon, they'd turn their attention to the vista in front of them. The future.

"The man"—again, Falk glanced at his notes—"Jonathan Melvin Strand. We think he and Campos hooked up in Vegas. Strand has a few felonies under his belt, but this was his first assault."

"And his last, I hope," Daniel said.

"Should be spending a good chunk of his life in prison," Falk said. "The evidence against him is overwhelming. Strand took Zoë into the same room where Siple was bound. He tied her up and got some recordings and then—"

"Wait," Daniel said. "Recordings of...?"

Camilla knew the answer to that. "Of her talking, so when I asked for proof she was alive—"

"He made me say a few different things," Zoë said. "'Mom, I'm scared.' 'Come get me.' Stuff like that. He wanted me to sound afraid, which, you know..." She shrugged. "I was totally terrified, so that wasn't hard."

"I'm so sorry," Camilla said. "I should have gone with you. I shouldn't have—"

"There was no way you could have known what would happen." Zoë sounded almost annoyed.

Jeremy added, "Besides, if the guy could take out an FBI agent, he could've taken you out too. Like you told me earlier, it's not all about you."

The words stung, but Jeremy softened them with a smile.

"You have to stop blaming yourself." Daniel leaned forward

to meet her eyes, his soft and warm. "None of this was your fault."

"Strand had Zoë unlock her phone," Falk said. "Then, he injected her with the same drug he'd given Siple."

Daniel's eyes narrowed at that. "He could've killed her."

"But at least I got to sleep through it," Zoë said. "I don't remember anything after that until someone was waking me up."

"Still." Daniel looked furious, but it wasn't as if the kidnapper had been concerned about anybody's health. Camilla felt fortunate they'd all come out of this relatively unscathed.

Falk nodded to Camilla, who explained how Campos had tricked her into thinking he'd taken Zoë.

Bachir picked up the story. "I saw you being escorted out of the hospital. I didn't know who the man was, but the fear in your eyes told me something was wrong. I regret now that I didn't alert security right away, but I feared there was a reason you were going with that man. I didn't want to put you at risk. I thought I would get the license plate number, which I did, but then the man who'd taken you stayed at the hospital, so I stopped him."

"How?" Daniel asked.

The man's eyes sparkled. "I tackled him and yelled for someone to alert security."

Falk said, "They detained him, and then he called me." Facing Daniel, his eyebrows lifted. "I guess you gave him my number?"

"Seemed prudent," Daniel said.

Falk continued. "That's when we discovered you two"—he nodded to Camilla and Zoë—"were missing. Along with our agent. We found them pretty quickly, since Siple had checked in with her location when Zoë went to shower." Falk shifted to Camilla. "Tell us what happened from there."

Before she could answer, a knock sounded, and the nurse who manned the desk stepped inside. “Did you guys order food?”

“We’ll be done here in a minute,” Falk said.

“Actually”—Daniel pushed back from the table—“we need to eat.” He sent a wink Camilla’s direction. “I can hear my wife’s stomach growling from here.”

She laughed. “You cannot. We can wait.”

Daniel tipped his head toward Falk. “*He* can wait.”

Falk waved them off. “Go ahead. We have all the time in the world.”

All the time in the world. That sounded pretty good.

CHAPTER FIFTY-TWO

DANIEL STILL COULDN'T BELIEVE it.

He'd never dared hope that he could be reunited with his family. Now, he was afraid to blink, afraid this was all a crazy vision. A nightmare-turned-dream.

He couldn't stop touching them. Kissing them. Gazing at them. Zoë, Jeremy, and Camilla. His beautiful family.

It was more than he could take in, way more than he deserved. But if God was willing to offer him this...

Thank You. Thank You.

Once he'd distributed sandwiches and bags of chips, he pushed his chair and Jeremy's wheelchair back so his daughter and his wife could move in closer. If this was going to be the first meal they shared together in four years, they were going to face each other.

Falk and Bachir got the hint and stepped out.

Daniel helped Jeremy unwrap the sandwich and settle it on his lap but stopped him before he ate it. "You guys mind if I pray?"

Nobody spoke as they held hands. Daniel gripped his son's

arm above the cast, needing the connection, and bowed his head.

But words wouldn't come. He couldn't speak past the emotion in his throat. Four years earlier, he would never have cried in front of his wife and kids. Today, he couldn't hold back the flood. Finally, he simply said, "Thank You, God. Thank You."

That was it.

And then Camilla said, "Amen." And they ate.

Zoë, who'd always hated tomatoes, didn't pick them out of her sandwich. Apparently, she'd gotten over that.

Jeremy, who'd never sat still long enough to eat an entire meal, managed to polish off two sandwiches.

And Camilla. She'd lost weight since he'd left. And she'd aged, but in good ways. She looked older, sure. But also wiser. More beautiful. More...he couldn't even come up with a word for it.

Despite everything she'd been through, she looked radiant.

She ate an entire sandwich and almost a whole bag of chips. Daniel had guessed what she needed and taken care of her. For the first time in four years, he'd done his job as a husband.

Two weeks earlier, he'd been working at a mission in South Sudan, believing he'd never see his family again.

Now...

Thank You.

The break didn't last long enough. Even though Daniel wanted to know what had happened to bring all this about, mostly, he wanted to hold his wife and kiss his kids and hear their stories. He wanted to stare at them. To memorize their faces and never, ever look away.

But Falk and Bachir returned.

Daniel tossed all the trash, kissed Camilla on her head, and then sat between his kids again.

Marveling at them, at God's handiwork.

Falk nodded to Camilla. "Tell us what happened after you left the hospital."

While she shared about a terrifying drive through the snow while that madman watched her through a camera lens, emotion filled her words and dripped from her eyes.

Daniel couldn't help but cry with her. He'd come so close to losing her. So close.

To Bachir, she said, "When I saw you on my way out, I hoped maybe you knew something was wrong. How do you know Daniel, anyway?"

"I was raised at the mission where your husband worked. I came home from college one summer—I did my undergraduate work in England—and met him. I wanted to be a doctor, so he let me follow him around. I learned more from watching Dr. Daniel than I will ever learn in medical school. Not only did he teach me, but he helped me pass my MCAT. I owe everything to Dr. Daniel."

"You'd have done it without me," Daniel said. "God created you to be a doctor."

"And He sent you to help me do it." He turned to Camilla. "Dr. Daniel helped me get into the school here in Utah. When he called to tell me his family was here and might be in danger, I offered to help."

"Thank God you did," Daniel said. "This would have ended very differently if not for you."

"And the rifle?" Falk asked Bachir. "An AR-15. Not exactly an everyman weapon."

"It is similar to the weapon I learned to shoot when I was a boy. I wanted to buy something I was familiar with."

"Cool," Jeremy said. "I'd love to see it."

Bachir's smile was easy. "I will show it to you."

Beaming, Jeremy shifted in his wheelchair. When he

winced with pain, Daniel almost suggested he return to his room and rest, but Jeremy was practically grown up. He knew what he could handle.

Seeing his boy as an almost-adult was going to take some getting used to.

"Where was this mission?" Jeremy asked.

"South Sudan," Daniel said. "I'll tell you all about it another time."

Camilla reached across the table. "Bachir?" He took her hand. "You were a great comfort to me. Your prayers, your presence. It seemed whenever I needed somebody to talk to, you were right there."

"I admit that wasn't only Providence. I might have missed a few classes in my desire to speak with you in the cafeteria. But when I saw you in the neuro ward, that was all God. I really was there to see someone."

"Right when I needed you," she said.

"Anyway." Falk seemed eager to get the conversation back on track. "Bachir told us what happened. He got the license plate number, but the SUV—a black Toyota Highlander—is a pretty common car. And the traffic was terrible, and the snow..." He shook his head. "A perfect storm. We never found it." He glanced at Daniel. "We figured we could find you through Strand."

Daniel scoffed. "I told you—"

"Yeah." Falk ran a hand over his short hair and focused on Camilla. "Daniel called and told me what was going on. He tried to convince us Campos would take you up into the mountains, but after some threats and promises, Strand directed us to a safe house in Ogden where they'd been holed up. We got there and watched the place. I was sure you would turn up there."

Daniel's frustration spiked. "Even though I knew—"

"We had solid information," Falk said. "We were wrong, but we made the right choice. The guy had no reason to lie."

"So why did he?" Camilla asked.

"We think Campos lied to him." Falk's voice quickly resumed its calm tone. "He believed that was where you'd be taken."

"I knew better." Daniel forced himself to relax before he leaned forward to face Camilla. "I'd been up in the mountains for days. I'd followed tracks and found that cave. I knew he'd take you there. And he knew I knew."

Falk said, "There was no way—"

"How?" Camilla asked at the same time.

Daniel needed to move. He stood and paced behind the chairs. "He knew I'd been..." He took a deep breath, knowing he needed to fess up. He sat and faced his son. "I hope you're not mad. I hacked your social media accounts. It's how I knew what you were doing."

Jeremy's eyes widened.

Daniel turned to Zoë. "Yours too." Where Jeremy had seemed surprised, nervous even, Zoë narrowed her eyes, looking irritated.

"I just wanted... I needed to be sure you were safe. And, honestly, I missed you guys so much. I watched your public posts, but I couldn't get enough."

After a moment, Zoë said, "Okay. I guess."

"Don't worry. You're not in trouble, though"—back to Jeremy—"you need to clean up your language."

"Yes, sir."

Daniel mussed his hair, then leaned down and kissed his head. He couldn't stop touching them, kissing them.

How had he survived four years without these two in his life?

Would he ever be able to repair what he'd done? Yes, he'd

been trying to protect them. But the cost...the cost was so high. Too high.

"What happened next?" Falk prompted.

"When I showed up at the accident site," Daniel said, "Campos knew—"

"Wait!" Jeremy's jaw dropped. "When *you* showed up?"

"I'm the one who pulled you from..." The memory of that moment hit him. Watching the car flip. Seeing pieces of it fly off and slide across the desert floor. Knowing what was happening, what could have happened... He swallowed hard. "I saw the whole thing." His voice didn't sound right.

Camilla stared at him, eyes wide. "You *watched* it? I only saw pictures, and..." She shook her head. "Wait. You were on the dirt bike?"

"I thought Campos would be there," Daniel said. "I planned... I had a rifle." He couldn't look at Camilla anymore, the wonder and horror in her expression. Instead, he focused on his son. "I thought he might try to kidnap you to get to me. I thought I could protect you."

"Is that why you were in the US?" Falk asked.

"Originally, I thought, if I was sure Campos knew I was alive, I'd go to you, tell you the truth, and beg you to protect us. But, for all I knew, the person who'd messaged Jeremy was just pulling a prank. I didn't want to risk exposing everybody until I knew. I was there to protect the boys. I thought I could handle it. I never imagined..."

"I lost control of the car," Jeremy said. "It was my—"

"Don't start that," Daniel said. "None of the blame for any of this lies with you. Got it?"

When Jeremy nodded, Daniel continued. "After the accident, I didn't want to be seen or questioned. I was afraid Campos would keep shooting, maybe hurt someone. I didn't know what to do. I told the 911 operator about the gunshots, and then I took off, hoping to draw him away. I figured Camilla would tell the authorities about Campos. Then Bachir saw you two"—he indicated Camilla and Falk—"in the hospital cafeteria. He took a photo and sent it to me, and I knew you were involved. I thought you'd keep them safe."

"I still don't understand," Falk said. "You knew Campos was there. You saw him."

"I never saw him." If only he'd gotten eyes on Campos before the boys got there.

"He saw you," Camilla said. "He knew it was you. He told me you were at the accident site. I thought he was crazy."

"Why not call me right away?" Falk asked.

Camilla leaned forward, waiting for the answer. She looked...afraid. "Were you... Did you not want us to know you were alive? Were you going to leave again?"

"No." He rushed to reassure her. If not for the audience, he'd pull her into a hug and never let her go. "I wanted to be with you." He met his family's eyes, each one. "More than I can ever express, I wanted to be with you again." He turned to Falk. "I didn't want us to live in fear. I'd planned... I stayed up in the mountains because I wanted to..." He looked toward the ceiling. He really didn't want to say this.

Not in front of his wife, his children.

But this was a time for truth. If they were going to move forward together, he needed to be honest. He focused on the FBI agent. "I was hunting him. I knew he was up there. I was hoping to get a shot at him. Somebody'd been staying up there in that old copper mine. There's a shack with heat, and I figured it was him. I kept watching it, thinking he'd come back. I guess he was in that place in Ogden, though. I didn't know."

"You were going to kill him?" Falk asked.

"Yes." Daniel held Falk's gaze. "In cold blood."

Camilla exhaled as if she'd been holding her breath. He was afraid to look at her. And then he did.

And she smiled at him.

Falk's pen tap-tap-tapped on the table. The man just watched it, silently.

"He almost killed my son," Daniel said. "I'm just lucky he didn't kill me."

Nobody spoke.

Finally, Falk looked up. "Contemplating murder isn't illegal. Can't exactly throw you in jail for having murderous thoughts. If I could, we'd need a lot more cells." Falk shifted his attention back to Camilla. "So Campos knew it was him at the accident site?"

She nodded slowly, facing Daniel. "He knew you'd come," Camilla said. "He was convinced you'd show up to save me. But I don't understand how you knew."

"He left a message on Jeremy's app." Daniel found it on his cell and angled it so she could see.

It had been posted at about six that evening. It read, *I've got the place all ready for her.*

That was it.

It wasn't even posted under the same name. Before, he'd used the name Roger. Now, it was...

Little brother.

"I gotta get my phone back," Jeremy said. "I didn't even see it."

"He knew exactly what he was doing." Daniel slid his cell into his pocket. "I'd gotten a hotel in Provo, but when Bachir called with the news that you'd been taken, I headed into the mountains."

To Camilla, Falk said, "He called me. But we'd gotten the tip about the house, so we were there."

"Even though I told you—"

"You were right." Falk glared at Daniel. "I was wrong. It all worked out. Let's leave it at that."

Easy for him to say. It wasn't his wife who'd almost died. Turning away from the agent, he faced Camilla. "I think I was behind you on the road."

"That was you?" Wonder filled her voice. "I kept praying somebody would see, somebody would do something. And then I turned, and you kept going."

"I had to. I had to wait for Bachir. We found another road up the back side of the mountain. It only went so far, and then we had to get out and hike. In the snow, it took forever. Bachir went around to the ridge across from the cave's entrance, and I went through from the old copper mine. I'd discovered the way earlier in the week and had even rigged that grate you saw to open."

"How?" she asked. "Campos shook it, but it didn't budge."

"I'd cut all the bars and secured them with u-shaped metal riggings." It took forever because he'd had to make them look weathered, so Campos wouldn't suspect. "You had to lift it to open it. I'd even greased the joints so they wouldn't creak. If he left you alone, I was going to get you out. He was way too big to fit through that hole. We could have escaped."

"But he never left me alone." Camilla sounded amazed. "That was you. I thought I'd imagined... I'm so glad I didn't recognize you. I'd have been so shocked, I'd have given you away for sure."

"We planned to wait for the Feds to arrive." Daniel continued to focus on his wife. "Much as I wanted the guy dead, the idea of murder didn't sit well with me. I wanted to protect you, but if there was a way to get him without killing him in cold blood, I wanted to take it. I mean, I'd ruined our lives to put a murderer behind bars. Was I really going to become just like him? I couldn't do it. I didn't want to do it."

He met Jeremy's eyes, then Zoë's. "I was in the cave with your mother. I was armed. I could have crept out of that grate and shot Campos, and maybe I could have even claimed I'd had to do it."

"Killing in defense of another," Falk said.

"But I knew he wouldn't kill her until he had me. Even if the courts would have bought it..." He met Camilla's eyes. "I would have known. God would have known. I had to trust Him to save you, to save us all."

Camilla swallowed. The action seemed painful. "I'm glad you don't have to live with that."

"Easy to say now that everything has worked out." Daniel could imagine so many other ways it could have ended. "I risked your life, your safety. Again."

"You did the right thing, again," Camilla said.

Hearing her say that raised a lump in his throat.

"The guy's dead." Jeremy looked from him to Camilla. "Right? You said he's dead." His face was pale, and his hand pressed against his injured ribs and lungs.

"He's dead," Daniel said. "Campos pulled your mother out of the cave and started screaming threats. Bachir came out from hiding and kept him talking. Kept him from hurting her. Meanwhile, I crept out of the hole in the cave and got behind him. Bachir had a gun aimed at Campos. Campos's gun was..." He squeezed his eyes closed, seeing it all again. Knowing he'd see it in his nightmares for a long time.

Zoë said, "What?"

"It was aimed at me," Camilla said.

"Your mother decided, wisely, to let her feet go out from under her. Campos fired, but he missed. And I whacked him on the head with a big rock. He went down. I thought I'd hit him hard enough to at least stun him, and I just wanted..." He looked at Falk. "All I could think about was getting Cammie away. I don't really know what happened after that."

Bachir leaned forward. The smile he'd worn was gone now. "The man was down, but he moved. He lifted his gun. I thought he was going to shoot you, so..."

"You saved our lives," Daniel said.

Again, Camilla reached across the table and squeezed his hand. "Thank you."

"I hate that you have to live with it," Daniel said. "I didn't want to, and now you do."

"I am okay with it. I saved the lives of two good people and took the life of a murderer. I can live with it." Bachir sat back. "All that training when I was stolen from my family and given a gun, God had told me He would use it for good someday. This was the good."

"There won't be any charges, right?" Daniel asked.

"This is Utah," Falk said. "No law against carrying a weapon."

"And the shooting?"

"We don't prosecute people for saving lives."

"And the Vipers? Are we safe?"

"Far as we can tell, they know nothing about this. We still have a man on the inside in St. Louis, and he said there's been no mention of you or the hitman or any of it."

"What about Alfredo?" Daniel asked. "Has there been any backlash?"

Falk closed the file in front of him. "Punta was murdered last week. He'd relocated to Phoenix and gotten involved with a local gang. We believe that, when Campos found out you were still alive, he tracked him down and killed him."

The image of the kid who'd walked into his ER so many years before filled his mind. Stupid, skinny kid who'd turned evil so fast. "I told him to change his name. I gave him enough money to change his life."

Camilla's eyes found Daniel's. "Is that what happened to the money?"

"I'd hidden it in a locker at the bus station. I offered it to him in exchange for my life. Told him I'd tell him where it was when I was free. I thought...I hoped I'd be able to come home someday. I wasn't afraid to die, but the idea of not seeing you three again..."

"And Punta believed you?" Falk sounded skeptical.

"He knew where my family was. He knew what I had to lose." Daniel turned to Camilla. "I was sure you'd have me declared dead and live off the insurance money. But you didn't."

"I wasn't ready to give up on you. I wasn't ready to give up hope."

He closed his eyes and absorbed that. She'd stuck with him through it all. Despite all evidence to the contrary, she'd held onto hope he'd return.

Even though it made no sense whatsoever. "You were supposed to," he said. "That was the point of all of it. The blood—my own blood, which I'd been carrying around in a plastic bag strapped to my leg for weeks, just in case. The funeral home, the oven... You were supposed to believe I was gone."

She reached past Zoë and took his hand. "Hope doesn't die so easily."

Zoë laid her hand on top of theirs and gazed up at him.

Jeremy leaned in from the other side.

Had they all continued to hope? Or had Camilla's hope carried the children?

"How did you know how to use the crematorium?" Falk asked.

Daniel squeezed Camilla's hand, and his family backed away—

slightly. "Had a patient once who loved to talk about his funeral business." Daniel's lips lifted at the corners. "Who knew I'd need that information? And Alfredo was all over the idea. I don't think he wanted to kill me, and walking away with a hundred and fifty grand sounded good to him. Why didn't he just do what I told him?"

"Guys like that," Falk said, "they don't know how."

"If he'd just—"

"You blaming yourself that the guy who almost killed you ended up dead?" Falk chuckled. "It was between you and him. I, for one, am glad it was him. It's not like he changed his ways after you. Local cops think he's responsible for a couple of murders in Phoenix, and that's on top of all those he pulled off in St. Louis. The world's better off without him."

"Seriously, Dad," Zoë said. "You can't save everybody."

He smiled at his little girl—who wasn't so little anymore. "You're right, sweetie. We're safe. Campos is dead. Bachir's not in any trouble." He squeezed Zoë's hand, leaned over to kiss Jeremy's forehead, and met Cammie's eyes. "It's over. It's really over."

Now, he just had to figure out how to go on from here.

CHAPTER FIFTY-THREE

THE ROOM in the Ronald McDonald House stayed empty that night. Daniel couldn't bear to leave his children, and Cammie couldn't bear to leave him. Daniel sat in the middle of the couch in Jeremy's hospital room, and Zoë and Camilla sat on either side of him. It was cramped and uncomfortable.

And the best night she'd spent in a long, long time.

Jeremy was released from the hospital later the following afternoon.

Bachir let them borrow his car. He was standing beside it when Camilla, Daniel, and Zoë walked beside Jeremy's wheelchair out of the hospital into the chilly sunshine.

The air was crisp, the sky blue, the fresh blanket of snow sparkling. The world was brighter than it had been for years.

They'd rented a suite of rooms at a nearby hotel, where they would stay until Jeremy could safely get on an airplane.

They were all exhausted, but Daniel had contacted his family the night before to tell them he was alive. Though most of his brothers would be arriving the following day, his parents and his brother Sam flew in that afternoon. Marcy fetched them from the airport and then watched the reunion scene from the corner of the suite, holding Camilla's hand. Tears streamed down both their faces.

All of their faces.

Camilla had never seen so many happy tears.

That evening, after Daniel told more of his story, filling his folks and his brother in on everything that'd happened, he took Camilla aside.

"We're going out, you and me."

"But your parents—"

"Will survive without us for a couple of hours."

He ordered room service, kissed the kids goodbye, and ushered her to the door.

Sam had gone for a walk earlier, clearly overwhelmed that his big brother was back. The most successful brother—if one counted success in dollars, anyway—the one she'd once dubbed *the charmer,* had been subdued all afternoon, watching more than talking, choking up and trying to hide it.

Like everyone else, Peggy and Roger, Daniel's parents, couldn't stop staring at him, touching him, asking him questions. Just being with him seemed to melt years off their faces.

Camilla felt guilty leaving, but when she looked back to offer an apology to her mother-in-law, Peggy smiled. There was no censure there. Just love. "Go. Enjoy your husband."

She and Daniel walked hand-in-hand along the chilly sidewalk. It had been cleared of snow, though a few patches remained here and there.

Every once in a while, she looked to make sure the man at her side was really Daniel. And when she did, she'd find him glancing her way.

They'd grin at each other.

She didn't know about him, but she felt overwhelmed.

There were so many questions, so many things she needed

to tell him, but she hardly knew where to start. Just being together… That was enough.

But it wouldn't last, this feeling of calm. Because she'd lived four years without him. He'd lived four years without her. They had stories to share. Some good, no doubt. Some not so good.

The thought of what she had to share twisted her insides.

How did she tell her husband that she'd nearly married his best friend? How was she supposed to explain away the attraction she'd felt for Paul? The time they'd spent together? The way she'd come to rely on him?

How was she going to confess their kiss?

She glanced at Daniel and caught him looking at her.

"You're still there."

He squeezed her hand. "I'm not going anywhere. Ever."

The sidewalk was crowded, young people headed toward the restaurants and shops in the busy downtown area. Music filtered from up ahead.

A new thought intruded. Did Daniel have something to confess as well? Had there been someone in his life?

Had Daniel fallen in love?

The fear made her steps falter.

He gripped her more tightly and slowed. "You all right?"

"Yeah, sure."

But she wasn't.

Did he have someone else? They'd been apart for a long time.

And she'd been such a shrew back then, demanding his time, his attention. Demanding her own way rather than being content with the life—the amazing, beautiful life—she'd had.

Had he found someone who appreciated him?

They were ambling now, annoying locals, who rushed past. She peeked up at him again. His easy smile was gone. When she caught his eye, he said, "What's wrong?"

"Nothing."

He pulled her to the side of a building and faced her. "I know there are a million things we need to tell each other. But we need to be honest. Tell me what you're thinking."

"So much has happened. Some of it..." She couldn't finish.

He cupped her cheek. "We can do this, Cammie. Together. We can handle anything." He leaned down, kissed her forehead. For a brief moment, he pulled her close.

She told herself everything would be fine.

And willed herself to believe it.

CHAPTER FIFTY-FOUR

THEY CHOSE an Italian restaurant and were seated at a round table in the back, the scents of oregano and garlic hanging in the air. Faint music played overhead. The place was crowded and dark. Intimate.

"Wine?" he asked.

"I don't drink anymore."

His eyebrows hiked.

"I was afraid I'd open a bottle and crawl right in."

He blinked, swallowed. Didn't say anything until they asked the server for two sodas. They studied the menus in silence until their drinks were delivered. Daniel downed about half of his drink in one shot. "Heaven over ice."

"Seriously? Dr Pepper?"

"It's weird the things you miss. I didn't wish for television or the news. I didn't miss the hospital."

"You didn't?" It seemed impossible that he hadn't missed the place that had meant so much to him. "I'd have thought—"

"That I'd miss the place that ruined our lives?" His head shook slightly. "I made so many mistakes. I regret so many things." And then, the tension slipped away. "You read my letters?"

"I could recite them word for word."

"Really?" That seemed to please him. "So you know how I feel. I'm sorry about all of it. I'm sorry I screwed it all up."

"And I'm sorry I expected you to be someone you weren't. I'm sorry you didn't feel needed at home. I'm sorry for all those things I said." She shook off the emotions filling her eyes.

She didn't want to cry tonight. She wanted to celebrate.

"I understood your fear, Cammie. I was never angry with you. My biggest regret was that those were the last words you spoke to me. I knew you'd blame yourself. But what happened next wasn't your fault. I shouldn't have taken off. I just needed a minute to get my thoughts together. And then...and then Alfredo was there, and I was out of time." He downed the rest of his soda. "So we're both imperfect, we're both sorry, and we're both forgiven. Yes?"

"Forgiven." Mostly, but she wasn't ready to delve into the only thing still nagging at her.

She didn't want to ruin their night. And she needed more time to process. "So, you didn't miss the hospital?"

"The work I did at the mission was fulfilling. And reasonable. No long hours, no competition with other doctors. No administrators or insurance companies. It was about healing people, nothing else. I liked that."

He'd found work he liked *better* than the hospital? After all the hours he'd spent at that place?

"Suddenly I had all the time in the world, and no family to spend it with." Before she could respond to that, he continued. "Other things I'd thought I'd miss... I had a phone, but not like the one I had here. The internet was spotty, but I didn't care about any of that. I missed Dr Pepper and"—he looked around the restaurant—"pepperoni pizza and that delicious roast beef you make and western worship music."

"Like, country music?"

"No, no. American-style music. Don't get me wrong. Their worship was amazing. The people who run the mission love the Lord, and I'm sure He enjoys their music and the way they worship. It was...indescribable. But I missed English lyrics. I missed standing beside you, watching you praise God. I missed seeing the joy of the Lord reflected on your face."

The joy of worshipping God. Honestly, she missed that herself. In the years since Daniel left, she'd learned the meaning of the phrase *the sacrifice of praise.* It hadn't been easy to worship for years.

He leaned his head back and looked at the ceiling. When he lowered it, his eyes were red with tears he was trying not to shed. "I missed you and the kids so much. I didn't have a choice. It was pay Alfredo off or die. And I didn't want to die. But, wow, it hurt so bad, knowing you thought I was dead. Knowing I'd never see you again. I don't know if I'd have survived if I hadn't had the people in the mission, the work. I hope you can forgive—"

"You stayed alive."

They could go back and analyze all their choices. They could nitpick every decision they'd made, hate themselves or each other for them. But what would be the point?

It was over, and he was here, and she didn't want either of them to wallow in regret. "How can I fault you for trying to protect us?"

"I lied to you. To everybody. I did it to save you, but—"

"It came at a cost. Testifying came at a cost. But the cost of not testifying... You did the right thing."

His eyebrows lifted. "You weren't convinced."

"I was selfish. I cared about the wrong things. I cared about our home and income and status. A million times after you left, I repented of that. Of course you had to testify. If you hadn't, you wouldn't be the man I fell in love with."

He swallowed hard but said nothing.

"Why didn't you reach out to us? We could have joined you."

Daniel rubbed his lips together. He was about to speak when the server stopped to ask what they wanted to eat. He ordered their favorite pizza, and they watched her walk off.

Camilla waited for an answer.

"I wandered around for a long time," Daniel said. "I started in Mexico, but it felt too close to home. I got false papers and flew to Africa. It was a year before I stumbled on the mission and found my place. You couldn't have joined me as I wandered the world.

"And then, honestly... You'd bought a house in Oklahoma City. You seemed settled and happy. I didn't want to disrupt your lives."

"You're my husband. Their father. How could your existence not be anything but good?"

He looked away, licked his lips. His Adam's apple bobbed before he sighed and faced her again. "I was afraid. Of Campos finding out I was alive. Of him targeting you guys. Of ruining your lives. I'd already almost gotten you all killed. I thought maybe you were better off without me."

"How could you think that?"

"You would have come to Africa, lived as a missionary? Left everything? Your friends, the kids' schools? Think about it, Cammie. Really think about it."

She tried to imagine it, but the picture wouldn't come.

"I'm sorry," he said. "I didn't know the right thing to do. It seemed kinder to let you believe I was dead."

Kinder.

Was that what it was?

She didn't know. But she wasn't going to ruin the homecoming with her doubts. Over time, she'd learn to live with what he'd done. She'd probably even come to understand it. For now, it was enough that he was home. "Let's live free of the past." Maybe if she said it aloud, she'd figure out how to do it, somehow. "Let's start fresh from here."

Almost fresh. Because she hadn't told him her secret. And didn't want to. Ever.

But he was studying her, head cocked to the side, squinting. Seeing through her in a way nobody else ever had. "What is it you want to say to me?"

She sat back, heart pounding. "What do you mean?"

"A lot has changed, but I can still read you. Whatever it is—"

"I was dating Paul." She blurted the words, and now she wished she could shove them back in her mouth. She lowered her gaze, unable to look at him. She shouldn't have said it. Their first opportunity to be alone, and she'd wrecked it.

Would it be their last night together?

He tipped her chin up with his finger. She didn't want to look at him, she didn't. But he was there. Daniel was *there*. How could she not stare at him? Even though she dreaded his response, how would she ever look away again?

"I know."

"We dated for a while." She rushed to get it all out. "I mean, we weren't really dating. Just seeing each other sometimes. And talking a lot. But then this week..." His words registered, the even tone of them. "What do you mean, you know?"

"I hacked your accounts too. You two shared a lot of messages. When he moved to Oklahoma City..." His mouth was set in a grim line, the wrinkles she was still getting used to deepening, but he shrugged as if it didn't bother him.

She tried to focus on his words, not the face she'd never get enough of. He'd hacked her accounts? He'd been watching her? All that time?

He'd known all about her life, and she'd known nothing...

"I'm sorry." He spoke quickly, again reading her mind. "It's unacceptable, my spying. I shouldn't have, and I'm sorry I did." He shook his head. "I mean, I'm not sorry, but I know I *should* be, and I know that's also unacceptable. But I just missed you so much." It was so unlike Daniel to babble that she let him go on. "I'm telling you, even though maybe I should've kept it to myself tonight. I don't want anything to ruin this, but I also don't want anything to come between us. I love you, and I don't want to lie to you. I don't want secrets between us. So, there it is. Not that I saw everything that you were up to. Like I said, the internet was—"

"You knew about Paul?" There was so much to process in his words, but she couldn't get past that one fact. That one tiny, enormous fact.

"I knew you two spent a lot of time together. I saw his posts too. He posted more photos of the two of you than you did. His feelings for you didn't surprise me. I'd suspected back in St. Louis that he was in love with you. He's a great guy. I figured it was just a matter of time..." He ran a hand down his face and covered his mouth, maybe trying to force himself to shut up.

"And I saw your posts about your business," he said, as if the bomb he'd just dropped hadn't exploded between them. As if they could just move on. "I'm so proud of what you've built."

Did he really want to talk about her *job*? Irritation sent adrenaline through her veins. "You knew about my relationship with Paul. You were *okay* with it?" She heard the volume in her words but didn't care.

A muscle ticked in his cheek. "That's not what I..." He leaned forward, volume low, maybe hinting that she should lower hers. "I abandoned you. You deserved to be happy, and I didn't deserve—"

"If I'd married him and then discovered you were alive..." She closed her eyes to try to imagine it, opened them quickly. The image was too painful. How would she have managed it? The man she really loved alive. While she was married to a man she cared for, but not enough, not nearly enough. "I'd have divorced him. I'd have had to. I'd have been a...a bigamist. And I'd never have loved him like I do you. It would've been... I can't even..." She glared at Daniel. "You really would have let me marry another man? How could you?"

He leaned back against his chair. A beat passed while emotions played across his face. "Please, hear me."

She swallowed her anger, or tried to. "Hear what? You didn't want me?"

"Oh, sweetheart. No." His anger seemed to melt away. He leaned toward her again and reached his hand across the table, palm up.

She didn't take it.

"I trusted God with you. I had to. I had no claim on you. More than anything in the world, I wanted you back."

"For the kids," she added.

"Not *for* the kids. Yes, I missed them. Yes, I wanted them too." His hand was still lying there, waiting. If anything, it inched toward her a little more. "You, Camilla. You are the most important person in my life. It was your image I took to bed with me every night. It was memories of you that helped me get through every day. Barely an hour went by that I didn't pray for you, think of you. I love the children with everything in me, but you're..." He choked up, blinked a couple of times and swallowed hard. "You're part of me. I'm part of you. It felt like...like half my heart was ripped away when I left you."

Yes.

That was exactly it. She'd felt the same way. As if she'd never be whole again. And now, despite all the questions and fears and worries, her heart was already stitching back together.

"I didn't want you to marry him." That muscle in Daniel's jaw ticked again, the one that told her he was angry but fighting it. Not at her, though. She could see that. "The thought of you two together made me jealous, furious." The dark emotions on his face slid away, and his expression softened. "But I had to leave all of that with the Lord. I had to trust that He would do what was right. If I was never going to come home to you, then He would provide all you needed. If that meant Paul, then it meant Paul. So, no, I wouldn't have been okay with it. I'd have been heartbroken and crazy jealous. But it wasn't about me. It was about you and the kids and what you needed."

"We needed you."

"I know." His voice broke, and he paused a long moment before he said again, "I know. I needed you too."

The truth of it hummed on his words, showed in his expression.

She took his hand and let it all go. All the frustrations and the questions. All the fears, all the worries, all the unknowns. God would work it out. Hadn't He already?

They were here, together. That was God's doing.

Was Daniel perfect? Did she love all his choices? No. But...

But.

This amazing, wonderful man. He'd loved her enough to sacrifice everything for her. He'd loved her enough to leave her. To watch out for her and their kids from afar for years. He'd loved her enough to fight for his life and come back to her.

How could she not trust him? How could she not give herself to him again?

"Our lives were not complete without you." She brushed at her tears impatiently. This was a time for celebrating, not tears.

"We will all be richer and happier because you're home. We missed you so much. There was a Daniel-sized hole in our family that nobody could ever have filled."

He nodded a few times but didn't speak. She could feel the emotion rolling off him in waves. He pulled back, breaking their contact. "Not even Paul?"

She didn't want Paul to take up one more moment of her time with Daniel, but she might as well get it out there and be done with it.

"We were close friends, and I cared for him. But this week, when I thought we might have to go into witness protection, he wanted to come. He wanted to marry me and leave his business and start over with me."

"Of course. He loves you." Daniel's words were flat, his face unreadable.

"But I don't love him, and I never have. I told him that, and he left on Monday. We'd already decided not to see each other again. He realized I'd never love any man but you."

Daniel blinked several times. "Really?"

"I never stopped loving you. Deep down, I never really believed you were gone."

He stood, leaned across the table, and kissed her lightly on the cheek. He didn't say anything, but she guessed he was too choked up to speak.

She touched the spot his lips had warmed, wanting more. They hadn't had a real kiss since he'd been back. She decided she needed to remedy that tonight, no matter what. Even so, she needed to ask her own questions.

"Did you...?" She took a fortifying breath. "Was there anyone you ?"

"Never."

"But you didn't know if you'd be able to come home, and I thought you were dead. And I was seeing someone, sort of." She hated to ask it, felt sick even thinking it. "I would understand if you'd—"

"There's never been anyone but you."

She took those words in, let them plant themselves in the fresh soil of her healing heart. Daniel loved her. He'd returned because he loved her. Despite all her faults and fears, despite all she'd done wrong, he was here. With her. For her.

Her heart swelled, nearly exploded, with gratitude and love.

The server appeared. "Large pepperoni, half mushroom?"

Their eye contact broke, and they both chuckled. She'd forgotten they were in a public place.

The server set the pizza on a tray by their table. "I'll get you another Dr Pepper. Lemme know if you need anything else."

"Will do." Daniel slid a slice of pepperoni onto Cammie's plate, took one with mushrooms for himself, and then pulled her hand into his, enveloping it in warmth. "Mind if I pray?"

Her mind reeled as she listened to his simple prayer. She didn't have all the answers. She didn't know what the future would hold. She didn't know anything except that her husband was home, her children were safe, and her God was good.

Her heart filled with peace.

They tried the pizza—salty, cheesy, and delicious. He had a few bites, wiped his mouth, and sipped his soda.

She nodded to his drink. "That caffeine's going to keep you up all night."

"I haven't had a decent night's sleep since... I can't even remember."

"You'll need to tell me everything. About when you got here and—"

"Not tonight."

Fine by her. They had forever to ask each other questions. "I want to hear everything about where you've been and all you did."

"And you'll tell me all about your business and your house."

"Our house," she said.

Daniel wiped his mouth. "Here's the problem. My medical license lapsed. I couldn't exactly attend continuing ed courses to keep it current. I have nothing to offer you. I'm basically penniless and jobless and—"

"Do you still want to practice medicine?"

"It's going to take time for me to get reinstated. Maybe a couple of years."

"I guess I'll let you freeload for a little while." She winked and took a bite of pizza.

"I'll get a job. But it'll be a while before we're back to the lifestyle we—"

"I don't care about that. I don't care about any of that. We have a nice house in Oklahoma. I can pay the bills, and now that you're home, we have everything we need. If you want to practice medicine, great. If you want to do something else, that's fine too. I can work from anywhere and, once Jeremy graduates and goes off to school, we'll have lots of choices. Whatever you want, wherever you want." She peered at his pizza slice until he took a bite. After he did, she continued. "I think we should consider moving to Maine—or at least closer to your family. Now that you're back, they're going to want to be near you."

He swallowed his bite. "Really? You wouldn't mind? That's a long way from home."

"Wherever you are is home. Besides, your parents are going to need you. They took your...death hard. Your brothers too."

"I hate what I did to them." Grief darkened his expression. "To you and the kids."

"You stayed alive, sweetheart. You did what you had to do. Nobody blames you."

He took that in, then smiled. "I guess I can freeload off you for a little while. And Maine... I would love that."

She would too. They'd lived in the same state as her parents most of their married lives. She looked forward to spending more time with Peggy and Roger and the Wright brothers.

After dinner, they walked back to the hotel and found Zoë sound asleep on the pull-out couch in the living area. Peggy, Roger, and Sam were quietly watching TV. They stood when Daniel and Camilla walked in, each hugging Daniel as if they hadn't seen him in years. As if reassuring themselves that he was real.

Peggy finally backed out of his arms and kissed Camilla's cheek. "We'll see you in the morning. You two call us when you're up and ready for company. I'm sure you need your sleep."

They'd rented a suite down the hall, not wanting to be any farther away than that.

In the smaller bedroom, Jeremy was groggy when Daniel woke him and gave him his pain meds. After assuring them he didn't need anything else, Jeremy fell back asleep.

Camilla cleaned up and changed into her pajamas, then stared at her reflection in the mirror. It'd been four years, four long years, since she'd slid between the sheets beside her husband.

She was four years older. She was grayer, weathered and wrinkled.

And as nervous as a bride on her wedding night. More nervous than she'd been on her wedding night, honestly. She and Daniel were married, but they were different than they'd been. They'd had so many experiences apart from each other. There'd been so many changes.

But this was Daniel, her Daniel.

Her husband. And she loved him desperately.

She stepped into the bedroom.

Standing by the bed, he opened his arms, and she stepped into them and lifted her face to his. He covered her lips with his own, and for the first time in four years, she was truly home.

THE END

...of this story. But the next afternoon...

Sam Wright wasn't exactly a break-down-and-cry type of guy. But his brother, his big brother, the one he'd idolized as long as he could remember, was back from the grave.

He was still processing. He couldn't imagine how Camilla and the kids felt. And Mom and Dad, who'd never gotten over losing their oldest child.

It was a lot to take. That morning over breakfast, they'd learned the whole horrifying story. But the bad guy was dead, Camilla was safe, and Jeremy and his cousin were both recovering. Daniel and Camilla were visiting with Mom and Dad, and Jeremy and Zoë were watching a movie.

Sam figured he'd take a walk, get out of everyone's way.

He'd left the hotel a few minutes before. The air was cold and dry, snow pushed to the edges of the sidewalk. He'd never been to Salt Lake City before, and the pictures he'd seen hadn't done it justice.

The streets were wide and clean, the city nestled right up against a rugged mountain range. He figured there was good skiing up there, not that he'd hit the slopes on this visit. He was here because, after he'd heard about Daniel's—resurrection? Return from the dead?—he'd needed to confirm the crazy story in person. He'd needed to hug his brother and hear his voice and see his face.

Sounded kind of sappy when he put it like that.

It almost made a man believe in miracles.

A woman stepped out of the building in front of him—a pharmacy, he noted.

It wasn't her, of course.

This woman had dark-brown hair pulled up in a ponytail—much longer than Eliza ever wore hers. The stranger had on a thick beige cardigan that hung off her narrow frame. She wore ugly uniform-type pants that looked two sizes too big. She carried a fabric book bag over her shoulder.

Far from the high fashion Eliza preferred.

The stranger stopped on the sidewalk and peered up the street in the opposite direction.

Then she turned his way.

And recognition slammed into him.

Forcing a measured pace, he moved toward her and stepped into her line of sight, half expecting to see the face of a stranger. "Eliza?"

Her eyes widened, and not in that gosh-I'm-so-happy-to-see-you way he was used to getting from women. Which...okay, maybe he deserved her reaction. But was she still holding a grudge?

He was no prince, but he hadn't done anything *that* bad. Certainly not bad enough for her to dump him, block his number, drop off social media, and disappear.

Not that he'd been looking for her. Not exactly. Not in a while, anyway. But...yeah, he'd wondered what happened to her. Worried, when she never turned up on Instagram. When he never bumped into her at her favorite places.

What was she doing in Utah?

And so skinny? And dressed like a...homeless person? Okay, it wasn't that bad, but really, where was the Neiman-Marcus wardrobe? She was still gorgeous, of course, but you had to look beyond a lot of ugly to see it.

He ached to touch her. The way she crossed her arms told him a hug wouldn't be welcome.

"I thought that was you."

Her gaze darted past him. "Hey, Sam." She looked behind her, then across the street.

Hey Sam? Her attitude threw him off. They hadn't seen each other for years. After everything they'd been through together, he deserved more, didn't he?

"What are you doing here?" Her question sounded more polite than interested.

"That's a long story. I'd love to tell you about it. Is this where you live now?"

She nodded, then shook her head. "Not exactly." Her gaze barely paused on him as she continued scanning her surroundings. But not like she was eager to be done with him. Not like she had better places to be.

She was scared.

The thought had adrenaline flooding his veins.

He needed to tread carefully, keep her from running.

"Why don't we get some coffee and catch up?" There, that sounded nonthreatening, right?

"I can't. Sorry."

"You looking for someone? You need a ride, or—?"

"They should be back. They were just circling the block because there wasn't anyplace to park."

He couldn't help the quick glance at her left hand. No wedding ring. He'd analyze his relief later. "Who are you waiting for? Friends?"

"Uh-huh. Friends."

Yeah...no. She was lying. "What's going on, Eliza? What's wrong?"

"I'm fine." But she didn't meet his eyes. Her reaction—the fear, the avoidance, the way she barely looked at him. All of it was wrong. They'd once been close. They'd once shared everything. Even if she still hated him, she should respond in some way. He'd rather see fire in her eyes than this...disregard. As if he didn't matter at all. As if he never had.

It occurred to him that maybe the thing she worried about was much bigger than running into her ex.

"Can I do anything for you? Do you need—?"

"I don't need anything. Everything's fine."

Obviously not, but he couldn't exactly force the truth out of her. He reached beneath his jacket and slipped a business card and pen out of his shirt pocket. He looked away from her just long enough to jot his personal phone number on the back. She'd had it, once. But she'd blocked his phone number a long time ago. For all he knew, she'd deleted it. For good measure, he added his home address. Not something he generally gave to people he met on the street, but this was Eliza. If she looked for him, he wanted her to find him. He wanted to be there for her.

"I gotta go." She started to walk away, but he gripped her elbow and shoved the card in her hand.

"If you ever need anything..."

She looked at it like it might bite her, then up at him, blinking in confusion. Or fear. "I'm fine."

"Just keep it, okay? It'll make me feel better."

She shoved it deep in her pocket.

And then she took off across the street and hopped in an SUV that had just stopped beside the opposite curb. As soon as she was settled, the driver eased into traffic.

Leaving Sam to stare after the only woman he'd ever loved.

Daniel and Camilla are back together, but what happens next? Download the bonus epilogue for one more chapter. Click the

link, use the QR Code below, or find it here—> https://dl.bookfunnel.com/99iw3mbran.

You'll notice that I couldn't help giving you a little tease of *Running to You,* the first book of my new series, *The Wright Heroes of Maine.* Amnesia, a second-chance romance, and a mystery you're going to love. Turn the page for more about *Running to You.*

Running to You

Sam never understood why Eliza left him five years ago, ghosting him without explanation. He's avoided romance ever since, focusing on building his business. Money might not keep him warm at night, but it can sure buy a lot of blankets.

Then Eliza shows up on his doorstep and throws herself into his arms. She can't explain her bruises or the head injury that's left her with no memories of the past five years, including their breakup. No matter how good it feels to hold her, though, there's no way he's getting sucked into romance again.

He'll deliver Eliza to her mother, and that will be that. But instead of finding her mom, they're met by two attackers and barely escape alive. Despite the danger to his life and his heart, he can't leave Eliza to fend for herself.

Together, they embark on a journey to reconstruct her past while evading the men chasing her. As Sam and Eliza close in on the truth, their romance reignites, but her secret threatens to destroy them both.

Prepare to be enthralled by this gripping story of amnesia, a second chance at love, and a secret baby. *Running to You* is an edge-of-your-seat Christian romantic suspense set in Maine that will keep you reading all night long.

DEAR READER

If you follow me on social media or receive my newsletter, then you've probably already heard that the accident in *A Mountain Too Steep* is very similar to a wreck my son Jacob and his cousin, Joshua, suffered in 2018.

Marcy's words when she called Camilla in Chapter One were almost identical to my sister's words that terrible July night.

My husband and I felt very much like Camilla did, trying to figure out what to do, what to pack, how to get to Salt Lake City as fast as possible. I tried to sleep—and did a little. Eddie didn't even bother.

Like Camilla, I texted or emailed everybody I knew would pray. I also posted on social media, asking for prayer. I am convinced that all those prayers saved our boys' lives.

If you're curious about the true story, I've blogged about it on my website, robinpatchen.com, a few times. The first post was written not long after the accidents. Note the plural, *accidents*. In real life, three days before Jake's wreck, my daughter fell and crushed both her wrists. I didn't put that in the story because, really, who'd have believed it?

Jacob suffered exactly the same wounds as Jeremy in the story. The intubation, the need to put back in the chest tube, the reaction to ketamine—all of that really happened. (I changed Evan's wounds and recovery a little, for the sake of the story and my nephew's privacy). Both our boys recovered completely, praise God.

Some of you have asked me why this is part of the Coventry Saga. If you read *Courage in the Shadows,* then you met Camilla, Zoë, and Jeremy. Daniel is Grant's oldest brother. I thought about locating this story in Boston and bringing the brothers in, but I wanted to keep the events as close to what really happened in our family as possible.

If you liked *A Mountain Too Steep,* I'm betting you'll want to read about the rest of the Wright family. Sam's book (*Running to You*) releases in October, and I think you're going to love it.

God bless you!

Robin

ALSO BY ROBIN PATCHEN

The Wright Heroes of Maine

Running to You

Rescuing You

The Coventry Saga

Glimmer in the Darkness

Tides of Duplicity

Betrayal of Genius

Traces of Virtue

Touch of Innocence

Inheritance of Secrets

Lineage of Corruption

Wreathed in Disgrace

Courage in the Shadows

Vengeance in the Mist

A Mountain Too Steep

The Nutfield Saga

Convenient Lies

Twisted Lies

Generous Lies

Innocent Lies

Beautiful Lies

Legacy Rejected

Legacy Restored

Legacy Reclaimed

Legacy Redeemed

Amanda Series

Chasing Amanda

Finding Amanda

ABOUT THE AUTHOR

Robin Patchen is a *USA Today* bestselling and award-winning author of Christian romantic suspense. She grew up in a small town in New Hampshire, the setting of her Nutfield Saga books, and then headed to Boston to earn a journalism degree. After college, working in marketing and public relations, she discovered how much she loathed the nine-to-five ball and chain. After relocating to the Southwest, she started writing her first novel while she homeschooled her three children. The novel was dreadful, but her passion for storytelling didn't wane. Thankfully, as her children grew, so did her writing ability. Now that her kids are adults, she has more time to play with the lives of fictional heroes and heroines, wreaking havoc and working magic to give her characters happy endings. When she's not writing, she's editing or reading, proving that most of her life revolves around the twenty-six letters of the alphabet. Visit robinpatchen.com/subscribe to receive a free book and stay informed about Robin's latest projects.

Printed in Great Britain
by Amazon

37867856R00205